To: Jacob

Between Dusk And Dawn

Enjoy!

Lynn Emery

Lynn Emery

Copyright © 2012 Margaret Emery Hubbard

All rights reserved.

ISBN-10: 0983930910
ISBN-13:978-0-9839309-1-4

"CONTRE LA FORCE Y A PAS DE RÉSISTANCE"
(Against strength there is no resistance)

Chapter 1

LaShaun sat on her back porch gazing in fascination at the glowing dots. Tiny beams flickered against the dark orange and blue sky as the day quickly faded into night. Lightening bugs danced along the edge of the woods that started at the end of her neatly manicured lawn. They seemed to be thanking her for creating a habitat in which they could thrive. She got up from the cane rocker and went down the back steps. Standing still, LaShaun held out one hand and was rewarded. One of the little flying beetles settled just above her wrist. Soon three more of her sparkling friends decided to join the party. LaShaun smiled as they blinked on and off like tiny flashlights.

"I'm so glad you decided to visit. Next time I'll open a tiny bottle of vintage nectar just for you." She laughed as their little bodies lit up as if accepting her invitation.

The peaceful night was a welcome respite from the chaos of dealing with people. The residents of Beau Chene still whispered that the Rousselle family practiced voodoo, the same tale that had been passed on for over one hundred and twenty years. In hushed tones they spoke of ghosts and goblins. It was said that there were strange ritual gatherings in the woods on their land. Like most Louisiana natives, they possessed a mixture of fascination and fear when it came to the supernatural.

But the same house and land that inspired so many dark tales whispered in Vermillion Parish, and the parish seat Beau Chene, brought tranquility and comfort to LaShaun. The restored Creole style home first built by their ancestor Louis Volant in 1830 had been lovingly restored at least twice. Her late grandmother's second husband had done the last renovation in 1950. At Monmon Odette's direction, her husband had kept the old Creole nineteenth century look and charm intact.

LaShaun breathed in the cool air of the October fall evening. She gazed at the house, once more thanking her ancestors for their business acumen and love of the land. She was about to go inside when a rustling in the brush caught her attention. She faced the woods cloaked in shadows. The wild, verdant growth stood in contrast to the neatly mowed lawn that surrounded the house. Curious, LaShaun tilted her head to one side and listened. Something untamed moved through the thick leaves. She could feel the essence of the creature, savoring its freedom of movement in the night. The creature didn't fear LaShaun, but sent out waves of equal curiosity at the strange upright being in sight. It was cautious not to approach and felt secure hidden among the vegetation that cloaked it. Then a high pitched keening sound cut through the tranquil surroundings. LaShaun's visitor went from calm to tense in an instant. Seconds later it skittered deeper into the woods away from the danger signal. Another keening wail echoed sounding a little closer. The haunting sound brought silence. Even the crickets and small frogs hushed. LaShaun took three steps towards the woods to investigate, but stopped when headlights swung down her driveway. The mystery in the woods forgotten, she walked across the grass until she reached her driveway made of crushed rocks.

The lights shut off, and seconds later the door to the light gray F-10 Ford truck swung open. Deputy Chase Broussard, dressed in civilian clothes, waved. "You out enjoyin' this pretty evening? Thought you might want some company."

LaShaun walked up to the six foot two handsome Cajun lawman. She tilted her head up and was rewarded with a quick but sugar sweet kiss. "Hmm, you thought right Deputy. Come on in the house. I'll make us some supper."

"Hope I'm not being presumptuous coming out here. I tried to call, but you're too busy communing with nature to hear your phone." Chase wrapped a muscular arm around LaShaun's waist as they walked down the driveway to the back porch.

"I do lose track of time when I'm breathing in this sweet Louisiana fall air. You can't blame me. We only get nights like this twice a year." LaShaun looked up at the evening night sky. "I don't miss Los Angeles anymore. I thought I would at first, that I'd become used to the excitement of a big city. There was always a cultural event to attend, and nobody cares if you're different. In fact, being different is normal."

"Not like being in a small town where different is seen as dangerous you mean," Chase said.

LaShaun shrugged. "Beau Chene is different now, and so am I. Coming home is what I needed. Not to mention I've made some nice new friends."

"You got that right, lady." Chase pulled her close and kissed her again, this time longer and with more passion.

When they pulled apart LaShaun smoothed back his dark brown wavy hair. "You hungry?"

"Hmm, but we can eat a little food first," Chase replied with a wink.

She gave him a playful push and darted up the porch steps. "That moon is bringing out the beast in you."

Chase followed her into the house and locked the back door. "No, a beautiful woman with the taste of honey and cinnamon brings out the beast in me. Be careful, cause I just might bite."

LaShaun laughed as she entered the kitchen. "Then I definitely better feed you, and fast."

"That won't stop me from nibbling on you later, girl."

Chase gave her butt a playful swat then ducked when she tried to hit him back. He turned on the radio to a local station playing zydeco and Cajun music. LaShaun hummed along with a lively tune as she took shrimp from the freezer. Already cleaned, she set them under cold running water while she mixed up a tomato roux. She had fresh loaves of French bread from a local bakery. She would make shrimp and sausage in a Creole sauce over rice. Without asking, Chase pitched in. He filled the rice cooker and set it. Then he spread garlic butter on the bread and put it in the oven to warm. LaShaun savored the cooking smells and the cozy feel of their togetherness.

For most of her life she'd felt separated from other people. The exception of course had been her relationship with her grandmother, Monmon Odette. They were both socially apart from the locals who whispered about the Rousselle family voodoo legend. The Rousselle extended family was large, but contentious with battling factions. Monmon Odette, the matriarch at the center of this feuding brood, kept them in line. But with her death ten months ago, and the fight over her estate, the fragile ties had frayed even more. LaShaun kept in touch with a few cousins, but they weren't close. The legacy and resentment of LaShaun being Monmon Odette's favorite meant that she wasn't close to her family. When LaShaun inherited the bulk of her grandmother's estate, those delicate ties were strained even more. So to have Chase in her life meant she wasn't isolated anymore. She'd even managed to make friends with Savannah Honoré and Deputy Myrtle Arceneaux. LaShaun was still getting used to not being on her own.

Chase gathered salad fixings from the refrigerator. "I hope your day was better than mine."

"Being Chief of Detectives not as fun as you thought it would be, huh?" LaShaun asked.

"Fun isn't anything close to the words I wanna use to describe work these days. But it's better than the Army," Chase said.

"I'll bet." LaShaun didn't say more. Chase had only recently told her he was in the Army, and had been in Afghanistan. But he didn't like to talk about it, so she didn't push. He'd tell her when he was ready.

So what have you been up to?" Chase seemed content to get steeped in domestic chores.

"I'm still untangling Monmon Odette's business interests and getting a crash course in mineral rights, timber rights, stocks and bonds. I knew she was sharp, but I didn't have a clue she was such a whiz at being a tycoon. Thank goodness she hired an accountant and lawyer I can trust."

"Your grandmother looked out for you in every detail, honey. That's real love," Chase said as he sliced Creole tomatoes into the big wooden bowl of salad and carrots.

"I miss her so much," LaShaun said softly. She added shrimp to the roux and stirred the simmering mixture in her grandmother's favorite deep cast iron skillet.

"I know, but she's resting in peace knowing you're well taken care of." He finished the salad and wiped his hands on a towel. Then he joined her at the stove, pushed aside her thick braid and kissed the back of her neck.

"Yeah, but sometimes I can feel her spirit." LaShaun smiled at the thought of her beloved grandmère hovering nearby.

"Oui, cher," Chase said quietly. "My mama swore that the spirit of her grandmother protected her all through her childhood after her mama died. Miss Odette was a strong life-force on this earth. Wouldn't be surprised if she carried that after passing to the other side."

LaShaun sighed as she covered the skillet and lowered the flame under it. She turned to face him. "Oh, I'm convinced she did."

"You had some sign?" Chase no longer questioned LaShaun's "gift" of being in tune to the supernatural.

"Not really, just a feeling." She smiled at him and playfully tapped the end of his nose with a fingertip. "She's glad that I'm happy."

"Hmm, can I claim some credit for that?" Chase smiled back.

"Mais oui," she replied with a wink. "Now let's have some supper."

LaShaun pushed aside talk of sadness and spirits as they filled their plates and sat down to eat in the kitchen. After saying grace, they exchanged small town talk about the weather and local news. Chase had LaShaun laughing as he described his latest family news. A younger cousin had become a local high school football hero, and had gotten a little too friendly with more than one cheerleader. His account about the teenager's conservative mother's embarrassment had LaShaun in tears.

"Glenda hoping he'd be a priest," Chase said in between chuckles. "Guess she can scratch that."

LaShaun put away leftovers as Chase stacked the dishwasher. "Back to your day. I take it you had a rough one?" she asked.

Chase grunted. "The usual knuckle-headed nonsense. I had to chase down some fool who shoplifted a crate of cigarettes from the Stop-N-Go on Oak Road. A couple of drunks got into a fight."

"That's what you signed on for when you became a lawman," LaShaun teased.

"That I can handle, but dealing with dead livestock is definitely not my favorite thing." Chase pushed the button to start the dishwasher then leaned against the counter watching LaShaun.

"The owners should call the local vet for that," LaShaun said as she sealed a plastic container with the shrimp Creole.

"Frank Jeffers over on the other end of Black Bayou first called in that somebody was stealing his cows and goats. That was two days ago. Today he found three goats slaughtered." Chase wore a slight frown. "I mean really ripped up bad."

"Sounds like wild dogs." LaShaun felt a prickle along her arms as she remembered the keening animal like call in her woods.

"Or coyotes." Chase wrapped the remaining loaves of bread in wax paper.

"Around here?" LaShaun put the rest of the food in the fridge and faced him.

"Believe it or not, Louisiana has a growing coyote problem. The population has gotten bigger, and they're moving up from snatching small house pets I guess. I'm no authority on the damn things. Frank is in a big uproar about it. He' demanding that we protect his property."

"Okay, you're going on a coyote stakeout. Guess I better start fixing you coffee and homemade donuts for those long night watches," LaShaun teased, covering her mouth to hold in a giggle.

He crossed the space between them in two long-legged strides and grabbed her around the waist from behind. "Me chasing mangy animals is funny to you, huh?"

"I think you're very qualified to chase down all kinds of criminals, included the furry ones. Quit that," she squirmed as he held her tighter.

"I'll have you know I was trained by the FBI for real police work, missy." He lifted her from the floor.

"Put me down," LaShaun ordered, though she didn't try very hard to get away.

"Take back that crack about a coyote stakeout, and I may turn you loose." Chase pulled her closer to him and buried his face into her hair.

"Maybe I don't want you to let go."

Instead of trying to get away, she pressed against his pelvis. Chase took in a slow breath and exhaled. LaShaun felt his growing passion, and let her head fall back. His long, strong fingers pulled her hair loose from its braid until it was around her shoulders. They kissed as they unbuttoned, unclasped and pulled free of clothing.

"Here?" LaShaun murmured, her lips still against his.

"Hmm," was his only reply.

He lifted her against the countertop, and LaShaun wrapped her legs around him. Soon they were locked in a steady rhythm of sweet passion. He entered her, letting her rest on the warm granite surface. The sensation of floating in his arms combined with his steady thrusts pushed LaShaun over the edge, but each time he eased her back by slowing his pace. Soon even he couldn't hold back. As the heat between them rose, LaShaun cried out begging for more. She reached her peak in an explosion of pleasure that sent the most delicious shock waves all through her body. Holding on for every last bit of delight, she savored the force of his release inside her. Chase moaned and gasped as the fever took control of every inch of his being. He called her name, urging her to move with him. LaShaun bit into his shoulder, crying out once more as she rode the wave of a second orgasm. Seconds later they grew still. Then Chase lifted her from the counter. LaShaun trailed kisses down his chest, and led him to her bedroom leaving their clothing scattered don the kitchen floor.

Once in her private sanctuary, she pulled back the comforter and they climbed into bed. LaShaun snuggled against him. "I love that you wanted to be with me after a trying day at work."

"No place I'd rather be. Whenever you're ready we can make this forever, cher," Chase whispered as he stroked her hair.

LaShaun felt the disquiet of her doubts threaten the sweet moment. "I know. It's just..."

"Times have changed, LaShaun. Nobody would question us being together, or hold that against me being elected."

"Not out in the open, but you know damn well they have plenty to say behind closed doors. With you running for sheriff things could get nasty." LaShaun wanted to protect him, but the thought of letting him go for his own good left her feeling weak with despair.

"Girl, how many times I got to tell you; I'm a big boy, and I can handle these small town folks just fine," Chase said in a light tone.

LaShaun finally manage to get free of his arms. She sat up next to him. "The subject of me being a political liability has come up. Tell me the truth."

"Joe Castille brought up the Trosclair murder investigation, and your cousin's case. I forcefully reminded him you were cleared in both cases.[1]

"The chief alderman is an influential man, and he knows what folks think. Maybe he's got a point." LaShaun pulled the sheet up to her chin. She looked at him steadily.

"He's got a lot of bull is what he's got." Chase gazed back at her for a few moments as silence stretched between them. "Honey, I'm not psychic. Say what you got to say."

"I've never been as close to a man as I feel to you; having someone who looks out for me, even though I can stand on my own," she added quickly.

"I know."

"What we have is good; real good, but..." LaShaun took in a deep breath and let it out.

"Okay, I didn't need a sixth sense to hear the 'but' coming at me." Chase smiled at her, but her somber expression made it fade away. He stroked the arm LaShaun used to hold the sheet up as though it were a shield. "Baby, come on."

"No, listen to what I'm saying. Dealing with funny looks when you walk by and the comments are going to be a way of life if you're with me. You need to think long and hard. I'm used to being on the outside. But you've been part of a supportive community and family all your life. Popular guy in high school, accepted around town as one of the white hats. I'm not sure you grasp the reality of having people judge you based on being with me," LaShaun said as she closed her eyes and swallowed hard.

There. She'd said it, and she knew the danger. He could very well consider her words and the way he was being treated, and decide he couldn't handle the subtle ostracism. But she needed to know sooner rather than later. Maybe she should have been more forceful in pushing him away before they'd shared such sweet moments. Learning to be alone again, to settle for the occasional lukewarm love affair would be gut wrenchingly painful. But that would be less painful than seeing the love light die slowly in Chase's dark Cajun eyes.

"I'm going to think about what you said, seriously think about it. Because I know this means a lot to you, for me to be absolutely sure I've made the right decision. But I have to tell you, giving you up ain't the answer, cher. Being Sheriff just wouldn't be enough without the love of my life." Chase gently tugged LaShaun's arm until she lay nestled against him again.

LaShaun let out a sigh of relief inwardly at his response. "Don't say I didn't warn you."

Chase reached under the covers and lightly smacked her bare bottom. "And I'm warning you, get used to putting up with me a lot longer than you figured."

She wiggled with pleasure and managed to get even closer to him. "What did I do to deserve a spanking?"

"Trying to talk me out of a good thing, that's what." Chase kissed the top of her head. Then he threw back the covers and stood up.

"And where are you going?" LaShaun sat up in surprise. She enjoyed the view as he bent over to pick up his underwear. The dark blue briefs had somehow landed on the hardwood hallway floor just outside the bedroom.

He turned around and stepped into them, then stood with one hand on his waist. "I'm going home, ma'am. I'm not going to get into the habit of spending nights at your place."

"Good idea. That will generate less gossip." LaShaun nodded, though the bed already felt colder without him.

"Forget politics. When we start keeping house I want it to be for real. Right now we're still dating, and I'm letting you get comfortable with being part of a couple." Chase went out and came back with his shirt and pants. "I don't want you to get too skittish on me, more than you already are that is."

"I'm thinking of you," LaShaun protested with a huff.

"Uh-huh, I believe it. Being alone is a way to feel safe. So maybe a little part of you is afraid?" He pulled on his pants and zipped them, then paused, still holding his shirt.

"Now you're the one talking nonsense." LaShaun slapped at the beautiful quilt that served as her bedspread as though straightening it. She avoided looking at him for a few seconds. When he didn't say anything she glanced at him. "What?"

"LaShaun Rousselle, dangerous magic woman, is a scared of me. I'm one powerful dude."

"So full of yourself, Mr. Deputy Sheriff," LaShaun retorted. She snatched up the round accent pillow that matched the quilt and aimed it at his head.

Chase laughed and caught it. "Okay, darlin'. I won't tease you. Now give me a goodnight kiss to send me on my way."

"I'm not sure you deserve one." LaShaun didn't resist when he leaned down to her. In fact she wrapped her arms around his necked and kissed him hard. "Now get on home."

"Yes, ma'am. I'll call you tomorrow. Oh, and be careful to..."

"Lock the door, keep my shotgun handy and the phone close by," LaShaun repeated his favorite mini-lecture on safety each time he left her alone. She put her lips to his ear. "If you stayed the night more often I would be well protected."

He gave her another pat on the bottom. "When you're ready. Now come on and lock up."

"What does that mean?" LaShaun pulled her robe from a hook on the closet door and padded after him down the hallway to the back door.

Chase tipped an imaginary cowboy hat at her. "You know exactly what I'm talkin' about, ma'am." He blew a kiss and went out the door.

"Smart ass," LaShaun muttered. She clicked the locks in place then hugged herself and smiled.

*****

Two hours later the musical bells from her landline phone finally cut through the fog of sleep. LaShaun rolled onto her back and looked at the red numbers on the digital clock next to her bed. Her pulse picked up as anxiety flooded through her. Nobody called with good news at two o'clock in the morning. The soft glow from the night light in the hall kept her from groping around in the dark. She found the phone on the fifth ring before her voice mail picked up.

"Hello," she said, forgetting to check the caller ID first. When she did glance at it said, "Unknown".

"Don't let 'em get her. You got to help," said a raspy female voice raspy, desperate and like she was in deep trouble.

Chapter 2

Tuesday morning, and just four hours after that early phone call, LaShaun sat at her kitchen table. Bright sunshine, still new to the day, lit up the lovely fall day. Fatigue kept sneaking up on LaShaun, but she fought off the urge to yawn several times. The mystery surrounding that call had made it hard for her to go back to sleep, but an hour after that intense ten minute conversation, she'd managed to drop off. LaShaun's visitor, on the other hand, looked as though she hadn't slept at all. LaShaun had agreed to this crack of dawn meeting because Mrs. Clothilde Arceneaux had sounded so disturbed. Two china cups of strong Louisiana dark roast coffee sat between them on the table. LaShaun waited patiently for Miss Clo, as she was affectionately called around the parish, to get to the point. The grandmother of Acting Sheriff M.J. Arceneaux, who had become one of LaShaun's only two female friends in the town, Miss Clo wore a plain pink blouse tucked into a long floral skirt. At seventy-four, she still looked good and kept active.

LaShaun had more waiting and less patience after another fifteen minutes of listening to Miss Clo. She chattered about local church events, her grandson's school awards and the weather. LaShaun was about to push her to the reason for her visit when the older woman put down her cup and sighed.

"I expect you're tired of me blabbing on like a nervous squawking hen." Miss Clo patted her lips with a napkin.

"No, ma'am. You take your time," LaShaun said, hoping she would ignore that invitation.

Miss Clo smiled at her. "Your monmon did a good job teaching you manners. But I've been testing your patience long enough. I just don't know how to tell it. And she wouldn't come with me." She sighed and fidgeted with the floral cloth purse in her lap.

"Just start with something simple. Now, who wouldn't come with you?" LaShaun asked.

LaShaun got up and took the warm biscuits out of the oven. She reasoned that not staring at Miss Clo might make it easier for her to gather her thoughts. LaShaun retrieved softened butter and fig preserves she made from the ripe fruit of her own trees. She set the simple country breakfast on the table and poured them both more hot coffee from a ceramic carafe.

"Joyelle LeJeun. We've been friends since childhood. She's a good person, devoted to her church work and her family. Some of the nasty talk goin' around is enough to make me get out my husband's pistol and let them bullets be my answer."

"How would it be if M.J. had to arrest her own monmon?" LaShaun pressed her lips together to keep from laughing at the image.

"She'd do it, too! Myrtle Jean believes in obeyin' the law," Miss Clo said with a grin. Then she became serious.

"Who or what has you this fired up?" LaShaun put a biscuit and a spoonful of preserves on a saucer for her.

"Thank you, cher. I'm hungry, mais oui." Miss Clo nibbled delicately on the biscuit then put it aside. "You know Joyelle?"

"No, ma'am, I don't recall Miss Joyelle right offhand, but I was gone for a few years living in Los Angeles," LaShaun replied.

"She lives over in Bayou Rouge. Her daughter has that beauty shop on Magnolia Street in Sweet Bayou." Miss Clo looked at LaShaun as if that should explain it all.

"Yes, ma'am." LaShaun knew the little village about six miles away from the center of Beau Chene, but still didn't place the LeJeun family.

"Anyway, Joyelle is blessed with a gift from God." Miss Clo looked at LaShaun and cleared her throat. "Not exactly like yours, of course."

"I'm sure," LaShaun replied quietly.

She knew what it must have taken Miss Clo to visit her. The Arceneaux family was well respected in Beau Chene as devout Christians, hard-working people who would help anyone at anytime; polar opposite of the popular opinion about the Rousselle clan.

"But Myrtle Jean says you're good people. She's a bit hard-headed like her daddy, but she's got good commonsense. Just wish she'd use some of it to see she should marry Ben Volant. You know Ben? He's been crazy for her since they was in high school and—see, there I go rambling again."

"That's okay," LaShaun said. Despite her desire to get to the heart of Miss Clo's visit, that tidbit about M.J.'s love life was worth a bit of digression. She smiled and nodded at the Acting Sheriff's grandmother.

"Back to the reason I'm here. Joyelle is a traiteur." Miss Clo said the word softly and with reverence.

"Yes, of course. My grandmother spoke often of the traiteurs using prayer and herbs to treat all kinds of ailments." LaShaun remembered once more why being home in Creole country made her feel whole. The old ways made her feel even closer to her grandmother and other ancestors.

"Oui. Lots of folks living in the bayou still call a traiteur before they call a doctor. When prayers go up the blessings come down. It is not for us to know why Le Bon Dieu touches some and not others. His ways are not our ways," Miss Clo said. "Joyelle hasn't told another soul, not even Nolan; that's her husband by the way. But she's had a lot of strange cases for the last year or so. The first two or three folks, she thought some kinda strange virus was going around. Then back in August a lady from over in Iberia Parish brought in her boy child. She said he was having fevers and running away at night. Then he'd come home all filthy and covered with scratches."

LaShaun felt a prickle down her neck as Miss Clo's voice went lower, as though she didn't like speaking of these things above a whisper. "Boys like to sneak out and get into mischief, especially country boys."

"Joyelle thought so, too. He couldn't say where he went or what he was doin'. Me and Joyelle raised six boys between us, so we know how they can be. But Joyelle said this was different. The child had a couple of fevers around the same time. And he looked confused, like he didn't remember anything."

"He might not want to confess he's been playing with his friends." LaShaun shrugged.

Miss Clo nodded. "That's exactly what Joyelle told his mama. Then the mama pulled out his t-shirt and pajama pants he'd had on one of those nights. They had spots of blood on 'em. And the boy was cut, nothing but a few scrapes on his arms. Nothing that would cause that much blood."

"Maybe one of his friends got hurt, or they killed some animals. Even more reason he wouldn't want to tell what really happened." LaShaun gazed out of the bay window next to the table. Once again she was being drawn into strange events in the countryside. She had a growing prickle that this was not just a tale of naughty boys breaking curfew.

"Maybe so, but the boy looked so strange it gave Joyelle the jitters. Still she said prayers for him and his mama. For the fevers. Joyelle gave his mama some ginger root, cayenne pepper and cloves to make him a tea. She also gave her some cloth tea bags to put in his bath water." Miss Clo finished the cup of coffee.

"Yes, that's a common treatment for fevers." LaShaun remembered her grandmother tying small bags filled with herbs. "Monmon Odette used those to treat several of my cousins for fever."

"Oui," Miss Clo said and pursed her lips, but said no more about LaShaun's infamous grandmother and her reputation. "And the boy got better real quick."

"Okay, so why isn't that the end of the story?" LaShaun asked as she sipped her coffee.

"This week a woman came to Joyelle. She first complained of having strange dreams. Then the rest of her troubles came out. Her husband accused her of cheatin' on him because he caught her goin' out at night. She'd come back with her clothes all messed up and sayin' she didn't know what he was talkin' about." Miss Clo shook her head. "Somethin' ain't right in this parish. "

LaShaun put down her cup. "I'm not sure what you want me to do."

"Talk to Joyelle. She's worried, but she wouldn't come with me because... well." Miss Clo shrugged.

"She's scared of getting mixed up with the Rousselles, and me in particular, I know. But so far I don't see anything supernatural in what you told me. Because that is why you woke me up so early and showed up with the sunrise, right? I'm supposed to be the Vermillion Parish Voodoo queen." LaShaun gazed at her with a raised eyebrow.

"Let me tell you, I never called you evil," Miss Clo blurted out in a rush. "A little wild maybe, but that's all in the past. I know because my Myrtle Jean wouldn't say it if it wasn't so, and that's what I tell folks when they bring up gossip about you."

"I thank you for defending me, Miss Clo." LaShaun gave her hand a pat and smiled. "Tell your friend not to worry. All she's got is a little boy that just happened to get sick around the same time he snuck out at night to play. This woman is stepping out on her husband, but didn't have the sense or imagination to come up with a believable story when she got caught. No spirit possession, no mojo, nothing but plain old small town shenanigans."

"But what about Reverend Fletcher goin' around sayin' Joyelle is consorting with the devil? He's got people avoiding one of the sweetest and most good-hearted women on this earth." Miss Clo hissed with frustration.

"I don't know the name." LaShaun wore a slight frown.

"He's been in town about seven or eight months now. He took over as the new minister at Redemption Baptist Church, except now they done changed the name to the Church of Sweet Redemption. They're real strict on their members, especially the women I hear. Anyway, Pastor Fletcher even has a radio broadcast. Some members of the church left, didn't like his ways. But others who've known Joyelle for years told him about her. He says she's dealing in sorcery of some kind. He even convinced some folks she's the cause of their ailments, including that boy's mama."

"Adding me into the mix sure won't help that kind of talk die down," LaShaun said with a laugh. She grew serious at the look of chastisement from the older woman. "Sorry, but believe me I've faced that kind of treatment all my life, and so did Monmon Odette. One crazy pastor spreading gossip won't hurt her."

"But Joyelle's name is being dragged through the mud," Miss Clo said with heat. "Joyelle's husband has been hearing whispers from his co-workers. One of the supervisors at that plant is a deacon at that church. She's worried he'll lose his job because of her."

"The big oil refinery the Trosclairs own?" LaShaun thought of the rich, powerful local family she'd crossed swords with more than once.

"That's the one."

"He should sue their pants off if they fire him over something that crazy. But I still don't know what you want me to do, Miss Clo. In fact, your friend doesn't even want me involved." LaShaun shook her head.

Miss Clo sighed. "So you won't at least talk to the boy's mama, or Patsy? I told them you would try to help."

"You did what?" LaShaun squinted at her.

"I guess you too busy managing all that land and money, and thinking about your own affairs. Sorry to interrupt your mornin'."

Miss Clo rose and hooked her purse over an elbow. She started to leave, then came back to the table and wrapped two of the fluffy homemade biscuits in a napkin. With a curt nod, she headed down the hallway toward the front door.

On nothing but the strength of M.J.'s word, Miss Clo had ignored the advice of several of her neighbors to steer clear of Rousselles, and expecially LaShaun. She'd visited LaShaun in the days after Monmon Odette's death to bring comfort in the form of home cooking and kind words. She hadn't pushed her friendship on LaShaun. She seemed to sense that LaShaun was used to being alone. Still LaShaun knew she had an older woman to turn to, a grandmother figure, if she felt the need for one.

"I'm sure the talk will die down," LaShaun said as she followed behind her friend and tried not to feel badly about dismissing her concerns.

"Maybe so," Miss Clo tossed back over her shoulder. Once she got to the screen door leading to the long front porch she turned to face LaShaun. "I hope you have a good day, darlin'."

"Miss Clo--"

The proud mother of seven and grandmother of twenty raised a hand like a school crossing guard stopping traffic. "No need to beat a dead horse. You're right. These two poor things suffering from Lord knows what ain't your problem."

"It's not that I don't care, but..." LaShaun looked at a stoic and determined face. "I'll talk to one of them. If I say there's nothing odd or strange that should be the end of it."

"Of course. Joyelle and I will be here at two o'clock on Thursday. She said afternoon would be fine." Miss Clo started went down the steps then stopped and turned around. "I mean, if that's a good time for you."

"Thursday at two o'clock is fine. Should I bake cookies, too?" LaShaun quipped. Her sarcasm missed the target.

Miss Clo waved a hand in the air and continued on to her little Chevy Traverse. "No, cher. I'll bring some of my chocolate chip and walnut oatmeal cookies. You just make the coffee. Bye, now."

"Yeah, no problem. Make the coffee, eat a cookie, and get drawn into somebody else's drama. Happy to oblige," LaShaun grumbled, but waved at the departing force of nature with a smile. Then she burst into laughter at the smooth way she'd been played.

*****

The next morning LaShaun went into town to pick up a few groceries, and maybe a little gossip about Patsy Boutin. Thankfully there were a lot of new residents in Beau Chene, people who didn't seem to listen to local gossip. Or maybe they were more open-minded. Whatever the reason, LaShaun got an equal number of friendly smiles mixed in with the wary looks from residents born and raised in Beau Chene. Still, she had only two people she could turn to for insider news. Attorney Savannah St. Julien Honoré was one of them. Since becoming Acting Sheriff, M. J. stuck to the rules even closer than before. No way would LaShaun put M. J. in a bad position, especially by dropping in to chat with her at the station. So that left Savannah. LaShaun timed her shopping trip to make sure Savannah would be in her office. She parked in a space on Broad Street and walked a half block.

"Good morning. How can I help you?" A fresh faced young woman beamed up at her. Savannah's new legal secretary had big hazel eyes and bouncy reddish brown curls. Her smile suggested that any legal problem brought to their door could be solved. The name plate on her desk read "Ginger Roberts" in black letters.

"Hi. Nice to meet you, Ginger. I'm here to see Savannah. LaShaun Rousselle. I don't have an appointment," LaShaun added before the young woman could ask.

"Oh, I see." Her light brown face grew serious, as though not having an appointment meant LaShaun was in serious trouble. "I'll check with Mrs. Honoré right now."

"Thanks."

LaShaun grinned at the way the young legal secretary hustled off. Moments later Savannah led the way back to the lobby. Her secretary blinked rapidly at LaShaun.

"Good morning," Savannah smiled. Then she tilted her head to one side. "I hope this is purely a social visit."

LaShaun laughed. "It is, I promise."

Savannah grinned back and walked to her office. "Okay, then you can come on in. Otherwise I was going to send you over to my friend in Lafayette Parish. I can't take another action-packed episode in the life of LaShaun Rousselle."

"Hey, I'm not the only source of turmoil around here," LaShaun tossed back, and sank down in a comfortable leather chair in the seating area.

Savannah brought out a box of donuts, and then poured coffee in two mugs. She sat across from LaShaun in a matching chair and propped her feet on the seat of a third one.

"I'm not going to comment, except to say you provide the most interesting commotions at least. None of this routine, penny ante trouble. Why can't people manage their lives a little neater?" Savannah bit into a donut and chewed for a few moments. "I mean, is that too much to ask?"

LaShaun selected one of the glazed treats that had a filling. "Apparently the answer is yes. Life is messy."

"Oh well, I could have stuck to marine law, and mineral and oil rights practice. But I wanted the human side of law." Savannah sipped from her mug.

"Be careful going after what you want, as the old saying goes." LaShaun gave her shoulder a pat and laughed at the scowl on her friend's face. "Speaking of messy lives, Miss Clo came to see me. For once, somebody other than me is being accused of putting bad gris-gris on folks."

"Humph, that's small town Louisiana for ya. Your neighbor trips and breaks a toe after y'all get into a fuss, and bam! You must be burning black candles on 'em. It'll blow over soon enough."

"Like it blew over with me, you mean?" LaShaun looked at her.

"You have a point. So Miss Clo came to consult our local expert in the dark arts, eh?" Savannah smothered a laugh when LaShaun's eyes narrowed to slits.

"Funny. What have you heard about Patsy Boutin? She's younger than us, right?" LaShaun asked as she licked icing from her fingers, then grabbed a napkin and wiped her hands.

"Yeah, about twenty-four. Patsy was in school with one of my cousins on mama's side. She married her high school sweetheart. Vic ignored all the talk, and his mama's advice, and marched down the aisle with her anyway."

"What talk?" LaShaun said.

"Patsy's hobby is collecting male admirers. Rumor has it her current back door man is a handsome fella who moved here three years ago; a very *married* handsome fella." Savannah carefully selected a second donut and sat back in her chair. "Not that I'm one to spread gossip, you understand."

"Oh, of course not; you're simply sharing insights into human nature," LaShaun tossed back with a chuckle.

"Very important in my profession," Savannah said and grinned back at her. "I'm guessing you already know he finally got fed up and walked out on her."

"All a big misunderstanding according to Miss Clo," LaShaun said and frowned. "And she's not some gullible little old lady either."

"So somebody is saying she's sneaking around because somebody put a spell on her?" Savannah let out a sharp laugh. "Yeah, some hunky man with a nice package in his tight jeans."

"If your daddy and aunt could hear such earthy talk," LaShaun shot back. Then she tapped her fingers on the table top. "I'm totally sympathetic to a woman who's the subject of lurid gossip about her romantic life."

"I remember the big scandal when a local high school coach got caught with Patsy parked on a secluded country road in the back of his SUV. They weren't discussing sports. Lucky for him, she'd turned eighteen the week before. Instead of a jail sentence all he got was suspended from his job for the school year, and a cast iron skillet aimed at his head when he got home. He survived, and so did his marriage, but just barely in both cases. He walked around with stitches on his scalp like he was wearing a big letter 'A' for adulterer."

"You just made my life simple again. I'm eternally grateful. I can go back to my quiet bayou country existence," LaShaun said as she got up to refresh her mug of coffee.

"Glad I could help. But like you said, Miss Clo is pretty sharp. If she's sensing something is up, keep your eyes and your mind open," Savannah replied.

"I will. Your new secretary seems very efficient." LaShaun sat down again.

"A little wide-eyed and innocent, but we'll put an end to that with a few sordid small town scandals,"

Savannah quipped. "She just moved here from Indiana with her husband. He's an instructor at the University of Lafayette. She needed extra money, and my paralegal left for bigger things."

"Sounds good." LaShaun was about to go on when Ginger knocked on the door and came in.

"Sorry to interrupt, but there's a call from the sheriff's station. Detective Broussard is on line two." Ginger's eyes were wide, proving Savannah's description as accurate.

"Thanks, Ginger." After Ginger left Savannah glanced at LaShaun. "Your sweetie tracked you down, girl. Must be checking in to see if he needs to pick up milk or something before he comes home."

"Number one, no man keeps tabs on me. Number two, if he did I'd make him regret it and number three, we're not playing house," LaShaun shot back.

"Whatever," Savannah replied with an impish grin. She went to the phone and picked up the cordless handset. "Hello officer. You're right on time. Oh, you really need to talk to me. Never mind, what's up?" She listened for a few minutes before she grabbed a legal pad and wrote notes. "Right, I can be there in a few minutes. I don't have any appointments until after lunch. Got it. And don't answer anymore questions." She hung up, stood and grabbed her leather satchel that functioned as a brief case and purse.

"Is Chase okay?" LaShaun's heart started to hammer in her chest. "Why would he need a lawyer?"

Savannah checked to make sure her supplies were in the satchel. "Those instructions weren't for Chase. He put his suspect on the phone."

"Enjoy the more human side of the legal profession," LaShaun joked as she walked out with her. "I'm going back to simple stuff, like picking up some fresh vegetables from the Farmers Market."

"Don't get too comfy. I have a feeling you're going to get a call from Miss Clo before Thursday. Vic just got arrested for trying to kill Patsy, but he's claiming it was self-defense."

It was LaShaun's turn to stare at Savannah with wide eyes. "Oh hell."

"And her daddy is at the station demanding a few minutes alone with Vic to beat some answers out of him. Patsy has gone missing." Savannah pushed through the front door. "Just watch the evening news tonight. I'm sure you'll hear more."

"Oh double hell." LaShaun planted her fists on her hips as she watched Savannah get in her car and drive off.

Chapter 3

Two days later the weather was just as lovely as the day before; a perfect Friday to cheer up all working people. Noon day sunshine painted the landscape and made colors look brighter against the clear blue sky. LaShaun looked forward to the weekend. Chase had three straight days off after working long hours all week. They planned to shut out the ugliness of the past five days. But instead of thinking TGIF, LaShaun was entertaining potential trouble in the form of two country ladies. Miss Clo had shown up after calling early in the morning again. This time she'd managed to drag Joyelle along. LaShaun went back into the front parlor where her grandmother had entertained for three and half decades. When she walked in balancing the painted wood tray the two women stopped their intense whispered conversation.

"Here we are, ladies, tea with a touch of mint." LaShaun smiled at Joyelle to put her at ease. The taut smile in return said she needed a lot more convincing.

"Thank you, baby." Miss Clo picked up the tall glass and drank. "Hmm, delicious and just sweet enough." She nudged Joyelle.

Seeing her friend had no ill effects, Joyelle cautiously raised the glass to her mouth and sipped. "Yes, it's very good."

"Thank you. Now what can I do for you ladies today?"

Miss Clo and Joyelle exchanged a glance. Miss Clo cleared her throat, sipped some tea and put down the glass. "You remember I came to you a few days ago about strange happenings, and Joyelle seeing some of her clients."

"Yes." LaShaun raised an eyebrow.

"I don't care what nobody says, Vic didn't hurt Patsy," Joyelle blurted out. Then she pressed her lips together as if working to keep more words from escaping.

"Okay." LaShaun sat back in chair startled, and unable to think of any other response. She looked to Miss Clo for some coherent explanation.

"That body wasn't even Patsy, and they still don't know who she is. Was," Miss Clo added with a wince. "May the Lord give the poor soul sweet rest."

"Amen," Joyelle said softly.

"Yes, I saw the news reports." LaShaun nodded.

According to KATC, the Lafayette television station they picked up in Vermillion Parish, no one had come forward to identify a dead woman. Found in a swamp, she didn't fit any of the missing persons reported in either Vermillion or Lafayette Parishes. Chase had told her there really was nothing else that the department was withholding.

"It means Vic didn't kill Patsy," Joyelle said, this time with less force. She seemed to have relaxed a little.

"Well, it means no one knows where she is. She could still be alive," LaShaun said carefully.

"Plus that Tommy Daigle is missing. Did they run off together, LaShaun?" Miss Clo leaned forward as though LaShaun would go into a trance and solve the mystery.

"Seems likely, huh?" Joyelle stared at LaShaun as well.

LaShaun smiled. "There is nothing supernatural about two cheating people high-tailing it out of town together; which brings me back to Patsy going out at night."

"And having amnesia, don't forget that part," Joyelle cut in. "I knew Patsy's reputation, so I was gonna tell Vic to get some sense. But then I talked to her, looked into her eyes. Something ain't right with the girl."

"I believe most folks would agree. Let's just say Patsy has a problem with faithfulness," LaShaun replied.

"I wouldn't argue with one thing you're saying," Joyelle said with a firm nod. "I told Vic instead of me he needed to see one of them marriage counselors."

"Or a lawyer about a divorce. Reverend Fletcher should be preaching to those two instead of going after good people. Vic ain't no angel by a long shot," Miss Clo said and gave a grunt to punctuate her opinion.

"Really?" LaShaun became even more convinced no psychic abilities were needed figure this one out.

"The ones we really feel sorry for are their two little girls. Poor babies are caught up in Sodom and Gomorrah," Miss Clo replied. "Lord only knows what they seen and heard in that house."

"Bless their sweet little hearts," Joyelle added.

"This all sounds very interesting, but I don't know why you're here talking to me." LaShaun shrugged.

This time both women cleared their throats. Miss Clo nudged her friend with an elbow. Joyelle blinked back at her and remained silent. Then she studied some far off point visible through the window facing the sofa where she sat. Miss Clo heaved an annoyed sigh.

"Joyelle ain't only talkin' about Patsy. I told you about the little boy. There were two others who had the same problem. They all was disappearing at night, and would come home looking like they'd been running in the woods all night." Miss Clo nudged her friend again, this time harder.

Joyelle twisted her hands together. "I just thought at first it was some kind of strange sickness I never seen before. But after a while I thought... maybe somebody put something on these folks."

"You mean voodoo," LaShaun said out loud what they kept hinting around. Both women flinched, and then nodded in unison.

"I got a bad feeling about it all," Joyelle replied barely above a whisper.

"The facts don't point to anything strange. Since Patsy's lover happens to be missing now, I'd say you don't need to worry." LaShaun picked up the small plate. "Have a spicy cheese puff."

"No thank you." Miss Clo waved away the offer while her friend shook her head. "LaShaun, you haven't been listening with your full attention. You got to look past the surface here. There is a pattern."

"A dark, dangerous pattern," Joyelle added leaning forward for emphasis. "In the last year six peoples come to me, mais yeah. They all got the same kind of sickness. Finally with a lady over in Iberia Parish, I went one morning to see her. Her mama said she'd been out all night. Her eyes were red and wild, and she couldn't say where she'd been or what she'd been doing. She was covered with scratches."

"Tell her about the marks," Miss Clo said.

Joyelle put a hand to her mouth then lowered it. "She had bite marks on her neck."

LaShaun looked from her to Miss Clo and back again. "Bite marks?"

"Looked like something had just been nipping at her like, not deep wounds. Some barely broke the skin. God protect us," Joyelle said quietly. "I really think there is some kinda evil movin' through the land."

"Sounds more like hickeys. Her boyfriend got a little too affectionate." LaShaun grinned at them hoping to lighten the mood. The two women stared back at her.

"This ain't a jokin' matter, young lady," Miss Clo said.

"Yes, ma'am. Sorry. Tell me a more about these symptoms you've observed." LaShaun put on a serious expression.

"All of 'em have memory loss. Two of them had bad dreams that they was runnin' through the woods after something or somebody." Joyelle stopped and looked at Miss Clo.

"Go on, tell it all." Miss Clo nodded. She looked at LaShaun. "This part we haven't told anybody."

LaShaun felt an uneasy prickle along her arms. "Okay."

"I said it was six in the last year, but back in 2007 I had another case. I didn't think about it until all this started happenin'." Joyelle closed her eyes for a few seconds and then opened them again. "Manny Young came to see me, actually his grandmama brought him. He was runnin' wild. Ms. Flora Lee wanted me to pray over the boy." She stopped again. Her hands trembled in her lap.

Miss Clo put a hand on her shoulder. "You heard about Manny Young?"

"Yeah," was all LaShaun could manage from her now dust dry throat.

The entire country had heard about Emanuel "Manny" Young, the Blood River Ripper as some creative reporter had named him. Seven young women and five men had been found ripped apart, their body parts scattered in the prairies across three parishes. His lawyer had successfully put on an insanity defense. Manny was convicted in 2010, but in an unusual move, the judge ordered that he be committed to the Feliciana Forensic Hospital. The court found that he needed treatment. When he became mentally stable, he'd be sent to Angola State Penitentiary's death row.

"Manny was doin' the same thing. Goin' out at night, comin' back in looking all wild and crazy. He'd get drunk, like his daddy, and get into trouble." Joyelle drew in a deep breath and let it out.

"His mama took off when he was a baby," Miss Clo put in.

"They started finding the bodies in April 2008. Flora Lee should have come to see me early on, though I'm not sure it would have helped." Joyelle picked up her glass, emptied it with one deep gulp and then put it back down.

"His granddaddy said he'd grow out of it," Miss Clo said.

"I tried prayin' for him, but he got a little crazy and tore outta my house." Joyelle gave a shudder.

"The look in his eyes was terrible. A month later they found the next body, and another, and another."

"All of the women had a history of arrests for drugs and prostitution, so did the men," LaShaun murmured as the details she'd read when she lived in Los Angeles came back to her.

"Some came from out of New Orleans after Katrina," Miss Clo said. Everyone in Louisiana referred to the horrendous Hurricane Katrina by one name. The 2005 storm had killed hundreds, and changed New Orleans forever.

"So folks from around here just assumed it was all drug related, some gang or something." Joyelle seemed to age as she thought about the grisly events. Then she looked at LaShaun.

"If you read about it, then you know they finally found Manny's DNA on three of the bodies." Miss Clo continued to pat her friend's shoulder.

"And he confessed," LaShaun added.

"He'd told me about these dreams he had" Joyelle gripped Miss Clo's hand. "I don't think I can say them horrible things."

"You go sit out on the porch in the sunshine for a bit," Miss Clo said. Joyelle nodded and left. Moments later they heard the sound of the front screen door shut as she went out.

"She's really shaken up." LaShaun didn't feel any amusement now.

"Manny told her about several dreams. In one he was with a pretty girl, and they was having fun, of a sexual nature. He didn't know how much time passed, but he woke up in the woods with blood all over him. The girl was gone. Another one, he dreamed he was eating raw meat." Miss Clo put a hand to her chest before she went on. "That was six months after they found parts of a dead woman in St. Mary Parish. After Manny was convicted Joyelle saw pictures of some of the victims in the local paper during Manny's trial."

LaShaun's entire body hummed with a kind of electricity. She sat straight. "One of the victims fit the description of the pretty girl Manny saw in his dream."

"Yes," Miss Clo said, her voice shaking.

"Joyelle didn't go to the police?" LaShaun now had the sensation of a rock sitting in her stomach.

"She didn't know all the details until long after the trial was over." Miss Clo spoke with force in defense of her friend. "He was convicted anyway."

"I'm not judging her, Miss Clo, not at all," LaShaun replied quickly.

Joyelle came back inside. She looked somewhat revived. "Fresh air and sunshine did me good. Sorry for getting so nervy on you, Clo."

"Any normal person would get spooked by all these strange goings-on." Miss Clo patted her friend on the back when Miss Joyelle sat down next to her again.

"Anyway, I didn't see nothing strange when the first case came to me. But then after a third person wanted prayer and talked about bad dreams." Joyelle shook her head slowly. "Now Patsy is missing, and her husband is being accused of doing something awful to her."

"And they find a dead body?" Miss Clo gazed at LaShaun. "You tell me this is all just normal stuff."

"Does seem strange." LaShaun gazed out one of the windows. The scene beyond seemed peaceful and lovely. She was finding it hard to imagine a sinister undercurrent in Vermillion Parish.

"Thank the good Lord, you're gonna find out what's happening," Miss Clo said with a wide smile.

"Oh now wait a minute," LaShaun replied. The two women gazed at her in dismay. "I'm not even sure where to start."

"Manny's granddaddy says you can go with him on his next visit to the Forensic Unit," Joyelle blurted out.

"I'm not going to a secure facility full of violent men found to be criminally insane. No thank you very much." LaShaun looked at Joyelle as though she'd lost *her* mind.

Miss Clo put a restraining hand on her friend's arm. "That might not be necessary just yet, Joy. I happen to have a few things you can start reading."

"Really?" LaShaun blinked at her in surprise.

Miss Clo reached into her large quilted handbag. She pulled out a folder with a large rubber band around it. "I've got copies of clippings about Manny's case, the trial and all. I made notes on what Joyelle told me."

LaShaun took the folder. "You been listening to M.J. talk about work, or did she get her investigative skills from you?"

"A little of both," Miss Clo replied with a grin.

The two women waited as LaShaun looked through the packet of material Miss Clo had given her. Newspaper stories were organized in date order beginning with the discovery of the bodies, then with Manny's arrest, trial and conviction. A year later a psychiatrist wrote a scholarly article on cultural beliefs and crime. Though he didn't identify Manny, it didn't take a reporter much digging to figure out the "Louisiana case" was the Blood River Ripper. A year later the reporter did a follow-up story which included an interview with Manny's grandfather, relatives of the victims and the assistant district attorney who handled the case. Miss Clo had carefully typed up notes of Joyelle's account of how she met Manny and what she remembered.

LaShaun looked up at the two women. "I'm speechless. You've put a lot of effort into this."

"My daughter bought me a lap top and one of those fancy wireless printers." Miss Clo shrugged as if it was no big deal.

"Clo was always real organized, even in high school," Joyelle put in.

LaShaun closed the folder. When Miss Clo and Joyelle continued to gaze at her, LaShaun cleared her throat. "I'll call you in a day or so, maybe three. I want to read it thoroughly, and maybe do a little of my own digging."

"Well, that sounds reasonable. So we'll let you get back to your quiet Friday. We're in for a beautiful weekend." Miss Clo and Joyelle, taking her cue, stood as well.

"We thank you for helping us figure this out, LaShaun." Joyelle seemed relieved to hand over at least part of the burden to someone else.

"I can't make any promises. So I don't want you two to get your hopes up," LaShaun said as she walked them toward the front door.

"We have faith in you, don't we Joy?" Miss Clo said.

"Yes we do," Joyelle replied.

"Thanks, but folks staying out late and getting into mischief may be a coincidence." LaShaun tried to manage their expectations.

Joyelle's round pleasant face wore a sad expression. "It's not."

"Have a wonderful weekend, cher."

Miss Clo patted LaShaun's shoulder and the two friends left. As they walked away they spoke softly to each other. Once in Miss Clo's small car they waved one last time before they drove away. LaShaun watched the car disappear. She looked around at the land surrounding her house. No wave of danger or anything abnormal came to her. She saw beech, oak and magnolia trees. Green grass carpeted the ground that was her front yard. The wooded land she now owned, thanks to Monmon Odette, surrounded the house to the west for six acres. Her nearest neighbors were a good two miles away in that direction. To the east she could barely make out Xavier Marchand's horse barn. Their family home was three quarters of a mile to the east past the barn. Not even a whiff of anything sinister came to LaShaun on the slight autumn breeze.

She carried the folder into the house and put it on the antique desk where she did bills, and where her lap top sat. Determined not to think about stranger wanderings at night and serial killers, LaShaun did housework. She dusted around the folder, stared at it but kept going. She went into the kitchen and prepared the batter for homemade hushpuppies. All the while her mind kept going back to folder. What she wanted was to prepare for the days she'd spend with Chase. But she rushed through her preparations, finally filling up her grandmother's huge pot with gumbo ingredients so that it could simmer. Then she retrieved the folder and settled on the bench. For two hours she absentmindedly stirred the pot and read. When there was a knock on the door she jumped and looked out of the bay window. Chase stood waving at her.

"You plan to let me in sometime before it gets dark out here?" he called, his deep voice muffled by the glass between them. He was dressed in a red checkered flannel shirt. The sleeves were rolled back to reveal his muscled forearms. He wore blue jeans and a dark red cap covered his curly black hair.

"Sorry." LaShaun put the folder down, careful not to lose her place, and then went to the back door to let him in. "I got so involved in reading I didn't hear you."

Chase kissed her lips lightly. Then he walked in and tossed a small travel bag on the wooden bench near the back door. "That must be some good book. Smells good in here. I hope dinner's almost ready. I barely had half my sandwich at lunch before I had to get back to work."

"Long day with all the excitement, huh?" LaShaun took the cap from his head and hung it on a rack above the bench.

"Pooh, I don't wanna even talk about it. Crazy stuff. I just wish Patsy and her latest fling would let somebody know where they ran off to, and this circus can be over." Chase sat down on the small sofa in the seating area LaShaun had added to the kitchen. He turned on the flat screen television. Flipping the channels he found a sports network. "I'm just glad to have a few days off."

"I'll bet." LaShaun sat next to him and smiled when he took her hand in his without taking his eyes off the sports news. She tapped her foot for a few seconds. "Did anybody identify the dead woman y'all found?"

"No, we're circulating a drawing. I figure we'll get something sooner or later." Chase stretched out his long legs and settled back against the cushion. After a few moments he laughed at a joke one of the sports reporters made. "That guy's a real wise ass."

"Yeah, funny." LaShaun waited a few more moments. "So what's the cause of death?"

"Prelim says blunt force trauma, but there was some decomp so..." Chase looked at her sideways. "Hey, we're not talking dead bodies, murder and grim reaper stuff. For two days we're going to discuss nothing heavier than the weather or what we're going to eat."

"I know. You want to get away from crime and punishment. I don't blame you." LaShaun patted his hard thigh.

"Good." Chase kicked off his leather cowboy boots and stood up. He stretched, and then went to the stove. He lifted the pot and sniffed. "Is it ready?"

"Sure. I mostly cooked it the other day. The seasonings should be well into the shrimp and chicken by now. I'm going to drop a few oysters in, the way you like it, and let them simmer for about ten minutes," LaShaun said.

She got the covered bowl of oysters from the refrigerator. Chase went to the window and looked out as LaShaun dropped the oysters in and set the kitchen timer. He picked up the folder LaShaun has been so engrossed with.

"So this is what had you so hypnotized you couldn't hear anything." His voice trailed off as he flipped the pages. "Honey?"

"Yes, babe." LaShaun stirred the pot then covered it back up. She took out the electric fryer and filled it with oil.

"Why are you reading about a serial killer on the eve of our quiet weekend, the days we planned to love on each other and think nice thoughts?" Chase asked as he continued to scan the pages in the folder.

LaShaun watched the oil heat up quickly. She took out the hushpuppies, but waited longer for the oil to get to the right temperature. "I was just looking over information Miss Clo brought me."

"Sweet Miss Clo is riding around the country side with a serial killer scrap book," Chase said. He walked over to stand in front of LaShaun. "M.J. would be more than a little disturbed to hear this."

"You don't want to discuss this stuff on our special weekend." LaShaun reached for the folder.

Chase moved it just beyond her reach. "Maybe just a little bit."

LaShaun turned around and dropped six hushpuppies into the oil. They started to sizzle immediately. "Miss Clo and her friend Joyelle came to see me this afternoon. According to them, strange things are going on in Vermillion Parish, and... Joyelle said prayers over Manny Young about a year before he was arrested."

"And?" Chase prompted when she paid more attention to the cooking rather than telling him more.

"Joyelle says Manny was acting strange like Patsy Boutin and a few of her other patients, for lack of a better word. You know Joyelle is a traiteur." LaShaun took two ceramic gumbo bowls and plates to set dinner on out of the cabinet.

"Yes, I but I don't get the connection." Chase let out a sharp hiss. "Oh wait a minute, they're saying something supernatural is going on."

"Not really in so many words," LaShaun said calmly. She used a slotted metal spoon to remove the now golden brown hushpuppies. She put them on a small serving plate lined with a paper towel to soak up excess oil. Then she faced him and crossed her arms.

"If Miss Clo or Joyelle thinks there is a connection to a known crime, talking to law enforcement is what they need to do," Chase said, wearing his professional lawman expression.

LaShaun sighed. "Joyelle doesn't have anything more substantial than her experience and a gut feeling. You want to interview Joyelle about her intuition?"

"So they come to the local paranormal detective." Chase raised an eyebrow at her.

"Coming from anyone else I'd say you were mocking me," LaShaun shot back, and grabbed the folder from his hands. She put it on the small desk in a corner of the kitchen.

"You know better. The last time things got dangerous. Now we're talking a psycho serial killer." Chase grabbed her by both shoulders. "Yes, I know you can handle yourself in most situations, but why take chances?"

"So I guess you don't think visiting the Blood River Ripper is a great idea either, huh?"

"What the hell?" Chase stared at her with a stunned expression.

"I'm joking, ha-ha, a joke. Had you going there for a minute."

LaShaun wrapped her arms around his waist and smiled up at him. No need to mention that Joyelle brought it up. In fact, LaShaun was intrigued by the possibility of looking into the killer's eyes. She wondered what she'd see, and sense, from him.

"Visiting Manny Young maybe the *worst* idea of all possible ideas." Chase gazed at her pointedly. "You agree, right?"

"I can see the downside of visiting a vicious murderer," LaShaun replied. She gave him a peck on the chin then stepped away. "Let's eat."

"No more talk about murders, murderers, and cheating wives on the run. I'm going to wash up."

Chase padded on sock covered feet to the master bathroom. When he came back they feasted on hot gumbo, hushpuppies and cold root beer from a local soft drink company. Chase steered the conversation firmly away from his work. Even when they settled in front of the television, he turned off a popular crime show and found a pirate movie instead. The sweet comfort of being with him wrapped around LaShaun like one of her favorite quilts. Later in bed his kisses and the touch of his long fingers banished any other thought outside their own little world. Hours into the early morning, Chase snored softly next to her. LaShaun's eyes popped open to see the glowing digital clock show her the time. A strange howl echoed from a distance. Or had she been dreaming? She closed her eyes and tried not to think of Manny Young.

Chapter 4

LaShaun and Chase spent Sunday fishing in a pond only a few miles away from Chase's house. They took their time getting back to his house. There they showered and changed, and drove down river to a charming seafood restaurant. LaShaun suggested The Cafe Long Vue because of the delicious food; and because it was far away from Beau Chene in St. Mary Parish. She was still worried about Chase's election chances. The view of the water and boats motoring by outside wide the windows served as lovely a backdrop. Chase seemed totally relaxed as he talked about his nieces and nephews. His eyes sparkled as he recounted what made each one uniquely wonderful. Then he glanced up, and LaShaun knew what was coming.

"Too bad you couldn't come to our family barbecue Labor Day weekend," he said in a casual tone.

"We agreed that it would have been awkward," said LaShaun as she speared a plump grilled shrimp and dipped it in sauce before eating it.

"No, I agreed that *you* would feel awkward. My family would have welcomed you." Chase tilted his head to one side. "My daddy can put anybody at ease in any situation. The man is a born diplomat, and big teddy bear."

"We've only been dating a few months. Why don't we give them a little while longer to get used to having their son involved with the voodoo priestess of Vermillion Parish," LaShaun quipped, and then glanced out of the window. "Hey, there's my dream boat."

Chase reached across the table and grabbed her right hand. "I'm not going to push you on meeting the family. Just know that I'll issue the invitation every once in a while."

"Okay." LaShaun relaxed beneath his touch.

"Like right now. My brother and his wife always have a big blow out Halloween party, and it's Jessi's birthday," Chase said quietly, still holding her hand. "You've got a good three weeks to think it over."

"I'm sure I'll make a fabulous addition to the spooky festivities. The place will be packed to see if I stir up any real goblins." LaShaun once again felt the old sense of isolation in the midst of a crowd, the staring eyes directed at her as though she were an exhibit in a freak show. She attempted to pull her hand away, but Chase held on.

"The party is all about the *kids*. We have more princesses and comic book hero costumes than any ghostly kind of thing. We play old fashion games, but we also have some fun video games, too," Chase grinned. When LaShaun gave him a pointed look he sighed. "Okay sure, they decorate with fake spider webs and rubber spiders, a few old sheets made up like ghosts and maybe a scarecrow."

"Right." LaShaun freed her hand and crossed her arms.

"My sister is usually dressed as something goofy, like a lady bug. It's not what you're thinking at all. Good, clean harmless fun. They're not inviting you because of any kind of hidden agenda." Chase grew serious. "I wouldn't stand for it even if my family was like that, but they're not. They're caring, open-hearted people."

"Which is where you get it," LaShaun said softly. "Sorry for being so paranoid. I'm used to it being me and my grandmother against the world. She's gone now and..."

"You're not alone. Besides, you've got people who care about you. But I want you to feel completely fine with it when it happens."

"Thanks for understanding," LaShaun said.

She tried to sound hopeful. When he smiled and went back to his plate of baked trout, LaShaun felt a stab of guilt. Chase kept talking about his family, including uncles and aunts. Deep down she wasn't sure she could be the woman he needed. The thought left her cold. Although LaShaun had dreamed of having a sister she could confide in, or a big brother to stand up for her, the reality of an adopted family made her feel jittery. She tried to imagine having expectations and frequent questions directed at her. What Chase thought of as family closeness and caring made LaShaun feel claustrophobic.

"I'm used to being on my own. It can get lonely, but on the other hand it's..." LaShaun hesitated before saying the word "freedom".

"What?" Chase wiped his mouth with a corner of the cloth napkin.

"Having to attend family gatherings and talk about personal stuff is going to be tough for me." LaShaun knew she'd stick out like a sore thumb in a crowd of chattering people blurting out their business and getting into hers.

"Small talk with people you hardly know doesn't come easy to you. I get it." Chase tilted his head to one side and studied her for a few moments. "Which is why we'll take it slow."

"Thanks," LaShaun murmured.

What if she was never ready for the "meet the family" event? When she tried to look on the bright side point of view it didn't work. She was about to be more open with him, but the ringing of his cell phone interrupted. Chase's expression became serious when he looked at the call ID display.

"Hello, boss."

He signaled to LaShaun that he was going outside. He walked through the glass doors that led outside to the patio and found a corner away from the few diners out there. LaShaun didn't need her psychic gifts to tell her that call couldn't be good news. M.J. would only interrupt his day off for serious business. Chase walked farther away until he crossed the wooden bridge over a strip of water. Soon he was on the grass of a high bank overlooking the river, well away from anyone. LaShaun felt a familiar warm tingle along her spine, up her neck and across her shoulders. The news Chase was hearing involved death, specifically the dead woman they'd found that turned out not to be Patsy Boutin. As Chase strode back toward the patio doors, LaShaun waved to their waiter.

"We need the check and two boxes for our food, please," LaShaun said.

"Sure thing, ma'am." The tall thin young man left.

Chase sat down. "Sorry, but M.J. needs me to come in for a couple of hours."

"I've already sent for the check and to-go boxes." LaShaun nodded toward the approaching waiter.

"That 'seeing the future' thing throws me off every time," Chase said low so the family of four sitting at the next table wouldn't hear.

"You're a deputy. Lawmen have emergencies, and they're subject to be called in at any time. Common sense deduction, babe." LaShaun decided not to mention the rest of what she knew.

He smiled as he leaned closer. "I keep forgetting you're as smart a detective as Miss Marple, and a helluva lot sexier."

"I'm guessing I won't get to show you just how sexy a sleuth I can be tonight?" LaShaun made a soft kissing sound.

"Rain check," Chase said and winked at her.

The waiter returned and Chase sat back in his chair. He scowled when LaShaun insisted it was her turn to pay, but gave in. They put the remains of their dinner in the containers and left. On the ride back, Chase seemed distracted. He turned on the radio and tried to make small talk, but lapsed into long silences.

"Anything you can tell me? I won't gossip," LaShaun quipped.

He put a hand on her thigh and smiled at her. "I didn't want to spoil the last few minutes we have of our weekend."

"Last few minutes, huh? Must be bad."

LaShaun put her hand on his. There was danger, but LaShaun couldn't see if the threat was to Chase. When she noticed he wasn't wearing the necklace she'd given him, LaShaun started to ask. Then she saw the pendant hanging from a leather braided strap holding his keys. She sighed with relief. The sterling silver wolf's head set in onyx with a lapis lazuli stone beneath it had been given to her by her grandmother. Monmon Odette said the wolf was a symbol of power, and the onyx provided protection. Their Choctaw ancestors had handed down this wisdom. LaShaun touched the silver as she said a prayer of protection for him.

"Bad enough. We identified the dead woman. She disappeared from Baton Rouge about three years ago. She had a history of drug use and running off with men." Chase watched traffic as they turned onto Highway 14 and back into Vermillion Parish.

"Sad, but common. Her family got in touch when they saw her picture, huh?" LaShaun remembered in time to make that a question. She already knew the answer.

"Yes, and you're not fooling me." Chase squeezed her thigh then put his hand back on the steering wheel.

"Okay, so maybe I sense a few things. But don't forget I know just like everyone else that y'all spread that drawing far and wide." LaShaun sometimes wished she didn't see things ahead.

"Your gift doesn't bother me, honey," Chase said and smiled at her reassuringly.

LaShaun moved closer to him until their hips touched. "I sense that call had to do with the dead woman."

He nodded and his jaw set into his "on duty" look. "It sure does."

"What?"

"She's a member of a rich old Baton Rouge family. The kind of people that have a lot of money passed down from three generations back. These folks don't want to be in the news, not even the fancy society pages," Chase said.

"Okay, but... oh-oh." LaShaun let out a low whistle.

"Exactly. The media is swarming because someone has been spreading rumors about a supernatural serial killer." Chase glanced sideways at her then back at the road ahead.

"Well don't look at me. I've been with you." LaShaun poked his big bicep.

"What about your two buddies, Miss Clo and her sidekick?" Chase turned down the tiny highway that was a back route connecting to Rougon Road that would take them to Rousselle Lane eventually.

LaShaun shook her head. "No way. Joyelle had to be convinced to come see me, and she could barely talk about Manny Young. Miss Clo wouldn't gossip. She's worried about the backlash against her friend."

"Well somebody has been talking. I'll get the details when I meet M.J. at the station," Chase said.

"But why do they need you back? You've been working so hard," LaShaun protested. "They've got that other ambitious detective, Dave Gouchaux. "

"Yep, he's sharp. But M.J. wants me there, too. Dave can be a little too take charge sometimes," Chase said.

"I've seen him talk down to M.J." LaShaun gave a snort. "She's got more patience than me. I'd put that snot in his place quick. She's in charge, and you're going to be elected Sheriff."

"There's a little thing called an election, honey. Besides, M.J. can handle herself. She'll know when the time is right to check Dave." Chase smiled. "M.J.

might decide to run for Sheriff. It's not too late for her to fill out the papers."

"Oh, no. I don't want to choose, but of course I'd vote for you," LaShaun added quickly when he glanced at her. "I would!"

"Don't pretend that M.J. wouldn't make a fine Sheriff, and you like her a lot." Chase chuckled when LaShaun slapped his arm.

"I'm solidly in *your* corner, Deputy Broussard. Stop teasing. Besides, I happen to have it on good authority that M.J. doesn't want to run for Sheriff. She hates politics even more than you do. She told me being Sheriff is seventy percent dealing with asshole public officials." LaShaun laughed at the memory of the sour look on M.J.'s face when she said it.

"Gee, thanks for giving me something to shoot for. I really want the job now," Chase quipped.

"You'll do fine dealing with the people and police side of it," LaShaun said with certainty. "I just want you to be safe doing both."

"I'll be fine," he said. "If I even get elected remember."

"The folks in Vermillion Parish with any sense will run to the polls and press that button next to your name." LaShaun smiled at him, but it faded as they got closer to Beau Chene. The vibrations of trouble came to her in waves.

Fifteen minutes later they arrived at LaShaun's house. The outside security light at the end of her driveway and the one in her backyard had come on at dusk. It was only four thirty in the afternoon and already it was growing dark fast. LaShaun got out of Chase's truck and walked around to the driver's side.

She leaned in the open window and kissed his mouth hard.

"You owe me, Deputy Broussard."

"I always pay my debts, ma'am."

Chase claimed his own gentle kiss. He waited until LaShaun opened her front door and started to go in. She turned back and came out on the porch again.

"Hey you! Call me," LaShaun yelled after him as he turned around and drove away. He blew his horn in reply.

She watched the red glow from his truck taillights vanish as he turned the corner of her driveway and onto the road. LaShaun sighed. Even their shortened weekend had been wonderful. She breathed in the crisp night air. A huge October full moon glowed like a giant firefly in the night sky. Chase would admonish her about lingering outside at night, but the darkness and shadows once the sun disappeared had never frightened LaShaun. Leaning against the porch railing that ran the length of it, she gazed up at the sky. Her ancestors had been able to see a ceiling of stars. Even living far from a large city, it was hard to get the same view in these modern days. She looked at the lovely way shadows laced the woods in folds, a soft velvet midnight blue and black like a woman's cape. Suddenly a movement in her peripheral vision caused LaShaun to go still. Her senses kicked in. She calculated how fast she could get inside, slam the door and lock it. Plenty of time, she thought calmly. Even if this being, human or not, made it to her she could crash the carved oak rocker in that direction, and move quickly.

"Evenin', ma'am," the voice rumbled like a heavy rock rolling across the ground toward her. "I need to talk to you 'bout my boy."

Her breathing slowed down as LaShaun turned to face the figure standing on the edge of her driveway. He seemed to have come from a break between a huge swamp cottonwood tree and an oak, both planted over a hundred years ago. Was this another spirit stirred up by her ancestors in these woods? Her grandmother had taught her to fight back. She fingered the silver cross that hung from a chain around her neck.

"Who are you?" she asked, trying to project a fear she didn't feel.

Demons grew bold and proudly gave their names when humans cowered. Having his name would give LaShaun some power to strike out. The being didn't move. Waves of hopelessness buffeted her. She faced a man, not a specter.

"Step into the light, please," LaShaun said.

The man walked slowly across the driveway making gravel crunch beneath his shoes. He moved into the glare of the security lamp overhead. "I hope you don't mind me comin' out here unannounced. I thought maybe you'd find it harder to say no if I didn't call first."

"You still haven't told me your name, and why you're hiding. " LaShaun stood ready to either fight like a wildcat, or rush inside for her single barrel shotgun in the hall closet.

Headlights lit up the tree trunks suddenly as an all terrain vehicle rumbled through the brush east of LaShaun's property. The dark green camouflage buggy stopped, but the engine grumbled. "Hey neighbor, you all right?"

"Hi Mr. Marchand. I'm fine," LaShaun called back to her neighbor.

"I seen a truck head this way moving slow and swing onto your property. Didn't see it come back. Knew you weren't home." Xavier Marchand, Sr. jumped from the driver's side while his youngest son, Xavier, Jr. sat watching. "Kinda late for you to be out visiting strangers, fella."

"I got my cell phone ready to dial the sheriff's station, daddy," the seventeen year said.

"No need for that. Miss Rousselle ain't in no danger from me," the man said. No trace of alarm was in his tone.

Mr. Marchand took a few steps closer. He wore a surprised expression. "That you, Orin? Orin Young?"

"How you and the family been doin', Xavier? Haven't seen you in a while." Mr. Young nodded to the man.

"Yeah, since you stopped coming to the Men's Fellowship meetings at St. Anthony's," Mr. Marchand replied. "I'm good, and same for the family. How are you, Orin?"

"Can't say the same, Xavier. Can't say the same at all." Mr. Young replied. "I just want to talk to Miss Rousselle."

"I'm okay, Mr. Marchand." LaShaun knew the man was no threat.

"This is a bad thing," Mr. Marchand said low, as if speaking to himself. He backed up and got into the all terrain buggy again.

"Are you sure we should leave her? That dude showing up out here at night..." the younger

Marchand spoke quietly, but LaShaun could hear him. Xavier, Jr. shifted to hold the rifle in his hands so that it was visible, as a warning apparently.

"Let's get on home," his father said. He frowned at Mr. Young and then glanced briefly at LaShaun before shifting into reverse.

"We'll keep an eye out, Miss LaShaun," his son shouted over the noise of the vehicle's engine. His father did not look back, as though he was eager to be gone.

"Sorry, I tried to avoid anybody knowing I come out here. The whole town gonna know by tomorrow night. Guess I better leave." Mr. Young heaved a deep sigh. More waves of despair flowed from him.

"No point now. They're going to know anyway, so you might as well come in and say what you have to say." LaShaun looked at him.

"You ain't scared to talk to me by yourself?"

"I'm not scared. You can come in for some tea or coffee." LaShaun could feel that Mr. Young was wavering. His uncertainty warred with his desire to speak to her. "You've come this far."

"Yes." Mr. Young walked to the porch steps, but then hesitated again. One foot was on the first step. "Being seen with me won't be good for your reputation."

LaShaun's laughter startled him. "Mr. Young, you can't do my reputation any harm."

"What about your deputy? He wants to be sheriff I hear," Mr. Young replied.

Her smile faded and she looked at him with interest. "You better come on in then before anybody else sees you."

She opened the door and beckoned for him to go in first. After a few more seconds Mr. Young walked ahead of her into the house. LaShaun turned on the porch light and followed him into the formal parlor for visitors. Once he was seated on the edge of a chair, LaShaun went down the hallway to the kitchen. Fortunately she'd left the electric coffee maker prepared so all she had to do was flip the on switch. After setting up cups on a tray she went back to the parlor. Mr. Young stood staring at wood carvings on a side table. Then he gazed up at the landscape painting of one portion of LaShaun's family acres around the house. She'd taken down the portrait of Monmon Odette. The painting had a tendency to unsettle visitors. Instead she loaned it to the local museum, to the curator's great delight.

"The coffee will be ready in a few minutes. I have some homemade tea cakes to go with them." LaShaun smiled at the somber man.

"Don't go to no trouble for me." Mr. Young seemed accustomed to being shunned instead of welcomed.

"I didn't, Mr. Young. The tea cakes are waiting for guests, and the coffee was easy." LaShaun sat down knowing he waited for her to sit first. "How can I help you?"

"Lotta times folks just ask that outta habit. Don't really want to help. They just tryin' to get rid of somebody fast." Mr. Young sighed again.

LaShaun now had time and more light to study him. Mr. Young's thick hair was a silvery white. A long lock fell across his high forehead. Deep frown lines cut into both sides of his mouth, as though smiling was something he rarely did. He looked about seventy years old. His shoulders sloped down as though he was weighted with heavy burdens. She thought of the scripture in the Bible; he appeared to be a man of sorrows, acquainted with grief[2]. And yet she sensed something else beneath a shield to keep others out.

"I know you're Manny Young's granddaddy," LaShaun said, answering his unasked question.

Orin Young's shoulders slumped lower. The weight of acknowledging his kinship with a serial killer seemed to press him down even more. He nodded. "Most folks don't know he was a twin. His baby sister died, something called placenta failure. His mama always said Manny sucked all the life outta his twin."

His first victim? LaShaun felt a lump settle into her mid-section at the thought. "But you said he was a happy boy, so his childhood was normal. Right?"

"His mama wasn't right in the head. She took off, ended up living on the streets in New Orleans. My son, well he had problems with drinking. Me and my wife raised Manny. We'd go fishin' and huntin'. He loved to hunt." Mr. Young stopped and looked at LaShaun. "It ain't what you're thinkin'. He didn't take pleasure in killin' just for the sake of it. Lots of reporters said that, but they lied."

LaShaun wondered if Mr. Young's love for Manny made him blind to early signs of violence. Yet there were stories of killers who seemed no different from others; no horrible childhood to explain the burst of brutality later in life.

"I see. So his childhood was normal, even happy," LaShaun said.

"We did our best," Mr. Young said with strength. A light flared in his watery gray-green eyes.

"I'm sure you did, sir." LaShaun meant it. She felt his fierce love for the boy as he remembered him.

"Still he missed his mama, like any child would. Never could understand why she was gone. My son wasn't around, and when he did show up most times he was drunk and draggin' some bar fly floozy with him." Mr. Young scowled as though his son had walked into the room. "Manny had his problems when he got older, but he wasn't no killer."

"The state police had strong evidence that Manny murdered at least seven of the twelve victims."

Mr. Young blinked hard for several seconds and then rubbed his eyes with the back of one hand. He looked at LaShaun. "I don't think it was him. Oh, I know they had evidence he did it. I've never been one for superstition, all that hoodoo hocus pocus crap. But I seen his eyes, and it wasn't him."

LaShaun sat forward forgetting the scent of coffee that floated into the room. She wondered if he would have the strength to say it. "Explain what you mean."

"I looked in my boy's eyes. I don't care what nobody says, Miz Rousselle. What looked back at me wasn't my grandson." Mr. Young spoke with such force that the cords in his neck stood out. Then he lost steam again and sank against the cushioned back of the chair. "My wife lost her mind, too, when she looked at him. Been in a nursing home this past year. Doctors say it's Alzheimer's. I know different."

"Mr. Young, I can't help you by going to see your grandson."

He shook his head slowly. "Joyelle told me you said no."

"Then why did you come to see me, Mr. Young?" LaShaun studied him as he seemed to waver on how to answer.

"Whatever got hold of my boy is movin' in other folks. I knew your grandmama." Mr. Young wore a sad smile as he nodded at her surprise reaction. "My wife grew up not far from here, before her daddy lost his land. She'd play with Odette when they was kids. We never thought of her as evil. Fact is she helped us with our daughters. The girls went wild when they got to be teenagers. All three of 'em, only a year apart. Odette put a scare into them."

"How?" LaShaun raised an eyebrow.

"They were sneaking into the woods with boys, having liquor parties and such at night. Odette caught the kids out on her property and pretended to be workin' magic on 'em." Mr. Young wore a genuine expression of mirth for the first time. "They call it scared straight when they make kids tour a jail or prison, right? That's what she did. Scared those rascals straight. At least two settled down, finished high school and got decent husbands." The light died from his eyes.

"Must be hard on all the family," LaShaun said.

He seemed unwilling to broach that painful subject. Instead he stood up. "Listen to Joyelle, and talk to those other folks she told you about. Maybe you'll reconsider. I thank you for your time."

"Stay and have some coffee to take the chill off the night. We can talk some more and--"

"No, ma'am. I've lost the knack of being company for other folks. Besides, I don't have any more answers for you. All I know is Manny got taken over by something bad, real bad. He wasn't no angel, but he don't deserve to die with a needle full of poison stuck in his arm." Mr. Young gazed down at LaShaun solemnly. "You take care."

His last words didn't sound like a normal leave taking goodbye. He turned around and walked out of living room with LaShaun following him. The dour man's steps seemed heavy as he trudged across the porch, down the front steps and into the shadows. LaShaun saw the vague outline of a truck just off a path beyond a clump of azalea bushes. The headlights flared up and he backed out to the road. The rumble of the engine faded into the night as LaShaun locked the front door. For the first time a flicker of trepidation tickled the base of her spine.

*****

LaShaun came wide awake in the dark. She lay still as her eyes adjusted to the darkness in her bedroom. Every sense in her body told her she was alone. Yet her spiritual sense shouted the opposite. Nothing moved in the room. There was no sound except the occasional creak of wood settling in the old house. She was used to hearing the creaks and cracks. In fact they were oddly comforting. But she knew something was up. Coming fully out of a deep sleep always signaled she needed to be cautious. The antique brass clock on the table ticked off the seconds. The modern digital clock glowed on the nightstand next to her queen-sized bed. Fifteen minutes went by before she heard it; a soft insistent scratching. LaShaun rose slowly from the bed as though not wanting to startle the source of the noise.

Anyone else would think mice. LaShaun wasn't anyone else. Her supernatural alarm clanged inside her head causing a dull throb to take hold behind both ears. With catlike movements she pulled on a pair of jeans, a long sleeved t-shirt and a jacket. She found her leather walking boots at the foot of her bed and put them on, grateful she'd gotten the zipper version for fast dressing. In minutes she found the large hunting knife one of her male ancestors had used in the early eighteenth century. She clipped the leather sheaf that held it to her waist and walked down the hallway to her the back door leading to her porch. She unlocked the door, and the sound of the metal caused the scratching to cease.

LaShaun opened the wood door, then pushed through the screen door to step onto the porch. The soft glow from the tall security light reached the back yard, but only partially. Most of it was left in darkness, which LaShaun preferred. She scanned the quarter acre neatly mown lawn. Then she looked at the denser indigo blue where her woods began. Something in the distance moved; an outline different from the tree trunks and shrubs. LaShaun walked across the porch and down the steps toward the shape. It moved away. The thing wanted to put distance between them. Waves of apprehension and shame brushed across her senses like an unworldly breeze. LaShaun focused on sending a message of reassurance, of calm, to the thing. Instead it cringed even farther into itself. Then a sharp metallic taste flooded the back of her throat. A warning. She snapped back to her surroundings too late. Something hard slammed into her from the left and LaShaun hit the ground. She rolled onto her back as the man, or something crouched over her. Loud breathing above sounded like a cross between a human and an animal. The thing's fetid breath caused LaShaun to choke on bile rising in her throat. Whatever she faced had been feeding.

LaShaun made whimpering sounds to simulate being in fear. The being let out a low growl as if pleased. A yelp from the woods caused the head to whip toward the sound. LaShaun drew her knife from the leather case and slashed at where she thought the legs would be. The shrill scream of pain sent chills up her spine. Suddenly the shadow over her vanished, and the scream faded as it ran for the cover of her forest. LaShaun scrambled to her feet and whirled around to check all sides for more danger. Her senses told her they were gone. Finally she let out the breath she was holding with a long sigh. LaShaun backed her way up the steps, across her porch and through the kitchen door. She slammed it harder than necessary and snapped the metal locks.

Her whole body ached from the impact as she walked on shaky legs to her kitchen. Only the soft light of the oven hood glowed, so LaShaun turned on the fluorescent lights set in the ceiling. She looked down, but found no scratches on her skin or rips in her clothing. Then she looked at the antique silver knife, wondering why she'd chosen to pick it up in the first place. A thick deep red liquid oozed on the blade. After a few seconds it sizzled as if the metal held heat. The liquid turned to ashes. LaShaun found brown paper used to wrap meat for the freezer. She tapped the ashes onto it though not sure why. Folding the paper carefully, LaShaun went into her small parlor. She found one of seven old family books, each bound in soft leather. Selecting the one she thought would be most helpful, LaShaun spent the rest of the night reading.

Chapter 5

The musical chiming in her dreams sounded familiar. LaShaun shifted position without opening her eyes, and wondered why the rabbit she was watching suddenly played a flute. Then she snapped awake. She lay stretched out on the small sofa in the entertainment nook off her kitchen. The forty-six inch flat screen television showed the local morning newscast, but the sound was muted. The book she'd been reading lay face down on the braided rug in front of the sofa. LaShaun looked at the digital clock display on the televisions screen. Six forty-five. When the doorbell chimed again she pushed herself upright, stretched and went to the back door. Chase looked as sleepy as she felt. She let him in.

"Good morning." LaShaun yawned as Chase kissed her cheek. "You're off to work early."

"Good morning back. And no, I'm going home after working almost twelve hours straight." Chase went to the kitchen and straight for the coffee maker. He sighed when he saw it was cold. "Okay, I'll make the first pot. You're up pretty early."

"Not exactly. I barely went to bed," LaShaun said.

"You didn't even drink this batch you made last night. Why couldn't you sleep?" Chase emptied the left over coffee and wet grounds to make a fresh pot.

LaShaun remembered her family journal and retrieved the book. Chase had his back to her as he measured coffee grounds into the filter and then filled the water well. She slipped volume seven of the

Histoire de la LeGrange Famille into the book shelf below the television, not ready to share the remarkable Rousselle and LeGrange chronicles with him yet.

"Just restless I suppose," LaShaun replied and found the television remote. She turned up the sound a little.

"I see. Wouldn't have anything to do with Orin Young stopping by last night for a chat, would it?"

LaShaun spun around to find Chase gazing at her with both hands resting on his wide leather police belt. He still wore his handgun, safely holstered. He also had a set of handcuffs and various other tools of the trade. His marine blue knit shirt had the department insignia on the right shoulder in gold. Chase looked very official.

"I didn't think Xavier Marchand was one to gossip."

LaShaun gave him a brief smile as she went past him to the cabinets. She took out two coffee mugs and set them on the granite counter top. Moving fast she grabbed a small cast iron skillet, got eggs from the fridge and started breakfast.

"The Blood River Ripper's grandfather visits Monmon Odette's granddaughter, and you're surprised word got out fast?" Chase leaned against the long counter and watched her.

"I'm surprised you've been tied up with a murder and missing person, people. I guess Patsy and her lover are still gone without a trace." LaShaun figured her attempt to steer the subject in a new direction wouldn't work. She was right.

"What am I gonna do with you?" Chase shook his head.

She wrapped her arms around his waist and pressed against him. "I've got some real good suggestions if you want to take off that uniform."

"I'm serious." Chase pulled free of her embrace and crossed his arms. "First of all you shouldn't have let the man in here at night when you were alone. His grandson is a serial killer."

"Right, but he's not. He was a member of the Catholic Men's Fellowship ministry at St. Anthony's. His wife grew up with my grandmother." LaShaun spoke in a measured tone to sooth his irritated nerves.

"Oh, well that cancels out the fact that he raised a murderer who butchered people." Chase's hard expression didn't soften even a little.

"If it helps, Xavier, Sr. and his son came over to check on me. I'll bet they kept an eye out until he left. His wife called later to make sure I didn't need anything."

Chase gave a grunt. "Betty Marchand wanted more information she could add to the gossip that I'm sure is making the rounds right now."

LaShaun was more than a little annoyed with him for seeing through what she didn't say. "Maybe so, but what does it matter? I baked some tea cakes. I'll give you a bag to take home."

"What does it matter? Oh I don't know, LaShaun. Maybe you might consider that folks will think I can't be trusted to protect them. I have to be seen as objective, willing to follow the facts and not be influenced." Chase followed her.

"So this is about you running for office, huh? What about the fact that Orin Young wasn't convicted of any kind of crime. Unless loving his grandson despite what he is or what he's done breaks some law." LaShaun faced him with her arms crossed and her own scowl.

"All I'm saying is..."

Chase broke off and walked away to stare out of the bay window. He leaned on one of the chairs around the table next to it. He wasn't enjoying the view of her woods either. LaShaun was buffeted by his strong emotions: anger and disappointment. She knew her tone should stay calm, but her annoyance at his judgment of her got in the way.

"What? Spit it out," she said.

"You won't meet my family, and you seem to be doing everything you can to stir the pot when it comes to town gossip. First it was this thing with Miss Clo and her friend Joyelle. Now of all people you could be seen talking to, Manny Young's grandfather. We both know half of Beau Chene already knows by now. The other half will get the news by dinner time."

"Let's deal with one thing at a time. First about meeting your family, just two days ago you said there's no rush. Remember that? Apparently you didn't mean it," LaShaun said.

He spun around. "I did, I do... it's just. I can't keep explaining to my folks why you won't come to Sunday dinner. Or even an evening of dessert and coffee with just my parents. I can understand if a big family event would be too intimidating to start."

"I'm not scared of your family," LaShaun shot back. "I'm proud of my own family, and I don't need to explain or apologize for who they were, and who I am."

"I only meant you need to get comfortable with letting them get to know you," Chase replied evenly.

"Showing up so I can pass inspection isn't my idea of an enjoyable social event." LaShaun glared at him.

"That's not true," he replied with heat.

"You want your parents and the rest of your family to approve of me. That means I shouldn't be discussing supernatural stuff with Miss Clo and Joyelle. Maybe I should have run inside the house and refused to open the door the minute I knew who Mr. Young was, huh? Should I let you give me a list of people and places I should avoid and subjects I can't discuss?" LaShaun matched his hot response with her own fiery words.

"Don't be ridiculous," Chase shot back. He massaged his forehead with the tips of his fingers. "The reality is I want to make a life for us in this parish, and as the *wife* of an officer of the law you--"

"Oh wait a minute, Deputy Broussard," LaShaun cut him off sharply. "We haven't even gotten that far in this affair."

"Okay. Right. We're having an *affair*." Chase's leaden tone made the word sound dirty.

"Stop with the self-righteous act. You were more than eager to have this *affair*. Don't try to make it sound like I deceived you or something," LaShaun shot back.

"Being with you is something special. At least it was to me. Otherwise I wouldn't have brought my family into it." Chase gazed at her steadily.

The "was" stabbed into LaShaun. His words sounded like rejection because she'd failed some standard, some benchmark test. She didn't know what he wanted from her, or maybe she did and knew she couldn't give it to him. Chase was measuring her by some yardstick that applied to other women, not her. She was a Rousselle, and she was used to walking on the fringes of normal social interaction.

"You're special to me, too; but if accepting who and what I am doesn't work for you then..." LaShaun crossed her arms, but this time to brace herself for pain.

"Meaning you don't do commitment?" Chase stood still, arms by his sides.

"We started off talking about Orin Young, and now we're having a heart to heart about us." LaShaun went to the cookie jar shaped like country cabin. She filled a plastic bag with tea cakes and closed it with a twist tie. She held it out to him. "You're leaving so you might was well take these."

"Is this my goodbye gift?" Chase said quietly as he took the bag.

"That's up to you," LaShaun replied. She angrily swiped a stray tear from her cheek then looked at him. "You would have an easier time getting elected and a less complicated life in general if you do say goodbye."

Chase stood holding the bag and gazing at her. "I need to change clothes, get a few hours of sleep and go back on duty. I'm too tired and on edge, not good for us to talk right now. I'll call you later."

"Okay." LaShaun took pride in the fact that her voice didn't crack, even though her heart did.

He approached and kissed her lightly on the forehead. For a few moments he seemed about to say more, but went through her back door instead.

LaShaun didn't follow him as usual. She heard the engine of his truck start and the sound of gravel crunching beneath the tires as he drove away. Only then did something force her to move to the back door and lock it.

To dodge the empty sensation those thoughts brought on, LaShaun went over plans to work on the house that wouldn't violate the historical features. Her great-great grandfather, Lawrence LeGrange, had built the original house in 1878 as a gift for his daughter Marianne. LaShaun gathered research to submit her application to the Louisiana State Historical Society. The local museum curator had agreed to help her, so LaShaun had two good reasons to go see him. The other being she needed to get out of the house and away from bad vibes left after her fight with Chase. LaShaun finished a few housekeeping chores, put the box of her family's documents in her CRV and headed for the museum. A few hours thinking about history was more appealing than brooding about a possible future without Chase

Hours later LaShaun felt better, but not much. Thank God Pete Kluger, the curator, had given her homework. LaShaun climbed to the finished attic and happily sorted dusty boxes and old trunks. Decades of Rousselle family clutter helped keep her busy.

"Thank you, Monmon, for being a confirmed collector. Pete will be thrilled, and I'll get to clean out this place," LaShaun muttered looking around with satisfaction.

She'd even managed to find a wooden box of more family papers that dated from the late nineteenth century. At first glance, the letters seemed fairly dull. But Pete would delight at tidbits from everyday life in nineteenth century Vermillion Parish. The chiming of the front doorbell interrupted her reading a riveting account of taking hogs to market. LaShaun put down the journal, slapped dust from her clothes and went down the narrow stairs. She was surprised to find Savannah on the porch.

"Good morning and what are you doing out here?" LaShaun asked as she brushed a cobweb from her shoulder.

"It's after twelve, and have you listened to the radio?" Savannah gazed at LaShaun from head to toe. "Girl, you really do some heavy duty housecleaning."

"Historical research," LaShaun replied and sneezed from the dust.

"Well you better jump back to the present and pay attention." Savannah marched past LaShaun down the hallway to the kitchen. She threw her leather purse down and glanced around for the radio.

"You've either had too much coffee today or not enough." LaShaun went to the sink and washed her hands.

"Listen to this." Savannah pressed the button on the radio until she found a station, then turned up the volume. A male voice rang through the speakers.

"The good people of Beau Chene, and all of Vermillion Parish, need to unite against darkness that is spreading around us as I speak these words. Evil, dear Christian friends, is seeping into the very soil beneath our feet."

"Give me a break," LaShaun muttered with a snort.

"I know what some of you are thinking. Reverend Fletcher, you're saying, don't be so melodramatic." He paused for effect. "But if you good people believe in angels and in the Holy Spirit, then you can't deny that the Bible speaks of demons and evil. Turn to Genesis, and remember how the serpent told the first lie. And neighbors, he's been lying and deceiving us ever since then. Why he even tried to tempt Jesus himself!"

"The man has flair I must admit," Savannah said.

"So how can we dismiss the notion that evil and demonic influences walk among us right here in Beau Chene? Be careful, because this evil dresses itself in pretty faces, and nice clothes. This evil talks about history and culture, cloaking itself in academic pursuits and uses pretty language like secular humanism. But don't be seduced or lulled into complacency by all these smoke screens. The devil is busy, and he's looking for any opening into the lives of God's children. We have to be vigilant, steadfast and brave. We must be willing to stand firm even when it's not popular. Let's take a couple of examples I talked about early in the show, friends. I've spoken to your town and our parish leaders about Halloween celebrations, a most ungodly celebration. Why, Reverend, I can hear some saying, what's the harm in children dressing up and eating candy?Too many parents have been sucked into thinking this is a harmless night of fun, but look deeper. There are dark origins to these Halloween celebrations. The aldermen of this good town are being asked to stop having official trick or treating hours. Not only that, some have suggested that we use this unholy holiday as a tourist attraction, and discuss profit from evil. Shame, on you, Peter Kluger and Savannah Honorè. That's right I'm naming names. We need to call out those trying to lead us to destruction."

"What did you do to yank his chain?" LaShaun looked at Savannah.

"I wasn't the only one," Savannah blurted out. "A bunch of area businessmen said it would be great to have a town event. Some suggested we have a costume contest, and tell popular local ghost stories and legends. At least a dozen people, including two of the museum board members, were at that meeting at the mayor's office."

"Let's see if any of them step up to admit to it now," LaShaun said in a grim tone.

"We cannot condone these kinds of activities, or be idle while wickedness takes hold in high places. Yes, Mr. Mayor, I know you want to bring tourists and more businesses to Beau Chene. Be careful what else you bring in the process." Reverend Fletcher's voice dropped low giving the warning.

"Whoa, this guy doesn't play. He knows exactly which buttons to push. Mayor Savoie hates controversy." LaShaun looked at Savannah who nodded back.

"Finally, we have to be sure that those we elect to positions of authority are rooted in righteousness. We're not just talking about the city hall. Right across from that seat of power sits another important office. Sheriff Triche has served this town well, and we must choose wisely when we replace him. Values, my friends, are reflected in behavior and who they associate themselves with. Isn't that what we teach our children? That they should mind the company they keep? Of course. Then it stands to reason that we can do no less for those who are role models for us and our children."

"I'm surprised he didn't just come out and say Chase's name," Savannah said with a grimace of distaste. "He's a coward."

"No, he's shrewd. Chase is popular with a lot of the younger residents and people from urban areas who have moved here. Also Sheriff Triche is behind him, and he's even more popular." LaShaun clenched both hands into fists. "Chase isn't too happy about Miss Clo coming to see me. And now with Orin Young wanting me to help his grandson..."

"What the hell?" Savannah started to go on but LaShaun waved her to silence.

"Shush, let's hear the rest."

"But take heart. We can and we will stand strong to make this a decent atmosphere for our families. Speak to our local officials. Spend your money at businesses that support Christian values. Trust me; we're not just talking about these issues. We're taking action. Let us pray for this town, this parish and this great state."

LaShaun snatched the satellite radio remote from a corner and hit the button. "I can't stand hearing his voice another second. What a load of sanctimonious hypocrisy."

She wanted to laugh off his "holier than thou" diatribe, but couldn't. If it only involved her, LaShaun wouldn't mind. She and her grandmother had faced such animosity before. But now people she cared about were affected.

"Amen," Savannah chimed in. "Girl, I'm surprised he didn't mention you and Chase since he was calling folks out."

"He didn't have to. Reverend Fletcher knows that everyone got the message." LaShaun managed to keep her voice from breaking.

"Fletcher is on a religious bigot campaign, that's the bad news. The good news is we have a sizeable population of folks who are more sophisticated, and they want a smart, capable professional like Chase in office" Savannah replied.

"I can think of a few who are quietly rooting for Reverend Fletcher to keep stirring this particular pot." LaShaun stood. "They'll have a rich source of material to use against anyone who disagrees with them."

"I've got friends at the local radio and television stations. I can milk the media myself. They'll love having voices raised against this bigot. I'm going to make some calls." Savannah crossed her arms. "We'll show him."

"Maybe that's not the best idea. He wants a fight. Why not ignore him?" LaShaun said as she leaned against the counter.

"I don't think Reverend Fletcher will let up. He may have some more tricks up his sleeve. I say we need to speak up," Savannah said.

"Yeah, now if I can head off giving him more ammunition it might help," LaShaun muttered.

"So tell me about you and the Blood River Ripper," Savannah said as she pulled out a stool and sat at the breakfast counter.

"Don't say it like we're best buds or something," LaShaun retorted and then heaved a sigh. "His grandfather came to see me. He swears Manny wasn't responsible for what he did, that some kind of evil force possessed him."

"Orin Young hopes you can help him prove the devil made Manny rip people into bite-sized pieces? Oh please." Savannah rolled her eyes.

Hey, I'm not saying I believe him, or that I'm going to get involved.

"Good. Trust me; the evidence that Manny killed those poor people was strong." Savannah stood and helped herself to a tea cake from LaShaun's cookie jar. "Now I better get back to the office. I had lunch with the kids at school. My butt still hurts from sitting on those tiny chairs in the cafeteria. Meeting at two. Bye-bye."

"Bye, and thanks for the heads up. I think," LaShaun said.

"Can't believe I almost forgot more good news," Savannah swung her purse over one shoulder. "They found two people beat up, and no it's not Patsy and her boyfriend. Fletcher is gonna have a field day with that. I don't know anymore because M.J. is keeping a tight lid on this one."

"And no wonder," LaShaun replied.

She walked her friend out and locked the front door. Despite her best efforts, LaShaun couldn't concentrate on the past anymore. The present kept jabbing into her thoughts like an insistent accusatory forefinger pointed at her. She had almost succeeded in time travel with another section of the journal written by a great-great aunt when her phone rang. LaShaun made plans to clean up and go to town before she even answered.

*****

Thirty minutes later LaShaun sat in M.J.'s office. The acting Sheriff took phone calls. More accurately LaShaun watched her avoid calls from the media. At thirty-seven, Myrtle Jean Arceneaux looked a good ten years younger. Her thick hair was pulled back into a ponytail. She wore tiny sterling silver stud earrings, a brown jacket with matching slacks and an animal print shirt beneath the jacket. LaShaun liked her style, business-like but with a touch of fashion. No bland white shirt for M.J. She also excelled at being a law officer. What she didn't like was politics and reporters. Today she had to deal with both.

At least six reporters, two with video cameras, stood outside on the grounds between city hall and the sheriff's station. No doubt the local television newscasts would contain a combination of fact and speculation. LaShaun tried not to look, but she ended up glancing through the glass window. M.J.'s office looked out to the open station where deputies worked. Chase stood with his arms crossed talking to two of the two detectives he supervised. He wore an intense listening frown as one man gestured. When she'd walked in an hour earlier Chase had only given LaShaun a brief nod. Now she forced her gaze away from him. She felt no warmth reaching in the space between them. LaShaun turned to focus on M.J. just as the door to the office opened. The sheriff's new administrative assistant came in. Darlene gave LaShaun a tiny wave then faced her boss.

"Okay, Sheriff." Darlene held a tablet computer. "I made notes on the statements you've made to the two reporters you talked to. What about I type this up and Deputy Naquin issue this as an official press release?" She handed the tablet to M.J.

M.J., looking every bit in-charge, scanned the two paragraphs before handing it back to Darlene. "The smartest thing I did was to take you out of the clerical pool and make you my assistant. That's perfect. Have Bobby deal with that hungry pack out on our lawn. You can give him the phone calls for the next three hours or so. I already told him. Bobby Naquin is our information officer," she said to LaShaun.

Darlene beamed at the compliment. "On it."

When she left on her mission M.J. looked across her desk at LaShaun. "We got ourselves a real situation here."

"I'd say so, another dead body and a second victim, still alive?" LaShaun agreed.

"Only just. Xavier Marchand and his wife are understandably upset." M.J. looked down at a folder lying on her desk. "Prelim notes from the scene say it looked pretty bizarre."

"So you thought of me. That's not very flattering," LaShaun said in dry tone.

M.J. glanced up sharply. "They were actually found pretty close to your property line. Indications are they came from the direction of your woods."

"I haven't noticed anything unusual," LaShaun said. Monmon Odette would have been proud. Her grandmother had trained LaShaun to guard how much she shared with others.

"I see." M.J.'s neutral tone implied she would reserve judgment on the truth of that statement. "The man is hurt bad, but the doctor doesn't think his injuries are life threatening at this point."

"Could be a mugging, or a domestic dispute that got out of hand." LaShaun shrugged when M.J.'s eyebrows went up.

The door opened again and the short, gruff man that came in brought a smile to LaShaun's face. Recently retired Sheriff Triche looked much healthier than the last time she'd seen him. His silvery white hair was neatly cut, and the plaid flannel shirt tucked into his khaki pants made him look like a dapper retiree. LaShaun stood and gave him a hug.

"You look good, cher." LaShaun winked at him.

"I manage to get some rest in between workin' on a long honey-do list." He grinned back at her, and then the amusement left his expression. "Hey, Myrtle. Heard you got a real mess on your hands," Sheriff Triche said and let out a soft whistle.

"Good thing I had the best lawman around to train me." Myrtle stood and shook hands with him. All three sat down.

"You're top notch, and didn't need a lot of hand holding from me." He smiled like a proud parent. "The mayor called me. I told him in no uncertain terms that you're the boss."

"Thanks, but I'm not surprised. He and Dave put their heads together before he left, too." M.J. scowled as she glanced to her left and through the glass window.

"Humph. Candidate Dave looking for something to punch up his campaign against Chase," Sheriff Triche grumbled. Then he cast a sideways look at LaShaun and cleared his throat. "Don't tell me you up to your neck in this. I thought you was supposed to stay out of trouble."

"She's not connected," M.J. said quickly. "I'm asking her if she noticed anything strange since the victims were found in the general area the of Rousselle land."

"Uh-huh." The old sheriff grunted as he rose to his feet. "Well, I've had my share of chaos and dealing with weird crimes." He gave LaShaun a pointed look then gazed at M.J. again. "I just stopped by to let you know I put the mayor in his place. Let me know if you need me."

"Thanks, sir. I appreciate the support." M.J. stood as though in respect for her former boss. "Must be strange being in your old office."

"I don't even think about this office now. Funny how fast I'm getting used to being out to pasture. Bye now." The former Sheriff pointed a finger at LaShaun. "You don't give Myrtle no problems."

"Of course not, no more than I gave you," LaShaun shot and grinned his pained expression.

"Lord have mercy," he muttered and strolled out. Moments later they heard him exchanging hearty greetings with his former deputies and civilian staff.

"I miss having him grumble and fuss his way through solving the most complicated cases. And speaking of complicated, that brings me back to these two victims." M.J. sat down at her desk again and studied LaShaun. "We need to talk. I asked Chase to join us, but he's delayed."

"Okay." LaShaun hoped her expression was impassive at the mention of his name. But the way M.J. studied her made LaShaun fidget with the leather flap on her cross-body bag.

"I guess he'll wrap up with his detectives, but he doesn't seem to be in a hurry to get in here," M.J. said, probing more.

"Right." LaShaun sat straight and looked her in the eye. "So now you know I didn't see or hear anything last night or yesterday evening."

"Orin Young visited you." M.J. waited for an answer. When silence stretched a few moments she didn't seem disturbed at all. She just settled back in her chair and waited.

"He came to tell me that his grandson isn't really responsible for killing all those people several years ago. Something about thinking he was possessed." LaShaun shrugged again.

"My grandmother has been talking to you, too." M.J. frowned and sighed. "You want to tell me what's going on?"

"I don't know. Honestly, I have no idea," LaShaun said when M.J.'s expression darkened to one of annoyed disbelief. "Did Miss Clo tell you anything?"

"Her and Miss Joyelle came to talk to you about Patsy before she ran off with Al. There's nothing supernatural about a cheating wife. Or is there more?" M.J.'s grimace clearly showed she hoped not.

"I'm not sure. It could be a couple of overactive Creole imaginations, seeing something spooky when it's just same old story of a restless woman with hot pants." LaShaun paused. "But what's that got to do with this latest crime?"

"Not sure yet," M.J. said in a clipped tone. She gazed past LaShaun to the door of her office and nodded.

LaShaun turned around in time to see Chase through the glass top of the office door. He came in without knocking. "Hi."

"Hi." Chase gave her a curt nod then walked across the room and placed a sheet of paper on M.J.'s desk.

M.J. read the few lines then looked up at LaShaun. "The woman had a driver's license in the pocket of her jeans. Her name is, was, Brenda Singleton, twenty-eight years old."

"Never heard of her," LaShaun replied. "What about the guy?"

"We didn't find anything on him. His clothes were pretty torn up. Maybe he dropped his ID or it came out of his pockets." Chase rubbed his jaw and looked at M.J. instead of LaShaun.

"Well, I can't help y'all with this one so I'll be on my way." LaShaun started to get up, but M.J. waved her back into her seat.

"Hold on, there's more." M.J. looked at Chase then back to LaShaun. "The woman had a map in another pocket. Looks like a crude handwritten thing. It shows the woods around that small bayou off Vermillion Road and includes your land, with an arrow pointing to the old Rousselle family cemetery."

"I promise they weren't coming to my house for dinner. I don't know this Brenda whats-her-name or the guy." LaShaun felt a flash of irritation at the way they both stood gazing at her. "What?"

"You'd tell me if you were being threatened or anything, right?" Chase said quietly.

M.J. looked at him sharply, and then at LaShaun. She didn't say anything but leaned forward and concentrated on LaShaun's every move. Seconds ticked by as LaShaun looked back at Chase. She felt his genuine concern, not just that he was questioning her as a detective with the Vermillion Parish Sheriff's Office.

"Yes, I would tell you," LaShaun replied softly. She faced M.J. "Chase is talking about the occasional thrill seekers and oddballs who come out to get a look at the place with all the voodoo tales. For years Monmon Odette has had to deal with silly and just plain nutty characters showing up on our property around Halloween."

"I hadn't thought about that." M.J. stood. "It's been awhile, but I remember kids sneaking out there looking for ghosts." She gave a grunt. "Mostly to drink, smoke weed and get up to other no good."

"A few adults into the occult would show up, too. Some would try to get my grandmother to take part in silly rituals. Maybe those two were part of a group like that," LaShaun offered.

"If so, something went seriously wrong with their little ghost and goblins party," Chase added. "I'll check out the occult angle in the background check on the victims. The woman is from New Iberia."

"Ask the guy," LaShaun replied and looked at them with her head to one side. "You said he wasn't hurt that bad."

Chase looked at M.J. before answering. "He's not making a whole lot of sense."

M.J. let out a long breath. "He's hurt, and running a fever of some sort. Maybe he's got an infection."

"Okay, then wait until he gets better. I'm sure you two sharp officers of the law are all over this latest case. So since I don't know anything I'm going home." LaShaun did not move despite her words. She knew there was more, but she couldn't get a clear picture or message. "Right after you tell me whatever it is that has you sending out these weird vibes."

"He's hallucinating; at least that's what the doctor calls it. Though he's not sure how else to describe it. This guy is talking about running through the woods, feeling free like he's never felt before, and... mating with as many females as he wants." M.J. looked at Chase, sighed and then gazed at LaShaun again.

"Sounds like he's living every guy's fantasy," LaShaun retorted and laughed. M.J. and Chase didn't get the joke. "And?"

Chase pulled a couple of crime scene photos from M.J.'s desk and handed them to LaShaun. "Take a look at these. It's a long shot, but maybe you'll recognize one of them. These aren't the worse of the pictures, but this is after we could move them enough so their faces were visible."

The first one was of the woman. Dirt and deep scratches covered her face. Her matted hair had dried blood with leaves sticking to it. Then Chase showed her a picture of the man. He had so much filth and grim on him LaShaun wondered if his own mother would have known him. She handed the photos back.

"The man's got two deep cuts on his left leg. The wounds are getting worse, and the doctors aren't sure why," Chase added.

"And he keeps talking about the woods, specifically the woods around the powerful cemetery. And he keeps mumbling 'the Rousselle might be a problem,'" M.J. said and held up another shot of the man with his leg stretched out.

LaShaun gripped the arms of the chair. Heat moved through her body, her scalped tingled, and she heard a buzzing sound. The room seemed to sway a little as though the floor moved. She gulped in air to fight off the feeling of being smothered. When she closed her eyes images, blurred but colorful, flashed on her eyelids like a movie screen. An upright thing with hair growled. Spit dripped from its mouth as he hovered over her. Then there was darkness.

Chapter 6

"I could have driven home just fine. This is silly. Now I have to go back and get my car."

LaShaun gazed out at the landscape whizzing by as Chase drove her home. Sunshine and blue skies meant that they should have been enjoying the day. Instead LaShaun could only smell the musky odor of an animal she didn't want to know existed, and Chase wore a grim expression. It was two o'clock in the afternoon and LaShaun hadn't had lunch. Yet food was the last thing on her mind.

"I should have warned about that picture of the guy's leg," Chase said.

"I didn't pass out. I just got light-headed. I didn't eat much for breakfast. When M.J. called me over to the station I ended up missing lunch. I don't know. Maybe I've got some kind of vitamin deficiency." LaShaun heard her own voice, realized she was rambling and pressed her lips closed.

"I still think we should go to the urgent care clinic at the hospital," Chase reminded her.

"I'm fine. I'll go to the doctor later if I still feel weak," LaShaun replied sharply. "I'm not going to the hospital."

"Could it be you didn't want to be at the hospital where that man we found in the woods is being treated?" Chase spoke in a measured tone, like a policeman conducting an interview.

"No," LaShaun said with too much force. Even she heard the note of hysteria in that one word. She breathed in and out slowly, then turned to him forcing a smile she didn't feel. "Going to the hospital is a bit over the top for a little dizzy spell."

"Okay." Chase glanced at her briefly then back at the road ahead.

He turned onto Rougon Road, drove the two miles to Rousselle Lane and turned again. Another half mile down the private road led to the turn onto LaShaun's gravel driveway. Twin oak trees stood on either side with the large mail box sitting on a brick base to the left. Chase stopped without being asked, got out and retrieved a stack of envelopes for her. He got back into his truck and drove around to her back door. Both were silent as LaShaun got out and opened the locks. Chase paused as he passed the alarm controls.

"You should always set this when you leave home, and at night." He tapped the cream colored box attached to the wall for emphasis.

"Nothing bad was in the air so I didn't bother."

LaShaun sucked in a breath as though trying to recall the words. She didn't need to remind Chase that she was different. Once they were in the kitchen she tossed her keys and bag on the counter and faced him. Before she could thank him for bringing her home and tell him goodbye, Chase pulled her into his arms. His kiss was searching, as though he needed an answer from her. LaShaun didn't pull away. When he cupped her face with one strong hand LaShaun shivered with the effort to not let go. His tongue pushed through her partially opened lips, insisting. He tightened his embrace. Surrender seemed her only option as desire took hold of every nerve ending in her body. As she kissed him back, Chase let out a low groan in the back of his throat.

He guided them backwards to her bedroom. In minutes they were undressed and making love slowly, deliberately. Chase seemed determined to see and feel every moment, every movement. His dark gaze drove LaShaun to the brink of ecstasy three times, but he'd slow down and kiss her shoulders and neck. All the while he looked at her. Love folded around LaShaun, the unmistakable message that what he had for her transcended sex. Her world exploded into pure joy as she allowed him to rock her entire being, physically and emotionally. When he came, Chase whispered her name over and over as she held onto him.

They lay quiet, wrapped around each other for a full hour, drifting in and out of a light sleep. LaShaun watched the trees and leaves through the bedroom window dance in a gentle cool breeze. Chase smoothed a thick lock of hair from her forehead and kissed it gently.

"You aren't going to scare me away, you know. I'm tougher than any old Rousselle family curse, crazy voodoo demons and all," Chase said and laughed softly.

LaShaun looked into his eyes. "You deserve to be elected Sheriff."

"I would do a damn good job of it, too. But..."

"Don't give up what you want. Not for me."

"Listen, the election has to be postponed. The parish clerk hasn't announced it yet. The Department of Justice didn't get the legislature's new apportionment plan in time for review." Chase continued to stroked LaShaun's hair.

"What?" LaShaun sat up and stared at him.

"Because of population changes after Hurricane Katrina, Louisiana's political district lines had to be re-drawn. The U.S. Department of Justice had to approve any plans to assure no groups might lose representation in elections. Somebody made a mistake, either in the state or on the federal side. The bottom line is they approved the plan, but not in time for us to have the election in November. It's put off until April." Chase shrugged at the look she gave him. "It'll be in the papers tomorrow and on the news."

"So you'll have more time to campaign. Maybe we can get this mess cleaned up, and disarm Reverend Fletcher." LaShaun frowned as she mentally calculated how this development might help Chase.

"Small town politics again. I think they'd like for anyone but me to run. Dave is busy reminding everyone he's a real 'family values' guy." He laughed at the frown LaShaun put on at the mention of his only opponent.

"Dave Goudchaux has been bad mouthing you and M.J. And M.J. is way too tolerant with him if you ask me." LaShaun hissed at the thought of the big beefy ex-LSU football star.

"Dave's okay. A little sanctimonious, but he's okay." Chase sat up and swung his legs over the side of the bed.

"Don't tell me. He's joined Reverend Fletcher's church, and only to get more votes I'll bet." LaShaun gave a snort of contempt. She got out of bed and followed Chase into the bathroom.

"He didn't join, at least as far as I know."

Chase turned on the water and entered the walk in shower and gestured to LaShaun. They stopped talking. Between kisses they soaped each other's bodies then stood under the warm rainfall shower head to rinse off. Stepping out into the steamy bathroom they dried off with clean fluffy towels. After another ten minutes both were dressed again. They went to the kitchen, and Chase turned on the television. LaShaun, barefoot and in a comfy old T-shirt over jeans, fixed them both a sliced turkey sandwich on thick French bread. They sat at the long counter on the stools as they ate.

"I'm surprised your phone hasn't been blowing up with all the craziness going on," she said.

"Speaking of which, you want to tell me what's really going on?" Chase asked and put down his sandwich.

"What's going on?" LaShaun echoed and concentrated on taking a slow sip of lemonade.

Chase wiped his mouth with a paper napkin. "We've got some challenges in our relationship, the politics of election for one. Then there's my family wanting to meet you, and you're not too thrilled about it. Not to mention town tongues wagging about every little thing we do as a couple. Right?"

"Yeah." LaShaun cleared her throat and decided she needed more lemonade. When Chase crossed his arms to wait she lowered her glass.

"So if we're going to make it, we have to stick together. That means straight talk. No keeping stuff from each other, even if we think it's to protect the other person." Chase waited again.

LaShaun pushed away the plate with her half eaten sandwich on it. She heaved a sigh. "Okay. Right. Just don't get upset."

"All right."

"Then two nights ago I couldn't sleep." She sighed when Chase's eyebrows went up. "Being psychic must be contagious, "she muttered.

"Go on." He didn't relax his serious listening pose.

"I woke up feeling like something wasn't quite right. That happens sometimes when I'm asleep and my extra sense goes on alert. It's just like a tingling or a sudden jab in my chest. It's hard to describe, and I've never really explained it to anyone."

Chase sat forward with both elbows on the table. "Thanks for sharing part of you with me. So you came awake, then what?"

"I knew nothing was wrong inside the house, but there was something outside. So I got my knife and went out to the backyard."

"You did what? In pitch black night with no help? LaShaun."

"I knew you were going to freak out and go all Mr. Protection on me." LaShaun squinted at him. "I really can handle myself, and I always use good sense."

"Sorry, you're right. We've got to trust each other, too; even more than most other couples." Chase relaxed his disapproving frown. "So you went outside."

"So I went to the backyard and I saw the outline of some kind of animal moving in the woods. You know how when it's dark, but you see something that looks denser than the darkness around it, then it moves?"

"Yeah, I know exactly what you mean." Chase now listened intently. All judgment seemed wiped away by his interest in her observations. The investigator honed in on every detail.

"Right, I knew something was in the woods. I took the knife, and trust me I know how to use it. But then I didn't feel any kind of threat or malevolence from that figure. In fact I could almost hear it calling out for help, a desperate plea to understand what was happening. I know that sounds nuts." LaShaun shook her head.

"I have faith in that sixth sense of yours." Chase rested a large hand on her thigh.

Encouraged, LaShaun went on. "About the time I was going closer to try and offer some kind of comfort, or figure out how to help, things changed. I got a wave of alarm from the person, or animal. I don't know which it was, but it was warning me. I was concentrating on her so hard I must have missed the signals. I hardly had time to register the direction of the danger when something pounced on me."

"The only reason why I'm *not* freaking out right now is because you're obviously all in one piece," Chase said in a measured tone. Still he gripped her leg.

She smiled, put her hand on his, and leaned closer to him. "You just examined me from head to toe, so you know all my parts are working."

Chase let out a slow breath as though remembering her touch, then nodded. "Tell me what happened. Was it a man?"

"I'm not sure." LaShaun stopped smiling and frowned at what the possible right answer could be. "At the time it seemed to be upright with arms and legs, but I don't know. It had a funky gamey smell. Like a sweaty animal, or damp fur. I haven't been hunting in years, not since I was a kid. But that's the best way I can describe it."

"You used to hunt?" Chase looked surprised.

"Sure, my grandmother and Uncle Robert taught me to handle a hunting rifle. Monmon Odette bought a small one just for me. We didn't hunt for fun. Monmon would give the meat to some poor families around that she knew. I use a bow and arrow, too." LaShaun nodded as his eyes went wider.

"We'll talk hunting later, right now tell me about being attacked," Chase said leaning forward even more.

"Something jumped on me, pushed me flat on the ground. I should have been paying closer attention to my surroundings, but when I had the feeling that someone was in trouble I got distracted. I managed to get hold of the knife and was able to fight back. I just remember slashing for all I was worth. Whatever or whoever it was let out a howl of pain and ran off. I went back inside fast and locked the door. But there was no more danger."

"You should have called me," Chase said calmly. He rubbed his jaw as though thinking about her account.

"They were gone, both of them. I also knew they wouldn't be too eager to come back for more. I don't play." LaShaun chuckled, and then heaved a sigh when Chase glanced at her sternly.

"Let's see the knife," he said.

She went to her bedroom, found it in her nightstand and came back. When LaShaun pulled it from the soft leather sheath Chase let out a low whistle. He stood up and took it from her. The knife's blade was pure silver and thirteen and a half inches long with a ruby red bone handle. Chase turned it over in his hands in frank admiration. He gripped it combat style.

"You cut somebody with this thing, hell yes he's gonna run. I'm surprised. This is silver, but it doesn't feel heavy. How old is it?" Chase looked at LaShaun with a new appreciation in his dark Cajun eyes.

"My grandfather inherited it from his father. His great-grandfather got it from his father. The story handed down says it was originally made by a great Mayan warrior in Belize. This warrior was favored by the gods, and the knife is magical."

"Right," Chase said drawing the word out.

"I'm telling you the family legend," LaShaun shot back and grinned at him. "The warrior fought off the Spanish in a terrible battle. He killed his enemy and brought victory to his people against great odds; or something like that. How my ancestors ended up with it is a bit of a mystery. You know the story of a group of slaves who left Louisiana, moved to Central America and eventually settled in South America?"

"No, but I want to hear it one day, and more Rousselle family stories." Chase continued to slice the air with knife.

"Deal," she grinned, then grew serious. "However we got it, one tale is consistent; the knife is magical and can defeat supernatural beings."

"I'm going to borrow this beauty if I have to arrest a demon," Chase said. He moved away from her across the large kitchen and pivoted, gracefully making offensive moves like a soldier in combat. He stopped and walked back to her. "Whoever you cut is gotta be hurt bad."

LaShaun accepted the knife from him. "Exactly."

Chase stood with one hand on his slender waist. "What?"

"That male victim in the hospital has deep cuts on his leg. I slashed low and hard, to cause pain and disable whatever jumped me." LaShaun watched his expression go from confused to skeptical.

"Oh c'mon, babe." Chase pulled a hand over his face.

"You should check to see if his wound matches the shape of my knife," LaShaun said quietly. She looked down at the silver blade. "And if it does..."

Chase stared at her knife. "Damn."

Chapter 7

Two days later LaShaun drove to Vermillion Hospital. She had a mixture of wanting to go there, and wanting badly to stay away. The fact that her grandmother had died there brought back sad memories, but that wasn't the strongest aversion she had to it. The closer she got to the innocuous looking tan brick building, the more her stomach roiled. She'd even had to stop at small park downtown and breathe deeply to get over the queasy sensation. With the silver cross from Monmon Odette's prized rosary beads clutched in a fist, LaShaun closed her eyes and whispered a prayer. A male voice startled her.

"You alright, ma'am?"

LaShaun opened her eyes to see a teenage boy standing on the passenger side of her Honda CRV. He peered through the open window with a slight frown. Before she could answer a boy standing with two other teens called out.

"Dude, you're messing with the local voodoo queen. You best get your butt outta there before she puts something on you," a scruffy looking blonde kid called and let out a brash guffaw. The two girls with him giggled at his antics.

"I'm okay," LaShaun said and smiled at him.

Adolescent peer pressure was alive and well. With an embarrassed grin, he gave a slight nod and joined his friends. After a brief exchange with them his face turned bright red. LaShaun laughed and was about to start the engine when she saw a woman pointing to her. Two men, one carrying a compact video camera came her way. Although she always avoided reporters LaShaun decided that she should wait for these two. Actually her extra sense decided for her. She watched them approach. One man was stocky. He looked no older than LaShaun, but he already had an old man's beer belly. He carried the camera. The other man appeared to be in his late forties. Lots gray mixed in with his reddish brown hair. He wore a cap, dark blue denim pants and a plaid long-sleeved shirt. He grinned at her as he got closer.

"This is great!" the man called out as his long legs closed the space between them. His younger companion huffed with exertion to keep up. "A happy coincidence, but then we know that everything happens for a reason. There is some invisible clockwork that sets in motion events that are meant to be. Ms. LaShaun Rousselle, am I right? I'm James Schaffer. You might know me from my show, Ghost Team USA. This is Adam Moore, a member of the team." He stuck out his hand and seemed pleased when LaShaun accepted it.

"You won't get any kind of read from touching me, Mr. Shaffer," LaShaun said quietly and let go of his hand. She looked at the second man. "You *do not* have permission to take my picture or tape me."

"Yes, ma'am." Moore and Schaffer exchanged a brief glance.

"You're a legend in Beau Chene; in fact your whole family has quite a reputation. I'm not surprised you can mask parts of your aura." Schaffer studied LaShaun as though looking for a sign anyway.

"I'm not masking anything," LaShaun said mildly.

"You're just naturally immune to others who have clairvoyant ability then?" Schaffer scanned LaShaun's CRV as though committing every detail to memory.

"Nope, don't have to mask or be immune. You guys aren't psychics," LaShaun said.

Schaffer's smile slipped a notch, but he recovered. "We're investigating a series of unusual events here in Cajun Country. An interview with you would be a great addition to our research. We hope to..."

"Let me save us both some time. No, thank you." LaShaun broke in to head off a long-winded attempt to flatter her into talking. She didn't need to be clairvoyant to know this guy loved the sound of his own voice.

Schaffer didn't bat an eye at the rebuff. He lost the ingratiating grin and grew serious. "There are a lot of wild rumors. We would respect your desire for privacy if you want to speak off the record. I promise we'll present a fair and balanced account of the remarkable series of events that have occurred here. This is a golden opportunity for you to get your side of the story told to a wide audience."

"Is that right?" LaShaun turned toward him and rested a hand on the steering wheel.

"Absolutely. I'm sure you know some residents claim you have a part in these unusual phenomena. Things like people seeming to be possessed, doing things they wouldn't ordinarily do. And two badly mangled victims were recently found on your property, one of them dead."

Schaffer leaned his tall frame forward as though he didn't want to miss a word of her response. Both men stared at her intently. The younger man blinked and looked away when LaShaun raised an eyebrow at him.

"They weren't on my property for one thing. And I haven't heard anyone talking about possession. You better do more research. So far you've got a bunch of gossip and not much else," LaShaun said, and waved a hand at them as though slightly bored.

"The facts are solid, Miss Rousselle. Two murders, a victim who is badly mauled, and all this in the hometown of the Blood River Ripper. Some say Manny Young isn't done with Vermillion Parish."

James Schaffer pulled up to his full height. He had to be six feet four if he was an inch. With his serious air and deep voice, the man seemed made for dramatic performances. LaShaun squinted at him for a few moments. She made a note to do her own research on Schaffer. His partner seemed less inclined to press LaShaun. Adam Moore cleared his throat and took a step back.

"I know what the rest of the town knows. Maybe the mayor can tell you more. Sheriff Arceneaux keeps him informed." LaShaun eyed Moore when he tried to film her on the sly. She concentrated on his hands until she saw him flinch. Moore stared at his hand and then at LaShaun, eyes wide.

"Uh, hey Jim, the mayor's a public figure. We could film him." Moore moved a few feet farther away.

"Matter of fact there's Mayor Savoie now." LaShaun nodded in the direction of city hall several blocks away. A group of people crowded around the mayor. "Aren't those other reporters getting a statement from him?"

"I say we check it out. Maybe there's some new developments," Moore said with a jerk of his thumb, the camera balanced on his shoulder. "We promised an update during a break on tonight's show."

Schaffer glanced in the direction of the mayor and then back at LaShaun. "Please reconsider. I'm sure we can be of help to each other. Someone with your abilities could become quite famous."

"No, thanks. I'll leave stardom to you." LaShaun started her engine.

Schaffer called out something else, but LaShaun ignored him as she drove off. When she pulled up to stop sign she saw the two men heading toward the square in front of city hall. Sure they weren't observing her, LaShaun drove down Parish Road to the hospital. Just to be even more cautious, LaShaun parked in the lot behind the extended wing of the hospital. Since it was farther away from the entrance, only a few cars were scattered around the available spaces. She locked the CRV and entered through a side entrance. LaShaun paused. Even if she knew the man's name she wouldn't have asked which way to his room. But she didn't need directions.

LaShaun walked into the first floor lobby of the modest three story hospital. Despite being in a small town, Vermillion Hospital had a reputation for excellent care. Contributions from two local wealthy families helped buy state of the art medical equipment. An agreement with Tulane Medical School meant top residents and their instructors were on staff as well. As a result patients came from all over the parish for treatment. LaShaun took care to blend in with the few people who were walking around. She pretended to study the list of departments on a large wall sign. In reality she narrowed her focus on the image of the man from the photos Chase had shown her. She felt a tug inside, like an invisible cord pulling her toward the elevators. A bell announced one had just arrived. Three people stepped out when the doors opened, one woman crying. LaShaun ignored the strong emotion of shock and grief to keep her focus.

Once on the elevator she had a moment of indecision. No clear signal gave her a clue which floor to choose. A man hurried in just as the doors started to shut causing them to pull back.

"Third floor, ma'am, thanks. Got to go up and visit my brother." The tall man wore jeans and fancy cowboy boots. In the typical southern way he started a conversation as though they knew each other. "Least they moved him out of ICU and into a room."

LaShaun gasped at the sharp jab she felt. She hit the button to take them to the third floor. "Sure."

"You okay?" The man glanced at her nervously. "Visiting family, huh? I'm sure they gone be fine. Good care in this place."

"Thanks, I'm okay." LaShaun swallowed hard and forced a brief smile.

"Don't you worry. These nurses keep a sharp eye on all them fancy monitors and such. My sister-in-law wouldn't have Kent in here if the care wasn't tops. Don't wanna get on the wrong side of that little woman. No, lordy." The big man gave a gruff laugh.

Moments later another bell announced they had arrived, The doors slid open. LaShaun stood looking at the opposite wall for a few seconds then blinked when she realized the man was waiting for her to go first.

"Thank you," she murmured and smiled at him again.

The man nodded and strode down one of the four hallways. LaShaun lingered for a few seconds, and then followed him. The tug on her mid-section told her she should go that way as well. The tall man's heavy footsteps echoed in the silence. He turned down a hall branching off to rooms three hundred-six through three hundred fifteen. A nurse stood in front of a wheeled cart reading the computer screen and entering information. When she looked up and said hello, LaShaun replied with another forced smile. Soon she would have to pick a room or her presence would look odd. If anyone asked she wouldn't be able to give them a name of who she was visiting. When she walked by room three hundred thirteen the skin on her arms tingled, and the sensation in her stomach felt like a light punch.

LaShaun looked down the hall to her left and right. The nurse had been joined by one of the nursing assistants. They were too busy talking to each other to notice her. No one else was around, so she pushed open the door and went into the room. The man's left leg was elevated on a foam wedge. He had gauze wrapped around on wrist. His breathing was raspy and loud. As LaShaun took a few steps closer he grimaced. He moved his head and lips as though trying to speak, but his eyes remained closed. She went still until he seemed to settle down again. Suddenly being in the room with this stranger didn't seem like such a great idea. The sensations of danger, dread and horror hit LaShaun like a body blow from a wrestler.

"Damn," she blurted out and staggered back half a step.

She grabbed the back of the single chair in the room to steady herself, took in a few deep breaths and let them out. When she looked at the man again he stared back at her. His dark brown eyes were glassy, but he seemed alert. His lips moved for a few seconds, but no sound came out. Then he looked at the bed table. A plastic pitcher sat on it along with a small cup with a straw. He looked back at LaShaun.

"Water?" was all she managed to get out.

When he nodded she took a cautious step forward. Feeling nothing she kept going until she got to the table. She poured water into the cup. After a second of hesitation she went to the bed and held the cup close to his mouth. He got the straw between his lips and with effort sucked on it. His throat worked. Seconds later he turned his head slightly to let go of the straw. He resumed staring at LaShaun.

"Can you help me?"

"I'm not a nurse," LaShaun replied.

"I know," he rasped, and then stopped to rest, panting for a few seconds. "Can you help? Please. Please."

LaShaun offered him more water. He took the straw into his mouth once more, drank and rested between three sips. His eyes closed and opened again. Dark circles under his eyes looked like bruises. She glanced up at the dry erase board. The name of his nurse, Crystal, was listed along with the schedule of how often his vital signs would be checked. When the door swished open LaShaun jumped.

"Didn't mean to scare you, hon. I'm just checking to make sure our patient is okay." The short plump redhead bustled about. She activated a blood pressure monitor attached to his arm, and then wrote down the last reading. Next she stuck a thermometer in his mouth.

"You a family member or friend?" The nurse smiled at LaShaun.

"Yes, ma'am." LaShaun nodded. She looked at the man who stared at her.

"Which one, baby?" The woman prodded.

"What? Oh, sorry, uh, family friend. I decided to see how he's doing." LaShaun rubbed her hands together. She fidgeted with the strap of her cross body bag.

"That's nice."

The nurse turned her back to check his pulse, and then she carefully touched the bandage wrapped around his leg. When the man let out a groan she stopped. She checked the IV tubes and adjusted the sheets. Then she turned to face LaShaun again.

"I can't stay long, I just wanted to pop in for a minute," LaShaun said to head off more questions.

"No problem. You live close by?" The redhead looked at her patient. A slight frown pulled her arched red eyebrows together.

"I'm a good ways off, so like I said I won't wear him out with a long visit," LaShaun replied.

"Stay," the man whispered hoarsely without taking his gaze from LaShaun. "Talk."

"Well, let me know if you, uh, need anything." The nurse looked from the man to LaShaun as she walked to the door again.

"Thank you so much." LaShaun smiled at the woman, trying not to look impatient for her to leave. Once the door whisked shut she walked to the bed again.

"Tell me what you mean," LaShaun said.

His lips moved, but she couldn't make out what he was saying. LaShaun leaned over and tried to understand, but the words sounded garbled. The man seemed to strain with the effort to be heard. He stopped trying for a few moments then looked at her. He wore a frightened and frustrated expression. His mouth opened, and LaShaun moved closer.

"Don't want to live like this. Help me." Quick as lightening he reached out and gripped LaShaun's left arm.

She fought down panic as the heat from his breath hit her in the face. "I have to know more."

The man seemed to lose his burst of strength. He let go and his eyes glazed over as he looked past LaShaun. "God have mercy on me."

"You'll be alright. The medical care here is..." LaShaun's voice froze in her throat at the wild look in his eyes.

Without warning the man sat up, pushed her away and shouted. "Get out now. I can't control it."

LaShaun backed away until she bumped against the wall. The man's expression seemed to melt and change, his skin moved like the rubber of a mask. He face became elongated as she watched. His eyes grew brighter as he glared at LaShaun. When he tried to sit up, thick cloth restraints jerked him back. LaShaun felt smothered by a flood of hostility beating against her entire body. Air seemed sucked from the room. One restraint strap broke, and he lunged across the bed at her. Frustrated that three other straps held, he knocked aside the table. LaShaun stared at him in fascination for a few seconds. She shoved the chair between them when he lunged again. The nurse rushed in with a male orderly.

"What in the world?" The nurse took one look at the man and gasped. She spun around and yelled down the hallway. "Code blue! Restraints off."

Two male medical aides hurried into the room. They went past the nurse, and paused to take in the situation. One of them stood with his arms out by his sides as though to show he was no threat. His bicep muscles bulged, and LaShaun judged he could use as much force as necessary. Only LaShaun knew the two men weren't facing a totally human force.

"Okay, man. Remember me? Joe. I brought you breakfast this morning, and helped you get cleaned up. Everything gonna be alright." Joe nodded slowly. When the other aide moved sideways the man grunted and glared at him with wild eyes.

"Lord have mercy," the nurse whispered.

"Don't let him bite you," LaShaun blurted out. She shrank back when the wild man looked at her.

"Believe me, lady, that's something we don't intend to happen," Norman whispered back to her. He wrapped a towel around his right forearm.

"Come on, now, calm down. What do you need?" Joe spoke in a calm even voice. The man blinked back at him, but didn't move.

"Get him tied down again, and I'll give him some Ativan." The nurse circled to get closer to the IV tubes still attached to the patient's left arm.

"May God give you peace, and may he free you from the evil that binds you," LaShaun whispered.

She repeated the short prayer three more times as the man struggled against the thick straps. After several minutes his movements slowed until he slumped back against the pillow. Tears rolled down his face. He shook his head slowly, let out a long breath then looked at her again. His expression of sadness and hopelessness brought LaShaun close to tears as well. His eyes glazed over, and his lips parted. The man's bottomless despair engulfed her like a plastic bag over her nose and mouth. She backed out of the room fighting to catch her breath. When she stumbled out into hallway and leaned against a wall, staff and patients who had gathered stared at her. The lone hospital security guard finally arrived. As he ran toward the room he barked information into a cell phone.

"Get some deputies over here fast, man." The guard stuffed the phone in his pocket, and went into the room.

The crowd lost interest in LaShaun for a moment. She took advantage of that small window of distraction and walked quickly toward the elevators still heaving in gulps of air. As she waited LaShaun could hear the nurse describing her to the security guard, so she dashed to the stairs instead. Minutes later LaShaun was in the lobby, out through a side entrance and in the parking lot. Avoiding the exit to the main street, LaShaun chose a side parking lot exit. She took a series of small streets to drive home. By the time she got to Rousselle Lane the feeling of suffocation had completely stopped. But her hands shook badly. She gripped the steering wheel and gasped when she saw the figure of an elderly woman sitting on her porch, in Monmon Odette's favorite spot. The Chevy Traverse sitting in the driveway reassured her. With a long shuddering sigh of relief, LaShaun parked the CRV and got out. Miss Clo waited for her wearing a grave expression.

"Something wrong is loose in these parts, baby. Something that I don't like to think about."

"You have the most unusual way of greeting me, Miss Clo." LaShaun wiped perspiration on her brow and sat down. Miss Clo sat again.

"Sorry to bring more trouble to your doorstep, child. If your grandmother was alive..." Miss Clo rocked back and forth.

"Monmon Odette's spirit is with me always," LaShaun said softly.

"Oh my Lord." Miss Clo made the sign of the cross. "Please tell me she's not here now."

LYNN EMERY

Chapter 8

"Relax, I didn't mean she's lurking," LaShaun replied wearily.

"Good." Miss Clo still glanced around as though looking for signs.

"At least not right this minute," LaShaun said. When Miss Clo jumped, she patted her should. "I'm teasing you, cher. Calm down."

After a few moments LaShaun unlocked the front door, went inside and came back with two glasses. She put the tray on the small round table between their chairs and sat down. Both sipped tea and gazed into the distance deep in thought. The blue skies had gradually been blocked out by a cover a clouds, giving the day a gloomy feel. For at least fifteen minutes neither woman spoke.

"I went to the hospital to see the man they found in the woods," LaShaun said finally.

"Those two were runnin' around like wild animals. The talk is all over town. Sounds like the folks Joyelle has been treatin'." Miss Clo looked at LaShaun.

"Exactly like it. Is that why you came?" LaShaun looked back at her.

"Nope. Patsy showed up at Joyelle's house last night. Patsy begged her to stay, and Joyelle gave in. She always did have a soft heart. When Joyelle called me I gave her a good talkin' to about obstructin' a police investigation." Miss Clo gave a sharp nod.

"Like you've been completely forthcoming with your granddaughter, the acting sheriff?" LaShaun burst out laughing. When Miss Clo glared at her she got control of herself.

"I'll talk to Myrtle Jean soon enough." Miss Clo stopped rocking her chair and leaned forward. "The woman is dead, and they say he's not far from it. They say he's got some strange infection. What's he like?"

"Never mind him for now. Tell me about Patsy." LaShaun drank more tea.

"Humph. Patsy showed up in perfect health, but she wouldn't tell Joyelle much of anything. She just kept saying she was glad to be home, and talked about how she was so tired. Joyelle says she's skinny as a matchstick with dark circles under her eyes. Joyelle's husband wasn't happy, but they let her stay in the mother-in-law suite they have built on their house." Miss Clo shook her head. "Something's wrong, and she's part of it."

"So tell me what else happened." LaShaun drained the last of her sweet tea.

"Joyelle didn't get much sleep. She called me around five o'clock this morning. I told her to call M.J., and not to give me any argument." Miss Clo shook her head. "I don't like none of this one bit."

LaShaun thought about her last point. "So M.J. went to interview Patsy?"

Miss Clo nodded with a grim expression. "She took two deputies with her. One was that new lady deputy she hired. Seems like a nice enough person. The other was Chief Detective Broussard." Miss Clo glanced at LaShaun with one raised eyebrow.

"Go on." LaShaun did not react at his name.

"Patsy got an attitude with M.J.," Miss Clo said with a frown. "Ungrateful little snip. She wouldn't say if she knew where her lover boy is hidin'. His wife's daddy and three brothers are looking for him, so he best stay undercover for a good long time."

"Tommy Daigle is still missing, and Patsy shows up." LaShaun rocked her chair back and forth a few times.

"Yeah, he's probably tryin' to think of some good story before he shows up to face the music."

"So what happened? I mean with M.J. and Chase," LaShaun said.

"Nothin' really. Patsy hasn't broken any laws so it's not like they could haul her down to the station. She said she knew her rights, and they had no reason to hold her. Patsy sashayed out to her little Pontiac Grand Am and drove off." Miss Clo shook her head again. "M.J. wasn't too please with Joyelle, but she hadn't broken any law either. So I came to tell you that's that. Maybe this thing with Patsy is over."

"I wonder why she went to Joyelle instead of her family?" LaShaun looked at Miss Clo.

"I get a headache tryin' to figure out why Patsy does anything." Miss Clo sighed. "That girl won't be satisfied until she gets somebody killed."

LaShaun was about to express her opinion on Patsy's morals, or lack thereof when the sound of a car stopped her. Two Vermillion Parish sheriff's cars pulled into her driveway. M.J. parked and got out of the first one. Despite the clouds M.J. wore sunglasses. She removed them and walked up to the edge of the porch. Chase cut his engine and got out of the second cruiser. M.J. stared hard at her grandmother.

"We're going to have us nice long talk later on, Monmon. Then you can explain why you keep playing detective."

"I'm not interferin' in your work, baby. I promise." Miss Clo put on her sweetest smile. "We're just havin' a little visit is all."

"You told LaShaun about Patsy being at Miss Joyelle's house I'll bet. Never mind," M.J. said cutting off her grandmother's reply. She stuck her sunglasses into a case hanging from her belt and looked at LaShaun. "We're going to have a talk with *you* right now, LaShaun."

"Yes, ma'am," LaShaun said promptly.

"Don't get smart with me. I'm not in the mood," M.J. shot back. Her dark eyebrows pulled together until she looked less like a pretty woman, and more like an annoyed officer of the law.

"I'm not being smart-alecky, honest. I want to cooperate fully," LaShaun said with the most sincerity she could muster.

"You could start by not interviewing our suspects," M.J. snapped back. She stabbed a finger in the air between them. "And don't think I won't arrest your butt for interfering with a criminal investigation, and that includes this mess with Patsy."

"I wasn't trying to get in the way or anything. I just wondered if I might recognize him cleaned up." LaShaun blinked at the wrath she felt from M.J. "Okay, I should have told y'all and not gone over there alone."

"Funny you didn't think of it *before* you went," M.J. said before LaShaun or Miss Clo could speak. "Both of you are going to tell me what the hell is going on, and you're not gonna leave out even one tiny detail. Otherwise, I'll charge you both with obstruction of justice and anything else I can think of!"

"Myrtle Jean Arceneaux you wouldn't dare. Your mama and daddy would have your backside if you did." Miss Clo frowned at her.

"Mama would be the first to agree with me. Now start talking. Or we go down to the station and make this a formal interrogation. What's your choice? I'm fine either way." M.J.'s voice cut at them like a steel blade.

"Of course we'll cooperate. You don't have to get all testy." Miss Clo lost some of her steam under M.J. withering gaze.

"Something has happened, hasn't it?" LaShaun looked at Chase.

M.J. raised a hand before Chase could reply. "Yeah, you could say a few things have happened. I've got a preacher whipping up folks for witch trials like this is the middle ages, strange people wandering around the swamps, a crazy man tearing up the hospital, and three murders. Yeah, you damn sure could say something has happened."

"Three?" LaShaun honed in on that number.

Chase glanced at the three women then stepped forward. "The state police called us an hour ago. They found Tommy Daigle's body in Cameron Parish near Grand Lake."

"You brought in Patsy to find out what she knows about Tommy," LaShaun said. It wasn't a question.

"We would if we knew where she was," M.J. replied. She looked at her grandmother.

Miss Clo shook her head hard. "Don't give me that evil-eyed stare. I have no idea where she could be."

When Chase and M.J. looked at LaShaun she started. "Don't be silly. I've never even met the woman. Why in the world would you think--"

"I need help."

All four of them jumped at the voice that spoke. Patsy stepped from behind the wide gardenia bush on the south end of LaShaun's long front porch. When Chase spun to face LaShaun his jaw worked for several seconds. He seemed too enraged to form words.

"Damn," was all LaShaun could manage to get out. "I'm going to jail. Again." 3

*****

Six hours later LaShaun made it back home. Drained of every ounce of energy, she made sure the house was locked up. Then she sank into a tub of suds in her master bathroom. The scent of the honeysuckle and vanilla filled the air. The bath oil created huge bubbles that shimmered with rainbow colors. Steam clouded the wide mirror over the sink. The pale green and ocean blue colors should have combined with the heavenly fragrance should have soothed her. Instead LaShaun reclined against her bath pillow feeling lonesome. No amount of soap could wash that away. She tried closing her eyes, but that didn't work. Even the soft jazz streaming through the speakers of the small flat screen television made no difference. What she needed most wasn't anywhere near her house.

Chase. She didn't expect him to come over. He had his hands full with three murder investigations. Not to mention he was furious with her. As the jets made their best effort to ease her tense muscles, LaShaun tried to think of why he shouldn't lose trust in her.

"Guess you better get used to being celibate and single, girlfriend," LaShaun muttered. Giving up her attempt at a Zen moment, she grabbed the TV remote and switched channels.

"This is a KATC news break. Missing Beau Chene resident Patsy Boutin has been located, and the man she reportedly ran off with is dead. Find out how a local psychic is being used by the Sheriff's Department to unravel the mystery. Details at eleven. " The pretty young woman the color of caramel candy beamed as if she could see LaShaun and was saying "Gotcha!"

"Good Lord."

LaShaun hit the remote until she found the jazz music channel again. The bubble bath seemed like a good idea, but she was too keyed up to let work its magic. She stood and let the big fluffy suds slide down her body. The bathroom door swung slowly inward, and she stood still. She looked for any object to use as a weapon and wondered why the alarm hadn't gone off. Calmly she steadied her breathing for a fight. Chase stood gazing at her with a frown.

"I was about to jump on you," LaShaun blurted out, relieved and very annoyed. "How'd you get in here, and why didn't you call first?"

"You gave me a key, and you can jump on me later."

Chase stood with both hands on his hips. He still wore his duty belt with the gun, handcuffs, and other tools he needed to keep law and order. Even angry he looked deliciously sexy, maybe more so. LaShaun brushed suds from her breasts and down her stomach.

"You're right to be a little upset with me." LaShaun looked down at the floor and then at him again.

"A little upset doesn't quite cover it." His gaze traveled down her neck but he seemed to check himself, and he looked into her eyes again. "You've got more explaining to do."

"Well at least let me dry off and get dressed before you shine a light on me and make me confess." She didn't ask him to leave, and he didn't move.

As he watched she picked up the flexible handheld shower want attached to the wall, used her foot to turn on the water and rinsed off slowly with warm water while the tub drained. LaShaun also rinsed more bubbles from the sides of the wide tub. She attached the shower wand to the wall again. Chase strode forward and put his arm out for her to grab on and held up the bath towel with his free hand. LaShaun steadied herself by holding onto him.

"Be careful. I don't want to get you all wet."

Chase breathed heavily as he looked down at her. "That's what folks keep telling me about you, to be careful."

"Are you listening to them?" LaShaun took the oversized blush pink towel, but he continued to hold the other end.

"Not really," he said huskily.

He carefully took off his clothes, folded them and placed everything, including his duty belt, on the cushioned bench along one wall. He turned back to LaShaun and sighed at the sight of her. LaShaun walked to him.

"I'm not trying to cause trouble for you, cher," she said between planting kisses on his chest.

Chase let out a shuddering breath. "We'll talk, but not right now."

He picked her up, and carried her to the granite surface of the built long vanity. LaShaun squirmed against him, her legs around his waist. With a soft moan Chase put down on the counter and entered her. Soon the steam came from them instead of hot water from the tub. With each caress Chase let go of his anger and tension. He rested his head on her shoulder. They made love hard and fast, crying out in pleasure. They came together and held each other tightly for a few moments before Chase disentangled himself. He walked on unsteady legs to the glass enclosed shower. LaShaun joined him, and they stood under the warm stream for several seconds. She exited; leaving him to finish alone and lather his muscular body.

"I'll make you some dinner," LaShaun said as she pulled on her cotton pajama bottoms. When he merely waved in response, LaShaun pulled on the matching T-shirt top and went to the kitchen.

She heated up leftover red beans, steamed three cups of rice and mixed up a pan of cornbread. The beans had sat overnight, so the seasonings would make them even more flavorful. As soft swamp blues played in the background, LaShaun set the table. Soon the kitchen filled with the smell of onion, garlic and the cornbread baking in the oven. LaShaun hummed along with a familiar tune as a local artist, Tray Delacroix, sang about a sweet love affair. Tray alternated between verses in Creole French and English. When the singer cracked a joke about his Louisiana hot sauce LaShaun laughed. Chase slipped his arms around her as she stirred the pot of beans.

"I know just what he means," he said, his words muffled as he pressed his mouth against LaShaun's neck.

"Don't mess with the cook," LaShaun pretended to try and shake him off.

"Fine. But I'll tell you this much, I'm spending the night," Chase said and back away.

LaShaun turned to stare at him. Chase wore a loving smile as he gazed back at her. He was dressed in tan pajama pants and matching muscle T-shirt. "I thought..."

"Yeah, but I'll feel better being here tonight. I brought a few things."

"After I the trouble I caused." LaShaun turned to the large pot again and shook her head. "Those folks are right, your family and friends. You should stay away from me."

He reached around her and turned down the fire under the pot. He checked on the bread and then grabbed her by the hand. "The food is okay. You come over here."

"But the bread..."

"Ten minutes left on the timer. I checked." Chase sat on the sofa in the small family room right off the kitchen. Then he pulled LaShaun onto his lap. "I want to tell you something."

"We have to be realistic." She started to say more, but couldn't make the words come out.

"I'll talk, you listen." Chase gently turned her face to his forcing LaShaun to look him in the eyes. "We're a team. I may get irritated... okay... mad as hell, at you sometimes. But I'm not going anywhere. I want to marry you."

LaShaun tried to jump from his lap, but he held her firmly with two strong arms. "The last few hours should be enough evidence why that's a bad plan. I'm always getting into these complicated situations," she replied.

"More proof you need me to bail you out," Chase said with a grin.

"Be serious. I don't want you to suffer because I was born under this cloud. I care about you," LaShaun finished in a shaking voice.

"I love you, and you love me. Yes? Saying it won't bring some supernatural disaster down on our heads." Chase pressed his face against neck.

She brushed his thick dark curls with the tips of her fingers and nodded. "You're one stubborn Cajun Cowboy."

He laughed and looked up at her. "Then it's settled. We're engaged."

"What the..."

"I even got the ring," Chase said and fished around under the seat cushion, finding an emerald green velvet box. He opened it to reveal an oval multicolored ametrine stone set in eighteen karate gold with round diamonds on either side.

LaShaun finally managed to catch her breath and speak. "This looks just like Monmon Odette's ring, the one she got from her grandmother."

"Acting as her attorney, Savannah had strict instructions to give me a package two months after her death. Mrs. Rousselle also included a letter that told me not to tell about it, not until and unless I wanted to spend my life with you. And I do." Chase slipped it on LaShaun's right ring finger.

"Monmon Odette showed this to me once when I was a little girl, and then she locked it away." LaShaun stared at the ring mesmerized by the play of color as the green, gold and pink stone shimmered.

"Now you're grown up, and going to be a married lady."

"You have an election coming up. Reverend Fletcher is already plotting against you, and all these murders with me smack in the middle of it all. Oh no." LaShaun tried to wriggle off his lap.

"Oh yes." Chase held on tight.

"I can't let you risk everything..." LaShaun started and stopped when he clamped a hand over her mouth.

"I have no intention of losing the election. I'm going to start speaking out to the people in Vermillion Parish who care about the issues and won't be fooled by intolerant scare tactics." Chase lost his serious expression and grinned at her. "You like it? M.J. helped me practice."

LaShaun blinked at him. "You really have lost your mind."

"Crazy like a fox. Dave is mostly unknown. The mayor and three aldermen are with me for now. Of course those politicians might jump ship if the winds get to rough. Who knows?" Chase shrugged. "But it doesn't matter. I have faith in the wonderful people who will come out to vote for justice and common sense. Hey, I'm getting better at speech making on the fly."

"My past may be held against you, Chase. And more" LaShaun frowned at him, and gazed at her light brown skin against his. Even with his skin tanned from the sun, the difference was evident. "I don't want you to lose your dream of being Sheriff because of me."

"I'm not saying we're the most progressive place, but when it comes down to it good old Cajun common sense wins out."

LaShaun thought about what he said for a few moments. "Oui. Monmon Odette said our culture has been unique down through history. We've tried to treat each other decent for the most part, before Louisiana became part of America that is. Seems like there is always somebody eager to point out the differences and whip up hatred."

"We don't plan to let that happen. With the election delayed I've got more time to campaign. And we can concentrate on these murders, and figure out what Patsy's been up to." Chase frowned.

"Did she have anything to say that would help?"

"I can't go into details, but she gave a little bit that might lead to something. The biggest part of being a cop is dealing with people who don't tell the truth, or at least don't tell it all."

"I hear her husband won't let her come home or see their kids. Maybe she doesn't want to admit she ran off with another man. If they divorce she could lose custody of the children," LaShaun said.

"*Unless Vince is really dumb he's already figured out the story with the rest of the town,"

Chase said, then he kissed LaShaun tenderly. "Speaking of marriage."

LaShaun looked at the ring on her finger. Light danced in the facets as the colors seemed to come alive the longer she gazed at it. Would it be selfish to grab a chance for happiness? Chase would likely face ostracism from family and friends.

"I know what I'm getting into, cher," Chase whispered as though he could read her thoughts by looking at her expression.

"You have to promise me something, "LaShaun said after a few moments. She looked into his dark eyes.

"That's what this night is all about, promises." Chase kissed shoulder and neck.

"If at any time you feel the going is too tough, or you can't cope with the whispers and..."

"I won't, but go on," Chase broke in.

"You'll tell me honestly. Don't keep it in, or brood about it. Like you said, we've got to be honest with each other. Sometimes it might be us facing the world. Make this decision with a clear head, no hearts and flowers to make things look rosy." LaShaun pulled away from him. The love in his eyes tugged at her soul, but she resisted the urge to melt into him. "This is a huge decision for you. I'm already an outsider."

"Stand by me, love, because I'm more than ready to stand by you," Chase said firmly, no trace of doubt in his voice or his dark gaze.

LaShaun gasped at the impact of his honesty. No matter what, they would be a force of love that would meet every test thrown at them. She bent her head and tasted his sweet lips, savoring his eager response. When she pulled back LaShaun nodded. "Yes."

Chase closed his eyes and nuzzled her neck. "Yes," he repeated. Several minutes went by as they held each other before he spoke again. "Darlin'?"

"Yes." LaShaun sighed.

"Can we please eat? I'm starving." Chase grinned at her.

With a burst of laughter LaShaun gave his arm a swat. Then she jumped from his lap. "The bread!"

For the rest the evening the darkness just outside the windows looked romantic and cozy, like a country quilt around their special world. They didn't look at the news, or talk about death, crime and the mystery of what was happening in their beloved bayou parish. Later LaShaun drifted off to sleep cradled by Chase's long body. A howling far off in the woods barely registered in her semi-conscious haze of contentment. Her eyes flew open for only a second or two then closed again.

Chapter 9

The next morning LaShaun woke up in a strange mood, she wasn't quite sure what she felt. Anxiety floated around her like a sticky swamp fog. She should have been happy. And indeed looking at the drop dead gorgeous ring on her finger brought a rush of joy to her heart. Then she would feel anxious again, and the good vibe faded as the implications of saying "Yes" to Chase's proposal sank in. She also had a vague sense that more bad events would soon happen.

Still she greeted Chase with a smile when he woke next to her. They cooked breakfast together and exchanged small talk. LaShaun sent him off to work with a loving kiss. Anyone watching would see a normal scene. Except LaShaun had to admit she agreed with Reverend Fletcher. Something sinister had settled in Vermillion Parish. She washed the few breakfast dishes left, unloaded the dishwasher of dinner dishes and put them away. She hummed a light tune hoping to banish the unsettling feeling inside her gut. It didn't work.

She went to the small parlor and found the leather bound book she'd tucked away in drawer. The rare volume from Monmon Odette's library felt warm and heavy as she picked it up. LaShaun turned to the section where she'd placed the antique copper bookmark her grandmother used so often. The text described a creature LaShaun didn't want to believe existed. Turning a page she gazed at the drawing of a half human, half animal monster. Finally she decided. After calling the museum she drove into town to meet with the curator, Pete Kluger. One of the employees, a young student named Nyla, grinned at LaShaun when she walked into the lobby.

"Good morning. It's a beautiful day," Nyla said.

"I'm glad someone is feeling cheerful," LaShaun grinned back at her. "New fella? No, wait. You reunited with an old love; one that you feel sure really cares about you."

Nyla's stared at LaShaun with her mouth open for several seconds. "Damn, you really are psychic."

"Watch your language, young lady. I have to keep repeating myself," Dotty muttered as she walked to the reception desk. The office manager ran a tight ship.

"Hi Dotty. I hope you're having great morning," LaShaun chirped. "Pete is expecting me." Before Dotty could reply LaShaun zipped past her toward his office.

"Thinks she owns the place..."

Dotty's voice faded as LaShaun kept walking down the hall. She entered the small ante room decorated with antique furniture and through a second door into his office. She stopped when she saw Miss Clo and Joyelle seated in two chairs. Joyelle sniffled and blinked hard when she saw LaShaun and then whimpered. Miss Clo patted her back and made soothing noises. Pete blinked rapidly and kept rubbing his forehead as he gazed at them. Pete seemed to let out a sigh of relief at the sight of LaShaun. He met her at the door.

"I'm glad to see you," he blurted out. "So glad."

"Hello everybody. What's going on?" LaShaun looked a bit bewildered.

"I was discussing local legends with these ladies. Um, maybe they took something I said too literally." Pete hefted a large leather bound volume to show LaShaun.

"I don't believe any of it," Miss Clo blurted out. She glanced at her friend. Joyelle merely shook her head, took out a tissue and dabbed her eyes. "Honey, don't get upset. There's got to be another explanation."

"Explanation of what?" LaShaun sat down across from Joyelle on a large upholstered chair.

"Maybe I shouldn't have upset you, Mrs. LeJeun. I sometimes get excited about Louisiana Cajun lore." Pete looked at LaShaun as though asking for help.

"He does," LaShaun plunged in, and gave him a pointed look. "What legend are we talking about?"

"Rougarou.[4] Mrs LeJeun described the behavior of her... patients, and I may have hastily extrapolated to reach a conclusion. I didn't mean to suggest that--"

"That I've been consorting with evil, and helping a pack of rougarou prey on the innocent," Joyelle said. She sobbed quietly into the bunched up tissues in both her hands.

"Don't be silly, dear," Miss Clo said quickly, and put a consoling arm around her friend.

"I'm sure Pete said no such thing, did you? " LaShaun said, her voice strained.

"Oh no, I just said that the behavior of the individuals sounded like local stories!" Pete protested.

"Joyelle insisted we talk to Mr. Pete because he's an expert on history in the parish." Miss Clo looked at Pete who shrugged.

"I knew he had a lot of old books and diaries from long ago. When I was a girl, my monmon told stories about her granddaddy. He was a famous traiteur. He prayed over this man, and he was a rougarou." Joyelle made the sign of the cross. "Protect us Holy Father."

"You don't really think Patsy is roaming around because she's a werewolf, do you? We all know she ran off with Tommy Daigle." LaShaun put calm and reason into her tone.

"And he's dead," Pete said. He winced when LaShaun glared at him. "But there is something distinctly human about the whole story. Faithless wife and angry, jealous husband. Or maybe Tommy wanted to return to his wife and Patsy became enraged. The sheriff will figure out what happened." He broke off from rambling and cleared his throat.

"We have no reason to think this is anything but a lot of horny young people behaving badly," LaShaun quipped. "Pete's right. Between the sheriff's office and the state police all the dirty details will be sorted out soon."

Joyelle stared at LaShaun steadily. "Have you seen anything, you know, with your extra sight?"

"Nothing," LaShaun replied promptly. She walked over to Joyelle and put a hand under her elbow. Joyelle stood, and LaShaun glanced at Miss Clo who followed her lead. "Why don't you ladies do a bit of shopping and then have a nice lunch. It's a beautiful day. Sunshine and blue skies will chase away those nerves over old fairytales."

"You don't believe in rougarou?" Joyelle asked.

"In the old days people didn't understand strange behavior. They had to explain things some kind of way. My grandmother told me a lot supernatural stuff was just people acting crazy or being mean on purpose." LaShaun laughed.

"Exactly what I was going to say after I mentioned the rougarou thing," Pete put in. He smiled and nodded at the two older women.

Miss Clo squinted at him and then glanced at LaShaun. "Right."

"Our competent sheriff and her deputies are making sure the parish is well protected," LaShaun said. "I'll walk y'all out."

"Let me visit the ladies room first," Joyelle said demurely. She sniffed and wore a shy smile. "I do feel a bit foolish getting so upset. The truth is my grandmother admitted great-great grandfather Landry told a lot of whoppers, and he enjoyed moonshine a bit too much. I'll be back in a few, Clo." She laughed and went down the hall.

Miss Clo watched her friend disappear around a corner to the ladies restroom. She faced LaShaun and Pete. "Now you two quit spinning that bull, and tell me the real deal."

"There aren't any werewolves roaming around Vermillion Parish," LaShaun said quietly, looking over her shoulder.

"But you do have a clue that *something* more than just bad behavior is at work. That wasn't a question, young lady," Miss Clo said sharply when LaShaun opened her mouth to reply. "I've heard the rumors about that man at the hospital acting crazy. Somehow this all ties together."

LaShaun sighed, exchanged a glance with Pete and nodded. "He's human, Miss Clo."

"But I believe you're going to find out soon enough, and no, I'm not claiming to see the future," Miss Clo whispered. "But I agree we shouldn't say anything more in front of Joyelle."

"I'm can't promise," LaShaun started, but footsteps on the tile floor caused her to break off.

"Well, I'm ready to go. Thank y'all so much for humoring a jumpy little old lady," Joyelle said with a chuckle.

"Not at all," Pete said beaming at her. "You ladies have wonderful day."

"Thank you. You do the same." Joyelle waved goodbye.

LaShaun walked with them to Joyelle's Pathfinder. "Bye, now. And don't you worry."

Miss Clo pulled LaShaun close to whisper. "I'll be calling you later, Missy."

"C'mon , Clo. We can get to the store early, and then beat the lunch crowds at the restaurant," Joyelle called out.

"Goodbye, LaShaun," Miss Clo said in a normal voice volume.

She glanced at LaShaun and pointed a finger at her to emphasize she'd be in touch. Then Miss Clo got in the car, buckled up and started chattering as though they hadn't only moments ago been discussing demonic half animal/half human predators. LaShaun waved goodbye and put on her best cheery smile. Then LaShaun marched through the museum as Dotty and Nyla stared. She entered Pete's office and shut the door firmly. When she spun to face him, Pete stuttered.

"Joyelle's imagination took over. Okay, maybe I did go on about some local legends, but of course I wouldn't put any stock in those old stories." Pete gave a nervous laugh and then sighed. "Thank God you came in. Weeping women scare me worse than any werewolf ever could."

LaShaun rubbed her eyes and let out a slow breath. "Joyelle is on edge with Reverend Fletcher all but saying that she's 'consorting with the devil'."

"Don't get me started on that nincompoop," Pete said. He dropped the heavy book he still held onto the round table in the corner of his office. "She's got more Christian charity in her pinkie finger than that so-called man of God has in his entire body. I hope to never meet that man in person. I probably would be ex-communicated."

"You haven't attended any church on a regular basis in several years, and aren't you Unitarian anyway?" LaShaun helped him put away more books.

"Let me. Some of these volumes are heavy." Pete took one large tome from her. "Knowing Fletcher he'd try to get me thrown out of any and everything, even have my car club membership revoked." He laughed hard at his own joke.

LaShaun stood at the window as Pete continued to go on with sarcastic comments about Reverend Fletcher. She looked out at the tree lined street. Going west it led back toward the picturesque business and shopping district of Beau Chene. South it became a small two lane road that connected to Highway 35 leading into swamplands.

"Hmm," LaShaun said as he kept talking. His voice sounded like a steady buzz in the background. Finally she heard her name repeated.

"Sorry to go on a rant but intolerance galls me. Let's have some hot chocolate to wash away the bitter after taste." Pete bustled out and came back with a ceramic pot. "Filled this up with the delicious brew. Oops, better not say such things too loudly. Some of Fletcher's congregation might think we're having a witches' conference."

"Hmm," LaShaun repeated, still taking in the country autumn scene.

"Things go better with chocolate, eh? Come on, LaShaun. No more brooding," Pete said. He walked over to her carrying both dark green mugs with the museum's name on them in gold. He handed her one.

"Thank you," LaShaun mumbled as she took it.

"Now, my friend, why did you come to see me?" Pete smiled at her and sipped hot chocolate.

"To discuss an infestation," LaShaun said and held the mug without drinking from it.

"Are we talking about termites, ants, or nutria?" Pete chuckled.

"Werewolves," LaShaun replied.

Pete choked and sputtered hot chocolate down the front of his sweater, then fell down. Fortunately for him the wide window seat broke his fall.

*****

Two hours later LaShaun left Pete, who was by turns excited and terrified. LaShaun helped him sober up from dreams of becoming a superstar historian. She reminded him of victims ripped to pieces. Pete decided his research would turn to wiping out the creatures. Still he also wanted to preserve at least one specimen, he insisted;

preferably dead with no chance of coming back again. That was just fine with LaShaun. Now she faced the task of telling Chase. That vow to always be honest with him was about to bite her on the butt. She could only imagine his reaction. She drove to his house after calling him.

Chase had been walked through two crime scenes again, this time with state police forensic techs. Both were located on the country back roads of the parish, which meant he could easily drive out to his house for lunch. He opened the door to LaShaun with a delighted grin. She was about to ruin his good mood.

"Hey, babe. Nice break after looking at weird photos and then the real thing." Chase kissed her firmly on the mouth then let her go ahead of him to his kitchen. "At least we have cool weather with low humidity. No fighting off flying insects the size of model airplanes trying to bite my butt."

"I don't blame them, nice butt," LaShaun quipped and winked at him.

"I accept your admiration, the bugs not so much. I've got sliced smoked turkey, beef and a selection of cheese for po-boy sandwiches. You get the chips and soft drinks." Chase pulled out a French loaf from a bread box. Minutes later he had mustard, mayo and sweet relish on the counter. "How's your day been?"

"Interesting I guess you could say," LaShaun replied. She found a bowl and poured corn ships into it.

"Yeah, well mine was boring and routine. But it's the kind of police work that solves crimes," Chase said as he sliced bread for their sandwiches.

"Hunting for evidence to crack a case sounds pretty exciting." LaShaun went to the stainless steel fridge and grabbed two dark brown bottles of ginger ale made in Louisiana.

Chase licked mustard off one thumb. "No matter what folks see on television, real police work is a lot of sweaty, unpleasant stuff that goes on for hours. We end up sorting through garbage of one kind or another a lot."

"So those sites in the woods have anything helpful?" LaShaun got the answer she expected.

"Nothing I can talk about. But don't expect any breaking news reports, I'll tell you that much. Lots of paper baggies full of icky stuff you wouldn't want to discuss over lunch. All of it is off to the lab. At least once we collect it we're done. The lab guys have to pick through it, stare at it and jiggle it for more hours. I thought about going into forensics, but changed my mind." Chase grimaced. "I'll stick to the field work."

"So no big breaks, huh? No clues why those folks were in the woods?" LaShaun watched him finish spreading condiments generously on one set of slices. "Ease up on the mayo for me. Gotta watch the hips."

Chase looked around at her and let out a low whistled. "I'm watching 'em for you. They're doin' just fine from this man's point of view."

"Thank you, sir." LaShaun blew him a kiss. "Too bad you guys can't wrap up this case soon. I'm sure M.J. feels the same."

"Yeah. The longer this drags on, the more Reverend Fletcher can whip up a Salem witch trial mood around the parish. Thank the good Lord we haven't found any voodoo dolls or farm animals with their throats cut. Still it's freaky."

"What?" LaShaun kept her tone casual. She filled two large glass mugs with ice and put them on the center counter.

"People getting their kicks running through the woods at night. First we have Patsy sneaking out at night, and tales of her coming home with leaves and grass stains on her clothes. I mean, dang, girl. Get a cheap motel room like normal folks cheating." Chase laughed as he put plates with the sandwiches on the counter and sat down.

"Yeah, freaky." LaShaun watched him crunch on a handful of chips and then wash them down with some of the ginger ale.

"Then we have this last couple romping around the sticks in the dark. We don't have a full moon for nothing this fall. I tell you that much." Chase dug into his sandwich.

They ate in silence for another few minutes. Chase made most of the small talk between mouthfuls. LaShaun took a few nibbles. Food wasn't on her mind. She tried to think of a way to lead into telling Chase her latest theory. She absentmindedly turned on the radio and searched for some music. Chase subscribed to a satellite channel so there were plenty of choices. A snatch of news report came on and Vermillion Parish was mentioned. Though she tried, LaShaun wasn't quick enough changing to another station.

"Wait, go back to that one." Chase wiped his mouth clean of crumbs. He reached over to adjust the volume and made the male voice louder.

"Halloween approaches in a picturesque Cajun Country town as the forces of good and evil seem poised for battle; at least that's what a local preacher has to say. Famous phantom chaser James Schaffer is in Beau Chene, Louisiana tracking down tales of ghouls and goblins. Ghost Team USA promises to break news by All Hallows Eve that will send chills up our collective spines. Can't wait, Edie," the man said.

"You think Schaffer's finally got more than shadows on a wall this time?" The female radio personality made it clear she was skeptical.

"I don't know. We're talking about the state where Marie Laveau worked her magic. Louisiana is known for being a place of mystery, voodoo and haunted plantations," the man replied and did his imitation of ghostly sounds.

Edie laughed. "Well folks, guess we should tune in and see what lurks in the swamps. Ghost Team USA airs on your local Fox Channel, so check local listings."

Chase turned the radio to a station playing eighties music. He gave a disgusted grunt. "Exactly what we don't need; some idiot spreading nonsense to a national audience. We'll have kooks coming out of the woodwork, calling the station with wild stories."

"Even you admit the goings-on have been weird," LaShaun offered.

"So far all I see is a bunch of crazy human behavior, but just barely. What is wrong with people, running around the woods half-naked some of them, acting like dogs in heat."

"You're getting warm," LaShaun mumbled.

"What was that, babe? You've barely touched that masterpiece of a po-boy I made for you." Chase downed the rest of his ginger ale and sighed. "Now what did you say about the weather getting warm?"

"Nothing."

"I'll tell you this much. Looks like somebody has been hosting wild sex parties out in the woods. Chances are they had drugs and liquor to help them commune with nature. Jumping each other in the woods like a pack of animals." He shook his head.

"What you're seeing may be canine behavior. Just not dogs... exactly. I'm talking about lycanthropy," LaShaun said as she looked at him.

"What?" Chase chewed on a few chips. He wore a slight frown.

She took a deep breath, let it out and jumped in. "Well, I think a lot of this peculiar running around in the woods stuff is related to lycanthropy. Remember the old stories about rougarous? "

Chase swallowed hard and stared at LaShaun. "You're serious."

"Lycanthropy is a clinical term. A lot of doctors and scientists say it's a mental illness where the person believes he or she can become a wild animal. In this case we're talking about wolves."

Chase slapped his hands together to dust off salt and crumbs. Then he stood up and put both hands on his trim waist. "You're right. Those folks are crazy as hell if they're howling at the moon and chasing around the swamps hunting rabbits for food. Lycanthropy."

"The rougarou legend says people are punished for not observing holy seasons, in this case Lent. They're cursed to become half human and half wolf."

"Those were ghost stories told around the fireplace to make us kids behave. My grandmother scared my sisters straight more than once," Chase said as he gave a short laugh, but the sound died away when he looked at LaShaun. "You really are serious."

"Listen, I don't know if rougarous are real or not, but if people believe that they're wild animals it could explain this behavior. Think about it, animals don't follow the same rules as humans. They run free. Wolves also follow the law of the jungle. If somebody invades your territory, you kill 'em." LaShaun nodded.

Chase scowled. "Lycanthropy, rougarou or werewolf; all of it sounds like an excuse. Some psychologist shows up to give 'em an insanity defense. I don't buy it."

"A lot of what our ancestors talked about wasn't just superstitious nonsense. I told you about my grandmother, and her grandmother and great-grand parents. You know what I've faced. I didn't make that up." LaShaun watched as Chase closed his eyes and pulled a hand over his face.

"When I signed up to be a deputy sheriff I expected to fight *human* crime. Damn!"

"I know, honey," LaShaun said and rubbed his arms.

"Are you sure?" Chase looked at LaShaun.

"No, but the signs are there. I've been reading this book from my family's library. One of the old stories talks about what Joyelle described. Then this morning they talked to Pete, and he let slip--"

"Oh hell," Chase blurted out. "Please say Pete didn't tell those two little old ladies that Vermillion

Parish has a pack of werewolves roaming the bayous."

"I convinced them Pete was talking about the legends, and that he didn't mean to say that rougarous were real."

"Our traditions run deep as the Gulf of Mexico, LaShaun. Before you know it talk about rougarou will be all over town. We got another full moon coming, and Halloween is just two weeks away."

"I'm sure they're planning the next church bake sale and gossiping about their friends." LaShaun smiled at him.

"M.J. is gonna love this."

"We're not going to tell M.J.," LaShaun said quickly.

"She sure as hell won't hear it from me. But you did say lycanthropy is considered a form of mental illness. That could explain a lot. Yeah, so if we do have to bring this up to M.J. that's the explanation I'll emphasize. And stay away from the rougarou stuff." Chase let out a long sigh. "Not so bad after all."

"Except that guy in the hospital has a cut that won't heal, and he's getting worse," LaShaun murmured.

"The doctor says he's got some kind of infection, no mentioning silver knives in front of M.J." Chase shook a forefinger at LaShaun. Before he could continue to lecture his cell phone went off. He grabbed it from the case clipped to his belt and glanced at the caller ID. "Speaking of the boss, this is her calling."

"I'll wash the dishes." LaShaun slipped from the stool and picked up the plates.

"Hi, Sheriff. What's up?" Chase spoke in a light tone. He shrugged when LaShaun glanced at him over her shoulder. "Yeah, I'm home having lunch. Uh-huh. Uh-huh. Yeah, LaShaun does happen to be here."

Hearing her name, LaShaun forgot about drying the wet plates and spun around. Chase's expression went tense again. The muscle along his jaw bone jumped a few times at whatever he was hearing.

"What?" LaShaun mouthed at him.

Chase waved to her to wait. "I don't think that's a great idea. The guy is unstable and-- okay. Put the fear of God into the hospital staff, and make sure they know that if this gets out there'll be hell to pay. Right, I'll call you back." He tapped the key to end the call.

LaShaun didn't like the deep frown creasing his handsome forehead. "I hope it's not another murder."

"No. Our suspect, the crazy guy in the hospital, has stabilized. He's talking pretty clear." Chase looked at LaShaun for a long moment. "And he's asking for *you*."

Chapter 10

At ten o'clock that night LaShaun and M.J. met the on-duty hospital security guard at a service entrance. He silver metallic nameplate had "James Collins" stamped in black. M.J. made terse introductions, including that she and James had been high school classmates. The husky man led them down a hall to one of the elevators used only by doctors and other employees. LaShaun felt flutters in her belly at the cloak and dagger routine, but M.J. had insisted. Not only did M.J. aim to thwart the small town grapevine, she didn't want the reality show team to appear with their video cameras rolling. The security guard led them down a brightly lit empty hallway to an elevator used by staff only. Bland white tile floors and gray walls gave the place a sterile look. LaShaun pulled the denim jacket she wore closer to her body.

"It's freezing in here, colder than outside," she said.

"Keeping the temperature cool reduces bacteria growth, and keeps viruses from spreading. Something very important with a lot of sick people," the security guard replied.

"You know your stuff," LaShaun said.

The man grinned and nodded. "I learn all I can, and take classes. That's the reason I've been promoted. I'm thinking about nursing school. Got three growing kids to feed and educate, ma'am."

"Good for you." LaShaun smiled back at him. The elevator bumped to a stop, and LaShaun's stomach flipped again as they stepped out.

"We're going around this corner," James said with a nod, and then led the way.

M.J. glanced around the hallway, and then down three that branched off to other wings. "You're sure we won't see anybody?"

"It's after visiting hours, and tonight we enforced that rule on this floor more than usual. I checked to make sure visitors left," James said in a grave tone.

"Good," M.J. said, her voice just as solemn.

"Your guy was moved to a wing with two empty rooms, but it's still close to the hub. That's what we call the nurses' station. You're in luck," the guard said. "Mildred Jones is the charge nurse on duty tonight. She takes confidentiality so serious she could head up national security."

As if she'd heard her name, a tall woman with "M. Jones, RN" strode from an office next to the nursing station. She cast a brief glanced at LaShaun before nodding to M.J. "Evening, Sheriff. I hope we can get this over fast. My people are jumpy enough as it is."

"We won't be staying any longer than we have to. How is he?" M.J. looked at two nurses who looked away and got busy doing something else.

"He's still able to talk sense, if that's what you mean. I hope you can track down his next of kin," the charge spoke low.

"We're trying," M.J. said quietly.

"You know who he is?" LaShaun looked from the nurse to M.J.

"Not here. Let's go, James," M.J. said with a glance at the security guard.

"Right." James led the way.

They walked several feet from the nursing station and around another corner. Chase stood with a deputy outside the second door to their left. Both of them seemed just as tense as their boss. The blonde deputy had a fresh-faced boy-next-door look . He appeared to be barely out of his teens. His hazel eyes were wide as though he expected some unpleasant surprise soon. Chase whispered instructions to him then approached them.

"One of the male aides is in there with a male nurse. They've got something to calm him down fast if he gets violent again," Chase said to M.J., but he was looking at LaShaun. "Let's cut it short if he even looks like he about to get crazy."

"Definitely,"M.J. said and signaled James they were ready to go in.

"Okay," James whispered to no one in particular.

He pushed open the room door, and then stood holding it as the others entered the narrow room. Chase led the way followed by M.J. and Nurse Jones. LaShaun tried to move forward to see the man, but M.J. shook her head. Two men stood beside the hospital bed, both dressed in light blue scrubs. They looked at the charge nurse who gave a slight nod toward M.J. and Chase as though saying, "This is your show now".

The male nurse cleared his throat, and looked at his boss. "He drifted off to sleep a few minutes ago. His vitals haven't changed."

"His name is Willie Dupuis. He won't tell anyone but you his story," Chase whispered. "If we try to ask a question he shuts down."

"The doctor says he's a little stronger, but whatever kind of infection he has is weird and persistent," M.J. added.

"Let him do the talking, don't ask a lot of questions. At least not at first," Chase said.

The male nurse and aide moved aside. M.J.'s expression tightened into a grimace. Chase put a protective hand on LaShaun's shoulder for a few moments. LaShaun nodded to indicate she was fine, and that she would follow his lead. Then she looked at the man.

"My God."

Lying beneath the white light above his bed, the man looked like a creature from another world. Willie Dupuis's skin had turned a shimmering shade of silver with a bluish tinge. LaShaun pushed past Chase before he could react and stood close to the bed. The male nurse glanced at the charge nurse. When she didn't object, the men stepped back against the wall to watch. For several minutes no one spoke. LaShaun gazed at him steadily until her surroundings seemed to fade. She heard Chase speaking to her, but his voice seemed far away. Even that sound died when the first wave of bleak resignation hit her. LaShaun shuddered and let out a soft gasp. Willie Dupuis grimaced then opened his eyes. His gaze drifted to the opposite wall, up to the ceiling and then in LaShaun's direction. Yet he seemed not to see her at first. He blinked a few times. His lips moved, and the effort caused him to flinch. The aide got a plastic cup with a straw and let Willie sip for a few seconds. When Willie nodded he'd had enough, the aide retreated to stand against the wall again. Willie looked at LaShaun.

"Thank you for coming," he rasped. He made the effort to smile, but failed.

"How do you feel?" LaShaun glanced down the length of his body. A strange croaking sound came from his throat, and LaShaun realized he had laughed, or tried to at least.

"About as good as I look," Willie finally replied. Then took several breaths and winced.

Without asking, LaShaun got the plastic cup and straw. "You need to drink a bit more water I think. Try."

"'Kay." Willie looked at her with watery eyes as he sipped more. His lips parted and she pulled the straw away. "Time is winding down. I'm done with this life."

"The doctors are working hard to treat you," LaShaun said.

"They can't help me. You delivered the cure." Willie closed his eyes again.

"What does he mean by that?" Nurse Jones said.

"This whole scene is something out of a horror movie," the aide mumbled, and the male nurse nodded agreement. Both men radiated a desire to be anywhere but in that particular hospital room.

LaShaun barely heard their voices. She rubbed her forehead as if to clear away a fog, and glanced around. Chase stared at her with a frown of worry stamped on his handsome face. M.J. looked determined to endure. The charge nurse studied LaShaun with a mixture of curiosity and fear. LaShaun shook her head at them and put a finger to her lips asking them to be quiet. When she looked at Willie again his eyes were open.

"Say a quick prayer for me, the old way," he said.

LaShaun put her hand on his arm. The shock of his cold flesh startled her. The charge nurse bustled forward to pull her away, but LaShaun resisted. "I need contact with him."

"We don't know what kind of infection he has. At least come wash with anti-bacterial soap and then put on gloves. I have to insist. This interview may be a police matter, but I'm responsible for medical precautions," Nurse Jones said in a firm tone.

"She's right," Willie rasped when LaShaun started to argue.

So LaShaun followed the nurse to the small bathroom in the room. She washed as the nurse instructed, used the air dryer connected to the wall and put on disposable latex gloves. Oddly the light blue rubber made her hands look similar to the color of Willie Dupuis's skin. She went back to the bed. This time she found his hand tucked beneath the sheet and plain white cotton hospital blanket. Willie closed his eyes again, and so did LaShaun. She whispered a short prayer in Creole French as Monmon Odette had taught her as a child. The prayer ended with a request that God forgive the sin of consorting with evil spirits.

"Amen," Willie said when LaShaun ended the prayer.

"This is weird," one of the men whispered, and was shushed by several voices.

Willie looked at LaShaun for a few moments. "You know it was me."

"Yes," LaShaun said.

"I didn't want to jump you like that, but when it comes on me I can't stop from being an animal." Willie's mouth trembled and a tear slid down his left cheek. "Sometimes you make a choice, and there ain't no turnin' back. Not ever."

"There is always hope and forgiveness. Remember the prayer," LaShaun said quietly. She still held his hand.

"You think so?" Willie's gaze pleaded for reassurance.

"I know it," LaShaun said without hesitation.

Willie let go of a long sigh, and more tears came. Then he swallowed hard. "I've done a lot of bad stuff, knifed a guy once in a fight on Bourbon Street in New Orleans. I killed another dude in self-defense. Then there was lots of women, not all of them were willing. You know what I mean?"

"Yeah, we know," Chase clipped, an expression of disgust stamping his face into a grimace. His mouth clamped shut at the look M.J. gave him.

Willie's gaze flickered past LaShaun to where Chase and M.J. stood. "I deserve to suffer. High on drink and drugs, I got myself into some real bad company. At first I just thought we was partyin' hard. I should have stopped when some of the others started roughin' up folks off the street. But I was sweatin' to get next to Emelda. That girl could drive a guy crazy swingin' those hips when she danced."

"What's her last name?" LaShaun said softly.

"Good," Chase whispered so low his voice barely made a sound.

"I don't know. Said she grew up in Grand Coteau . Got tired of the small town scene. What a hot goodlooker." Willie smiled. For a moment he looked like a normal man remembering sensuous good times. "She took to me. Well, I had some money at the time. But still..."

"You had fun at first," LaShaun prodded to pull him back from memories of the woman.

"My mama used to tell me the fun wouldn't last, and she was right. Emelda bit me one night while we was makin' love, I didn't think nothin' of it. I mean that girl had some crazy moves. Oh Lord, have mercy." Willie started breathe heavy.

"Damn, that was some kinda woman," the male nurse mumbled and wiped sweat from his forehead.

"You right about that, sick as he is just talking about her gets him hot," his colleague replied with a leer.

LaShaun ignored the urge to slap sense into them. They were the kind of men who, like Willie, would be seduced into trouble that would suck them dry. Evil knew exactly how to appeal to the flesh, as she could bear witness to from her own weaknesses in the past. She gestured to Chase and M.J., and they drew closer.

"You better clear the room," LaShaun said.

M.J. studied LaShaun's expression for a few seconds then nodded. She turned to the charge nurse. "I'm gonna ask y'all to step outside during our interview with Mr. Dupuis. He may be about to give us sensitive information related to an on-going investigation."

Nurse Jones blinked rapidly. "Uh, but he might get upset and need medical attention. Or what if he gets aggressive again?"

"We'll call you." M.J. waved the three hospital employees toward the door. "Just stand by."

The two nurses looked disappointed, but the aide beat them getting out the door. LaShaun continued to hold Willie's hand. The latex glove annoyed her. She knew the sickness eating at Willie Dupuis wasn't contagious.

M.J. pulled the deputy posted outside into the room. "Don't let anyone come in until I say so."

"You got it," the young man replied and went back to the hallway. The door whisked shut blocking out the hum of voices.

M.J. heaved a deep breath and positioned herself at the foot of the bed. Chase moved closer to LaShaun. Both of them watched the sick man closely. LaShaun patted Willie's hand, a sign of reassurance and that he should continue his account.

"I got the fever first, that's what me and a couple of guys I was in jail with called it. I was used to havin' blackouts because of the drinkin' and drugs. That didn't seem unusual. I'd wake up with blood on my shirt. Just a few spots. I thought, damn, we must have gotten into some good fights. But one night I had had blood in my mouth, on my face, and even in my shoes." Willie shivered.

LaShaun pulled the blanket up to his chin. "It's all over now. But you need to tell us."

"Emelda loved it. I've seen some crazy stuff in my time, but I never saw somebody's eyes light up like hers would." Willie gulped in air and continued. "One night I didn't drink as much as usual. The party got started the same way, but then Emelda and the others changed."

He gripped LaShaun's hand tighter. When Chase started toward her LaShaun firmly shook her head to stop him. "It's okay," she whispered.

Willie's eyes were wide and glassy when he turned his head sharply to look at LaShaun. "The horror movie turned real. Their faces got long, and at first I thought my eyes was playin' tricks on me cause their skin turned dark. But it was hair growin' on 'em; right before my eyes. Then my jaws popped and I felt pressure on my neck. I was sittin' next to a window in that old shack we had out in the woods. My face was changin' the same way. Lord, help me. I didn't know." He stopped and whimpered for a few moments.

"Of course not. Even with all you'd done you would never have chosen to go that way," LaShaun said.

"Emelda came over and got on my lap, and then we had some of the wildest kind of sex. The others got to it, too. Six men and four women switched up partners like it was nothin'. When it was all over I thought it was my imagination. Besides that, Emelda had me by the balls. Pardon my language, miss."

"No problem," LaShaun replied, and glanced at Chase.

"I loved every minute of being with that girl. It was a high better than anything. We called ourselves 'The Pack'. The leader, this older guy, kept us in liquor and drugs. And fresh girls. Some would leave. At least I thought they would leave. I found out different later, when we killed one of girls; a hooker from Baton Rouge." Willie gazed at LaShaun as if asking if he had to tell it. When she nodded a tear slid down his cheek.

"We dragged her out to the woods I thought for more fun. After the older guy had her one last time he clawed her back. She started screaming about calling the police." Willie let go of LaShaun's hand. His skin turned grayer. "The leader gave a signal and... they ripped her to pieces. Blood and body parts was all over."

"My God," M.J. whispered.

"A few hours later we all woke up on the ground. We threw the parts into the swamp way out near the parish line." Willie's voice sounded empty of all emotion. "No use lookin' for it. I'm sure between the gators, turtles and fish ain't much left. Besides, I'm not sure exactly where we tossed her, or what was left of her. The old guy knew the back roads, and he did the drivin'."

"Give the officers a general idea maybe," LaShaun spoke gently to him though inside she recoiled in revulsion.

"I wasn't too clear-headed, and I'm not from around here." Willie squeezed his eyes shut. "Not much I wanna remember, but I can't get the pictures out of my head. Things didn't get much better from there. Tell him to help me. Please."

LaShaun moved closer to the hospital bed. "Tell who, Willie?"

"I don't know why he got me into this mess. Even my mama could smell the demon in me, told me to leave and not come back. With all I'd done mama had never said that to me. I've got no home now in this world even if I was to live. I don't wanna burn in hell." Willie strained forward and grabbed LaShaun's arm in a tight grip. He started shivering and coughed so hard pinkish spittle dripped from one corner of his mouth.

"Let go of her." Chase stepped between Willie and LaShaun, and worked to pry the man's hand loose.

"Calm down and give me a name," LaShaun said, but her words were drowned out.

The male nurse, male aide and young deputy rushed into the room with the charge nurse right behind. They helped Chase push Willie back onto the pillows. The nurse already had a syringe of medicine on a tray. The charge nurse briskly barked orders for the deputies and LaShaun to back away. Willie lay shaking, tears leaking from his eyes. He called out to God and his mother to forgive him. Two or three minutes later he slipped into a drug induced sleep. Nurse Jones disposed of the syringe in the sharps container attached to the wall, and stripped off her latex gloves. She stuffed them into another trash can with special markings and then went into the bathroom to wash her hands. Seconds later she came.

"Dr. Oliver is coming, and he's not happy," Nurse Jones said, and raised an eyebrow at M.J.

As if on cue the door opened. A short thin man with red hair entered. He went straight to the bed to stare down at Willie. Then he got gloves from a box on the table, put them one and examined him. He lifted his eyelids and put a stethoscope to Willie's chest.

"I need everyone who isn't medical staff out. Now." Dr. Oliver said without looking at them.

"Of course," M.J. replied.

Chase, the deputy and LaShaun followed M.J. as she left the hospital room. LaShaun glanced over her shoulder once. Willie's eyes fluttered open and his lips moved. He seemed to be fighting the drug to keep talking. His message came through loud and clear to LaShaun, and the sensation caused her stomach to lurch. She stumbled against the young deputy who caught her.

"You okay, ma'am?"

Chase put a protective arm around her. "Get a glass of water, please."

"Sure." The deputy looked at them curiously as he walked down the hallway.

When the deputy returned, M.J. took the small plastic cup from him and sent him back to stand outside Willie's room. "You look shook up bad."

"I'm okay." LaShaun said. She accepted the cup and took a few sips.

"Let's go down there."

M.J. pointed to the end of the hall past the two empty rooms. They moved farther away from Willie's room and the deputy. A large window faced one of the parking lots. Beyond the pavement and circles of white light from large lamp poles trees seemed to hover like giants in the dark. LaShaun crossed her arms to ward off the cold she felt.

"What just happened?" M.J. looked to LaShaun for answers.

"Willie Dupuis seems to think LaShaun can help him get absolution." Chase rubbed his jaw.

"That makes no sense. He should have asked for a priest." M.J. continued to stare at LaShaun. "But instead he asked for *you*."

"She doesn't know anything about..." Chase stopped when LaShaun gave him a look.

"You're right, M.J. It's weird that he asked for me, but I've never met him before." LaShaun returned her gaze. "I don't like it anymore than you do."

"Then what the hell are we dealing with?" M.J. broke off when Dr. Oliver strode toward them.

"Don't upset my patient again." Dr. Oliver jammed his fists on his narrow hips.

"He asked to talk to us, and we've got a murder investigation to conduct. He's the main suspect," Chase said.

Dr. Oliver wore a grim expression. "Well I doubt he'll make it to a trial, or even out of this hospital. We tried strong antibiotics, but I'm afraid he's got a resistant bug."

"A strange infection is what the charge nurse said," M.J. replied.

"Strange is right. His grayish skin looks like silver poisoning, which is something I've never seen before. But it's rarely fatal, even if the patient has ingested large quantities." Dr. Oliver sighed.

"Why would people swallow silver?" M.J. asked.

"Folks have used silver for generations for various home remedies, despite medical advice to the contrary. But he didn't know what I was talking about when I asked. Even that doesn't cause his symptoms: fever, blisters, and that wound on his left leg won't heal. In fact it's getting worse, like the flesh is just rotting away." Dr. Oliver sighed. "Mr. Dupuis gave us next of kin contact information. His mother hung up on the hospital social worker after saying she didn't even want to speak his name. So Willie gave me permission to talk to you three about his treatment. If we don't figure out what he's got and how to treat it he'll take his secrets to the grave."

"Thanks for the information, doc. We talk to you first before we question him again," M.J. said.

"I wouldn't count on that. He's slipped into a semi-comatose state. I hope you got something helpful tonight." Dr Oliver gave M.J. a handshake, nodded to Chase and LaShaun and walked away.

"Sorry I couldn't get more information from him," LaShaun said.

"You did good," Chase replied. "You sure he didn't scratch you?"

"No, but it wouldn't matter if he did." LaShaun cleared her throat, but decided not to say anymore in front of M.J. "We need to find out who Willie was talking about, the guy that got him into the 'pack'. And the one he begged me to find."

"We know exactly who he is and where to find him," M.J. said. Her dark eyebrows pulled together to give her a seriously troubled expression.

"Yeah, and we don't have to worry about him going anywhere either," Chase added. "He's talking about his cell mate back in 2002 at the Lafayette Parish Jail."

LaShaun felt the rise of bile in the back of her throat. She swallowed more of the now tepid water in the plastic cup still in her hand. Then she looked at Chase.

"The Blood River Ripper was Willie's old pal," M.J. said quietly.

An hour later LaShaun was home. Chase checked her locks and security system thoroughly as she filled a kettle for hot tea. She'd tried to assure him there was no danger, but he made his rounds anyway. His cell phone rang twice as he did so. His muffled voice sounded clipped and to the point. When Chase returned to the kitchen he sighed.

"I've got to go, still on duty. But I hate leaving you alone." As he spoke, Chase strode to the window and looked out into the dark.

"I'm fine. Besides, I have it on good authority that Mr. Marchand and his son are keeping a sharp eye out. They've got rifles and know how to use them." LaShaun joined him at the window and pulled him away. "There's nothing to worry about."

Chase kissed her. "No going out to investigate strange noises or opening the door to late night visitors. Do it for my peace of mind."

"I'll follow your orders, sir." LaShaun planted a kiss on the tip of his nose. "Now go catch some bad guys."

Once alone LaShaun read through her family journal again. After a few minutes of reading she put it aside and did an internet search. She found the right company and clicked on the button to order the specialty ammunition, silver bullets for Chase and silver pellets for her shotgun.

Chapter 11

The next evening LaShaun's had dinner alone for the third straight night. Chase was working long hours, barely taking time to eat and sleep for a few hours. So she ate from a tray sitting on the sofa with only the television for company, not that she paid much attention to it. An old black and white zombie movie from the fifties played in the background. She laughed at the bad acting and an even worse story line. Her phone rang, and she picked up the cordless handset at the same time she hit the mute button on the TV remote.

"You better turn to Channel Six," Pete said without pausing for usual chit-chat.

"Good evening to you, too," LaShaun retorted. "Yes, I'm feeling fine and yourself?"

"Sorry. My Yankee directness comes back even after living in the south for eleven years," Pete said.

"You know we don't get to the point until we've rambled on for at least ten minutes," LaShaun quipped as she hit the button to bring up the local station. Her amusement evaporated when she saw James Schaffer and Reverend Fletcher on the local Fox affiliate.

Schaffer wore a black turtleneck, black jacket and sunglasses. Seated across from him was Reverend Fletcher. "So you believe that demonic forces are in Beau Chene? This is such a beautiful bucolic place. Amid the magnolia trees and Spanish moss draped oaks bathed in fall sunshine, it's hard to believe evil lurks here."

"Give me a break," LaShaun muttered.

"Look at Fletcher. He's trying to figure out what bucolic means," Pete said with a snort.

Indeed the preacher stammered for a few moments. He soon found his footing by honing in on the words he did understand. "Satan uses beauty to seduce those who aren't on guard to his cunning ways. Look in the Bible. There are so many instances of lovely women pulling men to their doom."

LaShaun flinched as if he'd aimed a direct hit at her and Chase. "I'd like to pull him into something unpleasant."

"Well, thank you for that insightful discussion. Reverend Fletcher." Schaffer turned in his chair as the camera moved in to show only him. "The story in this pretty little bayou town continues to get more and more extraordinary. Residents are buzzing about late night visits to interview a suspect rumored to be possessed, and another shocking murder has occurred. The local sheriff seems overwhelmed by the bizarre events. Our Ghost Team will have all of the shocking details in our next episode. We'll wrap after the break."

"What a ham," Pete blurted out.

"Yeah, but sounds like Schaffer knows about Willie Dupuis." LaShaun looked at the television screen without really seeing the next commercial about a local bank.

"Willie who?" Pete asked.

"The guy they found not far from my property, with the dead woman." LaShaun sat down on the edge of the sofa.

"I'm not surprised he's found folks willing to flap their lips," Pete said.

"Yes, but certain parties were supposed to keep quiet." LaShaun shook her head.

"When money starts talking, people start talking back. Guess we better tune in next week to see what Schaffer had to say. Maybe he's just blowing hot air for ratings, and he doesn't really know anything. Don't let it bother you. Call if you need any more research. And do keep me informed of anything you find out."

"Yeah, right," LaShaun mumbled and hit the off button.

Her appetite was gone, so LaShaun put away the remains of her dinner of Cornish hen, green beans and dirty rice. She was still wired about the Ghost Team interview two hours later when Chase showed up at her kitchen door. His morose expression meant she didn't have to ask how his day had gone. They kissed, and he trudged off to wash up while LaShaun heated up a plate of food for him. When he came back they exchanged small talk as he ate. LaShaun gave him space to wind down from work. In between bites of food Chase read text messages a few times. Finally LaShaun rubbed his shoulders.

"Put the phone away and have a slice of homemade pecan pie and a cup of coffee," she said.

"Thank you, baby, for making me a pie," Chase said with one last look at his phone before tucking it into his shirt pocket.

"I never said it was made in my house. Miss Joyelle brought it by earlier, in gratitude for easing her mind." LaShaun put a slice on a desert plate and poured Louisiana dark roast coffee into a cup for him.

Chase dug into the pie and washed down the mouthful with coffee. "Hmm, tastes might good. Speaking of which, let's talk about rougarous. Now there's something I never would have thought I'd be saying."

"At least Schaffer doesn't know *that* bit." LaShaun dumped the remains of food from his plate and loaded them into the dishwasher.

"He will soon, if he hasn't heard already. Joyelle joked to a relative about how silly she felt after talking to Pete about rougarou. The cousin repeated the story, and by the time it made the rounds it changed. You know how it goes. The original tone gets lost, and a bit more gets added to the story. By the time Miss Clo heard it, you had a starring role with Pete saying research by leading experts agree rougarou exist."

"Damn." LaShaun rubbed her forehead as if she already had a headache. "Pete is going to have a fit."

"The best we can do is damage control. Keep repeating that it's just a legend, no different from vampires." Chase's jaw tightened.

"What about Willie Dupuis? Schaffer dropped a hint that he knows, so Joyelle is the only one who's been talking," LaShaun said.

"I don't think anyone around town is making the connection. So far all the talk is speculation, so I'm sure the hospital staff hasn't talked," Chase added.

"How's Willie doing? I feel bad about cutting him, even if he isn't exactly a solid citizen," LaShaun said.

"You don't know for sure it was Willie," Chase said quickly.

"He *told* me it was him. How else did he know me?" LaShaun asked.

"You're somewhat of a celebrity around here," Chase replied with a shrug. "You told me yourself that a lot of wannabe goths and dabblers in the supernatural show up here. Maybe Willie and his pals heard about you."

LaShaun shook her head. "No, it was Willie. I'm certain."

When the doorbell rang Chase stood. He talked as he strode down the hall to the front door. "What I wouldn't give right now for a *normal* murder investigation."

Minutes later she heard voices and multiple footsteps approaching the kitchen. Miss Clo appeared first. She wore an apologetic smile. "Good evening. Sorry to bust in on you without notice."

"Hi. We should have called first. Sorry." M.J. glanced at her grandmother. "No pie for me. I wolfed down a hot meatball sandwich for lunch, and my stomach is fussing at me about that."

"Pie for you, Miss Clo?" LaShaun asked.

"No, thank you, dear." Miss Clo smiled at LaShaun. "But I'll take a slice to go for a late night snack."

"I'll wrap you up a couple of slices." LaShaun smiled back and headed for the kitchen again.

Miss Clo followed her. "This is such a cheerful room. I love the way you have a country feel, and how it flows to the den area."

"Thank you. I did a few renovations in the past few months." LaShaun went to the counter and pulled out plastic storage box. She uncovered the pie dish and sliced two generous helpings.

"Most folks wouldn't think that this house would be so warm and welcoming. Just goes to show you can't listen to silly old gossip." Miss Clo smiled and sat on another stool. "Why, you could have a wonderful holiday get-together in here."

"That's a great idea we can talk about later," Chase said promptly with a raised eyebrow at LaShaun. "But I'm thinking y'all didn't drive over here to discuss ideas for entertaining."

"No, not even close," M.J. said. "We need to discuss the visit we had the other night."

"Okay." LaShaun sat down in the over-sized chair that matched the two small sofas. Chase pulled up the large ottoman and sat next to her.

"Orin Young wanted you to go visit Manny. Joyelle and I thought it might be a good idea, too," Miss Clo said. She looked at M.J. pointedly. "Turns out we were on the right track after all. So much for my granddaughter's theory that we were just two old ladies butting in."

M.J. squinted at her. "No, you weren't. At the time there were no crimes committed, just a cheating wife and a lot of intuition based on old stories."

"She struggles with having to hear 'I told you so', from me and her mother," Miss Clo said, and pressed her lips shut when M.J. glared at her.

"Monmon..."

"She's just trying to help," LaShaun broke in, amused at the intergenerational battle of the wills. She looked at M.J. "She's right about what?"

"Willie Dupuis was in jail with Manny Young back in 2002, that's a fact. Now we have more murders that are similar to crimes Manny committed between 2002 and 2005."

"And at the time we weren't sure we'd found all of the bodies," Chase put in. When Miss Clo gasped and put a hand over her mouth he winced. "Sorry."

"The typical profile of the victims were women and men who had high risk lifestyles," M.J. added. "Folks who had lost ties with family."

"Or the families and friends were used to them disappearing for days, even months, at a time."

"So they might not be missed for a long while, if at all," LaShaun said.

"Exactly," Chase replied.

"Okay, but what does this have to do with Manny Young? He's been locked up since 2006, so he can't be suspect. And I know you enjoy being right, Miss Clo, but he can't know anything about folks roaming at night around here now." LaShaun suppressed a smile when the older woman pursed her lips in response to logic.

"Thank you," M.J. said firmly and shot a glance at her grandmother. "But based on what Willie said, Manny could give us more information."

"Either about Willie's movements, which means we could see if he's connected to more missing people or unsolved homicides," Chase said.

"Or maybe Manny will finally fill in some of the details about other murders he committed. It's not like he has anything to lose." M.J. stood up and walked around as though sitting still was too much.

"Or to gain," LaShaun replied gazing at Chase and then M.J.

"Good point. But Willie talked about how they hung out for a while after they were both out of jail. Manny got out first. Willie looked him up when Manny was hanging out in a rough part of town in

Lafayette." M.J. nodded when LaShaun's eyes went wide.

"They traveled together," LaShaun said softly.

"Yeah, around south Louisiana and east Texas. But how did you... Never mind." M.J. sighed. "We're waiting to hear back from law enforcement in Sabine and Newton counties."

"Great, but I still don't see what this has to do with *me*." LaShaun looked at from Chase to M.J. and at Miss Clo.

"We have solid connections to real crimes and Manny Young based on *facts*," M.J. said emphatically, looking at her grandmother. "We think visiting him for an interview might actually have some value. Willie implied toward the end that Manny got him into some stuff that even he's ashamed about."

"Okay, so one or both of you plan to interview Manny." LaShaun stared at her. "Right?"

"That's what I'd prefer, but..." M.J. tapped a fist on the duty belt around her trim waist she worked hard to maintain.

"He'll only talk to you. Seems his granddaddy has been talking to him about getting help. Mr. Young is still angry about us helping him get convicted, and he's convinced that you'll do Manny more good than any psychiatrist," Chase said wearing a stony expression.

"Manny hasn't been too cooperative or chatty with the therapists at the forensic hospital, including this psychologist who is eager to pick his brain," M.J. said. Then she looked at her grandmother. "Don't you repeat any of this to a single soul, Monmon. I brought you because Mr. Young has been confiding in you and isn't all that happy about dealing with me."

"Of course, Myrtle Jean!" Miss Clo snapped back. "You should know better. I won't even tell Joyelle, especially after that incident with her blabbing to her big mouth cousin. I got on her about it, too."

"In her defense, I hear she didn't mean to spread the story as though it was true." LaShaun gave Miss Clo a pat on the arm.

"Doesn't matter. We agreed not to discuss it with *anyone for any reason*. She wasn't thinking. But don't worry, dear. We've been friends longer than you been on this earth. We've had our little spats before. We've already made up. And she's very sorry about how the tale has grown and spread."

"I'll say it's grown and spread," M.J. put in. "All of the parish must be talking about the rougarou prowling the swamps around Beau Chene. The mayor has had more calls from Reverend Fletcher and his flock than you can believe."

"Oh I definitely believe," LaShaun said.

"More than a few are having fun with the story, too. With Halloween coming up, guess what will be the most popular costume this year?" Chase gave a grunt. "Even my sister and her kids are getting in on the act. They are so looking forward to their annual party."

"Back to Manny Young, his grandfather wants you to visit him. He's told the social worker that you're a distant cousin he grew up with, just in case. Manny is willing to talk to you." M.J. shook her head. "I'd prefer having one of my guys interview him, but Mr. Young made it clear that wasn't going to happen. And if we can solve some crimes or at least get more information..." She shrugged.

"We can't force Manny to talk to us, or even let us visit. He's been convicted." Chase let out a noisy breath and looked at LaShaun. "That place is supposed to be safe."

"Supposed to be?" Miss Clo's eyes went wide.

"Anything can happen with dangerous guys like him. They can be unpredictable. So if you don't want to go just say so. It's not like we're sure he'll even give us anything that will help." Chase spoke to LaShaun as if they were alone. He walked close to her and put a protective arm around her waist.

"They have plenty of security, LaShaun. Trained correctional officers staff the place. If he's been agitated or anyway showing signs he could cause problems they'll call off the visit. I don't think danger is a real issue," M.J. said squinting at Chase as though chastising him for trying to dissuade LaShaun.

LaShaun had no fear about her safety, or even coming face to face with a notorious serial killer. The others mistook her silence for indecision. In truth, she'd known all along that she would end up visiting Manny Young. She only waited for the inner sense and a sign that the time was right. Miss Clo chattered on about the Young family, Reverend Fletcher and town gossip. Chase glanced at LaShaun every few seconds. LaShaun gazed past Miss Clo and M.J. to the window beyond. A trio of moths fluttered against the window. The voices of the humans around her became background noise, muted almost to silence. Instead the LaShaun heard the fluttering of wings against glass. Monmon Odette always said seeing three moths meant there were secrets about to be revealed.

"LaShaun, did you hear M.J.?" Chase spoke close to her ear and gave her a gentle shake. "You look like you're in another world."

She blinked out of her reverie. She looked at him and smiled. Then she pulled free of his embrace and faced M.J. "I'll go. Set it up."

Chapter 12

The following day LaShaun worked on being patient with Savannah. They sat in the small office behind the gift shop Savannah's father owned a block from her law office. They had met for lunch provided by Savannah's aunt, known for being one of the best Creole cooks in several surrounding parishes. Two bowls of steaming shrimp and corn soup gave the room a wonderful fragrance.

"Just one more question. Have you lost your mind?" Savannah asked, dipping her soup spoon into the bowl, and then paused to wait for an answer.

LaShaun sighed. "You're starting to repeat yourself."

"Okay, let me list just a few reasons visiting a man with the nickname Blood River Ripper is a very bad idea."

Before Savannah could start, LaShaun broke in. "No, I don't believe law enforcement or the district attorney is trying to trap me into revealing that I'm somehow involved in these crimes. Yes, I do remember that Willie and the dead woman were found near my woods. Of course it's possible that Orin Young is using my involvement as a ploy to help get Manny off death row. And no, I don't think folks will get stirred up against me and my family again." LaShaun ate more of the delicious brew in her bowl and let the warm goodness slid down her throat. "No way could I have even gotten this in L.A."

Savannah's shapely dark eyebrows pulled together. "The DA still thinks you got away with something last year. He's not sure what it is, but he thinks you're guilty."

"Silly rabbit, wasting his time stewing about a case that's been stamped 'closed' for months." LaShaun fished out a succulent shrimp and enjoyed it.

"The man hates to lose. He sincerely thinks of himself as upholding right and protecting the citizens. That's a direct quote from his campaign talking points." Savannah grinned at the funny face LaShaun made. "I know, but it gets votes."

"What-ev. Guess a little thing like me being *innocent* doesn't matter around here," LaShaun said as she worked on making her bowl of soup empty.

"Visiting a psychotic serial killer in a place full of crazy criminals isn't affecting your appetite," Savannah said dryly.

"Hmm." LaShaun finished off one last piece of French bread and patted her mouth with a napkin. "M.J. assured me that the place is well run with lots of big, burly correctional officers."

"Oh well, then you should have a fine old time chatting with the grim reaper," Savannah retorted.

"You mean the Blood River Ripper," LaShaun corrected.

"Thanks for mentioning that while I'm still eating. Ugh." Savannah gave an exaggerated shiver.

"Okay, change of subject. What's up with Patsy and her husband? I heard that the guy's actually considering taking her back."

"Vince has completely forgotten his urge to strangle her. He looked into her big green eyes and believed her story," said Savannah as she walked to the small kitchenette area down the hall. One of the gift shop employees stopped her to ask questions. Moments later Savannah came back and closed the office door.

"Just what is the story?"LaShaun asked and sat back in her chair.

"You'll love this one. Patsy says Tommy chased after her until she was too afraid to resist his advances. He even implied he would hurt Vince and the kids if she didn't meet him for sex." Savannah rolled her eyes.

"So she was protecting her family. It could be true," LaShaun replied. She shrugged at the look Savannah gave her.

"That doesn't quite explain three trips to Victoria's Secret to buy sexy lingerie, or the hot love notes she slipped him every chance she got. And don't get me started on the sex-ting." Savannah waved a hand.

"The what?"

"Smokin' hot text messages. Not to mention the cell phone photos she sent. One had her wearing crotch-less panties, legs spread and blowing him a kiss."

"Grown folks stupid enough to do that stuff? Damn." LaShaun shook her head in wonder.

"Tommy's wife got her hands on his cell phone, and was kind enough to show them to Vince," Savannah continued. "I think she hoped Vince would do her the favor of bumping off the rival for her hubby's affections. Once Patsy gets her hooks in a guy she hangs on."

"She's a pretty little bundle of trouble. Probably realized men were easy targets while she was still in kindergarten," LaShaun said and laughed.

"Takes one to know one, huh?" Savannah tilted her head to one side

Instead of being offended LaShaun laughed harder. "I plead the fifth. I recognized her the minute she popped up at my house that night."

"Yeah, Vince is totally on her side and saying she's being falsely accused. He even asked me to be her lawyer. After I got over the shock at how gullible he is, I explained to him that I didn't feel comfortable with that. I mean, I was ready to represent him in divorcing her. That lasted all of one week." Savannah sat back and stared out the window. The narrow alley between her shop and the antique store next door had a few small trees and plant boxes.

"Patsy knew all she had to do was spend a few minutes with him," LaShaun said.

"You're right. He couldn't stay away from her for long. Now he's determined to defend her and protect his family," Savannah said with a sigh. "I never had a guy get that goo-goo crazy over me."

"Paul was and still is, so don't even start," LaShaun retorted. She nodded toward the photo of Savannah with her husband and twin girls on an antique side table.

"Paul wouldn't be dumb enough to overlook porn pictures and hot text messages," Savannah retorted.

"Okay, maybe Vince isn't the brightest bulb on the tree. Still love can make you do crazy things."

"Speaking of love and crazy, that is one fabulous engagement ring. Your fiancé is so romantic."

Savannah leaned forward and grabbed LaShaun's hand. "Damn, girl. I need my sunglasses."

"I hope he doesn't suffer because of me," LaShaun said softly.

Savannah let go of her hand and sat back again. "Don't *you* be silly now. Obviously Chase knows a once in a lifetime love is worth the risk."

LaShaun felt a warm shock like electricity at her words. She smiled softly at the knowledge that her own extra sense confirmed her friend's opinion. "You're right. But if he loses the election…"

"He'll chalk it up to experience and plan his next campaign. Or he'll keep being a top investigator. Either way he wants you by his side. Without the right person to share life with the other stuff means very little," Savannah said with certainty ringing in her voice. "Take it from a woman who found her wonderful soul mate. I almost pushed him away for good. Don't make that mistake."

"Yes, mother dear," LaShaun quipped.

"I'm serious. You're a loner, and you tend to be suspicious of people. That's okay if you haven't found *the one*."

"I know. Being alone won't do, and trying to be with someone else would feel even worse," LaShaun murmured.

"Exactly. Hold on tight, girl. He's worth it, and you deserve it. Chase is a good man, and they're too rare. He'd fight lions, tigers and bears for you." Savannah winked at her.

Or even wolves, LaShaun thought. She kept that to herself. No need in scaring Savannah, whose little girls would be trick or treating in a few days. Instead she pushed aside thoughts of supernatural killers. She smiled at her friend.

"Indeed he would. He's going with me to visit Manny Young. Mr. Young isn't happy, but I made it clear that was a condition."

"You're not scared to go alone, or ride with Mr. Young," Savannah said with confidence.

"Right again. Chase insisted, and I agreed so he wouldn't be worried. Maybe if Manny trusts me a little, he'll be willing to talk to Chase."

"I can't wait to hear about your visit with the guy. It's so strange to hear such conflicting stories about the same man. On the one hand he's a crazed killer, and folks say they knew he'd come to no good. Others claim he wasn't such a bad guy, at least not as a kid." Savannah's eyes were bright with interest.

"You would have loved being in the courtroom on that one," LaShaun said.

"When I was single, you bet. But that kind of a case can consume your life for months. Not to mention dealing with that kind of evil seeps into your pores. I wouldn't want my family exposed even second hand to that kind of bad karma." Savannah shook her head firmly.

"You almost sound superstitious, counselor," LaShaun quipped.

"Tante Marie and godmother always told me when you believe in God then you know there is a devil." Savannah pointed a finger at LaShaun to punctuate her sentence.

LaShaun got up and went to the photo of Savannah's family. "What you said about your kids, keeping them away from even the scent of evil. I don't think having a child is in my future, and maybe that's a good thing. "

"That's downright ridiculous talk," Savannah replied promptly.

"No, think about it. I stirred up something bad, real bad. I had to fight off that demon, and I'm not sure it's gone for good. What if going after an innocent soul is temptation enough to bring it back?" LaShaun put down the photo and faced Savannah.

"Look, I'm not an expert on that kind of thing. But I think your grandmother would say that you're wrong. Besides, she saw children in your future. Monmon Odette would have told you if she saw danger threatening them." Savannah used logic as usual.

"This gift we have is limited. We can't always know everything that is going to happen. I just wish I could be sure. Chase can make a choice, he knows about my past. But bringing a baby into my world is different." LaShaun crossed her arms tightly. The pain of that admission stung. "Chase wants children, a normal family."

Savannah stood in front of LaShaun. "So that's what keeps you awake at night."

"I have a responsibility to do the right thing, for the future. My ancestors called up that spirit over one hundred years ago. It lay dormant, waiting for another call; and I was arrogant enough to call it back again. Maybe I need to be the one to end it, once and for all." LaShaun spoke words to her friend that she had confided to no one else, except speaking aloud to the spirit of Monmon Odette when she was alone.

"You nudged 'it' awake, but your ancestors laid out the welcome mat long before you were born. He, she, it is gone. You destroyed it, remember?" Savannah sighed. "Stop rolling along in the guilt wagon."

"Thanks for the motivational speech. Hey, watch it!" LaShaun caught the white paper bag Savannah threw at her head.

"You're going to be happy with Chase. If you don't believe me, consult a psychic," Savannah quipped with an impish grin.

"How clever," LaShaun shot back with a glare.

"Have a butter cream cookie or two, and I'll fix us some coffee." Savannah went back to the kitchenette.

Seconds later, Kris, one of the gift shop employees came in. She glanced over her shoulder and whispered, "Uh, somebody here wants to talk to you."

"Who is it?" LaShaun blinked at her odd behavior.

"Sorry to bust in on y'all having lunch, but this is kind of urgent." Patsy brushed past the young woman.

"I asked you wait a minute, *ma'am*." Kris put a hand on one hip.

"It's okay," LaShaun said.

"Let me know if y'all need anything," Kris said with dubious glance at Patsy before she stomped out.

Patsy's pert nose wrinkled with ire, and her eyes glittered. Quick as lightening her expression changed to an apologetic smile. LaShaun sized her up in ten seconds. Patsy had an agenda.

"I don't mean to trouble you again, Miz LaShaun, honestly I don't. But as you know I could be in a heap of trouble. I think maybe you're the only one who could help me." Patsy sat down in a chair without invitation.

"You take cream with your... what the hell?" Savannah stood in the door holding a cup of coffee in one hand and a tiny cream pitcher in another.

"Hello, Mrs. Honoré. I hope you don't mind, but I just have to get some advice." Patsy looked at her only briefly before turning back to LaShaun.

"I can't be your lawyer. I thought we'd settled that," Savannah said.

"She's here to see me," LaShaun replied with a sideways glance at her friend.

"I just know you'll understand that none of this is my fault. If we could speak privately..." Patsy's voice trailed off as she looked at Savannah. "Please. I only have a few minutes. I'm supposed to be shopping with my sister. When I saw your vehicle I told Betty, that's my other older sister, that I would meet her at the dollar store in an hour."

"LaShaun, can I talk to you?" Savannah nodded for her to her follow out of the office.

"I'll be right back."

Savannah led the way through the kitchenette to a storage room that also had a desk. She shut the door firmly. "I'm about to shove her butt out the front door."

"I want to hear what she has to say." LaShaun grinned at the hissing sound that Savannah made.

"How can you tell Patsy is lying? Her lips are moving, that's how," Savannah said. "I sat with her for two hours, and she's a manipulative little..."

"But it's interesting she made it a point to track me down a second time." LaShaun raised an eyebrow at her friend.

"She wants you to convince her gullible husband that Tommy put her under some kind of spell. Either way I don't like it."

Savannah started to go on but stopped when LaShaun lifted a hand. LaShaun moved quickly to the closed door and pulled it open. The narrow hallway was empty. She closed the door again. "I'd swear she was creeping up to listen."

"Not possible, that wood floor would have creaked and given her away." Savannah waved away LaShaun's suspicion. "I'm going to tell her to leave and don't slam the door on her way out."

"Let me handle Patsy." LaShaun tilted her head to one side. "She's used to using whatever it takes to get what she wants. Now she's here to figure out what it will take to bend me to her will."

Savannah started to laugh but covered her mouth quickly. "Oh this is going to be good. This girl has not been paying attention to the local legends about LaShaun Rousselle."

LaShaun squinted at the reference to her infamous past. "Gee thanks. Stay cool and let me find out more about what makes our girl tick."

"Check. Work it," Savannah whispered.

She nodded for LaShaun to lead the way back to the office. Once they arrived, Patsy sat as if she hadn't moved an inch. She nibbled on a cookie. "I hope you don't mind. Betty and I haven't had lunch yet."

"Help yourself," Savannah said, and gave her a tight smile. "Just so you know I advised LaShaun not to talk to you. I'll leave you two alone."

"Is there a side or back door? I'm pretty sure no one saw me come in, and that way I won't cause either you any embarrassment." Patsy hung her head. She looked friendless and vulnerable.

"Off the kitchen," Savannah clipped. She turned away from Patsy and rolled her eyes at Savannah. "See you later."

"Bye." LaShaun pursed her lips to keep from laughing at the way Savannah mouthed insults about their visitor. She sat across from Patsy. "So, you said it was urgent that you talk to me."

"Miz Joyelle told you about me, how she was so worried and everything." Patsy looked to the side.

"She mentioned you would leave the house at night but said you couldn't remember anything about it."

LaShaun felt a shield come up between them. Patsy had indeed been listening to local stories about LaShaun. They were separated in age. By the time Patsy hit high school LaShaun and her contemporaries were long gone. The younger set would be too busy with their social scene to care about old stories long before their time. But Patsy knew enough to be wary. Someone had coached her how to resist being read by a sensitive. Despite Patsy's efforts, LaShaun could feel it. The traces appeared like invisible bread crumbs. She wore a black leather cord around her neck with an amulet with the letter "A" in a circle. LaShaun recognized the symbol of anarchy, of doing whatever one wanted.

"Most of the time I didn't. But I'm going to tell you something I haven't told anyone." Patsy paused as though gathering her courage. She still held the cookie in her hand. As though deep in thought, she broke off a small piece and chewed for a few seconds. She swallowed and sighed.

"I know this is hard for you." LaShaun knew exactly the opposite. Patsy relished the process of deception as much as getting what she wanted as a result. LaShaun watched Patsy's rosebud lips twitch in amusement briefly before she sighed again.

"I did remember sometimes." Patsy daintily used a napkin to brush crumbs from her lap and into one hand. She finished the cookie off and glanced around.

"I'll get you a cup of coffee," LaShaun said and stood.

"Water would be just fine. Y'all had lunch I see. You got any meat?" Patsy wiped her mouth with the back of one hand. Her purse slipped from her lap to the floor.

"No meat." LaShaun went very still as she observed her.

"Wow, I must really be hungry." Patsy blinked at her and let out a musical laugh.

"Yeah, I'll bet your feeling ravenous," LaShaun replied and smiled when Patsy glanced at her sharply.

Instinct made LaShaun keep an eye on her even as she left the room. She went to the refrigerator and got a bottle of water from a six pack. When she returned Patsy stood at the window looking toward the street. She turned when she heard LaShaun return and took the offered bottled water.

"Thank you." With one quick motion Patsy opened it and drank deeply. She started to wipe her mouth again, but stopped when she saw her pink gloss smeared on her hand. "My manners have gotten terrible."

"So you remember those nights when you snuck out of the house." LaShaun stood with her arms folded.

Patsy nodded and then sat again. She waited for LaShaun to sit across from her. "Tommy is so sexy, was so sexy. I resisted him for a long time," she added quickly. "But he had some kind of hold on me. I know you've heard about me."

"Not all gossip is accurate," LaShaun said.

"You do understand," Patsy said and leaned forward. "I'm not denying how much I enjoy sex with cute guys. Vince is nice, but..."

"Predictable," LaShaun filled in for her.

"Exactly. I thought being with him would settle me down, and it did. But Tommy set his sights on me, and I gave in to temptation. Then Tommy blackmailed me, and threatened to hurt Vince. I couldn't let that happen."

"Besides, the sex with Tommy was exciting. Part of you wanted to break away, and part of you looked forward to being with him." LaShaun nodded. "Yes, I can see how you felt trapped."

"At first, but I finally told Tommy it was over. That's when he got really pissed off." Patsy clutched the bottle of water with both hands.

"Why didn't you just remind him that his wife would find out, too?" LaShaun tilted her head to one side.

Pasty laughed and put a hand over her mouth. "Sorry, this is serious. Tommy didn't care about his wife finding out. He's cheated on her since they were high school sweethearts. She wouldn't leave him, not for good anyway. Guess she was under his spell, too."

"People do stupid things when they're in love, or lust," LaShaun said.

"You're right about that," Patsy said, her lips curving up for a second before she assumed her sober account. "Anyway, I think Tommy was in a cult. Once or twice we partied with his friends. At first I thought they were just regular old party folks. We'd go out to this camp way out on the bayou. I'm ashamed to say this next part."

LaShaun fought off the impulse to laugh out loud at that so-called admission. Patsy loved every minute of her confessional. "Go on, I won't judge you."

"Sometimes we swapped partners; me and Tommy would swing with his friend Jason and his girlfriend from New Orleans. That was wild even for me." Patsy twisted the cap from the bottle and drank again. She stared at the floor as if too ashamed to lift her head.

LaShaun felt light-headed for a few moments. She closed her eyes. Flashes of people partying in an old house filled her mind. Patsy's musical laugh echoed. LaShaun sensed no regret, only the heat of excitement. Suddenly the scene switched to the woods and a camp fire. Liquor flowed freely, and drugs were passed around. When LaShaun opened her eyes again Patsy looked up and frowned at her.

"Have I shocked you?"

"No, go on." LaShaun's head cleared and everything around appeared in focus as though she was in a high definition.

"I hear you left your mark with men and partying back in the day." Patsy said, her arched eyebrows going up.

"So these friends of Tommy's were rude, crude and lewd. Y'all had some good times until you started feeling guilty." LaShaun directed Patsy back to her story.

"When I tried to pull away Tommy grew angry. Then I started blacking out and not remembering. I was too embarrassed to tell Miz Joyelle the whole truth. But I didn't lie completely. When she told me that maybe I was under some kind of evil influence it all made sense." Patsy bit her lower lip. "I could feel something wasn't right about the whole thing."

Yeah, you jumped on the chance to use Joyelle like a bird on a juicy bug. LaShaun pursed her lips and frowned. "I can imagine that upset you."

"I was horrified. I've never messed with voodoo or witchcraft stuff. When I was in high school some of my friends got into Goth. Who wants to dress in black all the time?" Patsy tossed her glossy reddish blonde hair back over one shoulder.

"Good point," LaShaun said dryly.

"Anyway, I told all of this to that hot chief investigator everybody says is your boyfriend." Patsy shot a questioning gaze at LaShaun.

"Chief Detective Broussard," LaShaun replied matter-of-factly, not rising to the bait.

"Yes, he was more polite than his boss." Patsy grimaced as though she tasted something sour. "*Acting* Sheriff Arceneaux treated me like I was dirt under her saintly feet."

LaShaun figured that meant M.J. didn't pretend to be taken in by her stories. No doubt Chase didn't fall for her pert Cajun girl charm either, but didn't show it. "Sheriff Arceneaux has to be impartial, that sometimes comes across as being accusatory."

"She all but called me a bald-face liar. I'd call that accusatory," Patsy snapped. A spark of her temper flared up quickly then died down just as fast. "Anyway, maybe you're right. Accusing people is part of her job I guess."

"Hmm. By the way you didn't say what kind of cult," LaShaun replied.

"They didn't stand around chanting or cut the heads off of chickens or anything. But they were real secretive. They'd talk about dark stuff, like murders and groups that were into rituals. A couple of the girls said they didn't trust me with the 'mysteries'. That's what they called it. Like there was some level to their group that not everybody was allowed to join. One night Tommy and I got high... I'm not proud of it, but it's not like marijuana is a hard drug or anything."

"So you and Tommy were high," LaShaun prompted.

"I got him to talk about his pals that acted so guarded around me and some of the others. He said he'd show me some really hot times if I proved to him I was woman enough." Patsy squirmed in her chair as though imagining the carnal delights in store.

"And did he?"

"We went away together. He forced me," Patsy added almost as though it were an afterthought to keep her story consistent.

"When you disappeared you mean," LaShaun said and sat forward.

"I did enjoy sneaking off at first. Vince kept at me all the time about the house and cooking. The kids were screaming and needed constant attention. Tommy played on me being a little unhappy. When I tried to go home, he pretty much held me hostage. We was holdup at this old motel on Evangeline Thruway in Lafayette. Some of his creepy friends came by one night, but they didn't come in our room though. Tommy stood outside talking to them. Then he came in and said he had some people to see and for me to stay put."

"Why didn't you escape then?" LaShaun asked the obvious.

"I know, I know." Patsy shook her head. "But he pulled out the phone so I couldn't call nobody, and I didn't have a car or nothing. Besides, I was real high and not thinking straight. He made sure we always had some sweet weed. That was some strong stuff," Patsy sighed.

LaShaun got the distinct impression Patsy missed those fun times. Instead she pretended to be sympathetic. "Sounds awful, feeling trapped and part of it was your fault."

"You understand me in a way no one else ever has." Patsy smiled at LaShaun.

"Thanks," LaShaun replied and smiled back. "So Tommy and you went with his friends to find out about the 'real hot times'."

"No, Tommy didn't come back. That's the last time I saw him alive. I swear it." Patsy's bottom lip quivered. She even managed to squeeze a single tear out that slid down her rosy cheek.

"Here you go, calm down." LaShaun handed her a fresh napkin even though she was sure that one tear would dry up soon. "You told this to Chief Arceneaux and Detective Broussard, I take it."

Patsy shook her head. "No. I was afraid they'd arrest me for drugs. Anyway, that acting sheriff woman already treated me like trailer park trash. I was ashamed to tell it all. But I told them the important part; that those weird friends of his might have gotten him killed."

"Okay, so why are you telling me?" LaShaun gazed back at her waiting for the other shoe to drop.

"Please tell that hottie Chief Deputy Broussard that none of this was my fault. He'll believe you. And you know how to deal with that supernatural stuff." Patsy let out a long, noisy hiss of air. She retrieved her purse from the floor and stood. "I feel better already."

"You've given me a lot to think about," LaShaun stood as well and continued to study her.

"I'll bet," Patsy replied with a bright smile. She glanced at the wall clock. "I better get moving or my sister will start to wonder. I don't want her involved in any of this. She still thinks of me as her kid sister needing protection."

LaShaun wondered just how gullible that sister could possibly be. The entire town knew Patsy's misdeeds. Even they had no idea just what this little hometown girl had been up to though. Reverend Fletcher could preach a year's worth of sermons based on Patsy.

"It means a lot that you trust me enough to share all these details," said LaShaun, reverting to her old self, the one who could put on an award winning acting performance. She placed a hand on Patsy's shoulder. "My personal history isn't squeaky clean either. But people deserve a second chance. Call me if you ever need to talk again. Will you do that?"

"I most certainly will, LaShaun. I feel such a connection to you." Patsy blinked and sniffed. She brushed her eyes.

"I'm glad. Take care." LaShaun wore her best benevolent smile as she rubbed Patsy's shoulder.

"Thanks for being so kind." Patsy turned to go then paused and faced LaShaun again. "One more thing."

"Yes?" Ahh, LaShaun thought, here it comes.

"Tommy and his friends stopped going to that old house to party. They found this old place farther down the bayou. I think very strange things go on in those woods. That's in case you want to look into it one night." Patsy's eyes sparkled as she gazed back at LaShaun.

"I just might visit those woods one night." LaShaun smiled at her.

LYNN EMERY

Chapter 13

Two days later and a week before Halloween, Chase's dark eyebrows pulled together as he drove his Ford truck. LaShaun sat in the passenger's seat humming along with a song playing from the radio. The scenery along I-10 outside Lafayette flowed by. Sunlight warmed up the extended cab and banished the early morning chill. The Friday seven o'clock morning commuter traffic caused a steady stream of vehicles on both sides of the divided interstate highway. Mixed in with the smaller cars, eighteen wheelers moved in and out of lanes. But LaShaun knew watching the road wasn't the reason for Chase's intense contemplation. He was thinking ahead to their interview with Emanuel "Manny" Young, the Blood River Ripper. The bright morning and blue sky above contrasted with their mission, to visit a secure forensic facility filled with those judged to be criminally insane.

LaShaun looked at the green and brown vegetation flashing by as they drove. Occasional glimpses of swamps could be seen. They approached the elevated portion of I-10 over Whiskey Bay. As they got over the water she stretched forward to see more of what lay below. A string of four flat barges pushed by a white tugboat chugged through the muddy water way.

"This is another beautiful day. Kinda nice having fall weather even if it doesn't last all that long." LaShaun got one last look before their seventy mile an hour speed took them over the top of the twin span and down onto the ground level stretch of pavement.

"Humph," was Chase's only reply. "Did Mr. Young leave last night like he said?"

"Yes. He's staying with friends in St. Francisville, which is only a fifteen minute drive from Feliciana Forensic. He likes to stay the weekend and visit with Manny twice." LaShaun stretched her legs. "He's very devoted to his grandson. You have to admire him for that. A lot of families back away under the circumstances."

"The rest of the Young and Hebert families did just that. Mr. Orin and his wife are about the only ones who stuck by Manny. At first most of them were just as vocal that Manny was innocent. When the facts came out even they couldn't stomach him. Three weeks into the trial his granddaddy was in that courtroom all by his lonesome. His wife's health started going down about that time, too." Chase shook his head. "Tragic situation all around."

"I guess it was tense with the victim's families there, too. Had to have been hard on Mr. Young facing them." LaShaun looked at Chase.

"That's the thing, just two people showed up. A brother of the male victim came to the trial, and the aunt of one female victim."

Chase broke off to pay attention to a fast moving low slung sports car riding his bumper. He eased into another lane. The blue BMW 650 I zipped past them and blended back into their lane ahead of them.

"Idiot! Another reason I'm happy to be in podunk back roads bayou country." Chase blew out air.

"Relax and enjoy the view. We're driving through lovely country on a lovely day." LaShaun placed a hand on his firm thigh.

"Sure. Just an entertaining road trip to see a serial killer. To make it even more special we get to hang out with his equally crazy and dangerous roomies. Good times." Chase glanced at her sideways. "I don't know why you're in such a cheerful mood."

"I can't help loving extra time with you, even under the circumstances." LaShaun winked at him.

Chase covered her hand with his and rubbed the stone of her engagement ring with his thumb. "You're a sweet talker. In a minute you're going to convince me to have a good time."

"We've got sunshine and good music. We can stop at one of those great restaurants for lunch on the way back. Make it a day."

"Lunch, yes. But I've got to get back. We're meeting with the district attorney, state police and Iberia Parish Sheriff this afternoon." Chase shrugged when LaShaun pursed her lips in disappointment. "They're all eager to hear what I find out."

"And no wonder. He was only connected to twelve murders. Eight more are unsolved." LaShaun's bright mood dimmed.

He let go of her hand to hold the wheel again. "Yeah, that was some killing season Manny had."

"You don't know he did them all though. No conclusive evidence even though they fit the pattern. I've been reading up on the subject. Some experts believe there are at least two more killers in our area alone," LaShaun said.

"Have you been listening to that jerk Schaffer? Please." Chase gave a grunt of irritation.

"Give the devil his due. Schaffer interviewed some very credible experts on criminal behavior and paranormal phenomena. I watched his show Tuesday night."

"You've gone over to the dark side," Chase quipped.

She laughed. "Schaffer isn't 'the enemy' really. He's wants to grab the ratings and keep his show from being cancelled."

"We should be so lucky."

"There's another show that seems to be more popular, you know the one. They do investigations, and spend the night in so-called haunted houses or buildings. Anyway, Schaffer said something that made sense. Manny may have had a partner in crime. It's unusual, but not unheard of for two sadistic killers to team up."

"If Manny did have a partner he's good at leaving no traces behind. Must be a ghost," Chase retorted, then sucked in a breath. "I can't believe I just said that to you of all people."

"Better me than Schaffer," LaShaun said dryly.

"Amen. I can just hear the next commercial. 'A lead investigator with the Vermillion Parish Sheriff Department believes a ghost is stalking its next victim!' M.J. wouldn't fire me, she'd strangle me." Chase shook his head. When LaShaun laughed again he grimaced at her. "I'm not even joking."

LaShaun tried to answer, but couldn't stop laughing. Finally she brought herself under control. She breathed deeply a few times to recover. "Sorry, nervous energy."

"Glad I could help." Chase took one had off the steering wheel long enough to tickle her cheek.

"Orin Young would be all over that slip of the tongue." LaShaun grew solemn again at the thought of the grim faced older man.

"Yeah, his 'the devil made him do it' defense." Chase drove on wearing a slight frown. "Honey, you wouldn't happen to have any kind of vision about this whole deal. I mean it is kind of crazy that Willie Dupuis knew Manny."

She nodded slowly. "Patsy described some strange happenings going on that sound a lot like what Willie told us about."

"What?" Chase looked from the road too long and the truck drifted out of their lane. A blue Chevrolet honked at him, and Chase pulled the steering wheel with a jerk to straighten the truck again.

"You might want to pay attention," LaShaun said calmly.

"You might want to avoid shocking the hell out of me with bombshells about my investigation," Chase replied in a tart tone.

"I'm not sure how much of what she said was even true, Chase. Besides that there may be no connection at all. She and Tommy apparently met up with friends for drinking, drugging and sex. The parties were in some old house south of Black Bayou."

"Oh well that narrows it down," Chase said with a snort.

"Yeah, I know. Anyway, seems the whole point was for them to get wasted and laid. Pardon my crude and blunt description." LaShaun gazed at the road ahead as she thought about Patsy's tale.

"Wasted and laid parties fit Patsy's taste, and Tommy's. I'm not surprised those two found each other." Chase guided his truck up the incline to the large Mississippi River Bridge into Baton Rouge. "Nah, it's too wild to think that Patsy and Willie were running in the same circles."

"But possible." LaShaun looked at him.

"Sleepy Vermillion Parish has its share of folks who enjoy gettin' their freak on. Trust me. The French Quarter in New Orleans ain't got nothin' on us." Chase shook his head.

LaShaun raised an eyebrow at him. "You forget you're talking to the infamous wild Rousselle girl? I caused some spicy gossip about my behavior back in the day."

"I know," Chase glanced at her sideways. "I'm hoping at least some of those stories are true."

He laughed when she slapped his arm, and even harder when she glared at him. Before long they were laughing together and singing along with the Cajun songs blaring from his CD player. For a while longer LaShaun could almost believe they were on a pleasure trip. They passed through Baton Rouge quickly despite the morning traffic. Soon they were on historic Highway 61 heading out of East Baton Rouge Parish. Industrial plants spread out along the corridor that led into a portion of Louisiana's Plantation Country. They passed the Port Hudson Civil War Battle site, and decided they would return to visit the museum. Twenty minutes later they turned onto Highway 68 leading to East Feliciana Parish. The two lane paved roadway dipped down and back up over small hills. Tall trees and thick brush lined both sides and arched overhead to create a leafy tunnel. They had a brief glimpse of Asphodel Plantation around a curve. Minutes later yellow signs warned them not to pick up hitchhikers along the road. The white wooden fence and pretty pastures with grazing cattle gave way to chain fencing with barbed wire looped along the top. Dixon Correctional Institute looked deceptively peaceful. Less than a mile from the highway prisoners were outside. Some played basketball. Others lifted weights. Most stood or sat around in groups. LaShaun felt the simmering anger, frustration and confusion coming from them. She turned away in an attempt to shield herself from the onslaught of strong emotions. She had to get ready. Soon she would be in an even more tumultuous place.

"Anything wrong?" Chase said.

"I'll be okay in a minute."

LaShaun closed her eyes and mentally formed a peaceful image; her grandmother's garden in spring when she was seven years old. Her mother, Francine, was home for once and seemed happy. Francine played jump rope while Monmon Odette cut roses and gardenias. Francine's musical laughter made the sunshine warmer and brighter.

LaShaun focused on those memories, and the sick feeling gradually subsided. She recited a prayer several times as she took in and let out slow breaths. Strength flowed into her for what she knew would be the challenge to come. A gentle touch on her arm made her open her eyes. They were in a line of vehicles waiting to enter the grounds. A huge sign with white letters reading East Louisiana State Hospital told her they'd arrived at their destination.

Chase's dark eyebrows pulled together as he gazed at her with concern in his dark eyes.

"Maybe we shouldn't go through with this. I'm getting the jitters, and I'm no psychic."

"I'm okay. Don't worry." LaShaun sat up straight, took his hand and squeezed it.

"Would you tell me if you weren't?" Chase said.

"Yes," she said quietly.

Satisfied, he looked ahead again. "The white truck up there, that's Orin Young."

LaShaun followed his gaze. "He's staring into his rearview mirror, looking for us I think. Wave at him."

Chase waved several times to get his attention. The older man finally stuck an arm out of his window and waved back. "He's hoping you'll somehow make everyone believe that Manny isn't responsible. At the very least he wants to save him from death row."

"Like anyone would listen to me. I worry that we're raising his expectations," LaShaun said.

"Me and M.J. kept telling him the goal is to get information to clear up other murders, not to pull off some rescue for Manny," Chase replied.

"People hear what they want to hear, Chase. Every fake psychic and con artist knows that."

LaShaun tapped a foot as the line slowly moved forward. Orin Young's truck was three vehicles ahead of them. He slowly approached the guard station. One uniformed security guard stood checking in cars entering. Another guard stood on the exit side and examined vehicles leaving. Both glanced over the interiors of cars, and checked trucks or truck beds. LaShaun leaned forward. She was now eager to get in and meet the notorious Blood River Ripper. Chase gave her thigh a pat.

"I know, but security is too important to rush. I'm getting wound up about what we might find out, too. The cop in me likes to get all the answers." Chase observed the guards. "They're doing a good job."

"Remember, Manny won't let you be in the room with us," LaShaun replied.

Chase scowled to show how he felt about that. "Yeah."

Minutes later it was their turn. Chase flashed his ID and badge, and then assured the guard he'd locked up his handgun. The guard checked the metal locked tool box right behind the extended cab.

"We're going to visit a prisoner at the Forensic Unit, "Chase told her.

"Right. Got you on this list. Sorry for the wait. Y'all have a nice day." The woman smiled at him.

"Thanks." Chase drove on keeping to the fifteen mile an hour speed limit on the grounds. "Like coming here could ever start off a nice day."

"The grounds are beautiful. The hospital opened in 1848, and the first patients were brought on flatboats down the Mississippi River from New Orleans. The main building up ahead is on the National Historic Register. It looks like an old antebellum mansion, lovely with marble floors and even a ballroom on the third floor. But in the basement patients were kept in leg and arm chains attached to the wall. I stayed up late reading the history since I couldn't sleep."

"I'd hate to be working the night shift in there on Halloween."

They turned away from the main building. The truck tires crunched on the narrow gravel road as they went to a line of buildings south of the main building. Razor wire announced that this portion of the hospital was different. The Forensic Unit was separated from the cottages where regular patients were housed. Those patients walked around the campus with relative freedom. Some worked on the grounds.

Another guard directed them to the area for official vehicles since Chase was law enforcement. He parked and cut the engine. "We ready for this?"

LaShaun opened the passenger door. "I'm prepared."

Chase walked around the front of the truck and helped her down, though she didn't need him to. LaShaun gathered more strength from the firm grasp of his large hand. She smiled at him reassuringly. He led the way wearing a grim set to his jaw. They went through the security checks with no problems.

The Forensic Unit housed adults who had been admitted via court order for various reasons, mostly related to criminal cases. After signing in, Chase and LaShaun waited in a neat, but dreary waiting area. Chase walked around restlessly and stared at the pictures as he tapped the side of one thigh with a fist. LaShaun sat down in one of the vinyl covered chairs. Someone had attempted to lighten the atmosphere with plants. Yet the unit itself seemed to fight back, as if defying attempts to disguise the bleak reality. Dozens of violent men and women had to be contained to keep the public safe. LaShaun tilted her head to one side in a listening pose. When Chase approached again with a question in his dark gaze, LaShaun nodded.

"He knows we're here," she said quietly.

Before Chase could respond a short, plump woman wearing a white jacket walked out. She walked up to them briskly with a smile and stuck out a hand, first to Chase and after he let go she shook hands with LaShaun.

"Good morning. I'm Grace Norris, Mr. Young's treating psychiatrist. Glad to meet you. Can we get you anything? I'm sure you had to get an early start from Vermillion Parish. We have excellent biscuits from the dining room."

"No thanks. We ate on the way," Chase said. "This is Miss Rousselle."

"Manny has talked about you quite a bit since his grandfather told him you were coming." Dr. Norris studied LaShaun carefully.

"That's interesting. I'd heard he wasn't much of a talker." Chase's grim expression deepened into a frown.

"He's not usually." Dr. Norris started to go on, but looked around. Employees stared at them in frank interest. "Let's go to my office. Manny is visiting with his grandfather. We'll take you in once Mr. Young leaves."

She led them down a long hallway with offices on both sides. After turning another corner they went to a larger office. Mesh wire covered the windows. The pattern created checkerboard squares of sunshine on the window sill. Dr. Norris had managed to brighten the backdrop with plants and colorful ceramic figurines. She closed the door.

"Sure about that offer of refreshments? Contrary to stereotypes, my assistant makes delicious coffee." She waited for them to sit down before settling in the chair behind her desk.

"A cup of coffee sounds good." Chase glanced at LaShaun.

"My throat is a little dry. Something cool would be nice," LaShaun said.

"What kind of beverage would you like? We have fruit juices, iced tea or soft drinks." Dr. Norris picked up the handset of her white desk phone.

"Apple juice is fine," LaShaun replied with a smile of gratitude.

Dr. Norris nodded and spoke warmly to a woman named Ellie. She put the handset back on the cradle. "She'll be here in a minute. So Manny seems to be looking forward to meeting you. He doesn't get visitors, except for Mr. Orin of course."

"Of course," LaShaun echoed.

"Manny seems to think you'll understand what he's been through, and help in some way." Dr. Norris assumed the listening pose of a trained therapist.

"His grandfather may have over sold what I can do." LaShaun could tell Dr. Norris had a skill for inviting trust, and that she would honor it. "Manny's grandfather says your treatment has made a big difference."

Dr. Norris gazed back at her intently. "He's not violent, so you shouldn't worry. A security officer will be in the room with you."

"That's great," Chase said before LaShaun could reply. The tight expression around his eyes eased, and he relaxed against the back of the chair. "I wasn't too crazy about letting her be in there alone with a guard outside. A lot can happen in a few seconds."

"We're a strange hybrid, a combination of treatment and correctional facility. Security is always a consideration." Dr. Norris leaned forward with both elbows propped on her desk. "Manny is..."

A knock interrupted her. The assistant, a woman with bright auburn hair piled high, came in with a small tray. "Here you go, Doctor."

"Thanks, Ellie." Dr. Norris waited for assistant to leave. "Manny is eager to have a different visitor. The officer has been instructed to look for any signals that he's getting agitated. I have nursing staff on stand-by in case more help is needed."

"More help than correctional officers?" Chase asked.

"PRN medications," Dr. Norris replied. "Ativan and Haldol injections have been effective before."

"You said he wasn't violent," LaShaun said.

"Dr. Norris means recently. We know he has the potential for serious violence. That's how he got here." Chase looked at the psychiatrist.

"He's been calm and compliant for months," Dr. Norris said. "He can be a very pleasant and interesting guy to talk to."

"Yeah, when he's not hacking people to pieces," Chase mumbled.

"I'm sure your treatment techniques are very effective," LaShaun rushed to put in as Dr. Norris squinted at Chase. "We'll try not to upset him or cause any problems."

"Judge Trahan insisted this visit should take place, so... we'll see." Dr. Norris studied them both as seconds of silence on both sides ticked by. Her friendly manner slipped enough to allow LaShaun to see the iron will beneath.

"You didn't agree with us coming then." LaShaun raised an eyebrow.

"No, I didn't at first. Our main goals are treatment, security and following court orders. Not always in that order depending on the situation, but court orders trump treatment recommendations." Dr. Norris's thin lips pulled down at the corners for a few seconds. Another knock made her sit up straight. "Come in."

A correctional officer entered. "Hey, Doc. I just took Manny's granddaddy to the lobby. All clear for the next visitors. "

The tall man had arms that bulged against the short sleeves of his uniform shirt. His smooth skin had the look of African ebony wood. He sized up Chase, seemed satisfied and nodded to a fellow enforcer of laws. When he looked at LaShaun his eyes widened just for a second before his professional mask clicked back in place.

"Only Miss Rousselle, Roosevelt. We'll be with you in a minute," Dr. Norris said.

"Okay." The big man withdrew, closing the door with a soft thump.

"Miss Rousselle, Mr. Young is convinced you and Manny will establish some kind of connection." Dr. Norris's expression clearly showed she found such a thing implausible, but worrisome.

Chase spoke first. "Manny left some pretty big unanswered questions about the murders he committed. He's willing to talk to Miss Rousselle. The reasons don't really matter at this point. Maybe if Manny gets some stuff off his conscience he'll get better, well at least be less dangerous for the other inmates."

"And the criminal justice system can lead him to that lethal injection gurney even quicker," Dr. Norris raised a palm and cut off his response. "I'm not Manny's defense attorney. If Manny gets agitated, or the officer says it's time to end the interview please follow his instructions."

"Agreed," Chase said with a sharp nod.

"Excellent. I'm actually quite interested in the way local cultural beliefs in the supernatural interrelate with mental health issues. I wrote an article for a journal. I'm originally from upstate New York. I've found the subject of hoodoo or voodoo fascinating in the twelve years since I moved to Louisiana."

LaShaun smiled at her. "You explored the boundary between madness and belief in the supernatural."

"Very much so. A patient comes to the hospital convinced that snakes are in her stomach. Is she psychotic, or does she believe that an adversary has put a bad mojo on her? Before I came here the answer would have been obvious I thought. My diagnosis would have been swift and certain, paranoid delusions. Not now." Dr. Norris looked at LaShaun. "Mr. Young is convinced that Manny was possessed. Oh he hasn't said so in those words, but..."

"We're just here to talk," Chase said firmly.

"I see." Dr. Norris's gaze didn't shift from LaShaun.

"I didn't come to play mind games so that he'll confess to more crimes." LaShaun looked back at the psychiatrist.

"Manny isn't susceptible to mind games anyway." Dr. Norris stood to signal she'd finished all she had to say.

"I know. Manny is good at reading people, and not as gullible or simple-minded as folks think, including his grandfather." LaShaun stood also.

"We're not trying to trap Manny. We have plenty of evidence for the murders he's already convicted of committing." Chase continued to talk as Dr. Norris nodded. They left the office to join the powerful officer waiting in the hallway.

Roosevelt pointed down another long hallway. "We set up a room for the visit. My captain thought it would be better security wise. Just follow me."

Chase put a protective hand under LaShaun's elbow as they walked. He glanced over his shoulder and LaShaun followed his gaze. Dr. Norris still stood outside her office watching them. When LaShaun waved at her she waved back. Then they rounded a corner. Roosevelt led them to a large room with a table and two chairs. The window looked out onto an enclosed area. Men were outside smoking and milling around. Several laughed and talked to themselves.

"Be just a minute. Uh, Manny mentioned he was only going to visit with the lady." Roosevelt raised an eyebrow at Chase.

"Right." Chase scanned the room and turned to LaShaun. "Be careful."

"Manny wants something from us as well. Harming me won't suit his purpose." LaShaun squeezed Chase's arm.

Roosevelt's black eyebrows went up as he noticed the gesture. "The lady gonna be just fine."

"Thanks," Chase replied and left.

"Another officer is gonna bring Manny from the locked unit. We decided he'll stay in the room with you. I'll be right outside. Don't give him anything, no matter how small. No touching either. He's been told all this, too. Okay?"

"I understand," LaShaun said.

"You're not nervous at all, I can tell. That's good. Be back in a minute." Roosevelt left.

LaShaun took in the room. The walls were a pale green. Tan vinyl tiles had been mopped and polished. A slight scent of pine oil lingered from the last time the room was cleaned. No hint of emotion seemed to linger. LaShaun wondered at the typical use of the room. She guessed that it had been cleared out for this purpose. Then she felt a shift in the air pressure around her. Anticipation, pleasure at the break in routine and curiosity reached out to her. Animated voices sounded muted but grew clearer as the seconds passed. The rubber soles of shoes swished and squeaked on the vinyl floor. Suddenly the sound stopped outside the door.

"Okay, we cool?" came Roosevelt's voice, muffled by the door and walls.

"No worries, sir," came a reply.

When the door opened Roosevelt came in first. He swung it wide.. Emanuel "Manny" Young stopped for a few seconds before he took a couple of steps into the room. He looked around as though he expected to see more people. His greenish brown eyes lit up as his gaze settled on LaShaun's face.

LaShaun felt as if tiny electrified needles covered her arms and pricked the back of her neck. An unassuming man wearing a shy smile and with the manners of a polite country boy looked back. Yet a cunning assessment came through in the way he eyed her. Seeing her examine him as well, a veil dropped and once again Manny looked ordinary. She instantly knew how he had gotten close to his victims.

"Good mornin', ma'am. I appreciate you comin' so far to see me."

Chapter 14

LaShaun couldn't answer him right away. The correctional officer directed Manny to sit in the chair on other end of the table with his back to the window. LaShaun sat down in the chair closer to the door. The room was wide enough to be spacious, but LaShaun suddenly had the sensation of feeling crowded. Yet four and half feet of table was between them. There was no other furniture in the room. The security guard stood about six feet away. He leaned against a wall looking relaxed, but he also had the appearance of a strong man with speed of light reflexes. He observed every move Manny made without seeming to stare, or intrude.

Manny studied LaShaun for a few seconds. His dark brown hair had been cut short, and combed back in soft waves. He couldn't have been taller than five feet ten inches. With no bulging biceps, Manny did not look threatening at all. A long snake tattoo coiled down his left arm. The snake's head on the inside of his left wrist had large fangs. LaShaun blink a few times. The thing seemed poised to sink those fangs into Manny's bluish veins visible beneath his pale white skin. On his right arm a tattoo of barbed wire wrapped around his upper arm. More tattoos were on his neck.

"You don't look like I imagined. I don't look like you thought I would either, huh?" Manny shrugged and dipped his head as though apologizing. "But what is a serial killer supposed to look like?" he said softly and gazed out of the window for a second. Then he looked back at her.

"What did your granddaddy tell you about me?" LaShaun asked. The unpleasant, almost painful tingling had stopped. She pushed against the invisible shield he had up.

"Don't do that," he whispered with a quick sideways glance at the guard. When the guard didn't seem to notice anything Manny's gaze slid back to LaShaun. "I ain't always in control. "

"Mr. Orin feels like maybe you weren't responsible for killing your victims," LaShaun replied. His bark of laughter startled her.

"PawPaw done started believing that story. Lord, he needs to let it be. That scheme didn't come close to gettin' me outta this fix I'm in." Manny waved a hand as though brushing aside the explanation. "I'm done. Let's talk about somethin' more interestin'. Tell me about you."

"You know pretty much all there is to know. I live in Beau Chene, and my family is from there. My grandmother's house is off Rougon Road."

"Yeah, I remember where that is. You told Dr. Norris that you're a voodoo woman?" Manny leaned forward a little. "Bet she kept you down there talking a long time. She's got a thing about that sort of stuff."

"Did you tell Dr. Norris that your granddaddy thinks you're possessed?" LaShaun replied evenly.

"When the murders went down you mean." Manny shrugged again, and wore a boyish grin. His eyes sparkled making the green flecks in them come alive. "Course I don't remember the details. Maybe he's right."

"Did you ever dabble in voodoo or any kind of satanic rituals?" LaShaun felt him toying with her, so she went along.

"I might have, mostly to get next to girls that went in for stuff like that. You know the type, always looking for somethin' different. Drugs, heavy metal music and freaky sex, anything goes with that crowd. I got to convince these people I ain't crazy so I can get sent to Angola. At least I could party there." Manny's long thin mouth pulled up to one side.

LaShaun felt a chill. He actually looked handsome on the surface with that grin tugging his mouth up. She got an image of him in a black T-shirt with the embossed emblem of a popular band on the front, and a pair of black jeans. Yes, women would have found him attractive. Then the image winked off. LaShaun blinked back to the room, stunned at getting such a strong picture. Manny continued to wear a slight smirk like a wicked imp. Then he looked harmless again.

"What happened to you?" LaShaun said so softly that both Manny and the guard leaned as if trying to hear clearly.

Manny sighed. "I fell into a bad, bad crowd. I dabbled in some stuff I shouldn't have, and now look where it's got me."

"Stop lying, Manny," LaShaun snapped. She placed both palms down on the table top. "If you don't want to suffer some of the worse agony imaginable for eternity, you better get straight. I'm not talking about rotting in prison or a needle in the arm. Those are going to seem like a vacation compared to what comes *after* you die."

His skin turned paler as he blinked rapidly. Manny scratched his arms nervously. "I don't like talkin' about what happens in the next life."

"You better start thinking. Did whoever got you into this explain that nasty downside? Did you know ripping women into pieces was part of the deal? Well, answer me." LaShaun put enough force in her tone to rip at his psychic shield like a razor sharp talon. Manny definitely had not innocently stumbled into experimenting with the supernatural. "Yes, you were influenced, but you had a chance to walk away."

"It was too hard. You don't get it," Manny said. Gone was the forceful manipulator. He voice took on a whiny sound. "I can't... it's more complicated than you think." He brushed a hand through his hair.

"Sure, you had a rough childhood. Your mama loved drugs more than you, and then she disappeared, and your daddy cared more about partying than being a father." LaShaun repeated his family history without a hint of sympathy in her tone. "A whole lot of people go through worse, and they don't charm perfect strangers into trusting them and then slaughter them to get a thrill."

Manny slapped a large hand down on the table. The sound bounced off the walls, and made the guard spring forward. LaShaun held up her hand as a gesture he should wait. Manny hadn't moved toward her. The man stood at alert, but didn't take action.

"What the hell do you know about what I went through?"

Manny breathed in and out a few times, the sound loud in the silence. The green in his hazel eyes seemed to dance like flames. His gaze darted around the room as though he saw something move. A thick wavy lock of hair fell across his forehead and he turned his intense gaze on LaShaun.

"That's why we're here, isn't it? For you to tell me enough so that I can help your grandparents have peace. Tell the truth so Mr. Orin can stop having false hopes, and your poor grandmother can rest easy." LaShaun watched as his face twisted, transforming like a melting mask of rubber from one expression to another. He'd smile, then frown and bare his teeth. Manny hissed a few times and squirmed in his seat. Then he raked his hair with long fingers until several spikes of dark locks stuck out. LaShaun wouldn't have been surprised if his head spun around like something in an old horror movie. What she saw in him wasn't just an insane man going into a fit. The shimmer of something malevolent floated around him like an oily swamp mist.

"Don't talk about MawMaw Flora. She's been through enough." Manny swayed from side to side slightly, and then rocked back and forth in the chair. "Lord, that woman has suffered."

The guard spoke into a compact walkie-talkie on his shoulder then strode forward as the door swung open. "Okay, ma'am. I think that's enough for now."

"I'm sorry, Manny. I didn't mean to upset you," LaShaun said quickly. "I know you wanted to talk to me. Maybe if you get some water and calm down."

Roosevelt stood next to the other guard. "No, ma'am. I don't think..."

"Wait, wait. I'm gonna be okay. It's just that I've been real worried about my grandmama. Y'all can understand. Please, I'm goin' to calm down," Manny said and looked up at Roosevelt. "Please, she is tryin' to help me."

LaShaun saw Dr. Norris hovering just outside the door. Roosevelt glanced at the doctor. Some signal passed between them because he nodded to his colleague. The other guard took a position against the wall again, but remained vigilant. The door swung inward, but Roosevelt left a few inches of space so that it didn't completely close.

"My grandmama ain't been too well, and she's had to go through hell. Manny clasped his hands together tightly on top of the table. "Hearin' about the killin' and all was too much."

"Of course, the trial and stress took a toll on her health," LaShaun said.

His head hung lower. "I should have been stronger so I could be there to protect her. Not give her more grief."

"Your aunts are there to help Mr. Orin take care of her." LaShaun tried to reassure him. In spite of all he'd done, she felt a sliver of compassion for the man.

"Verlena got her family to think about, started over. I don't know where Diane is," Manny's voice broke and he blinked hard.

"Sorry to hear it," LaShaun said and leaned her elbows on the table. After a long moment of silence, she decided to stay away from discussion of his family. He seemed genuinely anguished, and might become too agitated to talk. "You remember an old friend, Willie Dupuis? He remembers you."

"Willie... Willie, hmm. Now let me see." Manny expression changed back to the wily truth twister again. "So you gettin' close to the real deal. I been readin' in here. They got a good library. Gettin' more educated than I ever did on the outside. I read this old saying, 'Be careful goin' after what you want cause you just might get it'."

"He says you got him into occult activity. Now he's caught up in a murder." LaShaun pulled back a few inches when Manny chuckled, his voice sounding hollow and deep.

"Shame on him. Can't put that one on *me*. I'm obviously not gettin' out nights to travel." Manny nodded at the solid stone walls around them.

"Tell us about the other murders, and if Willie was involved. Six bodies of women found along Lake Chenier and the wildlife area. That's a long way off. And two in Texas. Ripped up real bad." LaShaun had the sensation of feeling crowded again, as though there were more people in the room with them. She gazed at Manny and something happened.

A dark bubble closed around them as she stared into his eyes. Green fire caused his eyes to reflect a strange glow. LaShaun could not move. She felt pain down the middle of her back as though a large claw raked her flesh. She tried to move and speak, but a kind of pressure held her in place, and kept her silent. Manny smiled at her.

"I smelled you comin' miles away." He sucked in a deep breath and let it out, then licked his thin lips making them wet. "I could have you right here and they couldn't do a damn thing about it. I might have you yet, but not today. I got a bitch in here gives it up whenever I want it, and knows better than to say no. I bet you could handle my ten inches, couldn't you? Yeah, you could handle it real good."

"What have you done?" LaShaun heard her voice, but didn't feel her mouth move.

"I'm goin' to help you because I intend for you to come back. Highway 333 to Little White Lake is where they found the bodies, not Lake Chenier. Tsk, tsk, tsk. That was supposed to trap me, huh? Yeah, I know about Texas. I'm not the only one hungry for fresh meat and thirsty for blood. I'm not the first one either. You better watch your back, girl, cause they're getting wild and loose. They don't think anybody can stop them now. Find the house Willie told you about, and you should be able to track 'em down. If they don't come to you first. Use one of them GPS things. I'll bet your man has one."

"I can find it." LaShaun blocked out all thoughts of Chase to protect him.

"He must be givin' it to you good. I like loyalty." Manny wore a smile that made him look anything but friendly.

"Why are you giving me clues?" LaShaun ignored the taunt, satisfied that he didn't know about Chase. The less information he had about her personal life, the better.

"Because... I like you," Manny drawled. He made the simple sentence sound like a sexual threat. His gaze into her eyes intensified. "So you want to know."

LaShaun gasped as the air around them grew heavy and darker. Plunged into a night scene, LaShaun became lightheaded. She had the sensation of running. Leaves slapped her skin as she raced through woods. Instinct guided her around thick clumps of palmetto bushes and around tree trunks. A feeling of freedom coursed through her, and of power. The night belonged to her. Then she arrived at a clearing. Shadows moved, then came in closer. The others like her, sweating and exhilarated. Two of the group jumped on each other, not in attack. Their yowls softened as they mated. The rest of the group ignored them and trotted to another clearing. A woman lay on the ground looking wild. She smiled as they approached. Anticipation seeped from her pores as she moved toward a large member of the group standing tall, hair thick on his arms. The woman rose and slipped the pullover shirt over her head and shimmied out of her tight jeans. Gyrating in a bra and thong, she seemed eager for attention from her audience.

LaShaun struggled to scream a warning. This foolish woman, her brain fried by years of drug and alcohol abuse, expected a night of adventurous sex. Part of LaShaun felt the lust of the being whose eyes she looked through, and her stomach heaved. Yet she couldn't make a sound. The object of the woman's seduction grabbed her by the buttocks with both hand and licked her neck with a long tongue. Moaning and grinding against him, she dropped to her knees. He roughly forced her on all fours and mounted her from behind. His thrusts made the woman to cry out in pleasure. At first. Then she admonished him not to be so rough. But her lover didn't stop. Digging her fingers in the dirt, the woman tried to pull away. Her screams of anger gradually changed to pleas for help. Her lover raked long claw like fingernails over the flesh of her thighs, threw his head back and howled. Those watching answered until their voices mixed with the woman's screams. The mating turned into an attack. The man still clung to the woman as he sank his teeth into her back and ripped out a chunk of her. Blood dripped down his mouth as he continued to thrust. With a series of loud grunts he collapsed on top of the woman. Seconds later he appeared to sniff at the fleshy part of her arm. In shock, the woman whimpered and begged to be let go. Instead her attacker bit into her body again, and again. He flipped her over and ripped a hole in her neck. His pack moved in.

LaShaun shrieked at the horror movie playing out in front of her. With every ounce of psychic energy she had, LaShaun fought to block the vision. She'd never experienced being so fully pulled into the mind of another human being. Yet Manny did not feel human. The scent of a feral beast filled LaShaun's nostrils causing her to gag. A thick mist swirled around her in a burst of blood red and black streaks. As though a rope had fallen away, she became able to move her arms. She yelled and struck out at something dark that had come too close. That thing had finished one meal and now came for her.

"Calm down! LaShaun, calm down!"

"Get away, get away!" LaShaun pounded her fist against something solid.

"You're safe. The visit is over," a firm female voice said.

LaShaun opened her eyes, for the first time realizing that they were closed. She looked up into the worried faces of Chase, Dr. Norris and another man wearing green scrubs. She lay on a hospital bed. Chase held both her arms tightly as she panted for several seconds. "What's going on?"

"You passed out so we brought you to the unit medical clinic." Chase shook his head at someone.

She followed his gaze. Roosevelt stood on the other side of the bed. "I'm okay."

"Maybe you should stay in the bed for awhile," Chase said quietly.

"No, let me sit up." LaShaun had a strong need not to feel vulnerable.

Chase kept one strong arm around her. "You're still woozy."

Indeed, LaShaun felt weak. She managed to get upright only because Chase lifted her. "What happened?"

"Jacob said Manny was talking to you and then he got real quiet," Roosevelt said.

"Jacob?" LaShaun interrupted, and squinted against the light in the room. She remembered being in darkness.

"The officer who was in the room with you and Manny." Roosevelt glanced at Dr. Norris.

"Oh, right." LaShaun rubbed her eyes. "Go on, I'm okay."

"Jacob says y'all just sat there staring at each other. Then Manny started talking so low that the guard couldn't hear him clearly. You were nodding like you understood. All of a sudden Manny started yelping like crazy, and tried to jump across the table for you. About that time Jacob says you passed out and had some kind of a fit. By the time I ran into the room, Jacob had restrained Manny. Two other officers helped him while your friend here rushed in with Dr. Norris to help you."

"Did I say anything?" LaShaun looked at Roosevelt and then at Chase.

"Your lips moved, but the words didn't make sense. How do you feel now?" Chase sat next to her on the bed.

LaShaun sucked in air that tasted faintly antiseptic, and let it out. The images of the butchery she'd witnessed clung to her like spiders crawling on her skin. Her stomach still roiled, and her vision was still a little fuzzy. She rotated her shoulders feeling the stiffness in her neck muscles. "I'm fine."

"Yeah, right." Chase's arm tightened around her protectively.

"I guess the tension of coming here caught up with me." LaShaun managed a faint smile, but Chase's troubled expression remained.

Dr. Norris cleared her throat and turned to male nurse. "Thanks, Steve. You can go."

"Okay, but call if you need me again." Steve gazed at LaShaun and Chase. He seemed reluctant to leave. "I could get y'all some water; maybe get the lady something to settle her stomach."

"No, thank you," LaShaun replied quickly. The thought of trying to swallow anything made her queasy.

"I've never seen anything like this before, and I've seen some strange sights workin' here," Roosevelt said.

"You might need to check on the situation with Manny, Roosevelt. See if he's settled down. We don't want this to spill over into the unit." Dr. Norris looked at the big man and he got the signal.

"Sure, uh, I better get over there. Usually once he's in restraints Manny gets straight fast. He don't like being tied up." Roosevelt glanced at LaShaun sideways, shook his head and left.

Dr. Norris walked out with him speaking low, but came back a few moments later. She had both hands in the side pockets of her white coat. "Tell me what happened."

"I'm not sure. Like I said, maybe the stress of coming here and meeting a convicted multiple murderer got to me more than I thought it would." LaShaun massaged her necked with one hand.

"Manny can be quite graphic in his descriptions of his past behavior. With a new and attractive audience maybe he lapsed into an old habit." Dr. Norris gazed at LaShaun in waiting mode.

"Did he say anything about murders? Is that what freaked you out?" Chase added.

"I do remember he started talking about assaulting women, but things are fuzzy after that. I'm ready to leave." LaShaun sighed and leaned against Chase.

"You definitely need to get out of this place." Chase held on firmly as they both stood.

"Of course, get some rest. Call me if you need to talk." Dr. Norris held out a business card.

LaShaun looked at it for a moment before she took the card and stuck it in the pocket of her suede jacket. "Thanks, but I won't need that talk."

"You never know," Dr. Norris replied evenly. Her professionally arched eyebrows went high.

LaShaun nodded. Dr. Norris followed them out. Curious staff watched the trio as they left. Dr. Norris went with them to the door that led outside.

"Have a safe trip back to Vermillion Parish. An unusual place I hear, and for Louisiana that's saying a lot," Dr. Norris said. Once again she seemed to peer at them with the intent of seeing beyond the surface.

"Yeah, a beautiful part of the state." Chase smiled at her as he pretended to misunderstand her observation. He put a hand under LaShaun's elbow. "Definitely time to go."

"Thank you, goodbye," LaShaun said. When Chase held the door open LaShaun had a rush of relief to be outside. She inhaled and exhaled a few times. "Thank God."

"Damn, I knew he'd be out here waiting," Chase said softly.

Orin Young strode toward them. Despite his age, at seventy-five he had a spring in his step. His body seemed more agile than expected for a man his age. The steel gray eyes appeared alert and sharp as he studied LaShaun. He didn't wear glasses. LaShaun blinked at him as approached, trying to figure out some puzzle. When he got within a few feet he pointed to wooden benches beneath an oak tree, an oddly peaceful sight only a few yards from men like Manny. Chase and LaShaun followed him. LaShaun sat down while the two men remained standing.

"Well, you talked to my boy. You can see he's disturbed." Orin Young spoke as though they'd already been discussing Manny.

"Yes," LaShaun said quietly. She shivered inside her jacket in spite of the warm sunshine they stood in.

"Then you can tell them, you and Dr. Norris can explain. Something evil took hold of him long enough to make him kill. Bad spirits can take over a weak mind. That's Manny. He's always been a follower and eager to please. But with treatment he'll get stronger and not be a threat to anybody." Orin

Young spoke with force as his steel gray gaze bored into LaShaun.

"He may be crazy, but that doesn't mean he didn't know what he was doing when he killed those people," Chase said sharply.

"He was convicted of killing one woman," Orin shot back and held up a forefinger. "Just one. Those evil thugs killed the others."

"The only reason why we didn't purse the others cases is because he got the death penalty. Besides, the DA didn't want to put the other victims' families through hell. Did you see those crime scene photos?" Chase hammered home each word. "Did you really look at them, Mr. Young?"

"Chase, please," LaShaun said and stood between the two men. She put a hand on Chase's chest. His dark eyes flashed with outrage.

"I had to sit with the mother of one girl. She clung to hope that her daughter was alive, and then she just wanted to know she hadn't suffered. But we had to tell her the opposite. Your 'boy' tortured her little girl." Chase's voice rang out like gunshots.

"Her *little girl* was a transient dope head and prostitute. She let anyone use her body so she could get high. The girl had two sexually transmitted diseases. She was spreading filth every time she opened her legs to some stranger. So yes, I paid attention to the autopsy reports. All that damn DNA evidence proved was Manny was one among dozens of men who had her." Orin Young seemed taller as he spat back at Chase.

"So she deserved to die because she made mistakes? I'm telling you this; Manny ain't nearly as crazy as his granddaddy." Chase waved a hand at him and shook his head.

"Stop it, both of you," LaShaun shouted.

She glared a warning at Chase. Turning around he walked to his truck and leaned against it. Yet he continued to stare at Orin. The older man huffed a few times in anger, but said nothing as he glared back at Chase. One of the security officers watched them through a window of the Forensics Unit, but didn't come outside. LaShaun let a few more seconds tick by to allow Orin to calm down.

"Listen, Mr. Young. Manny is not going to be released," LaShaun said.

"If he gets treatment, he could be. A lot of people have been released and are followed by the staff. They call it forensic aftercare. There's this group home in Baton Rouge and--"

"He's a convicted murderer who is suspected of being a serial killer. His behavior is clearly too unpredictable. The best you can hope for is that he gets a life sentence instead of going on death row. Chase is right. District attorneys in three parishes, and at least one county in Texas, are willing to revive their cases if they think Manny has a chance of being put back on the street." LaShaun let out a long slow breath. "Besides, Manny killed and he enjoyed it."

Orin Young's eyes widened. He glanced from LaShaun to Chase. "I should have known. You're on their side in this thing. I know about you two."

"This has nothing to do with..." LaShaun started, but stopped when Orin raised a hand.

"Don't bother. You came here to get Manny to dig his own grave, not to help him. You had your mind made up, Broussard here made it up for you. Fine. I'll do it without your help."

Orin strode off to his pickup truck, got in and slammed the door. The engine roared to life. The gravel of the parking lot scattered as he pulled away. LaShaun sighed again and then joined Chase at his truck. She leaned against it beside him and crossed her arms.

"Real pleasure trip, huh?" Chase muttered.

Chapter 15

During the drive back to Beau Chene, LaShaun kept mentally replaying every word and image of the past few hours. She was sure she'd missed clues to what really happened, and what was still happening. Manny looked like his grandfather a lot when she thought about it. His eyes flashed giving him the same fierce gaze.

"That turned out to be a bust," Chase said. "At least we get a nice view of the mighty Mississippi River. Maybe we would have more luck at one of the riverboat casinos." He pointed toward the wide expanse of water as they crossed the bridge taking them away from Baton Rouge.

"I'm not so sure."

"C'mon, with my skills at the black jack table and your psychic tips we could get rich," Chase joked.

LaShaun reached over and turned down the radio playing lively country music. "No, I meant our visit might not have been pointless. Manny was giving me clues. I'm sure of it, but the question is why?"

"Tell me what really happened, LaShaun." Chase glanced at her sideways then back at the highway ahead.

"I've never had somebody actually connect with me and show me an entire scene. It was like watching a DVD." LaShaun's hands started to shake. She clasped them together to stop the unpleasant sensation.

"Of what, baby?"

"A murder," LaShaun said in a quiet voice that did not betray how sick recalling the vision made her.

"My God." Chase reached out and put a large hand over hers before pulling away again. After a few moments of silence he said, "You don't have to talk about it."

"No, I need to get this out of my head. Telling you will help. For most of my life I've only had one person to confide in. My grandmother always told me that our 'gift' meant that we would take in a lot of negative energy, see things that would drive many people insane. Sharing it with someone who cares, who we can trust, lightens the burden."

"Your grandmother left me that ring and a note with just one sentence. The note said, 'Take care of my girl, but I already know you will'," Chase said softly.

LaShaun glanced down at engagement ring on her finger. The sunlight caused the ametrine gemstone to catch fire with a kaleidoscope of colors. LaShaun whispered, "Merci, grandmèr."

"So it was bad, seeing this vision." Chase gripped the steering wheel with both hands.

"Horrible. But the thing is I couldn't distinguish if Manny was the killer or not, and he wasn't alone. The whole thing looked like a wild party that went way too far. Wait, that's wrong." LaShaun felt a sharp stab go through her. "Killing the woman was the high point of this party. Everybody knew she would die, except her."

"Willie Dupuis talked about this gang. You think these are the same people?" Chase switched to the slow lane to allow other vehicles to pass.

"There is a core group, maybe even an alpha leader. They pick up members now and then, some drop out and drift away to other groups. All of them tend to be transient." LaShaun closed her eyes to focus and then opened them again after a second or so.

"Street people into drugs, freaky scenes and willing to do just about anything for a thrill," Chase said.

"Right, right. But they choose their victims carefully." LaShaun squinted, but not because of the bright daylight.

"They made two mistakes though. They chose one victim from a prominent and wealthy family," Chase replied.

"Yes, but they didn't know that. She had mental problems and tended to live on the street. When she ran off from her family, she looked like any other homeless person." LaShaun shrugged when Chase looked at her in surprise. "Miss Clo kept a file and did her own research."

"I swear we need to put that little old lady on the payroll," Chase retorted.

"Over M.J.'s cold lifeless body," LaShaun replied. "What was the second mistake?"

"This group didn't know just how much Manny would enjoy killing. When bodies pile up too close together in time and space someone's going to notice. The police are only dumb in the movies." Chase frowned at the line of traffic ahead.

"Yeah." LaShaun sat silent.

Chase broke into her thoughts finally after ten minutes ticked by. "Are you going to tell me what you saw back there?"

"I had flashes of them running around woods and enjoying the hell out of themselves. They got to a clearing and..." LaShaun swallowed hard. "There was a woman on the ground. One of the males had sex with her. The woman wasn't scared at first. It was like a crazy partner swapping gathering with voyeurism as part of the cheap thrill."

"They stood around and watched. Damn."

LaShaun took in deep breaths and exhaled before going on. "Then the guy having sex with the victim started attacking her, during the act. The woman freaked out, but... the alpha took the first turn mauling her and then the rest of the pack joined in."

"Sweet heaven," Chase whispered and squeezed her shoulder again. "You said pack. You're not saying..."

"Yes, a pack of rougarous. Or at least they believe that's what they are." LaShaun squinted into the bright sunshine reflecting from the gray pavement and put on her sunglasses. Another few minutes of silence passed.

"Well, that's refreshing," Chase quipped.

"What?" LaShaun snapped out of her deep thoughts of sadomasochism and murder.

"That you think these scum balls have taken role playing too far. I'd rather face a bunch of delusional devil worshippers than real werewolves any day. I can't believe I just said that." Chase shook his head and sighed. "I've seen a lot of stuff, but nobody could have convinced me that being home would freak me out more than being in Afghanistan."

"How bad was it?" LaShaun glanced at him and saw his jaw tighten.

"Bad enough. Being a target 24-7 was no fun. Neither was raining body parts after IEDs went off," Chase said quietly. Then he looked at her briefly before staring ahead again. "Listen, don't be offended because I don't talk about my time in the Army. It's not about trust or anything. It's just..."

"If talking about the war bothers you then don't," LaShaun put in quickly. She moved closer to him on the seat and put a hand on his thigh.

"Thanks, baby. I've been out eight years, and I'm proud of the job I did. But I'm mighty glad to be home." Chase sighed. "I'm going to be interviewed on a local channel with the other candidate this Friday. So I expect my military service will come up. I don't want to be made out some kinda hero."

You'll do just fine. Say exactly that," LaShaun grinned. "And you'll sound like the honorable, strong and honest man who should be elected."

Chase laughed. "I should hire you as my campaign manager."

"Are you kidding? Any decent political advisor would tell you to dump me fast," LaShaun retorted. "In fact, I'd have to agree."

"Not going to happen, end of discussion. I'm surprised my opponent has taken any swipes at us." Chase shrugged.

"Can it be that the good folks of Vermillion Parish have become more open to diversity? Shh, I think angels are singing the hallelujah chorus," LaShaun said and laughed.

"The fact is a lot of the older generation has died out, so not as many people left to bring up your past."

"More than enough to remember and cause trouble, trust me," LaShaun replied.

"So far the campaign has been focused on crime and qualifications, which is how it should be." Chase nodded.

"Yeah, and at least we've kept the Ghost Team USA from finding out about Willie and Manny," LaShaun said.

"Me and M.J. are working hard to keep it that way." Chase cleared his throat. "Enough about werewolves and serial killers. Let's talk about something really scary."

"What?" LaShaun grinned and nudged him playfully.

"Umm, my parents invited us to have lunch at their house this Sunday." Chase glanced at LaShaun sideways. The air between them turned heavy with anticipation.

"Oh," was all LaShaun could manage after a few seconds.

With everything on her mind, the last thing she'd thought about was facing his family. She looked at the ring on her finger. Of course he wanted her to meet his parents. They were engaged. She couldn't expect Chase to leave them out of such an important part of his life for long.

"Sounds good," LaShaun said finally.

"Really? I know it came up kind of sudden, but actually they've been asking about you for a while now. I haven't told them about the ring just yet. This is going to be a good time for the family to..."

"Whoa, whoa, the family? You said we'd be having lunch with your parents." LaShaun's stomach tightened.

"It's kind of a tradition that my parents have a family lunch once a month. Usually we get together on the fourth Sunday after everybody goes to early mass. It's not this horde of people, hon. My two sisters, their husbands and kids and my three brothers come from Lafayette with their families. That's it."

"Oh, sounds like a real tiny gathering." LaShaun imagined a sea of eyeballs tracking her every move.

"Listen, to me; If I thought for one minute there would be some kind of ambush or judgments of you I'd have said no way." Chase's expression turned serious. "I love my family, don't get me wrong. But in some ways all I've seen in the Army and as a cop... I don't know. I had a hard time relating to them when I got home. And I can't talk to them about work."

"I think I understand," LaShaun said.

Chase gazed off without speaking for a few moments. "My mama says that traveling the world, the war and seeing the worse side of people all the time as a sheriff changed me. She's right, and I think she's not sure it was a good change either. Neither am I sometimes."

LaShaun knew that Chase had dark moments in the past. He didn't choose to stay in the old family home for sentimental reasons only. His grandparents' house sat several miles from the nearest neighbor. One of his sisters had lived there for a year or so after getting married, but moved to Lafayette when they had their first baby. She didn't want to be so isolated from other young families. The seclusion suited Chase. LaShaun also knew his parents worried about him.

"No, there is no darkness in your soul, Chase Broussard," LaShaun replied with tenderness. "

Chase's somber expression eased a little. "Is that the psychic talking?"

"That's the woman who has gotten to know you talking, cher." LaShaun smiled at him. "So, I better start planning what I'm going to wear."

"Tell you what; I'll explain to the folks that we should start out with just the four of us. We can plan the big meet the family event later. Better?"

"Thanks, Chase," LaShaun said, unable to hide the relief she felt. "I think that would suit me just *fine*."

Chase smiled. After a few seconds he whistled a tune, then broke into a popular song in Cajun French. His deep rich voice washed over her like a soothing balm. Yet LaShaun felt sadness pushing through as she pictured the faces of his family turned to her.

*****

Friday morning the temperature had dipped to forty degrees, but the sky was a brilliant blue. LaShaun drove down Black Bayou Road just outside of town to find more answers. A mile down the blacktop road she reached her destination. Not many cars were in the parking lot, which is why she'd come early on a weekday. She had her pick of spaces. After parking LaShaun got out, but stood studying a few minutes before she went inside.

The smell hit LaShaun's nostrils as she went through the glass doors of the Shady Moss Nursing Care Home; a stale odor of dirty mop bucket water mixed with a faint whiff of urine. The wide central hallway looked cheery enough with pastel landscape prints on the walls. A brass plaque announced they were from a generous donation by a local artist. A sandwich style board welcomed visitors, and also listed social events like bingo and Bible study groups. The main reception area was brightly lit. The decor struggled against any suggestions that Shady Moss was a place of despair. Except for the smell, and a group of sad, sleepy looking residents in wheelchairs lined up against one wall. Two of them drooled. Another woman with short gray and blonde hair waved gaily, smiling at LaShaun. She seemed eager to claim any visitor as her own.

"Hi," the woman lisped.

"Hello. How are you today?" LaShaun smiled back at her.

The woman nodded and kept waving one hand. "Hi."

"Good afternoon. Can I help you?" A tall woman with skin the color of cinnamon spoke from the center nurses' station. She wore a floral scrub top and white pants.

"Yes, I'm looking for Mrs. Flora Lee Young. I'm a friend of the family," LaShaun said.

"Sure. She's down the Rainbow Hallway in Room 269." The woman pointed down one of three hallways branching off to LaShaun's left.

"Thanks."

LaShaun had an explanation ready in case the woman questioned her. She didn't need to bother. The nurse had already gone back to making notes in a patient chart. A nursing assistant dressed in navy blue scrubs brushed by. No one seemed interested in a stranger walking in to visit. The television in the large dining room that faced the nurses' station blared noise from a game show. LaShaun glanced in the rooms as she walked looking at the numbers on the wall. Most looked fairly clean. The rooms were semi-private with two beds in each, with at least one bed occupied. Suddenly a man who looked no older than fifty whizzed out of one of the rooms in a wheelchair, his arms pumping as he pushed the wheels. He looked at LaShaun, but quickly averted his gaze. She felt his embarrassment. In a flash she had a picture of him as a strong healthy man working on a roof. More pictures of him with a series of pretty women. The man hated having her see him broken, sick and in an old folks home. LaShaun wanted to reassure the man that he had worth and dignity, but he was gone. And what could she have said anyway? With a sigh LaShaun continued down the hall with tan vinyl tiles. She reached Room 269. The door was half closed. She pushed it open. Both occupants were in bed. The name plate on the door indicated that Manny's grandmother was in the bed near the window.

"Hmm." A small woman lay in the first bed curled on her side. She blinked at LaShaun and smiled. Her lips worked for a few seconds before she could speak again. "Nice to see you."

"Hello Mrs. Richard." LaShaun remembered the second name from the room sign. "How are you doing today?"

"Goo--good." Mrs. Richard had difficulty speaking, but she seemed to be comfortable.

"Glad to hear it." LaShaun felt kindness from Mrs. Richard's soul, and it mixed with delightful mischief. "I'm just going to visit with Miss Flora Lee for a few minutes. I'll try not to disturb you."

"Humph." Mrs. Richard gave a little chuckle to signal she didn't mind a bit of disturbance to break up her day.

LaShaun nodded her understanding and went to the other bed. Mrs. Young sat up. To LaShaun's surprise she looked alert. A magazine lay in her lap, a copy of American Catholic. Yet her gaze was fastened on the scene outside the window. With any luck Mrs. Young was having a good day.

"Morning Miss Flora Lee," LaShaun said quietly so as not to startled her.

Mrs. Young blinked at the sound then slowly turned her head. Her gaze shifted from the window to LaShaun in slow motion. She blinked a few times as though trying to focus. "Who you be, child?"

"I'm LaShaun Rousselle, Odette's granddaughter. Francine was my mama." LaShaun carried a chair covered in rust colored imitation leather to the bedside and sat down. "We lived over on Rousselle Lane by Mr. Marchand. You know..."

"Odette and me used to roam them woods when I was a child. Francine was your mama, you say?" Mrs. Young blinked at her again. She pursed her lips and frowned.

"Let me get you some water." LaShaun stood and crossed to a side table with a pitcher on it. The ice had melted, but at least there was water left. She poured some into a glass and found a straw.

"Thank you," Mrs. Young murmured. She sipped from the plastic cup. Her hands seemed too weak to hold it for long.

"You're welcome." LaShaun placed the cup back on the table and sat in the chair again. Mrs. Richard lay on her side watching and smiling her approval. "I'm sorry to hear you're not feeling well."

"The good Lord watches over me." Mrs. Young looked out of the window again in a distracted manner.

"Then you're in good hands," LaShaun said.

"I always got along with Odette. Lots of folks talked against her, but I never had reason to pay that any mind. I was married and gone when Francine was still a girl." Mrs. Young eyes cleared as she studied LaShaun. Her thick eyebrows of gray and black hair lifted.

"Your husband told me y'all were friends," LaShaun said. The older woman's mind was clearing, LaShaun sensed it.

"Orin talked to you," Mrs. Young said softly.

"He came to see me about your grandson." LaShaun didn't want to upset Mrs. Young. She seemed frail, mentally and physically.

"Manny." Mrs. Young said the name and sighed.

"Yes. Mr. Young thinks maybe I can help him, so I visited Manny." LaShaun glanced at Mrs. Richard. The other woman's eyes had closed and she breathed steadily.

"You saw my boy?" Mrs. Young's heavily lined face brightened.

"Yes, he's doing well." LaShaun nodded.

"Thank you Blessed Mother." Mrs. Young almost smiled. Then she seemed to remember where Manny was and why he was there. The lines of sorrow and gloom took over her face again. "So many wanted him dead, you know. I thought those police or the guards would kill him and make it look like an accident. Or say he'd tried to escape."

"No one has hurt him," LaShaun replied.

"Not yet. I know what they gonna do to him. Stick a needle full of death in his vein, and watch him gasp his last breath. Vengeance is mine saith the Lord, but man don't care." Mrs. Young's voice trailed off. Her lips moved as she mumbled softly.

"The evidence went against him." LaShaun said. Mrs. Young startled her by looking at her sharply, her eyes gleaming with fire.

"I know what the boy did. I pray for his soul." Mrs. Young reached beneath the pillow and pulled out a beautiful rosary made of wooden beads with a silver crucifix.

"Yes ma'am. I think he's sorry about the life he's led."

"No," Mrs. Young said with such force her upper body shook. "I love that boy, Lord knows I do. But he ain't sorry. Part of it's my fault."

"I don't understand."

"I didn't have nowhere to go, not to my family for sure. My daddy... by the time he died mama was in the grave, too. I had them children. The girls, they blame me. What could I have done differently?" She strained forward, her eyes wide and filled with tears. "I took 'em to mass. I tried to soothe their hurt much as I could. Lord, please have mercy on me."

"Flo-rahee?" Mrs. Richard blinked at them, her head raised.

LaShaun left the chair and eased the distraught woman back against the two large pillows. "Manny takes responsibility for his own choices."

"Can't stop thinking of their sad eyes." Mrs. Young gasped and breathed hard. She shook her head. Tears flowed down her face.

LaShaun found a box of tissues and wiped her cheeks dry. "My grandmother had many regrets about her children. But she did the best she knew how at the time, and so did you."

"You're kind-hearted, not at all like folks say. But the Lord is punishing me." Mrs. Young twisted the wad of tissues in her hand. "I'm forgetful about a lot of things, but I can't forget... some things just stay on my mind. My girls needed me."

"I'm sure they know you tried, just like Mr. Orin. He's still trying to take care of Manny." LaShaun sat back in shock at the way her expression twisted with bitterness. Then Mrs. Young laughed, and the sound scraped across LaShaun's nerves like ragged fingernails. Even Mrs. Richard flinched and shook her head.

"My husband likes being in control, but Manny showed him. All of them finally got away you see, "Mrs. Young whispered, and cackled softly to herself. Her perverse grin crumpled, and her expression change again to one of sorrow. She covered her face with the now tattered tissue and whimpered.

A picture formed, not a vision this time. Pieces of a puzzle formed from snatches of what Manny had said and now from this poor woman. LaShaun leaned forward and tried to pull Mrs. Young's hands away, but she resisted. Voices in the hallway came closer then faded as staff went past the door. Mrs. Richard lay still, but her gaze was watchful.

"Did he hurt the girls, touch them the wrong way?" LaShaun said. She moved closer. Despite the growing sense of repulsion for the ugliness she would uncover, LaShaun pressed on. "You knew, but didn't feel like you could stop him?"

"I prayed Manny wouldn't be like him, but God punished me for not doing enough. The Bible says faith without works is dead." Mrs. Young nodded wearily. "I deserve to suffer."

"Manny turned out like his daddy, Ethan," LaShaun said, thinking of what Miss Clo had said about Manny's father.

"Poor Ethan got beat down. He took to drinking and then drugs. That was his way out. I didn't protect him either."

"That's why your daughters don't want to come back even to visit." LaShaun spoke more to herself than to the distraught woman.

"I don't blame them, not after they was free. They're right to hate the sight of me," Mrs. Young said, her voice flat with pain.

"Wait, you said Ethan used drugs to escape. Was he--"

"I didn't give you permission to come here." Orin Young stood in the doorway.

"I wanted to check on my grandmother's old friend." LaShaun stood as she spoke. Her smile tested her facial muscles. Suddenly she didn't like this man.

"We was talkin' 'bout the weather is all, and old times... with Odette. Nothing else," Mrs. Young glanced at him briefly.

Orin Young walked over to the bedside and gazed down at his wife. "Talkin' too much ain't good for you, Flora Lee. It wears you out, and strains your heart. You know that."

"You're right, Orin," Mrs. Young murmured. Her fingers picked at the crocheted throw that lay across the drab nursing home bedspread. "I just thought it was nice of Odette's girl to come see me. That's all."

LaShaun sensed the tiny hint of rebellion in her voice. Orin Young's neck muscles pulled into tight cords, but he said nothing for a long time. His wife gazed out of the window. Mrs. Richard made no sound, but LaShaun could see the dislike in her chocolate brown eyes when her glance flickered to Orin Young. A few seconds of charged silence stretched.

"Is there some reason I shouldn't visit, Mr. Young?" LaShaun pushed back. He shot a heated look in her direction. Her answering gaze dared him to make a scene.

Mr. Young's face strained into a smile. "I'm just concerned about my wife. She's not that strong."

"Well, you don't have to worry. I was just about to leave anyway. Nice to see you, Miss Flora Lee. Thanks for the stories about Monmon Odette when she was young. She was certainly a character." LaShaun leaned down and gave the older woman a gentle hug. As she did so LaShaun said, "You take care now, and I'll come see you again."

"Thank you, darlin'. I don't get any other visits now that the girls are gone and Manny..." Mrs. Young's lips trembled.

"Lay back and take your rest." Mr. Young walked to the bed and smoothed her gray hair down with one hand.

Mrs. Young's eyes blinked rapidly at his touch. She pushed deeper into the pillows and turned to face the drab faded green walls. LaShaun watched

Mr. Young fuss over his wife, patting her covers. He turned on the twenty-four inch flat screen television on a table. The sound of a game show with bells ringing came from the speakers.

"There's your favorite show. You and Miz Richard can watch." Mr. Young angled the screen so the other woman could see it as well. "There now, you girls are all set for a morning of entertainment. I'll see your little visitor out and be right back."

He turned and gestured to LaShaun, a clear signal that it was time for her to leave. As she walked past Mrs. Richard's bed, those dark expressive eyes told a story. LaShaun had the clear sense that Mrs. Richard wished dearly that she could slap him. Once they were in the hall Mr. Young closed the door gently.

"Thank you for taking an interest in Flora Lee. Don't think I'm not appreciative, but call me if you want to visit again." Mr. Young put a hand under LaShaun's elbow as they walked. He moved closer. "My poor wife's mind is feeble, but she never was too stable."

LaShaun felt the strange heat coming from his body. "She seemed fairly clear today."

"She has her good days, but she talks and rambles on not making sense. And of course she doesn't remember things. I hope she didn't upset you with any kind of crazy stories." Mr. Young nodded to the nurses.

One woman, about forty with flaming red hair, grinned at him flirtatiously and glared at LaShaun. "Hello, Mr. Young. I have a summary of your wife's progress. We can go over the results in my office."

"Thank you, Mrs. Wascom. After I visit with Flora Lee I'll come by on my way out." Mr. Young never stopped walking, and the nurse didn't seem pleased.

"I don't want to keep you from being with your wife. I know how much she means to you."

LaShaun pushed through the glass doors leading out of the nursing home. Bright sunlight bounced off the surface of the light gray concrete of the parking lot. She put her sunglasses on and faced him. They stood beneath the covered front patio where attractive wooden rocking chairs were scattered. A couple of elderly men sat smoking. A blues song came from a portable CD player on a table.

"There's no rush getting back to the poor dear." Mr. Young glanced around. "They try to make this place hospitable, but there's still some sadness here. I find it difficult at times, and feel so alone when I leave."

"I'm sure you miss your wife after being so close all these years." LaShaun nodded as if in sympathy.

"I'm blessed to be in good health. This is a lonely life. After all the years of hard work paid off, we're more than comfortable when it comes to money. But what is wealth without someone to share it with, eh?" Mr. Young stood tall, his chest out. "All that land and a big old empty house."

LaShaun figured that line must have worked wonders on the redhead inside. With a step back LaShaun gave him a full body appraisal. His iron gray hair looked sleek and thick. Well-built, he no doubt cut a fine figure in his youth. Even at his age he looked strong and vital. And LaShaun found him quite repellant.

"You could bring Miss Flora Lee home and hire sitters. I can recommend an excellent agency, the same one that helped me take care of Monmon Odette. That way you wouldn't be so alone in that big house." LaShaun smiled back at him.

"I 'll consider your suggestion. We could get together to talk about it more." Mr. Young tilted his head to one side.

"I'll leave the information with the social worker when I come back for a visit." LaShaun let her smile freeze in place.

"After you call to check with me first of course." Mr. Young's demeanor seemed a bit less friendly.

LaShaun let a few beats pass before she answered. "Of course. Goodbye."

She nodded once at him and walked off. LaShaun didn't need to look back to know his scrutiny included not only her body, but her motives. The man had a creepy, controlling kind of aura about him. Before he arrived his wife might have told LaShaun more. Yet Miss Flora Lee had given her clues, and so had Manny. Now it was up to her to follow them.

"I need to find out more about the Young family," LaShaun murmured as she got to her Honda CRV and hit the remote to unlock the driver's side door.

Chapter 16

Chase stood at the double wash basin in LaShaun's master bathroom shaving. He stopped every few seconds to wipe steam from the mirror. LaShaun stood at the other end of the long marble vanity. She rinsed with mouthwash and spit into the toilet. They were getting ready leave for lunch with his parents. The weather had turned warmer, and rain splattered against the bathroom window. She hoped the gray clouds and storms weren't a sign of how her first meeting with the Broussards would go.

"Absolutely a bad idea," Chase said, and paused before swiping the last of the creamy lather from his left cheek. "I don't think driving over to see one of Manny's sisters will help at all. Plus Orin could influence Manny not to talk to us again if he gets wind you're digging up family dirt."

"She lives in Beaumont, Texas and doesn't even speak to her parents anymore. That tells me a lot. He won't know. And no, I don't want you to come with me," LaShaun said when he started to speak.

"I wasn't going to offer. With all that's going on I can't be running down shadows a couple of hundred miles away. The deputies over in Cameron Parish found another body. Tuesday I'm driving over to Rockefeller Wildlife Refuge to look at the scene." Chase wiped his face with the fluffy towel then tossed it into the wicker hamper. "I'll load the washer when we get back."

"My, my, a sexy man who does laundry." LaShaun eased up behind him and wrapped her arms around his waist. She snuggled closer to him provocatively. "Now why don't you get your agitator working on me."

Chase twisted around in her embrace until they faced each other. He nuzzled her freshly washed hair. "You smell delicious, and you feel even better."

"So do you." LaShaun wiggled in his arms.

"But you haven't distracted me from the subject. I'm asking you not to take a trip to see one of those sisters," he whispered. "I might want to follow that lead later on since one of those bodies was found in Texas."

"Mr. Smart-ass," LaShaun said with a scowl and slapped his shoulder lightly. "Besides, you just said there wasn't anything important to find out. So it's my time to waste."

"I need to get you married and busy taking care of our kids." Chase turned on the blow dryer just in time to drown out LaShaun's angry growl.

"Oh no you didn't just turn into a cave man! If the phrase 'barefoot and pregnant' ever comes from those hot lips I'm going to barbecue you." LaShaun yelled to be heard over the hum of the hair dryer.

Chase laughed and kept combing through his thick black hair as the hot blast of air ruffed it, making him look even sexier. LaShaun combed through her own hair, putting jojoba oil on it to moisturize the thick curls. She glared at him a few times in the mirror, but he simply grinned back. When he flipped the switch the sound from the dryer died.

"Are you still speaking to me?" he said.

"Let me think about it," LaShaun tossed back.

She brushed his hand away when he tried to touch her arm. He tried again, and she didn't stop his long fingers from stroking her bare skin. Chase tugged at one strap of the tank top that matched her cotton flannel pajama pants.

"Okay, we can't go see my folks not speaking to one another. We have time to make up," he said softly.

"Smooth talking politician. Those tactics won't work on me." LaShaun tilted her head back as his lips trailed kisses down her neck.

"Then let's stop talkin'," he whispered.

Chase backed through the bathroom door to the queen-sized bed. Not bothering to undress, he pulled down her pajama pants but didn't wait to take off her top. He managed to kick free of his drawstring pajama pants as well. Like two college kids rushing before being caught, they made love on top of the covers. Fast and intense, Chase got right down to business. No foreplay except a few nibbles at her breast through the soft cotton tank top. The sensation sent her libido into high gear. For a long delicious time he went fast until LaShaun gasped, then slowed down.

"More," she whispered.

His answer was a groan as he plunged deeper inside her. They came at the same time gasping words of love, and then lay wrapped together for ten minutes before LaShaun's head cleared from the rapture. Eyes still closed, Chase had one long leg thrown across both of hers.

"Now we have to shower again," she said finally.

"Worth it," he replied and let out a sigh.

LaShaun kissed his forehead and then pushed him aside. He grunted in protest. "We better get a move on. I don't want us looking like we've been foolin' around just minutes before we get to your parents' house."

"We *have* been foolin' around," Chase said. His eyes were still closed as he smiled.

"I've got enough strikes against me. I'm going to look as close to saintly as possible."

LaShaun hissed at his loud laugher and padded into the bathroom and turned on the shower. Minutes later she dressed in fresh lounge pants and a t-shirt. Chase took his turn standing under the waterfall shower head. While he sang hard rock songs from the eighties off-key LaShaun went to kitchen and put on a pot of coffee. Then she cooked scrambled eggs and made toast for a light breakfast. She gazed at the wall clock. Nine o'clock. In an hour or so they would get dressed and drive to the small town of Meaux, Louisiana where his folks lived. They were going for lunch, but LaShaun felt like she was headed for a trial of some sort. And honestly she felt unprepared and guilty as hell. Having her fresh fingerprints all over their baby boy sure wouldn't help. Chase came in whistling. The ends of his dark curly hair were still damp from his most recent shower. He sat at the table and scooped up a serving of eggs from the still warm skillet on the table.

"Thanks for the breakfast, babe. I would have fixed it when I finished getting pretty." He winked at her.

"I needed to work off this nervous energy." LaShaun drank coffee and swallowed hard.

Chase gazed at her. "You don't have any reason to be nervous. My folks aren't going to bite. Besides, they know to be on their best behavior."

"I'm not scared, much..." LaShaun stared out of the bay window to the sun drenched lawn of her backyard.

"You're the woman who faces down dark forces from the other side. Surely two middle-aged Cajuns don't make you jumpy."

"No. I mean, well... yes." LaShaun gave him a weak smile. "I know it sounds silly."

"You're going to be part of my family. You're already part of me." Chase wore a serious expression as he squeezed her knee beneath the table. "Case closed. My parents will accept you."

"There's so much baggage attached to the Rousselle name, not to mention my bad rep." LaShaun sighed. "And it could cost you the election. That interview Friday night was tense. Your opponent kept talking about how he's a family man, and believes in good Christian values. He might as well have come out and said my name."

"We discussed facts and issues." Chase chewed on toast.

"Yeah."

LaShaun didn't see it that way. Dave Godchaux had taken every opportunity to imply that he was the good clean man for the job of Sheriff. "What about that stuff he said about being careful of his associations, and not giving even the appearance of impropriety? I was the elephant in the room that he didn't mention, but kept nodding toward."

"I think it went well." Chase stuffed more toast in his mouth.

"You did good." LaShaun smiled at him.

She had to admit Chase had been poised and professional, every inch the lawman. He'd talked about hiring more officers, getting the veteran deputies more training at the Louisiana State Police Academy and the new equipment the office could use. While his opponent had spent more time staking his claim on being a solid good old country boy with down home morals. Chase sounded like he was prepared for the job of being sheriff, young and ready to do his best. LaShaun wondered if it would be enough.

"The election is in April. I just hope nothing happens between now and then." LaShaun chewed on a thumb instead of the food on her plate.

"Like what?" Chase squinted at her. "What have you been up to?"

"Nothing. Really," she added when his expression didn't change. "Well, not much. I went to see Manny's grandmother at the nursing home. She didn't seem all that senile to me; more like she was full of remorse, sadness and scared of her husband."

"Scared of Mr. Orin? That doesn't sound right. I've always heard he provided for the family, and was a solid citizen. There's old gossip about a few flings he had with women back in the day. But..."

"So you have been doing a background check on him," LaShaun said eagerly. "Mr. Clean has his skeletons in the closet. Now that makes sense. He seems like a man who likes the ladies."

"Whoa, slow down. I didn't say he was all that bad, and from what I hear that was a long time ago."

"Yeah, you didn't see the way this middle-aged nurse at Shady Grove got all possessive." LaShaun squinted. "And Miss Flora Lee didn't talk about how good he was to her and the kids either. In fact, I got the impression that she'd led a miserable life. She went on and on about how she should have protected her daughters. At first I thought she meant from their brother or even Manny, but maybe she was talking about *Mr. Orin.*"

"I haven't heard any such talk," Chase replied with a shrug.

"Lots of family secrets stay hidden for years when it comes to abuse." LaShaun leaned forward warming to her line of logic.

Chase started to object then stopped. His expression darkened. "You're right. I've seen enough in my time on the job to know that's the truth."

"Mr. Orin wasn't happy to see me at that nursing home talking to his wife. I got the distinct whiff of dirty secrets. Which is why I'm going to go visit one of their daughters in Texas," LaShaun said casually and then took another sip of coffee.

"We're back to that. Naturally I can't order you not to go to Beaumont," Chase said.

"I wouldn't advise it, Chase Jules Broussard. You already walked across thin ice with that crack about me being busy having babies," LaShaun warned.

"My grandmother used to call me by my full name when I was close to getting a whippin'," Chase quipped.

"That's what I'm talkin' about," LaShaun pointed at the end of his nose.

He raised both hands like a suspect surrendering. "Fine, I give up. Just be very careful. Which daughter are you going to see, and do you plan to call her first?"

"Verlena Joubert. I got the name from Miss Clo." LaShaun sprang from her seat and found her smart phone. "She's married to Guy Joubert. He took a job with a trucking company about two years ago and they moved from Lake Charles to Beaumont. Miss Clo says she always wondered why the girls just disappeared. But everybody says Mr. Orin was real strict. Verlena and her two sisters all left one by one home in their late teens. Diane is the oldest, not that much older than Manny. I think she was fourteen when he was born. Miss Clo says they treated Manny more like a little brother."

Chase sat with his arms folded at she talked. "I wish y'all would leave the detecting to us professionals."

"She's been real helpful. Now would you have known all of that so fast? No." LaShaun said before Chase could take a breath to respond. When she sat at the table again she brushed a hand over his thick curls. "I promise to drive the safely, obey all traffic laws and watch my back."

"Well I'll guess that will have to do since it's obvious you're going to Texas. Just stay away from Orin Young. I hear he has a temper when he gets riled up." Chase finished his cup of coffee.

"I'll bet he does."

LaShaun gazed off in thought for several moments. She hardly registered that Chase cleared the table and loaded the dishwasher. He unfolded the Sunday paper and sat in the family room off the kitchen. For the next half hour LaShaun divided her thoughts between choosing the right outfit, and what she knew of the Young family. Her instinct told her there was more beneath the surface to uncover, and it could be unpleasant. Miss Flora Lee didn't mention warm memories of her family life with Orin Young.

LaShaun was standing the walk-in closet dressed in only a skirt and a bra, still sorting through her impressions and bits of what she'd been told. Chase's voice startled her and she dropped the soft brown sweater she was holding.

"That skirt is pretty, but the topless look won't go over real big with mama. Besides you're gonna be chilly." Chase leaned against the door frame.

"Cut the comedy act." LaShaun picked up the sweater and held it to her chest. "What do you think?"

"You look mighty fine, as usual," Chase said with a grin and wink.

"Right answer, but I'm serious. I want to look...normal."

LaShaun stepped to the full length mirror on the open closet door. The skirt was a print of brown, red and green leaves in a softly abstract fashion. Since the hem fell to her mid-calf, LaShaun intended to wear light brown suede boots. Chase appeared behind her.

"I want you just the way you are. If I can accept you, then so can they. " Chase gazed at her reflection in the mirror.

She turned to face him. "I don't want to cause any friction between you and your family. I'm used to be isolated."

"Any conflict happened before you came along," he replied and turned away. "Now I better get dressed myself."

"Okay." LaShaun wondered what he meant, and if she'd get a sense once she met his family.

*****

Almost two hours later they pulled onto the driveway of the Broussard home. The front of the two story home had lovely rust colored brinks. A long porch stretched painted white held huge planters and six rocking chairs. By its pristine condition, LaShaun also guessed that porch didn't get much use. Everything about the property and house said that appearances meant a lot. LaShaun glanced at Chase. He seemed to sense her gaze because he gave her hand a squeeze.

"Here we are; mama's pride and joy. And yes, the inside is just as perfect. There's a wide back patio where we hang out in warmer weather. A smaller screened in porch is back there as well." Chase parked his truck in front near the end of the circular driveway.

"It's beautiful," LaShaun said. "Parking out here in case we need to make a quick getaway?"

Chase laughed hard. "We're going to be fine. Now come on and let's get this ordeal over with."

"What?" Her mouth fell open.

"I'm teasing," Chase said and pointed at her. "Gotcha."

"You--" LaShaun stopped when the lovely stained oak front door swung open. A tall woman with dark brown hair waved to them.

"Y'all come on in," she called out and gestured eagerly. "Everybody can't wait to meet your friend."

LaShaun looked at Chase. "Your friend? You mean..."

"We're going to announce our engagement today." Chase swung open the driver's side door and pulled LaShaun across the seat. "Hey, mama. You lookin' good as usual."

"Go on. I put on ten pounds this year, and my hairdresser is having a time covering all the gray hairs." His mother grinned as she patted her short hairdo.

"LaShaun, allow me to introduce you to Elizabeth Graves Broussard. We call her 'Queen Bee' cause she rules her house with an iron hand." Chase bounded up the porch and into her embrace.

"Stop being a rascal," his mother replied and gave him a hug.

Chase held out his hand to LaShaun who took it and joined them on the porch. "This beautiful woman is LaShaun Rousselle. She's as gifted as she is good-looking."

"I'm so glad to *finally* meet you," Mrs. Broussard said.

"Thank you for inviting me." LaShaun accepted the cool appraising glance that went with Mrs. Broussard's southern lady greeting.

"Y'all come on in." Mrs. Broussard led the way through a wide foyer. A large round oak table stood in the center of it with a beautiful tall vase filled with fresh flowers. "We're in the family room. No need to be formal I thought, so I didn't set the dining room table. You're from Beau Chene. My husband's people owned land just outside of town."

"Yes, Chase's home and the property around it are gorgeous," LaShaun replied.

Mrs. Broussard paused in the archway that led to the family room. Her perfectly arched eyebrows rose as she glanced at her son. "I hope Chase hasn't turned it into a messy bachelor pad."

"Oh no, he's quite the neat housekeeper. You set a great example. I love your home."

"Thank you."

Every piece of furniture or decorative item positioned just so a bit sterile, but the compliment was genuine. Decorated in shades of green, gold and blue, the home could have been featured in a magazine. "Queen Bee" took great pleasure in having everything just right. Mrs. Broussard described several antiques inherited from both sides of the family.

"But I'm keeping y'all all to myself when everybody is waiting to meet you," She said after a few minutes.

"Everybody? We agreed it would just be the four of us, mama dear," Chase said in a measured tone.

"You know my house is like Grand Central Station on a Sunday. Your sisters dropped in to see what I cooked, and asked questions when they saw my special red velvet cake that I only make for special occasions. Bruce, Jr. and his family saw their cars and stopped after they left morning mass." Mrs. Broussard seemed not to notice Chase's squinty skepticism. "I always cook a big meal because my children love Sundays at our house. It's a tradition."

"Wonderful," LaShaun murmured. She stifled a giggle at the dark look Chase gave his mother, which was totally wasted.

"Here we are in all our glory," Mrs. Broussard said and swept out a hand to take in the large family room.

Six kids of various ages scampered about the room. Two older ones were engrossed in playing a video game, a fast paced tennis match. The cartoon characters of the game were displayed on a sixty-inch flat screen television mounted on a wall. The den stretched the length of the house it seemed. An oak dining room set sat at one end of the room. Two large L-shaped sofas with chairs and two wide ottomans were on the other end.

"Baby brother!" A willowy younger version of Elizabeth Broussard strode across to them and wrapped Chase in a bear hug.

"LaShaun, meet my sister Katie," Chase said with a wide smile.

"So nice to meet you." Katie gave LaShaun a discreet, but thorough head to toe examination.

Within minutes LaShaun and Chase were surrounded by family members, all except the two tweens. They were forced to stop playing the video game and be introduced. They made polite noises, smiled shyly then scurried back to the more interesting pursuit of competition. Bruce, Sr. had a warm approachable manner. He seemed more laid back than his wife. Chase's other two sisters, Elaine and Sharon, came next with their husbands. Finally his older brother, Bruce Broussard, Jr. stepped forward to introduce his wife and baby girl. Bruce Jr. stared at LaShaun until his wife poked him.

LaShaun wondered if Chase had prepared his parents and siblings to be nice. Even after twenty minutes of chatting to break the ice, no one asked about LaShaun's family. Under the circumstances someone should have had questions. As time went on the LaShaun's family and personal background became the elephant in the room.

They ate delicious rotisserie chicken, macaroni cheese casserole, green beans and yeast rolls.

Conversation over the meal continued to hover around safe subjects. The weather, the Saints football season and decorations for the Halloween party were exhausted. LaShaun wrestled with the powerful urge to giggle when, after a period of heavy silence, Chase's sister-in-law went back to the weather. She covered her mouth with a napkin and pretended to clear her throat when she lost the battle not to laugh. Chase nudged her with an elbow.

"Are you okay, dear?" Mrs. Broussard raised an eyebrow at them both.

"Yes, ma'am," LaShaun managed to get out. She grabbed her glass of iced tea and drank.

"We really appreciate y'all being so polite, but really you can ask us any burning questions," Chase said. He took LaShaun's hand and glanced around the table.

"What burning questions are we supposed to ask?" one of the two older children asked. Jessica had intense brown eyes and dark brown hair to match. The other children grew attentive.

"Let's clear these dishes," Chase's father said. "That way we'll get to dessert quicker. Your mother baked her red velvet cake, kids. And we've got homemade vanilla ice cream."

"Yaaay!" came a chorus of childish voices. The older kids forgot to be too cool to join their younger siblings and cousins. When LaShaun attempted to help the rest of the adults clear the table Mr. Broussard intervened.

"No, no. We can't have guests carrying dirty dishes. You get this one freebie since this is your first family gathering. After this all bets are off." Bruce,

Sr. winked at her. "You won't be a guest the next time."

"I won't insist then," LaShaun replied with a smile.

Jessica hovered near her grandfather listening in. "She won't be guest, paw-paw? What will she be?"

"I'm guessing from that rock on her finger, she's going to be family for sure," he said with another wink.

"Gee thanks, dad," Chase muttered.

"What?" His father blinked at him.

Then Bruce, Sr. noticed the adults had all frozen in place between the table and the archway leading to the large kitchen. Mrs. Broussard still held the now empty large casserole dish when she came back. She stared at LaShaun and then sat Chase. Hard. Her thin lips pressed together.

"Ooo, let me see." Sharon, Chase's youngest sister, pushed her husband aside and hurried to LaShaun.

"Well..." LaShaun glanced at Chase for direction. When he nodded she extended her hand.

"Yes, we're engaged," Chase said. He put a protective arm around LaShaun's waist.

"My oh my," Bruce, Jr. said softly, which earned him another poke from his wife, Adrianna.

"Congratulations. More reason to celebrate with cake and ice cream," Adrianna said with a wide smile and hugged LaShaun. "Now I won't be the only outsider."

"Nonsense, Adrianna. You're part of this family," Mrs. Broussard replied quickly, with a trace of tartness in her tone.

"Of course, Mrs. B, I meant the only one of the family that has lived outside Louisiana. I grew up in Colorado." Adrianna smiled at her widely as Chase's sisters exchanged glances.

"Thank you, Adrianna." LaShaun filed away a memo to have a chat with Bruce's wife later.

"Yes, congratulations on finding the right girl," Bruce, Jr. said with a chuckle. He seemed not to notice the way his mother glared at him.

Bruce, Sr. rubbed his chin. "Sorry I stole your thunder, son. Guess you wanted to make a formal announcement."

Katie put an arm around her father's shoulder and kissed his cheek with a laugh. "Daddy, clueless and lovable as always."

"So when is the big day?" Mrs. Broussard wore a smile that threatened to crack the lines in her face.

"We haven't picked a date yet, probably in the spring. Don't you think, babe?" Chase said and looked at LaShaun.

"Yes, spring," she echoed.

"That would be perfect," Sharon blurted out. "What about April? It will be just cool enough we won't swelter in the heat outside."

"Outside?" Chase and LaShaun said at the same time.

"Yes, under the oak tree on the family property where our great-great grandfather proposed. Such a romantic story." Sharon grabbed LaShaun's arm and led her to the seating area of the den. "He was dirt poor, but adored Marguerite. He promised her father that he would one day have his own property and treat her like royalty. He made good on that promise and..."

"Okay, little sis," Katie broke in. "Let's not get carried away and plan their wedding. That's the prerogative of the bride-to-be and her mother."

"Her mother and grandmother are deceased," Mrs. Broussard put in. Her husband gave her a look of censure and she clamped her lips together again.

"My mama died when I was young. My grandmother, Odette Rousselle, died nine months ago," LaShaun said.

"I'm so sorry." Sharon took one of LaShaun's hands. "I'm officially volunteering to help in any way I can. You two just let us know what you decide. A wedding is so exciting."

"Yes, exciting," Mrs. Broussard said with none of her youngest daughter's warmth or enthusiasm.

During the awkward silence the two older children hovered, watching the adults closely. The four younger children happily played with toys on the floor in the seating area several feet away. They apparently didn't notice anything usual. Chase's father cleared his throat loudly. He clapped his hands together loudly, and his wife and daughters jumped.

"Let's get to that dessert, shall we? Liz, come on and help me. You kids go relax on the sofas and we'll serve ya." He firmly guided his wife out of the room with a hand under one of her elbows.

"Kids, go outside with all that racket," Sharon said. "The weather is beautiful. Enjoy the fresh air."

Jessica and her cousin shook their heads, but she spoke up. "No, we'll stay here."

"Take your little sister and cousins outside," Elaine said firmly. "Now."

"Come on, Jessi," the boy, Kevin, said. "Paw-Paw Bruce has the radio controlled helicopters set up."

He didn't wait for her to reply before turning around and heading for the sliding patio doors. Jessica frowned at her aunts and mother for a few seconds then flounced out. Moments later the adults were seated on the comfortable sofas and matching chairs. Bruce Jr. turned the television to a college football game despite the frowns the women gave him.

"I'll keep the sound low," he said, unperturbed by their displeasure.

"Odette Rousselle was your grandmother. She's a legend in Vermillion Parish," Elaine said. "Don't give me the evil eye, Chase. We might as well talk about it."

LaShaun smiled. "I'll answer any questions you might have."

Adrianna leaned forward eagerly. "I'm not from here, so tell me all about your grandmother."

"Ahem, I don't think..." Sharon glanced toward the kitchen as though looking for her mother.

"It's okay. My grandmother has always been thought of as the Vermillion Parish version of Marie Laveau. That's a bit of an exaggeration. Monmon Odette's people came from Haiti in the eighteenth century. I have African, Indian and French ancestry. One of my ancestors was a French plantation owner in Natchitoches Parish. I have the land grant document from 1797 in fact." LaShaun gave a shortened version of the lecture she'd given in Los Angeles at the museum where she worked while living there.

"How fascinating," Adrianna said.

"Of course! So you're *the* LaShaun Rousselle. I love that show Ghost Team USA. Are you working on the Blood River Ripper story with James Schaffer?" Sharon's eyes were wide with interest.

"No, she's not. And don't believe anything they say on that stupid show. The guy's full of it," Chase said hotly.

"That's right. He's making everyone around here look like superstitious lunatics," Elaine said with a grim set to her mouth.

"I was in school with two of Manny Young's sisters, but only for a year or so. They were all older than me. Elaine had classes with two of them. But she won't talk about it." Sharon spoke in a low voice to LaShaun and Adrianna as though they were alone.

"They were his *aunts*, and I'm right here listening to you, Sharon," Elaine snapped at her younger sister.

"Did you know Verlena?" LaShaun asked quietly, hoping the excitement she felt didn't show.

"We worked on the newspaper together in high school, and she was a nice person. I don't blame her and her sisters for leaving. People treated them like they were killers right along with Manny," Elaine said.

"I thought they were his sisters, they treated him like a little brother. He was a cute kid. They brought him to a couple of basketball and football games at school," Sharon said. "I couldn't believe he turned into a crazed serial killer."

"With that peculiar grandfather and father he had? I'm not surprised, "Elaine muttered.

"Ooo, I forgot about that." Sharon turned to LaShaun and Adrianna. "Some of the girls at school said Mr. Orin gave them the creeps the way he looked at them, and..."

Chase waved to his sisters and then stood up. "Here comes mama's cake. Yum-yum."

"Shush, Sharon," Elaine whispered. "No more gruesome talk."

Over dessert Elaine and Chase made sure to keep the conversation away from voodoo and murder. Sharon and Adrianna talked about wedding details with delight. Mrs. Broussard wore a strained smile as they chattered. Finally the conversation wound down. Chase's father and brother pulled him away to talk about a possible fishing trip. Elaine went with her mother to the kitchen.

"Listen, let's have lunch. Bruce and I got married here, so if you want any tips on the best florists and dress shop to visit I can help," Adrianna said. Then she grinned at LaShaun. "Who am I kidding? I want to hear more about your voodoo grandmother."

"Adrianna, I can't believe you said that!" Sharon put a hand over her mouth.

"My grandparents are from Costa Rica, so I think Queen Elizabeth suspects I'm an illegal alien," Adrianna murmured.

"Really?" LaShaun laughed.

"Mama can be a bit... conservative," Sharon admitted. "But she thinks of you as a member of the family, Adrianna."

"Well, this one is sure gonna take the heat off me," Adrianna said with a laugh. "She's got my Latino heritage beat with the whole voodoo priestess thing. Wow, this year's birthday and Halloween party for Jessi is going to be the best ever."

"LaShaun, you must think we're awful." Sharon giggled and looked over her shoulder.

LaShaun burst into laughter and the two women joined her. In moments they were all in tears, slapping each other on the shoulder. Each of them tried to speak, but would dissolve into giggling. By the time the others joined them again, the three had mostly recovered. Chase gave LaShaun a questioning glance and she shrugged. Chase was the first to announce they would be leaving. His father gave LaShaun a bear hug that felt totally sincere. Mrs. Broussard gave LaShaun an air kiss, her cheek close enough to make it appear they were going to be such good friends. Sharon followed them out to Chase's truck, mischief in her hazel eyes.

"I'll call you about lunch. We'll have a great time." She waved to them as they drove off.

"Well, that was a lot of fun," Chase said. His expression looked fierce because of the way his jaw clamped tight.

"I know that announcement didn't go the way you planned. Bless your daddy's heart. He's adorable." LaShaun patted his thigh.

"I'm sorry about the way my mother came across. She's not as... intolerant as she seems. She just grew up a certain way." Chase's face flushed a light red.

"Don't be angry, honey. I'm not sure members of my family would have open arms for you either. Of course that could be because you're a cop, too. The Rousselle clan isn't known for being law abiding citizens." LaShaun moved closer to him. "It will be okay."

"Yeah."

Chase drove in silence for a few more miles, but LaShaun talked about how she enjoyed his sisters and turned on the CD player. After another twenty minutes she felt him relax and let go of the tension from the first family gathering. LaShaun kissed away the last traces of his frown with a peck on his cheek. He smiled at her and the sunshine looked a little brighter.

Chapter 17

Early on the Tuesday morning after her Sunday fun with the Broussard brood, LaShaun set out to meet Verlena Young Joubert. The drive was uneventful. The GPS system in LaShaun's Honda CRV took her down Interstate 10 out of Louisiana and into Texas. With only two stops, she made good time. About three hours of driving brought her into the city limits. She followed the directions to a modest two story older home on Palm Street in Beaumont. She'd done her homework with help from Miss Clo and Miss Joyelle. Chase shook his head as LaShaun told him about the details the two women had gathered. They had better information than the FBI could have dug up on short notice.

Verlena Joubert , age forty-one, worked in a medical clinic but had been laid off. Now she was a stay at home mother. She kept in touch with one former friend from high school, a young woman who happened to be the cousin to a friend of Miss Joyelle's second daughter. Between Miss Clo and Miss Joyelle, LaShaun got Verlena's address and phone number. Fortunately the friend convinced Verlena to meet with LaShaun, but only briefly and without any word to Verlena's husband.

LaShaun drove slowly to the corner of Palm Street and Brandon Ave. She parked the CRV on Brandon Ave. halfway between Verlena's home and the house next door. Verlena had been vehement that her husband not find out. So just in case Verlena's husband came home LaShaun could ask to be shuttled out a back door. LaShaun's sixth sense told her there had been strain on Verlena's marriage. The almost frantic tone in the woman's voice over the phone set off alarm bells. The last thing LaShaun wanted was to bring her grief. She had a feeling Verlena had seen her share of trouble.

LaShaun went up the wooden steps painted gray to match the porch and pushed a square button next to the front door. Sheer curtains covering a narrow window to her left parted and closed quickly. Metal clicked and the door opened a few inches.

"Hello, Mrs. Joubert. I'm--"

"I know who you are," Verlena said cutting her off. "I seen your picture a few times in the paper back when that man got killed."

"Right." LaShaun could have asked which man, but decided not to dwell on anything that might scare her more. "I appreciate you talking to me, and I won't take up much of your time."

"Uh-huh. If I thought Guy wouldn't call the house I would have met you somewhere. But he gets upset when I don't answer." Verlena stepped back and opened the door wider, her only invitation for LaShaun to enter.

"Thanks." LaShaun entered a surprisingly cheerful looking living room. "You could take your cell phone. If you feel more comfortable leaving..."

"No, come on in," Verlena cut her off again. She closed the door and faced LaShaun. "Have a seat."

"Are you okay? You seem nervous about your husband." LaShaun let the statement hang in the air.

"Guy is a good man," Verlena said defensively, and too quickly to be quite convincing. "He's just protective of me."

"I understand," LaShaun murmured and sat on the edge of a chair upholstered in a floral fabric. She looked around the room. A forty inch flat screen television with a game system attached sat in one corner. A softball catcher's mitt lay on the floor.

"No, you don't, but I guess that's why you're here." Verlena sat on a dark tan recliner across the room near the sofa.

"Pardon?" LaShaun stopped taking in the details of the house and looked at her sharply.

"I get the paper from home. They brought up Manny's case again with the killings y'all just had. My husband doesn't want our two boys to know about all that, or me to get upset. So I burned the paper. We finally have a decent life away from all that mess." Verlena's bottom lip trembled. She had traces of both her mother and Orin Young in her facial features. "How's mama doing? My friend Stacey says you been to see her at Shady Grove."

"She's frail, but doing fine," LaShaun said.

"Uh-huh." Verlena rocked back and forth. Her tone conveyed that she either didn't believe LaShaun, or didn't care if her mother was doing fine or not. "So you drove a long way just to spend a few minutes talking to me."

"Your daddy asked me to go visit Manny. He's hoping..."

"To get him off death row. Yeah, I didn't need a crystal ball to tell me that," Verlena said with a bitter laugh.

"You think Manny should get the lethal injection?" LaShaun said, surprised at the turn their talk had taken so quickly.

Verlena looked at LaShaun with her head tilted to one side for a few minutes. "You shocked that I'm so blunt. About the only thing I'll claim from Orin Young is being direct. Took me long enough to figure out how to stand up for myself."

"You're father is trying to do his best for your nephew," LaShaun replied.

Verlena's hands gripped both arms of the recliner, her fingers making deep pits in the fabric. "My friend says I should trust you, but I'm not so sure if you're set on helping daddy."

"I'm trying to find out the truth, and maybe help some families find out what happened to their missing relatives."

Verlena's face went pale. "Them poor folks not knowing is the worst part. Made me sick to see that one lady on television crying her eyes out."

I didn't promise to help Manny be released or to cover up anything." LaShaun watched as Verlena studied her as though looking for a sign to help her judge.

"You know what it's like to have folks look down at you," Verlena said finally.

"Well, hmm, yes. Mostly because of..."

"I heard all about the Rousselles." Verlena nodded. "So you know how it is to feel like a freak, like everywhere you go there's some kind of shadow hanging over you."

LaShaun did not have to pretend to be intrigued, and baffled at the sharp turn their conversation took. "I heard you and your sisters had friends, and you even worked on the high school paper. Your sister Diane sang in the choir and..."

"Sure, we put on a good front," Verlena said, continuing her trend of interrupting LaShaun. "I still felt like a freak. Pretending to be something I wasn't, nerves on edge cause you just know somehow the truth will come out."

"Your mother mentioned there were problems at home," LaShaun said carefully.

"Humph, is that what she called it? Problems?" Verlena's gray blue eyes so like her father's sparkled with anger.

"She didn't give me any details."

"Now I know for sure you talked to her," Verlena said with a harsh laugh that like sandpaper had rubbed her throat raw. "Never talk, that's what she preached to us. Don't tell anybody. When I finally did say something my high school guidance counselor helped me get the hell out. Thank God for her, and for my husband. I went to Kaplan College here in town, got a degree in medical coding. I tried to get Diane to listen and go to school. She left with the first man that offered her a ride out of town."

"How is she doing?" LaShaun knew the question would keep Verlena focused on the story of their lives.

"Diane doesn't keep in touch with me and my other sister. Too much we don't want to remember or talk about. She's had a couple of nervous breakdowns so maybe it's for the best." Verlena swallowed hard.

"I'm sorry," LaShaun said softly.

Verlena let go of the chair arms and flexed the fingers of both hands. "Anyway, you came here to get the real story. You sure you want to turn over that particular rock?"

"If it's too hard for you to talk about I understand. Manny seems to sincerely feel bad for Miss Flora Lee. He misses you, your sister and his grandmother."

Verlena's expression softened for the first time. Her bottom lip trembled again, and then she seemed to shake herself back to being strong. "He's not totally to blame what he turned into. Me and my sisters tried, but daddy had too strong a hold on him. No different from the way he had a hold on the rest of us."

"Manny was like your baby brother," LaShaun offered. She was guessing that Orin Young was the villain.

Verlena balled up a corner of the oversized sweater she wore over her jeans. "Manny wasn't our like our baby brother. He *is* our baby brother."

"Wait a minute. Repeat that," LaShaun said and leaned forward.

"In the spring of 1979 daddy brought home this girl. I guess me and Diane didn't give him enough variety." Verlena spoke as though the words tasted sour on her tongue as they came out. She stopped talking. Her body became stiff and straight in the chair. "Daddy introduced her as my brother Ethan's wife. They shared her until daddy decided he wanted her all to himself. By that time Ethan had fallen in love with Karla. Him and daddy got into it. Karla was hooked on drugs, and daddy kept her supplied. Naturally she chose him over Ethan. That's when Ethan's drinking and drugging got bad. He just took off one day in 1980. Karla moved to New

Iberia, and daddy would go see about his daughter-in-law. One day a year later he showed up with the baby."

"And you all told everybody that Manny was Ethan's baby." LaShaun gazed at her, feeling the vileness of what she was saying.

"We did as we was told like always," Verlena said quietly, her voice husky with emotion.

"Your daddy sexually molested you and Diane?" LaShaun said as gently as she could.

Verlena nodded and let out a ragged breath. "After all these years it's still hard to come out and say sometimes. I went through therapy. Diane wouldn't. We managed to protect our baby sister. I brought her with me when I got married. She lives in Austin now, but don't tell nobody," Verlena said quickly. "I don't want daddy to know where she is."

"Oh God." LaShaun began to see glimpses of the damage one man had done.

"Daddy thought of us as his possessions to do with as he liked. It stopped only because we escaped. Mama just pretended she didn't see. She was just as much a prisoner in some ways I guess. But she should have done something, anything to protect her children."

"I'm so sorry for all you've been through," LaShaun said after a few minutes of silence.

"I don't see how this makes a difference to anything." Verlena stared at LaShaun waiting for an answer.

"I don't know either. Manny seems to be connected. And no, law enforcement doesn't think so," LaShaun added quickly when Verlena started to speak.

Verlena rocked the chair back and forth. "Manny is locked up, and that's exactly where he needs to stay. Is daddy in the house by himself?"

"What?" LaShaun blinked in surprise at another sharp turn in their conversation.

"Daddy likes having somebody to control and manipulate. We're all gone now, so who's he ruling over? No, I'll bet he's got him somebody. Lord, I hope it's not a child." Verlena placed a hand over her heart.

LaShaun cleared her throat. "I got the impression one of the nurses at Shady Grove had a thing for your daddy."

"I'm sure she's doing more than sweet talk with him. But if she's an older lady, that's just for show. Daddy likes 'em young." Verlena rubbed her chin. "He enjoys slapping women around, and he's even meaner if he's drinking. But I don't know about killing people the way it was described in the news."

"Did you think Manny would become a serial killer?" LaShaun asked the question in a soft tone to blunt the blow.

Verlena flinched and her eyes filled with tears. "He was a sweet baby, but as he got older he acted strange. Daddy would hit him, said it would toughen him up because life was hard. Ethan hated the sight of Manny, and let him know it. He'd knock Manny around if daddy wasn't there to stop him. When he got to be about twelve, daddy started taking him on 'outings'. Lord only knows what he taught that boy. By that time Diane and me was trying to have our own lives with high school activities."

"You did your best," LaShaun said.

Verlena looked away through the sheer curtains covering one window. Tears rolled down her face. She didn't wipe them away. Soon her face was wet. "Maybe, maybe not. Manny might be blaming me like I blame mama."

"I don't think so at all. Manny expressed affection toward you and Miss Flora Lee. Where's the bathroom?"

"Down that hall to your right," Verlena whispered. She covered her face with both hands and sobbed.

LaShaun followed her directions and grabbed a box of tissues. She went back and handed them to Verlena. For a long time the woman continued to cry, not paying attention to the box or LaShaun standing next to her. Soon she was wailing as though all of the agony caused by Orin Young coursed through her body. LaShaun put an arm around her and let her weep. After several minutes Verlena quieted. She grabbed a handful of tissues and pressed them to her face. Then she blew her nose.

"I'm sorry for breaking down," she said hoarsely. She breathed in and out a few times then sat straight. "Thought for sure I was all cried out about that part of my life."

"No need to apologize." LaShaun sat across from her. "I'm stirring up heartache, and I'm not sure if it even matters. I apologize for making you talk about these things."

"You're the first one I told about Manny. In fact I don't think anyone else knows." Verlena shrugged.

LaShaun felt a tingle up her spine. She leaned forward. "Does Manny know?"

Verlena's eyes became haunted again. "When Manny turned thirteen Ethan got drunk. He started pushing Manny around. Manny screamed that he was a sorry excuse for a daddy. Ethan said, "Then you don't need to worry, you little bastard, cause I ain't your daddy'."

"What a horrible way to find out," LaShaun murmured.

"Daddy beat hell out of Ethan, and the next day he was gone. After that daddy shrugged it off, said it was no big deal and told Manny to quit crying like a punk. Manny started to act as cold as daddy and Ethan after that." Verlena squinted at LaShaun. "Manny is locked up, so he couldn't have killed those folks in the last few months. "

"I'm not saying your father killed them either if that's what you're thinking," LaShaun replied.

"Honey, don't hold your breath waiting for *me* to defend Orin Young."

They sat talking about Verlena's current life and her family. LaShaun wanted to give Verlena a chance to recover from the ordeal of talking about her past. As she looked around at pictures of a teenage boy and little girl, LaShaun felt bad about bringing darkness to the life Verlena had built. She knew the smiles on the face in the pictures were genuine. There were no traces of a haunting secret on the faces of Verlena's children. Verlena had built a new family of friends. Scenes of church picnics and of her son's softball team were lined up on the mantle.

"This seems like a nice quiet neighborhood," LaShaun said finally. "You have a beautiful family. I'm sorry if I've stirred up awful memories."

Verlena waved a hand dismissing her concerns. "Don't worry about me. I survived. A couple of hours talking about it won't spoil my life. God brought me through it, and you're right. My life is good here. I love Beaumont now, but living in a big city was an adjustment after living out in the country. At least we had lots of land to run around in. Sometimes I could pretend I was in another world."

LaShaun started to reply then blinked at her. She heard Willie Dupuis's voice in her head talking about a house, and Orin Young bragging about all the land he owned. The familiar tingle raced up her spine and down her arms." Verlena, does your family own property on Black Bayou?"

"Sure did. Why?" Verlena replied.

"Where exactly, and was there a house? I mean other than the one y'all lived in. I need to know where it is. It could be important." LaShaun's pounding heart, sweaty palms and the insistent tingle told her she'd found a link.

Verlena wore a grim expression as she stood. "I'll be right back."

LaShaun heard scraping and a thump. After ten minutes ticked by LaShaun ventured through the house. The kitchen had a bright airy feel to it. The back door led to an open garage. A light blue Ford Focus was parked there. Another space stood empty with a grease spot on the concrete floor, no doubt where Verlena's husband parked his vehicle. Sounds from inside the house and footsteps caused LaShaun to return to the living room. She was seated again when Verlena came back holding a shoebox.

"Daddy married mama because her people owned property. Here's a picture of a house daddy built years ago. One night he took me, Diane and Ethan there. He said we was going to a party." Verlena held a shoebox out in front of her. She stared at it but didn't remove the lid.

LaShaun felt excitement coursing through her nerves like electricity. She had a feeling that house had seen more than a few parties. Willie Dupuis had been to them, and maybe Patsy. Then she realized Verlena stood holding the box with trembling hands. She walked over to her.

"You don't have to look," LaShaun gently and pulled the box from Verlena's stiff fingers.

"I've kept it all these years. You know why? I'm hoping that daddy drops dead one day, and we get it all. No, it would be better if *he* ends up in a nursing home. Then he'd have to watch me sell off everything he's got." Verlena breathed hard, and her eyes sparkled with wrath. "I'll put some money away for my kids to attend college. I'll send some to Diane, though she'll probably send it back. We earned every cent he has in this world, and I intend to get it one day."

"Don't let anger burn you up inside. Orin Young is going to pay one way or another. Believe me, revenge isn't sweet at all," LaShaun said quietly.

Verlena blinked rapidly as though coming out of a trance. She gazed at the box and rubbed her right cheek as though waking herself up more. Then she looked at LaShaun. "You're right. I'm still working to set myself free from this rage that comes on me when I think about *him* and those years."

LaShaun shivered. Evil easily took root like a poisonous plant in the natural world. If Reverend Fletcher wanted to truly go after something demonic, he should look up Orin Young.

"Do whatever it takes to bring daddy down," Verlena said.

"I can't make such a promise," LaShaun said and shook her head.

Verlena ignored her protest. "You think he's mixed up in the killings somehow, and I *know* he's the reason Manny became a monster."

"I don't know for sure Mr. Orin has anything to do with the recent murders." LaShaun looked at the box in her hands. The strong tingle that seemed to travel from the thick cardboard and through her body implied differently.

"But you came here for a reason. There was whispers that you got the gift of sight even stronger than Miss Odette. You found the one that killed your cousin. Some say he was possessed, and you fought off a devilish spirit." Verlena placed a hand on top of the box. "I'll do anything to help, just tell me you'll stop him."

They stood facing each other in silence for several long moments. LaShaun looked into Verlena's eyes. She didn't see fury or hatred, but a plea to bring an end to more suffering. Verlena could have told her again about her sister's tortured quest to find peace, or how Manny's life had been twisted into something vile. She could have talked about the misery Flora Lee Young had endured. But she didn't have to speak. They both knew that Orin Young had grown to love causing pain and more as time passed. His sadistic nature had taken a horrific turn somehow.

"I'll do my best. I can't guarantee more because I'd be lying to you," LaShaun said finally.

"That's all I ask." Verlena hugged her hard for a few seconds and stepped back. She wore a sheepish grin. "I got to admit I was curious to meet you in person. You have a strong faith."

"Surprised I'm not wearing black clothes and fingernail polish with weird tattoos all over?" LaShaun smiled back at her.

"Are there normal tattoos?" Verlena wisecracked. She shook her head slowly, and her smile faded. "Thank you for trying. You're the first person from Beau Chene or even Vermillion Parish to come talk to me. Except for a reporter. She just wanted find dirt on the family to explain Manny's behavior."

"There was plenty to find it turns out. I'm sorry, I didn't mean..." LaShaun frowned at the way her thoughts slipped out.

"No, no, you're right. But you're not looking to exploit us for some tabloid. If I can help, burn some candles or help you make a gris-gris, just let me know."

LaShaun laughed hard. "You definitely listened to too many of stories about me and Monmon Odette."

"Maybe so." Verlena's face lit up when she smiled again.

LaShaun could feel that this woman now had love and joy in her life to fight the darkness from her past. Verlena's smile made her look like a younger, prettier version of what Flora Lee might have once looked like.

"No, cher. You go to church and light a candle. Say prayers for your brother's soul, that your mama finds peace; and pray for your daddy's soul, too." LaShaun nodded slowly at the shocked expression on Verlena's face.

"I'll pray for Manny to find redemption. I don't want mama to die miserable and full of guilt. But daddy?" Verlena's expression hardened. "I know the scriptures say we should forgive. That one I'm going to need the rest of my life to work on."

LaShaun placed a hand on her arm. "Take care. I'll be in touch."

On the drive back to Louisiana LaShaun considered what she'd learned. Her gaze kept drifting to the box she'd placed on the passenger seat. Once she crossed the state line, LaShaun stopped at a gas station that also had a sandwich shop inside. She went inside carrying the box and sat in booth with hard bright orange benches. Once again she looked at the contents. There were copies of land deeds going back ninety years. Two of the pictures showed vacant land. Another photo showed an old house being bulldozed. Then three more showed the construction of another house at various stages until its completion. The first photos were shot in the sixties. The dates on the photos showing the house being built had 1976 stamped on the bottom. LaShaun had wanted all originals, the items handled by Flora Lee, her family all those years ago. And by the youthful Orin Young. Her senses picked up the mystical timeline of how evil grew from a seed into a thick choking vine.

Chapter 18

Later that evening Chase came over to LaShaun's house just after six. The last fall daylight had disappeared. Dusk did not linger long past four in the afternoon that time of year. He didn't talk much, but the tense expression said a lot more than words could convey. Another body had been found near White Lake. He had a long night ahead. M.J. had coordinated a meeting with investigators from two other neighboring sheriff departments, Cameron and Lafayette Parish. Louisiana State Police detectives would also attend.

LaShaun sat on her bed, legs folded under her, when Chase came out of the shower. He brought the clean smell of soap with him when the bathroom door opened. He gave her a tired smile then pulled a forest green long sleeve t-shirt over his head.

"I wish you could just stay here and rest tonight," she said and watched his strong muscular legs step into a pair of indigo jeans.

"I'm lucky M.J. couldn't set the meeting up until seven thirty. At least that gave me time to come steal a kiss and some food," he joked.

"A decent night's sleep would be better. Talking about killing and wickedness after a long day of seeing it up close isn't good," LaShaun said.

Chase sat next to her on the bed and pulled LaShaun against his body. "You just summed up one serious occupational hazard of a lawman, and a soldier at war. We try not to let it, but this stuff seeps into your skin. We have to work hard to shake it."

"I know, cher. I know." LaShaun brushed the damp hair from his forehead.

"Yeah, you do understand. One more thing to love about you." He held her close for a few moments. The soft patter of all rain outside seemed to soothe him as he relaxed in her embrace. "By the way, what did you find out from Manny's aunt?"

"Orin Young wasn't a good father or husband." LaShaun gave him a quick summary. The longer she talked, the more Chase's expression tightened again.

"After ten years as a cop nothing surprises me. I've learned so many nasty secrets are kept inside families." Chase shook his head. "But it's not evidence Orin is a killer."

"Let's talk about something else. You need a break." LaShaun brushed his thick dark hair with her fingers.

"Yeah, long night ahead."

When he pulled away LaShaun shivered at the loss of warmth. "I fixed some gumbo and garlic bread. The temperature is going to dip down into the low forties tonight. You'll need something hot in your tummy rambling around the countryside in this weather."

"Thanks, hon," Chase said over his shoulder and continued to check the items on his duty belt. "But we won't be going out to this new crime scene. Too dark to see anything at this point. We've got pictures though."

LaShaun watched him for a few seconds. She wanted him to be safe, and not see any more ugliness than he'd already experienced. "How bad is this one?"

"Bad enough, but the good news is I'm sure this is plain old ordinary human evil." Chase turned around and rested both hands on his waist. "Nothing magical, we just have to find a guy who's got a lot of anger in him. We call it 'over kill'."

She nodded. "Way more violence than was needed to kill the victim, right?"

"Exactly. This murderer likes to watch them suffer. I've only taken a few of those profile courses, but I'd say he enjoys the moment when his victim realizes there's no way out; the terror in their eyes when they see their own death reflected in the killer's," Chase spoke in an even, professional tone. But his hands clenched into fists. "I'm going to work flat out to catch this sicko."

"The victim is a young homeless guy with a history of using and dealing drugs," LaShaun said without hesitation. In fact she didn't even realize for a moment that she'd spoken the words aloud.

Chase walked over to her and pulled LaShaun into his arms. "Try to unplug from whatever psychic wavelength you're on, LaShaun. Like you said, too much of this stuff can poison your soul."

She rested her head against his chest. "I wish you didn't have to follow trails of blood. After being in Afghanistan and seeing that carnage. It's already made you feel distant from your family. Being with me doesn't help."

Chase used a long forefinger to lift her face until they gazed into each other's eyes. "Being with you helps me feel connected."

They shared a sweet kiss, holding each other for a time to fight off the chill that came from brushing shoulders with ice cold evil. LaShaun wanted to pull off his clothes and feel the heat of his skin, but duty called. Forty minutes later Chase had finished a bowl of gumbo, dressed in his warm Vermillion Parish Sheriff's Department jacket and was gone. LaShaun turned on the television while she cleaned up after their meal. She found a station that re-played the six o'clock news they'd missed while eating.

"Chief Criminal Investigator Chase Broussard spoke at a press conference about the latest gruesome murder discovered near White Lake," a handsome anchor man intoned gravely.

LaShaun dried her hands of soapy water and went to the television. Footage from the press conference earlier that day in the afternoon played. Chase stood outside the station. M.J. was on his right, and Chase's opponent in the election stood to his left. LaShaun was convinced M.J. had made that concession so Dave Goudchaux wouldn't accuse her of playing favorites. He gazed at Chase as though he wanted to shove him aside and take the spotlight. Still he managed to affect an "I could do this better" expression.

Chase gave a brief description of the crime, the body of a man had been found by two Louisiana Wildlife and Fisheries employees. Reporters peppered him with questions once he'd finished his short statement devoid of details. Chase deflected most of them with a standard "Our investigation is on-going" response. Then James Schaffer took a step away from the crowd of about seven reporters.

"I'm Jim Schaffer with the Investigation News Network," Schaffer said in his best "I'm important" voice. "Is the Vermillion Parish Sheriff's Office close to stopping this slaughter, and is it true that an occult gang is linked these murders?"

M.J. changed places with Chase as he stepped back to let the boss take over. Her eyes flashed anger, but her voice held steady. "We continue to follow several leads, but an 'occult gang' isn't one of them. We have no such evidence."

Schaffer cocked an eyebrow with professional precision. He allowed the right amount of skepticism show in his expression. "Our team has spoken to several sources who believe otherwise. The words rougarou keep coming up."

"We don't deal in local legends, only facts," M.J. snapped back. "That's all the information we have."

LaShaun watched as M.J. led the rest of the law officers back inside the station. One reporter went on to repeat the fantastic details Schaffer had interjected into the press conference. She shook her head and finished cleaning up the kitchen.

Hours later the red numbers of the digital clock on LaShaun's night stand glowed softly, reminding her that it was after midnight. She'd tried to go to bed early since she intended to visit Manny again at the forensic hospital. This time she would go alone, and she would not tell Chase. He had enough on his mind; but mostly because she didn't want him to insist on going with her. Manny would be more talkative if she went alone. When the antique clock chimed the half hour LaShaun tossed the down blanket aside and sat up. The house was chilly, so she turned up the heat since she would be out of bed. The heavy leather bound book sat on the table in the seating area near her queen-sized bed. She gathered up the knit throw her grandmother had made and wrapped it around her. Then she sat in one of the two comfy chairs near the window. She began reading the yellowed pages, turning them carefully.

"Pete would have a fit if he knew I was touching the paper without using cotton gloves," LaShaun murmured to herself, and then smiled. "And Chase would have a fit knowing I'm here talking to myself."

She laughed softly, and continued to read. LaShaun knew the oils from her skin might damage the paper made of cotton, but she at least followed his advice and stored the collection properly. The florid handwriting alternated between Louisiana Creole French and English. Accounts of routine daily life were mixed in with references to strange happenings in early nineteenth century Vermillion Parish. Her great grandparents travelled to nearby Lafayette Parish and St. Martin Parish to help solve problems. Without realizing it, LaShaun's eyes closed. She suddenly jerked awake. It was three o'clock in the morning. She stretched to ease the stiffness in her shoulders and stood. A loud thump against the house rattled her bedroom window. Then a low growl seemed to start at the southwest corner of the house and spread out to surround it.

"Damn."

Two yelps from an animal seemed to answer her. LaShaun quickly pulled on jeans lined in flannel, weatherproof thick leather boots and a jacket. She found the short silver dagger and put it in one sleeve pocket of her jacket. In minutes she retrieved the custom made long knife her old teacher, Jean Paul, had given her years before. Carved with her initials in the blade, it looked like instrument used to hack thick stalks of sugar cane in the fields of Louisiana, a can knife with a slight hook on the end. But this knife of pure silver had never seen agricultural duty.

"Here we go," LaShaun said softly. Chase would be beyond freaked out at what she was about to do.

She punched the code of her security system, checking to make sure the remote with the panic button was in the front pouch pocket of her jacket. The growling stopped when she pushed open her back door and stepped out on the porch. A denser patch of darkness moved to her left, then to her right. LaShaun sniffed the air and tilted her head to one side. Three were near. Her sixth sense told her the leader hovered back in the woods to watch. He'd approach only when it was time to finish her off. He planned to let his minions have fun. Or so they thought.

"Come out to play, Orin Young," LaShaun shouted. "Or are you too much of a coward to handle a real woman?" This brought surprised silence from those circling her property. She heard a nervous grunt to her left as two heavy bodies bumped into each other. "Can you even still get it up old man? I've got something you've never had. I'll take on every inch of that supernatural joystick you've got."

LaShaun could sense the sexual excitement her words brought. The other males gave off the musky odor of going into heat at the prospect. One female let out a yelp to attract one of the males, but the leader barked a command. LaShaun didn't quite make out the words. The book from her ancestors said they sometimes developed a vocal language only they understood. His followers grumbled in protest, but complied.

"Only four of you, huh? First come, first serve. You'll get a bigger turn on if I cooperate up until the end. I want the thrill." LaShaun lifted the jacket to reveal her skin beneath. She rubbed her stomach slowly with one hand, and heard panting.

Despite a growl from the leader, an excited pack member bounded into the circle of light. The man wore a torn dark flannel shirt and ragged pants. A huge erection made a lump in the button fly of slacks. He reached into the pants trying to free it, moaning. Thick hair covered his neck, face and harms. LaShaun shivered with fear at the outcome if her precautions didn't work. She prayed the words of her ancestors were true, and that she'd translated the old French correctly.

"It's my turn to go first," a deep throated half-animal voice rang out. "You got the last one."

"Step back. This one is special," another deep voice reverberated in the air.

The sound shook LaShaun to the core. The force in the leader seemed to make the darkness deepen, as though he had more malevolence in him than any other she'd faced. Her huge security light dimmed as if on his command.

"To hell with that. I want this fine bitch." The rebel bounded forward.

"Stop him," the leader growled. "We'll have this one soon enough."

But the first pack member seemed in no mood to listen. Animal lust clouded his thick brain when LaShaun tossed her hair and nodded for him to come closer. Soon three others surrounded her muttering at the first to back off. LaShaun knew he wanted more than a first turn. This one wanted to be leader, and to have her all to himself.

"You got something sweet for me big boy?" LaShaun purred.

With a yelp he tore open the front of his pants and raced toward her. His companions closed in. With a prayer for strength LaShaun swung the huge silver cane knife and sliced into his mid-section. Using both hands she landed a second blow. Her arms felt the impact. Canine screams of pain filled the air and she swung again. The eager, rebellious creature writhed on the ground whimpering. Even suffering, his craving for sex continued. He pumped a hand up and down over his erection moaning in pleasure and pain. Disgusted at the sight, LaShaun felt nauseous. That second of distraction allowed the other three to throw her to the ground. The stench from a heavy body on top of her made LaShaun choke, and her eyes watered. Sharp claws raked the thick denim shirt jacket she wore as the animal tried to grab her breast. Other claws pulled at her pants. LaShaun fought back in panic that she would be infected. A face that looked vaguely female came so close to hers LaShaun could smell its breath. LaShaun fought against the urge to vomit as bared long teeth loomed over her. To her horror another figure appeared, and the spray can in her sleeve fell out when she swung her arm. One of the males snatched it up and grinned at her.

"Look, she's carrying perfume so she can smell pretty for me."

The other male laughed at his antics, while the female continued to stare at LaShaun. Saliva dripped from the right side of her mouth. Her long teeth seemed to make it hard for her to close her lips.

"You won't be so cute when I finish," the animal like female mumbled. "They won't care about your face. Not when I flip you on your stomach and watch them rape you."

"We're going to at least smell sweet for you hot stuff," the male said.

"Yeah, but she ain't gonna notice when we're going at it," his companion said and huffed a sickening laugh.

His friend responded with his own gruff laugh as he sprayed first his friend, and then himself on the neck. After a few seconds the second man rubbed his skin where the liquid hit, his wide mouth moved but no sound came out. Then the man holding the spray can rubbed his neck. First he grunted a few times, but then his groans turned to howls.

"What the hell is happening to me?" He spun around panting hard.

"Stop messing around and help me get her so we can all have some fun," the female started to go on, but then she stared at the other two in surprise.

Clumps of flesh fell from both men as they stumbled around. One fell over the first man who lay still in a pool of blood with his eyes open. LaShaun jammed her elbow into the throat of the female. The woman gagged and fell back. With her right arm suddenly free LaShaun slashed at her face.

"No, get away!" The filthy female lept away from the blade. Her terrified glance darted to LaShaun's first casualty lying in his own blood.

"I'm burning up. Make it stop." The man flung the small spray bottle away from him.

LaShaun jumped to her feet and caught the container in mid air. "Father, I pray that you give me the strength to fight and win, and if it be your will give these lost souls a chance to be delivered from this evil. Have mercy on us all. Amen."

As she spoke LaShaun hit the spray coating the three still on their feet. All of them screamed in unison for help from their leader, and then begged for relief from any source. Their howls continued until they were all on their knees. LaShaun saw the light reflecting from the long blade on the ground and picked it up. She stood with the big silver knife in one hand. Ignoring the sounds of agony around her, LaShaun tucked the smaller the spray bottle in her pocket. With her legs apart and the long knife in one hand, she assumed a battle stance. LaShaun stood ready to take on the bigger threat; their leader. Two big red eyes moved away and then winked out as the being turned to leave. LaShaun let out a slow breath but didn't relax. Her work wasn't done.

She was grateful that her neighbors had not come over to investigate. What would the Marchands have made of the macabre scene? Three human figures seemed to kneel around a fourth who lay in a pool of black blood. Anyone would think they were praying, maybe for him or for themselves. No longer able to speak, all the three made desperate hacking sounds.

"The spray isn't perfume, but then you probably figured that out. I mixed liquid silver in a suspension substance. The funny part is a lot of people are convinced that silver has medicinal benefit."

One pair of glassy eyes, the first man LaShaun had stabbed and slashed, stared up at the night sky. LaShaun continued to spray the ground. She walked around spraying a perimeter around her house, and then returned to the four figures trembling in silent pain. The female tried to crawl away but let out a muffled groan from the effort. Instead she gave up and lay whimpering.

LaShaun walked from one figure to the other. She studied them as though she were a scientist observing specimens. "Colloidal silver might be good for humans, but it's not good at all for rougarou. For us it has antibacterial properties. What if being a werewolf is a kind of bacterial infection? That's an interesting thought," she said softly.

"Arrgh." The female tried to growl at her, but the effort appeared to cause her pain.

"Or maybe you just *think* you're werewolves, and the pain you feel is all in your mind as well. Your leader must have powerful persuasive powers, almost supernatural. Unfortunately the most deadly megalomaniacs have that ability."

As she watched the four figures their skins seemed to disintegrate. The first male, the one so bold as to ignore the orders of their leader, stared up at her blinking. He seemed beyond pain. He tried to get up but only flopped around convulsively. His lips pulled back in what looked like an attempt to smile at her.

"Thank you," he rasped, sputtered out a few drops of blood then lay still.

"No problem." LaShaun squatted down to take a closer look at him, and made sure he was dead.

One of the other men panted, "Please. Shoot... head."

LaShaun walked over to him. "Gunshots would probably make my neighbor call the sheriff's station. I'm sorry. I can't do that. You won't suffer long."

She was right. Seconds later the man's mouth opened as though he tried to scream, but nothing came out. Ten minutes later the last three were dead, their bodies decomposing from the silver eating into them. LaShaun followed the instructions in the leather bound book. Even though she used a shovel, she wore thick rubber gloves that extended up to her elbows and safety glasses. She pushed the bodies close, straining at the hard work it took. Then she poured more liquid silver in a circle around them and added solvent naphtha.

"Dear Lord, I come to you in humility asking for spiritual cleansing. Make this land a safe place. I renounce and reject all sinful and evil acts committed by these lost souls. I renounce and reject all evil instruments ever used by them. I renounce all sinful things broadcast in the name of the enemy. All this is done in your name. Amen."

LaShaun took the electronic gas lighter and touched it to the soaked ground. Orange and red flames flared up. She tended the fire until five o'clock that morning, careful to watch for any stray sparks. Acrid smoke rose above the trees and up to the sky. The bodies gave off a strange sour scent, not the smell of burning flesh she'd expected. Twice she poured more solvent to keep the fire hot and destroy all traces of the creatures she'd killed.

"As though consumed by the fires of hell," she whispered, quoting the ancient instructions written by an ancestor who had died in seventeen ninety-three. A long howl echoed and seemed to bounce from tree trunk to tree trunk until it reached her.

The fire died down at last. LaShaun's limbs felt from numb from exertion. She went inside at about four thirty. Peeling off her clothes she examined herself for cuts. To her relief she only found bruising. She showered, and then used an ancient family remedy to reduce the bruising; a cold compress made of aloe, lavender oil and witch hazel. Then she pulled on flannel pajamas just as dawn turned the sky a grayish blue with orange around its edges. Within minutes of crawling into bed LaShaun fell asleep. She woke up when Chase returned at seven o'clock looking drained of energy. Another body had been found in St. Martin Parish.

"We've got us another serial killer," he said and yawned. "Sorry to wake you up so early, but I couldn't face my cold empty house." He undressed down to his briefs only and crawled into bed next to her.

"I know, baby." LaShaun closed her eyes and held on tight to his solid body, absorbing the warmth from his skin.

Chapter 19

Two hours later LaShaun eased out of bed and went to the bathroom. The bruising on her arms and shoulders had faded away. She sighed in relief. "Thank you, Monmon Odette. I won't have to explain being banged up just yet."

Even though Chase lay exhausted and fast asleep, LaShaun tiptoed around. She eased his handgun from the holster and went to the library. Alert to any sounds from the bedroom, LaShaun put the special bullets she'd ordered into the Glock 22. Just in case Chase woke suddenly, she returned to the bedroom and put the gun back. Then she went outside to his truck and replaced his ordinary shotgun shells with ones encased in silver and filled with silver pellets. These shells would explode causing the pellets to disperse and become embedded in the target.

LaShaun returned to the bedroom and was relieved to see Chase hadn't changed his position. She got back into bed, and he cuddled against her with a soft sigh. Moments later his kissed her face and body until she moaned with desire. Lying side by side, they made love slowly. It was as though the violence they'd both witnessed drove them to find solace in becoming one. An hour later he dressed and headed off for another crime scene with only a cup of coffee for breakfast. Fortunately he was too distracted to notice the circle of burned earth on her back lawn. LaShaun kept him talking as he went to his truck. The handed him a travel thermos of strong coffee and a brown paper bag with a sausage biscuit inside.

"You need to keep up your strength," LaShaun said with a smile.

"Thank you, ma'am. What you got planned today?" Chase sipped the coffee and climbed into the driver's seat.

"I'm going to run an errand," LaShaun replied vaguely.

"Have a good one, baby." He gestured for her to come close.

"I'll cook supper for you tonight and tell you about my day." LaShaun kissed his lips and stepped back.

"Deal. I'll call you later." Chase started the truck and gave her one last wave before turning the truck around and driving off.

Her neighbor arrived on an ATV just as Chase's truck turned onto the road. Xavier Marchand, Sr. wore sunglasses. "Morning, LaShaun. How you doin' today?"

"Just fine, and yourself?" LaShaun faced him with her arms crossed.

"Can't complain." Xavier cut the rumbling engine, but didn't get out of the seat of the ATV. His gaze swept the house and her yard before he looked back at her. "My wife says she smelled smoke and saw it coming from this way before daylight. Hope you're okay."

"I was burning trash," LaShaun said with an easy smile.

"Might early to be up doing chores," Xavier said.

"Sometimes it's best to get started first thing. Frees up the rest of the day. Got a lot to get done," LaShaun said with a smile. "Thanks for checking up on me."

"Just looking out for my neighbor," he replied as he looked around again. "Me and my youngest son sleep like logs. Don't even turn over. But my wife says she heard barking noises, like wild dogs running around. I'm going out into the woods to check. Don't want them dragging off any of my chickens or the ducks in our little pond."

"Those packs can get very dangerous for humans." LaShaun studied the woods. "But I don't think they'll come too close."

Xavier, Sr. looked around LaShaun's property instead of at the woods. "Well you call me quick if you need help. My son and me, we're good shots. Even my wife can handle a shotgun. Like you said, wild dogs will even attack people."

"I've got my own weapons. I'll be okay," LaShaun replied calmly.

"Yeah, right. Bye now." Xavier kicked up the engine again and drove back through the brush and across the invisible dividing line between their properties.

"Bye now," LaShaun echoed. He and Mrs. Marchand would have another strange story to tell about the Rousselle girl.

Twenty minutes later LaShaun drove down I-10. Manny's psychiatrist had been reluctant to approve another visit, but Dr. Norris finally gave in to her own curiosity. When she arrived, Officer Roosevelt met LaShaun at the door. Dr. Norris arranged it so LaShaun didn't have to check in at the main building.

"Ma'am, hope you had a pleasant drive," he said dryly, his tone suggesting her destination would be anything but.

"Something has happened?" LaShaun looked at him, but before he could answer Dr. Norris strode out.

"I started to text you and cancel. Manny is very upset, but he got practically hysterical when I suggested we put this off." Dr. Norris frowned. "I'm taking a big chance. The medical director had to be convinced. I told him Manny was linked to a new ongoing murder investigation."

"But you didn't mention that I'm not in law enforcement," LaShaun said and raised an eyebrow. Roosevelt cleared his throat loudly and walked away as though he didn't want to hear more.

Dr. Norris stepped closer and lowered her voice. "He didn't ask, and I didn't offer more details. I read the news stories about those latest victims. If there's a chance you can stop the blood bath... Let's make sure we don't get Manny worked up this time. I don't want to spend the holidays looking for another job."

"Understood."

LaShaun followed her back to the same room they'd been in the first time. Manny was already seated at the table. Another correctional officer stood in one corner only a few feet away from him. A husky male nurse stood on the other side of the room. He and Dr. Norris had a whispered conversation, and then nodded to the two officers. LaShaun was shocked when the four left her alone with Manny. Then she noticed he blinked slowly as though fighting to keep his eyes open. Both his arms were strapped to arms of the chair. Another thick strap around his waist kept him secured against the back of his seat.

"Hello again, sweetheart," Manny said softly. He pressed his lips together and reached for a paper cup near his right hand. His restraints were loose enough to allow him to pick it up, but he had to lower his head to sip. "The medicine they gave me dries out my mouth something bad. You see how much they trust me, and even after I promised to behave."

"You're not always in control, Manny," LaShaun replied. She helped him get a better grip on the cup. When their fingers brushed she felt a stab of fear come from him and pulled away again.

"You visited Verlena." Manny's dark eyes sparkled. "Did she tell you..." his voice trailed off.

"Everything, your sister told me everything," LaShaun said quietly.

Manny flinched as though the words stung him, and then he relaxed again. "We grew up in a crazy world. Nobody looking at us from the outside knew."

"I'm sorry."

"A screwed up family ain't no excuse for slaughtering people. You don't have to say it. I could hear you loud and clear." Manny chuckled softly to himself. "I agree. No excuses."

"You can find absolution if you help stop the killing," LaShaun said in a low tone.

"Don't worry. They're not listening. They don't really want to know." Manny jerked his head toward the door. Then his amused expression faded into a grim one. "He's pissed with you, so be careful. Don't go a lot of places alone at night for a long time. Stay away from Verlena, at least he doesn't know you went to visit her yet. See? I can keep secrets from him. Orin doesn't realize how strong he made me."

LaShaun felt another stab of fear, this time her own. "Tell me how to stop him."

Manny shook his head. "You killed three of his best pack members. All by your pretty little self. We're alike, you and me. We understand the value of being underestimated."

"That's how you got close to your victims." LaShaun fought off the shudder of horror at the way Manny smiled at her.

"Yes," he replied softly, hissing the word. He giggled. "And that's how you played it for good old daddy slash granddaddy. You surprised his ass. I love it."

"How can I surprise his ass one last time," LaShaun said carefully. Manny stopped laughing and grew still.

Despite the unspeakable deeds of Orin Young, he was still the only family Manny really had left. LaShaun also knew that even in abuse cases, children still loved their parents. The unspoken goal seemed to sober him. He looked through the window to his left for a few seconds then back at her.

"You've got what you need. I know because you're smart." Manny's head dropped until his chin almost touched his chest. For a few seconds he seemed to have dozed off, but then he lifted his head again. "He has one weakness."

LaShaun leaned forward when Manny didn't go on after more silence. "Which is?"

"Can you believe it? Daddy, dear, Daddy is afraid of eternal damnation. That's right, the man who has attended mass faithfully all his life while in league with the devil. He's scared of God. So he wants to live forever, his escape plan you might call it. That's why he found a rougarou and let it bite him."

"Madness," LaShaun blurted out and shrank back in revulsion. "We both know there is no such thing, not really."

"The mind is a powerful thing, and there is a devil; as surely as there are angels and a God." Manny waved a hand still tethered to the chair. "I'm going to tell you a little secret. Orin thinks you're grandmother raised you contrary to the Catholic Church. He's convinced that like him, you only pretended. What he doesn't know, and what I ain't gonna tell him, is that you got plenty faith. That's your weapon."

"My weapon," LaShaun repeated quietly.

Manny wore a wicked smile. "I let him believe you were just as corrupt as he is. Orin is bigheaded. Thinks he knows it all. Figured he could scare you off easy. But it didn't work out that way, huh? He doesn't know them rumors about you and your grandmother are wrong. You never gave in completely to your demons, and especially not now. I felt it that first day, as you got closer on the highway I knew. He's so defiled he can't tell."

"I see."

LaShaun didn't feel quite as confident. Years before she'd set loose a demon, literally. Was she so free from her past and the things she'd done? People she'd hurt might not believe so. Certainly few in Beau Chene would agree; not to mention Chase's mother. Now she'd selfishly pulled Chase into the chaos called her life. He had everything on the line for her, professionally and now personally with his family. How many of his friends would stick by him?

Her faith in herself was shaky at best; especially late at night when there was no running from the truth.

"In the Bible God used all kinds of rascals to do good deeds, even holy work," Manny said.

His voice jerked LaShaun away from self-examination. "Then I'll fit right in."

"I'd say so," Manny replied mildly with a twinkle in his eyes and a crooked smile that almost made him seem human.

LaShaun started at the clank of the heavy security door being slammed down the hall. The sound reminded her where she was. "Can you do some good, too? Even after the things you've done?"

Manny looked away. "He'll strike out at you, so keep your eyes open day and night. He's creative when it comes to making people suffer."

"Orin enjoys the power." LaShaun shivered as she remembered the vision Manny shared.

"I had to let you see how bad it can be," Manny said, his gaze still directed on some point far away. "You know what has to happen, and you have the tools you need."

LaShaun started to put a hand on his arm, but stopped. Instead she placed both palms on the table, pushed back her chair and stood. "You hate him that much?"

"What I feel is a lot harder than hate," Manny said in a flat voice.

"I won't be used as your murder weapon to punish Orin," LaShaun repeats.

Manny looked at her. The mischievous expression returned and made him look boyish. "I know your secrets. You'll do what's necessary to protect the ones you love."

LaShaun's temper flared. "Don't threaten me."

"I never did any such thing," Manny said, a pretend whimper in his voice. His eyes widened giving him a helpless and even beguiling look. The conniving serial killer assumed the act that fooled his victims.

She lowered her voice to make sure those standing at the window wouldn't hear; not even the intercom used to monitor visits. "I know your secrets as well."

"My life is an open book. The world knows me right down to my DNA." Manny let out a low chuckle.

LaShaun turned her back to the observation window and leaned forward. "I did some checking. After her second mental breakdown at age thirteen, Diane was admitted to a group home. What no one knows, not even Verlena, is she had a baby. Orin Young is your father. Diane is your sister, and your *mother*."

Manny put a fist into his mouth and bit down on it for a few seconds, breathing hard. For the first time he looked shocked. "Don't. I'm a devil spawned from a filthy union. Ethan got drunk and threatened to tell everyone, so me and Orin took care of him."

"He didn't run off." LaShaun worked hard not to let the revolted shock she felt show on her face.

"How could you know?"

"Don't try to manipulate me, and don't threaten me," LaShaun whispered in a tone as sharp as the edge of her silver weapon. She faced the observation window and spoke in a normal volume so they could hear. "Good luck with your court hearing. I'll tell your grandfather you said, 'Hello'."

Manny's expression darkened into a predatory scowl. He twisted in the chair until it wobbled. Roosevelt and the guards came through the door in seconds. Manny fought against his restraints and made rasping sounds like several snarling animals.

"Come out right now," Dr. Norris said sharply. She pulled LaShaun out into the hallway just as the male nurse injected medicine in Manny's left arm.

"Give *daddy* a special warm hello for me. Tell him I wish I was there to give it to him in person," Manny screamed.

Chapter 20

That night LaShaun combed through old books from the museum library that Pete loaned her. Most had wild legends that came more from the imagination of the authors than based on facts. Yet the stories her ancestors had written were no less fantastic. The rougarou legends held that the beasts were in league with imps of Satan. In return for physical power, eternal youth and earthly wealth the rougarou had to find more victims. One tale said Catholics who didn't observe lent would be devoured by a rougarou. But according to the Rousselle-LeGrange journals, anyone already prone to lusts of the flesh in any form was particularly vulnerable.

After reading for hours LaShaun stood up and stretched, stiff from sitting so long. She went to the informal parlor and put the books on the shelf made of acid free board. When she turned around the portrait of Monmon Odette gazed down at her.

"I wish Schaffer was right about talking to ghosts. Then you could tell me what to do next."

LaShaun jumped when a solid three knocks seemed to answer her. Looking out of the window she saw the rear fender of Miss Clo's car in her driveway. She was still laughing when she opened the door.

"Evenin'. Glad somebody's in a good mood." Miss Clo raised an eyebrow at her.

"Good evening to you. Come on in." LaShaun waved her in and closed the door. They settled in the informal parlor with Miss Clo refusing any refreshments. "So from that frown I take it you're not here bringing news full of sunshine and daisies."

"Joyelle would have come, but one of her daughters had to work late so she's babysitting the grand babies." Miss Clo folded her arms on top of the dark brown purse in her lap that matched her sensible shoes. "I came over to say we're sorry for dragging you into this mess."

"Now you don't have to..."

"Let me finish, girl," Miss Clo said in a "Mind your elder's" tone of voice.

"Sorry, go on."

"Me and Joyelle shouldn't have brought more trouble your way. And Patsy ain't exactly the 'poor lil thing' we thought either." Miss Clo's lips pursed in disapproval.

"What's she done now?" LaShaun said. So they finally accepted the general opinion about Patsy.

"She's slippin' around with that married high school coach again. His wife caught 'em in Coach Taylor's van. Then Patsy had the nerve to attack the woman. Fought Mrs. Taylor like the alley cat she is." Miss Clo huffed out a sigh. "I hate to sound like that Reverend Fletcher, but either folks have lost their minds or the devil is extra busy in Beau Chene. Now there are whispers that even I had trouble believing until he bailed her out."

LaShaun had a sharp stab like electricity up her arms. She knew the answer but asked anyway. "Who?"

"Orin Young. More than a few say Patsy and him are way too cozy. Not to mention rumors about him and a nurse at Shady Grove. I mean really! Carryin' on with Miss Flora Lee steps away." Miss Clo shook her head.

"Doing what comes natural to a canine," LaShaun murmured.

"S'cuse me?" Miss Clo blinked at her.

"Never mind, go on. "

"Anyway, I just want to say we should never have dragged you and your young man into this mess; especially with him running for sheriff. Dave Godchaux is a sly one, dropping hints about family values and old fashion morals. Everybody knows he's talking about you and Chase," Miss Clo said with a grimace.

"Don't worry, Miss Clo. I would become an issue for Chase no matter what," LaShaun said. Once again she wondered if Chase would consider distancing himself from her, at least until the election. She covered the ring on her finger as though already thinking of ways to shield him.

"Forget about helping Patsy. That girl deserves anything that happens to her from now on. Her husband came to his senses. Him and the kids have moved in with his parents, and Savannah Honoré is handling the divorce. The little boy Joyelle was treating is getting better. The storm has passed."

"What?" LaShaun looked up at her in confusion.

"M.J. says Willie Dupuis was the killer they been chasing. Nothing to do with Patsy, and obviously she's in good health, the little minx. But the good news is the trouble is over, well the killing at least."

"They just found two more bodies, Miss Clo," LaShaun said.

"According to the news those poor souls been dead several months." Miss Clo nodded with a solemn expression and made the sign of the Cross. "Willie Dupuis got punished in this life. They say he suffered something terrible in his last hours. No doubt he's facing eternal judgment in the next life right now."

"Yes, no doubt." LaShaun couldn't help but feel sympathy for the man, and silently said a prayer for his soul.

"Thank the Lord it's over. I don't know if Patsy was connected to Tommy's murder. More than likely their crazy idea of fun got them in with a dangerous crowd. She's going to get hers soon enough. As for Orin Young..." Miss Clo shook her head. "How he got tempted can be explained in one word: lust."

LaShaun considered the older woman's assessment and nodded slowly. When and why Orin became what he was didn't matter at this point. She guessed he'd turned bad early in his life, maybe even before he married poor Flora Lee. Orin had lust for sure, for sensual pleasure, power, money and eternal youth.

Miss Clo stood. "Maybe life will get back to normal in Beau Chene, if that Reverend Fletcher doesn't keep stirrin' the pot. Oh well, at least we've got enough folks with common sense to ignore his ranting and raving."

"Yes." LaShaun did not share Miss Clo's sense of closure at all. Her expression must have shown it.

"You okay, baby?" Miss Clo said quietly, a slight frown wiping away her smile.

LaShaun snapped out of her reverie and smiled as she stood. "Sure, I'm fine. Thanks for coming. By the way how is Miss Joyelle?"

"She's much happier, child. The little boy that she was seeing seems to be okay. It took a lot of prayer, but the good Lord smote whatever had him." Miss Clo laughed out loud. "Listen at me. I'm sounding like Reverend Fletcher, heaven forbid. You take care now."

"Bye," LaShaun said, forcing a light tone into her voice.

She walked out with Miss Clo and waved goodbye to her one last time as her little car backed out of the driveway. LaShaun stood on the wide porch gazing at the horizon. Nightfall seemed to spread ink blue paint on the sky as the sun slipped out of view. A chilly breeze caused the hanging potted plants to sway. Her woods looked dusty gray as light faded. A faint glow caught her eye, something flickering in shadows of leaves and branches. Could it be? LaShaun stood still and prayed what she'd seen was merely a trick of the fading light and wind. But there it was again, the unmistakable sign that her demon had come back. When she recited the prayer her grandmother had taught her years ago the glow faded. But for how long? She went to the small parlor. Concealed in the one hundred fifty year old desk handed down in her family were the items she'd turned to more than once.

LaShaun took out the figure of the Virgin Mary, three white candles, a lace table runner and Monmon Odette's rosary. She created an altar and began to pray. The air became oddly still in the room. A faint acrid scent of something burnt wafted around her, and overpowered the calming fragrance from the melting candle wax. She continued to pray. Wind blew stronger around the house causing the wood to creak. Barely audible, she heard it; the soft voice hovered just beyond the walls and pushed through the closed windows.

"I only want to help," it said.

***

After that evening LaShaun dared hope Miss Clo's confidence that the storm had passed was well founded. There were no more murders. She'd gone into her woods, and to the Rousselle family cemetery without encountering any hint of evil. Even the howling seemed to have stopped. LaShaun hadn't seen Orin Young, and she preferred to keep it that way. Maybe she'd destroyed the last few members of his evil entourage that night. Whatever the reasons, LaShaun worked hard to be optimistic like Miss Clo. Even so, she'd begun her own novena to Michael the Archangel. With two evil forces at work LaShaun needed major protection for sure.

Chase showed up at her back door at three o'clock in the afternoon on Halloween day. Being a southern gentleman, he rang the doorbell even though he had a key. LaShaun laughed when she pushed aside the short curtain covering the window of the door to see his grin. She unlocked that door and then the screen door as well.

"I've told you to just come on in." LaShaun kissed him lightly on the end of his nose and then led the way into her kitchen.

"I know we've kind of broken the rule about kissing before the wedding, but I think it's only right. I don't want to disrespect your grandmother's memory. This was her house after all." Chase perched on one of the counter stools.

"Kissing?" LaShaun looked at him with her head tilted to one side

"Okay, okay. I know that sounds a little nuts, but humor me on this one." Chase walked over where she stood packing up cupcakes and pulled LaShaun to him. "Maybe we should start planning the wedding a little sooner."

"Whoa, whoa, slow down, Chief Detective Broussard. I just got the ring a minute ago," LaShaun said. She tried to make a joke despite the way her heart hammered with anxiety.

"I want us to start our life together." Chase brushed a tendril of hair from her cheek.

"I hope you don't think we can plan a wedding in the next three weeks. Sharon and Adrianna would have fit. Not that your mother would care," she mumbled.

"Do we want to have a wedding with bridesmaids and flower girls?" Chase raised an eyebrow then nodded when LaShaun's eyes widen in alarm. "That's what I thought. Me neither. It's not about the big show for me either. It's about the vows and making it official that we ain't just playing around here. C'mon, girl, you know what I'm sayin'."

The soft purr of his Cajun accent became stronger as his voice became intimate, soothing away most of her uneasiness. But not all. "I know exactly what you're saying. But let's be practical. Concentrate on getting elected, and then we'll get married."

"Yeah, yeah, yeah. Practical." Chase nuzzled her neck.

"You know it makes sense," LaShaun insisted.

Chase sighed, gave her another peck on the forehead and sat down again. "Yes, it does. At least Dave and Reverend Fletcher don't have any ammo to shoot at me. We pretty much figure Willie killed those people. There's evidence he knew at least two of the victims, including the woman with him."

"That's good," LaShaun said faintly.

"And even better, there is no 'supernatural force luring victims to the misty Louisiana bayou each night to meet a bloody end'. James Schaffer knows how to ham it up." Chase gave a snort of contempt. "Luckily he didn't find a source to make a connection to Manny. Matter of fact I think him and the ghost busting crew of his packed it up and went home. Goodbye and don't come back."

"Speaking of Manny, I went to see him one more time. Don't get mad," LaShaun added quickly when Chase's dark eyebrows bunched together. "You had your hands full, and I didn't want an argument."

"We agreed, no secrets, LaShaun." Chase crossed his arms and stared at her steadily.

"I'm not keeping it a secret, right? It's just the timing of when I'm telling you." LaShaun tried to smile, but it faded when Chase didn't look appeased.

"Keep talking," he clipped.

"Don't ask me how, but Manny knew I'd talked to Verlena. Dr. Norris said after the first visit he actually seemed to be more stable. His outburst might have been some kind of emotional pressure release, and he talked more in therapy. So she agreed to a second visit. About the same time I called to ask permission, Manny asked to see me again."

"Serial killers are master manipulators and figuring out what buttons to push. Manny is one guy you don't want in your head," Chase said darkly.

"He's not," LaShaun protested. "Besides, I don't think there's any reason to see him again."

"Orin Young's solid reputation is history since talk about him and Patsy got around. This nurse he's been romancing heard about it, and she got pissed. So she's trash talking about him like crazy. Trust me, Orin has more on his plate than being mad at you," Chase said.

"You could be right." LaShaun stared through the window to the dense woods at the edge of her property.

"LaShaun, don't keep things from me, and don't try that timing argument either. It won't fly. Now what else? Cause I know there's more." Chase gazed at her, the lover and fiancé replaced by the seasoned cop.

LaShaun took a deep breath and gave him a full account of her battle the night with barely human opponents. She hastened to assure him she'd been well armed when the color drained out of his face. "I had three weapons; and the fourth one was knowing exactly what I was up against."

Chase pulled a hand over his face. "Saints in Heaven, given me strength. What the hell were you thinkin', girl?"

"They started it," LaShaun glared at him defiantly. "I didn't go looking for a fight a pack of rougarous, but I sure knew how to finish it."

"You didn't tell me because..." Chase spread both arms out as though waiting for a really big and excellent defense.

LaShaun cleared her throat. "You would have tried to stop me, and I needed to fight them my way. And I wanted you to be able to honestly say you weren't involved."

"Don't do this kind of crap, LaShaun," Chase snapped. Then he closed his eyes for a few moments. "We stand together no matter what. Your fight is my fight."

"Okay, let's talk about trust. I mean your trust in *me*," she added with force when opened his mouth to speak. When he didn't interrupt, LaShaun went on. "I know you're not totally convinced about a lot of supernatural folk tales. But you have to admit that there is something beyond what see around us every day. We good Catholics believe in angels and demons. The church still does exorcisms."

"I haven't studied the subject. Too many human evil doers runnin' around these days," Chase retorted. Still his frown relaxed as he leaned against the counter, as though willing to at least listen.

"I was born into the Rousselle family, with a long history of extra sensory experiences. My grandmother had the gift of sight and a rare ability to bend people to her will, under the right conditions. I have a gift, though it doesn't always feel that way," LaShaun added with a grimace. "But my point is I've got experience with these strange events, and like it or not this stuff seems to follow me. I'll do everything I can to keep you fully informed. Sometimes I need to act first, and talk to you later. But I'm not trying to hide anything from you."

"LaShaun..." Chase shook his head slowly.

"You're the law enforcement expert, and you can't tell me everything about your cases. I know it's not because you don't trust me, or because we're not a team. The supernatural is my territory. Trust me. Please." LaShaun walked close to him, pulled his folded arms loose and wrapped them around her body.

Chase rested his forehead against hers. "You're right. Trust goes both ways. I just want you to be safe."

"My big strong man," LaShaun said quietly, a gentle tease in her voice.

"Okay, okay, I'm a throw back. It's what guys do. We protect the people we love. It's genetic or something." Chase smiled as he spoke.

"I promise not to run around picking fights with demons, werewolves and other things that go bump in the night. How's that?" LaShaun snuggled even closer to his body.

"I feel so much better," Chase murmured. He kissed her long and passionately, his hands rubbing her back.

When they stopped he started to speak, but LaShaun put a forefinger on his lips. "No, we're going to be late for your niece's birthday party as it is."

Chase let out a mock groan of frustration when LaShaun pulled free. "Another hour and a half won't matter."

"Put on your coat and grab that box. I didn't spend hours making pecan candy and baking cupcakes so we can walk in late after everyone is too stuffed to eat them."

"Alright, but you owe me big time," Chase said pointing at her.

"I always pay my debts, Mister," she tossed back.

Ten minutes later they were on the highway travelling to Chase's parents' home. Since Jessi's birthday was on Halloween, every year since she'd turned five the family threw a birthday party with costumes. Over the years it had become quite a production, a social event not to be missed. LaShaun wasn't scared of ghosts and goblins. She feared facing more of the Broussard extended family and long time friends.

"Drive carefully so the cupcakes won't get all messy. I hope the candy isn't too brittle and ends up in pieces. Maybe I should check to make sure it's wrapped well." LaShaun twisted in her seat to check on the treats she'd made.

"I'm sure the food will be fine, and you look beautiful. Those jeans don't make your butt look big, and your hair looks great." Chase nodded. "That should cover all your nervous questions."

LaShaun laughed and slapped his arm. "Look who's psychic now."

They rode on through the velvet darkness that existed in rural Louisiana. There were no bright street lights to pierce the veil of night. Chase positioned her hand on his thigh, and then went back to driving and humming a song. LaShaun felt a flood of warmth. No matter what his family might say or do, at least she had him by her side.

Chapter 21

They arrived at four thirty, and Jessi's party was in full swing. In harvest style, pumpkins, hay bales and festive golden, dark green and orange streamers were wrapped around the porch posts. A few friendly smiling "ghosts" made of sheets bobbed on strings. A scarecrow sat in one of the rocking chairs. As Chase pulled into the crowded driveway they could hear squeals of delight from children and a few adults.

"See? Just good old Cajun country fun," Chase said and rubbed his hands together. "Us grown-ups have as much of a good time as the kids."

"You really do enjoy being with your family," LaShaun replied, a little prick of guilt and sadness going through her.

"We have our moments, and don't you worry. My mother will behave. She hates scenes." Chase put an arm around LaShaun.

"How encouraging," LaShaun said.

"We have to know what we're facing as a team, right?" Chase kissed her on the cheek. "I'll bet the grown folks are hoping you'll bring that legendary Rousselle family magic to the party."

"I plan to disappoint them for sure. Nothing but small talk and serving goodies to the children, that's all I plan for tonight."

"Well at least I know you're up for fighting off any kind of supernatural hobgoblin that decides to show up. I hope your brought you silver knife, garlic and some of that special dust you ghost busters use."

Chase laughed as he opened the driver side door and got out.

"I'm prepared, and so are you," LaShaun tossed back. She slid across the seat after him and brushed back her hair. Before she could finish explaining the front door flew open. Seconds later they were surrounded by a group of kids, led by one of Chase's nephews, Bruce Broussard, III.

"Here he is," Bruce announced. At fourteen he had yet to reach his growth spurt. "Hey, Uncle Chase. We're glad to see you two. Now we can hear some real stories, not that baby stuff Aunt Elaine has been telling the little kids."

"Yeah, we wanna hear about that serial killer they were talkin' about on Ghost Team USA. Is it true he made sausage out of his victims and put 'em in gumbo?" One lanky pre-teen made ghostly noises and guffawed with the rest of the boys.

"Hey guys, no talk of killing or other stuff that will scare your little brothers and sisters." Chase ruffled Bruce's auburn hair with a laugh then grabbed the container of pralines. "Where are you manners? Say good evening to Miss LaShaun."

"Evenin', ma'am," Bruce replied and nodded to her. His greeting was accompanied by a chorus of boyish voices shouting hello.

"Hello," LaShaun replied with a smile.

"Right, no scaring the babies," another boy with curly black hair replied and gave a snort. "My little brother will be up all night shaking in his jammies and swearing monsters are in his closet."

"Shoot, the kids won't be the only ones. My mama had the creeps for days after we watched old zombie movies," another kid said. "I'd knock on stuff and she'd jump three feet in the air."

"Shame on you, T-Ray," Chase said, barely able to conceal his grin.

The boys surrounded Chase and LaShaun like a group of lively jumping beans as they walked up the front steps and into the house. Decorations made the entrance just as inviting. Children dressed like popular cartoon characters played games and bounced around. There were at least three versions of Snow White, one Princess Jasmine and a tiny mermaid. The smaller boys were the usual variety of superheroes. One child dressed as a skeleton enjoyed creeping up behind other kids and dropping rubber spiders on their shoulders. He was rewarded with exuberant screams of fear, mostly in good fun.

"Hi you two." Adrianna waved at from across the large family, and other adults waved as well.

"Don't drop the cupcakes," LaShaun said as they managed to navigate the room full of kids going full blast to reach the group.

Chase smiled at them. "Hello everybody, this is LaShaun. Honey, these are my cousins Vanessa, Chuck, Bubba..."

"Don't start that, man. Hello, LaShaun. My name is Phil," the pudgy man said with a grin for LaShaun and a mock scowl at Chase.

"Nice to meet you," LaShaun said, and glanced at Chase.

"Family joke. Philip has a MBA no less, but he likes to be thought of as a good old country boy. Ahem, he has political aspirations," Chase said in a loud whisper as though telling her a secret.

"But we call him 'Bubba' so everyone will forget he's one of them educated, big city fellas," a second male cousin added with a grin and stuck out his hand. "I'm the real thing, Ray Grenier."

LaShaun shook his hand. "Nice to meet you."

"Give me those cupcakes. LaShaun and I will take these delightful treats to the kitchen. Hmm, I'm thinking one of those will get lost on the way," Adrianna said with a laugh.

"Couldn't we put them on the table?" LaShaun wasn't eager to face Queen Elizabeth despite her attempts to make amends since the brunch.

"No room. Don't worry though. At the rate food is disappearing your hard work won't be wasted. We rarely have leftovers." Adrianna held the handle of the large square container and looped the other arm through LaShaun's. "Come on. Might as well face The Queen early and get it over with."

"Is that how you coped?" LaShaun said with a laugh.

"Living miles away in Alexandria helps, *a lot*." Adrianna leaned closer as they got to the long hallway leading to the kitchen. "I learned one trick fairly fast though when we lived here. If I invited my family over for dinner along with the in-laws, Queen Bee would always find some other pressing engagement."

"Didn't she ever catch on?" LaShaun warmed to the fun. She would be sure to sit next to Adrianna at family gatherings.

"Nah. Then when we had the kids she sucked it up. One thing about her, she loves her grand kids," Adrianna replied.

"Wonder if she'll break that rule when we have a child," LaShaun murmured. She wondered if having bi-racial grandchildren would be more than Mrs. Broussard could take.

Despite the noise Adrianna picked up on her comment like she had special sensors. "Mr. Bruce might be easy going, but he won't stand for her going that far." Then Adrianna stopped in her tracks to stare at LaShaun.

"What is it?"

"Are you and Chase going to make another announcement soon? A little Chase running around, huh?" Adrianna launched into a string of Spanish.

"Whoa, whoa, whoa," LaShaun put in quickly. "No, we definitely *do not* have any such announcement to make."

Adrianna pouted. "Ahn, too bad. I would love to see you give Miss Queen Bee another shock before the wedding."

"You're terrible, and I kinda like it," LaShaun said and they both giggled.

They walked into the kitchen chatting about candy recipes and getting husbands to do the cooking. Chase's father was the only man present. He greeted LaShaun with genuine warmth. The other women smiled a lot and made small talk, but LaShaun could tell they weren't entirely comfortable with her. Much to her relief, Adrianna stayed close. The topics of discussion remained light, but finally they couldn't say anything more about the weather or how delicious Mrs. Broussard's Swedish meatballs tasted. After twenty-five minutes, Adrianna rescued them all with a suggestion that she show LaShaun all the games set up. Once they went out LaShaun let go of a deep breath.

"Whew, thanks for coming up with a reason to leave," LaShaun whispered as they went out to the large patio.

"No hay problema, mi amigo," Adrianna replied with good humor. "They're not too bad really, just trying to adjust to a brave new world. You know?"

"I'll take your word for it," LaShaun retorted. "I'm not one to talk recipes, housecleaning and whatever else they discuss."

"You did good," Adrianna said, and patted her on the hand. "Now let's have fun with the kids."

Beyond the paved patio orange and yellow paper lanterns were strung on poles and in the branches of two small trees. After playing several games, Chase's youngest sister Sharon organized kids and adults to play Black Cat Treasure Hunt.

"Okay," Sharon called out loudly until the kids settled down. "This is how it works. There are little kitty cats hidden all around with clues on them. Solve the clues to find Jean Lafitte's gold! Here is the first clue to get you started."

Bruce stepped forward and dropped his voice low to sound mysterious as he read the first clue. When he shouted "Go!" the crowd of kids scattered like mice looking for cheese. Two or three adults helped the younger kids, having and had fun as the children. LaShaun stood with Sharon and the others watching the chase.

"Jean Lafitte's treasure?" Chase said to Sharon laughing.

"I found an old trunk and filled it with those candies packaged in gold foil to look like coins, and threw in some trinkets and toys. The kids can divide up the loot, and take it home." Sharon took a bow. "Yes, I'm a genius."

Jessi ran up to them pulling her mother, Elaine, with her. "Thanks for the best party yet!"

"You're welcome, sweetie," Sharon said and swept out an arm. "I must share the credit."

"Thank you for coming, Miss LaShaun. The kids wanted me to ask something." Jessi nodded at her.

"Sure." LaShaun grinned at her.

"Do you feel any spirits roaming tonight, like some that might show up at my party?" Jessi looked at her with eagerness, clearly hoping for an apparition to make her party the talk of the town.

"Jessi," Chase said and rolled his eyes. The other adults leaned forward as though they wanted to know as well.

LaShaun affected a serious expression, closed her eyes for a few seconds and then opened them. "I sense spirits of fun, family love and friendship. Now go on before someone else gets that treasure."

"Aw, couldn't you stir up at least one ghost for us?" Jessi's eyes twinkled with mischief.

"Sorry, I think there's too much happiness around here. Ghosts like gloomy places," LaShaun joked and pinched her rosy cheek.

"Get on out there and hunt for gold, girl," her Uncle Bruce said with a chuckle.

"Hey, I found one!" a childish voice full of triumph squealed.

"Oh no you don't! It's my party, and I get the treasure!" Jessi shouted in protest and dashed off across the backyard.

The adults stood around jokingly taking bets on who would find the treasure first. Then they all exchanged memories of their childhood fun at Halloween and other parties. LaShaun began to feel at ease, even though Chase's mother made sure to keep her distance. The other older women kept her company. They didn't seem as eager to get to know LaShaun better either. Fifteen minutes later two exhausted adult staggered back with their four and five year olds.

"Thank God Sharon hid some mini prizes for our little ones," Jackie, another of the many cousins, said. Her three year old son clutched a toy action figure. "Now excuse us while we go collapse on the sofas." She left with another cousin who carried her three year old son.

The others laughed as the two women huffed and puffed their way along. Chase pulled LaShaun to him. "We better get started before we're too old to run after babies."

"Stop," LaShaun whispered close to his ear.

She could only hope no one else had heard him, especially Adrianna. Chase winked at her like one more mischievous kid at the party. LaShaun leaned into his embrace when he gently rested his arm around her shoulders. The younger generation didn't notice, but LaShaun glanced up to find Chase's mother staring at them. Her pink lipstick lips pressed together in a thin line.

For another hour or so the children seemed more than happy to keep the party going until they all dropped from exhaustion. The parents had no such plans since it was a school night. At six thirty Elaine, her husband and Jessi's baby sister performed the honor of rolling out Jessi's big cake. The birthday girl clapped her hands with delight. The decorations on it were from a popular television show about a girls club. Jessi cut the first few slices, and then her mother took over. Soon Mrs. Broussard and several of her middle-aged female relatives were busily wiping up gobs of butter cream frosting, and melted ice cream. The children, now fueled by more treats, began another spirited game of hide and seek. By seven thirty the adults were more than ready to round them up and head home. Elaine stood and got everyone's attention.

"Everett and I want to thank you guys for helping us with Jessi's party. I know some of y'all took off from work early, and we appreciate you." Elaine beamed. "We've got the best family around."

"You betcha," Bruce, Jr. chimed in. "Now we got to get our little revved up motors settled down."

"Lord yes. I'm about to round up my crew. Look at 'em running around like crazy outside," Sharon said and laughed.

A male cousin yawned and rubbed the back of his neck. "I wish I could suck up some of that energy."

The rest of the adults laughed. The group split into those helping clear the table, and those who went outside to gather up the children. The orange and yellow lanterns against the darkness gave the back yard a warm glow. LaShaun, Sharon and Adrianna were in the den laughing at Mr. Broussard's jokes when Elaine came in with one of their cousins, Debra.

"We can't find Melanie," Debra said, and twisted her hands together. Her husband walked in.

"Come on, Deb. You know Melanie likes to explore. She's probably in one of the rooms in this big old house."

"No, she was outside with the other kids. And she does like to wander off." Debra glanced out to the darkness. "Maybe she went into the woods."

"I'm sure she wouldn't do that. Little five year olds are afraid of the dark," Sharon said and rubbed her shoulders.

"No she's not. Melanie likes adventures, and the dark doesn't scare her." Deb looked around at her husband who nodded agreement. He stepped forward and took his wife's had.

"Adrianna and I will look in the house, starting with the back rooms," Elaine said.

"Yeah, Deb. We'll find her in no time," Adrianna said with a reassuring smile that Debra didn't return.

Chase came in. "What's up?"

"Melanie wandered off to explore, and we're going to find her. I'm sure she just found a great place to hide and then drifted off to sleep," Mr. Broussard said.

The adults started off in different directions calling her name. After twenty minutes the children joined them in the search for little Melanie. Chase and LaShaun were in the front yard when Elaine found them.

"Have you seen Jessi?" Elaine's face had lines of worry making her look ten years older.

"She's with the other kids in the backyard, right?" Chase said.

"We can't find her either." Elaine grabbed his arm. "She's gone and so is Melanie."

LaShaun felt the tingle that signaled trouble. "Maybe they're somewhere hiding together and thinking how much fun that we're all looking. You go back the house. We'll take outside."

Elaine nodded. She seemed eager to think the best. "Okay, you're right. I'll bet they're playing hide and seek, and they don't realize the game's over." She rushed back into the house.

When a long howl echoed in the distance LaShaun put a hand on Chase's shoulder to stop him. "Listen."

Chase shook his head. "I don't hear the kids."

"I'm not talking about the kids. I..."

Bruce, Jr. came out to the front porch. "Guys, we got a problem."

Inside the children sat around looking scared, and the adults stood in a huddle. When Chase and LaShaun approached, Mr. Broussard left them and walked up to Chase.

"We found the hair ribbon Melanie was wearing snagged on one of the shrubs," he said low. "We haven't mentioned this to Deb yet. She's on the verge of hysteria as it is."

"Jessi saw Melanie wandering off and went to get her back," LaShaun murmured.

Mrs. Broussard joined them in time to hear her. "So you know about this, huh? You carry trouble with you everywhere you go. If you--"

"Stop," Mr. Broussard said as he frowned at his wife. "This isn't the time to talk about evil spirits. Do you want Debra to have a complete meltdown, Liz?"

"Dad's right, mama. Let's focus on what's real," Chase said, reverting to law officer mode. "Since we haven't found them anywhere inside the house or the immediate area outside, and the ribbon was on a bush, then it's a logical conclusion that they've gone farther than we thought."

"I think we should to call the sheriff's office to help us look," Mr. Broussard said to Chase quietly.

"I agree, but we're short so only two deputies are likely on duty. And they could be miles away on the other side of the parish." Chase rubbed his chin. "If we don't find her in the next thirty or forty minutes, I'll call the guys on duty and all off duty deputies as well. They'll have big spot lights we can use in the dark."

"That's a plan," Mr. Broussard agreed.

"We'll let the some of the ladies keep the kids occupied. Then we'll split up in two or three person teams to search the woods. We'll need as many flashlights as we can find," Chase said. He and his father stood apart to discuss the search plan.

"You brought this on us." Mrs. Broussard spun around and stomped across the porch. Her footsteps rang out on the wooden surface until she yanked open the front door and let the screen door slap shut behind her.

"I'll get the others up to speed and organized." Mr. Broussard followed his wife into the house.

"Honey, I've got two big flashlights in my truck. Better get my gun, too. I didn't want to say that in front of the folks." Chase strode to his Ford F-10 with LaShaun taking long strides to keep up with him. He handed a flashlight to LaShaun. "We'll use these snake lights cause you can bend the handle around your neck so the light shines in front of you. That frees up your hands."

"Great." LaShaun positioned it so that the lamp rested on her chest. Then she pulled the silver knife and a derringer from the sleeve in her jacket and put both in an outer pocket.

"We're searching for two little girls, not going to battle." Chase stopped to stare at her. "Don't tell me..."

"I heard a howl, and we haven't caught up with the gang Willie Dupuis described. Orin Young is still on the loose with them." LaShaun pulled open the truck door after Chase remotely unlocked it.

"C'mon now, LaShaun. We have no proof that Orin is involved. As for the rougarou theory... geez, this would have to be on Halloween when we're talking about this crap." Chase kept moving as he talked. He unlocked a metal case under the front seat. He clipped his badge and then his gun holster to the belt he wore.

LaShaun lifted one of the two shotguns from the rack in the rear window of the pickup. She checked the shotgun even though she knew Chase kept it clean and in good shape. "At least we're ready for anything."

"Humph, too bad we don't have silver bullets," Chase retorted.

"We do," LaShaun replied and hefted the shotgun. She pointed to his Glock. "Your handgun, too."

"What the... Are you kidding me?" Chase froze in place.

"Monmon Odette always said, 'C'est mieux prend gar' que 'pardon'.'"[7] LaShaun jerked a head toward the woods. "Let's get started. You and me are a team. Right?"

Chase snapped out of it to follow her. "You can't be messing with my service revolver. I mean, silver bullets ain't regulation."

"I made sure they meet the same standards. Those bullets will stop anything coming at us, human or otherwise."

"Damn," Chase muttered.

He used his cell phone to call his father and tell him they were going in a northwest direction. Then they headed into the woods. They had gone twenty yards when another howl pierced the air. LaShaun felt the hair on her arms stand up. Chase, about ten yards to her right, flashed his beam in her direction.

"Probably just a dog," he said, though his tense expression implied he wasn't so sure.

LaShaun gave a non-committal shrug as her only reply and kept going. They left the boundary where Mr. Broussard kept wild plants hacked away. In ten yards they wove their way between tangles of prickly ash. Other thick shrubs pulled at their clothes. LaShaun reflected on the other name for the native plant, Devil's walking-stick. She shook off such thoughts so she could focus. Chase didn't notice she'd stopped and kept going. LaShaun stood and let the sounds around her sharpen. Six yards to her left a small animal hunkered down in fallen leaves. No harm from that direction. Then, as though issuing a challenge a low growl bounced off the oak trees. LaShaun caught sight of the light Chase had wound tightly around his left upper arm. She pushed her way through bushes and around tree trunks to catch up with him. He was headed away from the direction that she wanted to go. As the light receded LaShaun realized something was following Chase.

"Oh Lord, he thinks I'm behind him." LaShaun started to run, but a low growl stopped her.

"If you want to save those little pups you better follow instructions," the rumbling voice said just over her shoulder.

LaShaun spun and in the same motion let the strap holding the shotgun slide from her shoulder. She pointed the short barrel at a dark figure. "You better convince me those kids are safe, or I'll kill you."

The figure huffed out a nasty chuckle. "This ain't up for negotiation, bitch. You want those brats alive or dead? Your choice."

She heard distant voices of the other adults calling the names of both girls. LaShaun felt the cold damp air seeping inside her. "Move then."

"I figured you'd see the light. Keep up."

Then the figure loped off at a trot that turned into a jog. LaShaun got an idea from her adversary. She slung the light around so that it hung from her back. The figure seemed not to care about her flashlight, probably figuring she was cut off. He increased his pace and LaShaun struggled to follow. She stumbled over tree roots and other objects. She managed to pull her cell phone out of her jacket pocket but couldn't get a signal. Sweat made her hands slippery and she dropped it. The back light on the screen winked out. She spent precious seconds clawing through dirt and grass, but couldn't find it.

"Try to pull any tricks and they die," the voice hissed back at her, then took off again.

She gave up on the cell phone and followed him. After what seemed like forever the figure led her to a rough path through a meadow of long grass. In the distance a square of light glowed yellow surrounded by black night. And she knew. She'd arrived at the house Willie Dupuis described. The house Patsy talked about where they had such fun parties, but then Patsy had a decidedly twisted definition of good times. And this was the house Verlena had talked about.

The figure stopped and waved her forward. In a split second LaShaun decided she would not to go any farther. From the outline she gambled the figure was a man. Willie and Patsy described the gatherings as sexually charged, maybe fueled by drugs or alcohol. One thing was sure from their descriptions, the members were driven by lust.

"Wait a minute, handsome. I want to know what kind of party I've been invited to."

The figure turned around slowly. "Party is right."

"Manny told me a little bit. Before you have to share me, let's have some one-on-one action. Ten or fifteen minutes extra, and they won't miss us." LaShaun ran her hands over her body and nodded behind her. "There's a pile of leaves over there."

Breathing heavily, he walked closer to her. "What game you playin', girl?"

LaShaun swung the flashlight so that it pointed at her briefly, opened the top buttons of her shirt and then hid the light. "A game you're gonna like. On second thought, let's go on in. You can't handle me on your own."

The man drew the back of his hand across his mouth. "I'll make it so you won't be satisfied with another guy. You'll have the best night of your life, right up until we go inside."

LaShaun knew the real answer; right up until the time they kill her. She stood legs apart and rolled her hips. "I've always liked it rough. You got big hands, which means you're big all over."

"Damn, I like the way you talk."

"You'll like what I do even more," LaShaun said.

The man covered the space between them. "I don't know what you think you got up your sleeve, but it ain't gonna work. Now get in them woods, lay down and spread 'em."

LaShaun kept up a steady stream of graphic sex talk as she walked backward. "You ready?"

"Get on the ground. Hurry up before I bust outta these jeans," the man said, frantically pulled at the waistband trying to find the button. He stood close to her panting.

"Speaking of what I have up my sleeve," LaShaun hissed.

She aimed for his face and sprayed the silver solution. The man yelped in surprise, and seconds later in pain. His large hands covered his face, but he recovered faster than she'd thought he would. He slapped her so hard LaShaun heard ringing in her ears. Disoriented, she staggered and the man pounced on her. The spray bottle flew from hear grasp. Suddenly the flashlight around her neck felt like a noose.

"I don't need light. I can find what I want without it." He crushed the bulb into the hard earth. He growled when he touched the shotgun. In one movement he pulled it away from her and tossed it several feet away. "You won't need this either."

For a few seconds LaShaun froze as horror washed over her. His hot breath smelled of rotten meat and caused her to gag. When he grabbed at her wrists LaShaun came to life and slashed at him.

"I like a girl with some fight, but... what'd you spray on me." The man shook his head and then clawed at his neck. "Feels like I'm burnin'."

LaShaun pushed him aside and raised the knife to stab him. Suddenly a dark shadow came down with force. A loud thud of a solid object brought another sharp groan of pain from the man. She rolled away from him and felt hands pulling her up.

"You hurt?" Chase said.

"I'm okay. We have to make sure he can't make noise and bring the others out here. The house, over there." LaShaun spoke quickly as she went to the prone figure, no more than a lump of dark more dense that the rest of the night.

"How many?" Chase whispered.

"I don't know. Looks like he's knocked out," she said.

"Take off his shirt and gag him."

LaShaun used her knife to shred the man's sweaty shirt and then stuffed it into his mouth. Working together they dragged him to a tall pine. Chase handcuffed him so that the hugged the tree trunk.

"Please tell me they found the kids," LaShaun said and tried to catch her breath.

"No. The others went in the opposite direction searching. My cell phone signal is cutting in and out." Chase stuffed it into his jacket pocket after punching the keys in frustration.

They both looked at the house. Chase wore an intense expression for several seconds. LaShaun paced in a circle squeezing out every ounce of extrasensory perception she could to figure out their next move. Then she saw it, a flash in the trees.

"We need to confirm the girls are in there," Chase said finally. "You stay here while I take a look."

"They're not in the house," LaShaun cut him off. "Remember what Manny said? They like being in the woods."

"Damn," Chase muttered. He squinted into the dark. "I don't see anything."

"Just follow me," LaShaun ordered with certainty.

"No way. I don't want you to get hurt. Plus you can lead my deputies back here." Chase checked his shotgun then slung it back over his shoulder.

"If we both go we've got each other's back. Hopefully your cell phone signal held up long enough for M.J. to use the GPS tracker app. Maybe she's got the right general direction."

"Big maybe," Chase replied.

"We're wasting time. We stick together." LaShaun spoke fast and low to make her point.

"So much for me trying to be protective of you. Okay, let's go. *I'll* decide the next move depending on what we find. No debate. I'm the officer in charge." Chase checked the position of his handgun in the holster on his belt as he spoke.

"Yes, sir," LaShaun replied softly.

With a nod they set off. Both were careful to move quickly, yet quietly. Chase waved LaShaun to stay a few steps behind him. The leaves under foot were still soggy from rain in previous days, making their movements quieter. Still, LaShaun worried that their adversaries had the keen hearing and smell of wolves. She imagined Chase snorting in disbelief at the idea. The one they left handcuffed to a tree seemed quite human. Except for the furry feel of his hands, LaShaun thought grimly.

After going about another half mile east LaShaun touched Chase's shoulder. "Time for me to lead."

His only reply was a nod. The trees thinned out in places. A full moon provided a little light in those clearings. Chase stopped and pointed to the ground. LaShaun looked hard at the floor of dead leaves and twigs. Then she saw it, a narrow path leading northeast. They walked another quarter of a mile deep into the countryside. Only an occasional piece of litter gave a sign that humans ever visited this deep into bayou country. LaShaun mused that could just as well be walking through seventeenth century Louisiana. Chase seemed to read her mind.

"I don't see a light from not even one house out here. How long have we been walking?" he asked, and glanced around.

"Long enough." LaShaun stood still. Without saying more she walked past a ring of low palmetto bushes.

"I hear something." Chase took three long strides to catch up with her. "LaShaun let me go--"

His voice faded as LaShaun listened to another voice that led her on until she was running flat out. She jumped over large fallen branches and wove her way through a stand of trees until she reached the edge of a clearing. She gasped at the sight before her. In a circle of five oak trees, Patsy stood with the two girls. LaShaun eased the short barrel shotgun closer to her body, and then walked forward but stopped when a figure appeared. Orin Young stepped from behind one of the trees a few feet from Patsy and the children.

"Took you long enough to get here. Welcome to my parlor, said the spider to the fly." Orin wore a nasty grin.

Chapter 22

LaShaun worked on controlling the white hot rage that flooded her veins like volcanic lava. Patsy brushed her hands through Jessi's honey blonde hair. The smaller child huddled with her face buried in the older girl's plaid flannel shirt. Both were blindfolded with what looked like torn strips from a red checked table cloth.

"I been taking good care of 'em," Patsy said, a strain of defensiveness in her voice. "Nobody touched either of these girls."

LaShaun followed her gaze to Orin. "Thank you. Now send them over to me."

"I don't think so," Orin said mildly. He waved a .38 revolver. "You just come on in and join the party. The more girls, the merrier. Especially when the other guys get here."

"Your friend is hugging a tree trunk. He's not coming," LaShaun replied. She walked closer and heard Jessi gasp. "It's okay, sweetie. Everything is going to be alright."

"Don't make promises you can't keep." Orin stood with his legs apart. "Put down any weapons you have."

"I'm not armed. I came to find the girls just thinking they'd wandered off too far and got turned around in the dark." LaShaun listened for any sound, but Chase seemed to have melted into the landscape silently.

"Come closer so I can see," Orin said.

"Not with you holding a gun. You let the girls go. Then you and me can play," LaShaun said with a smile.

"We're going to play no matter what, and the young ladies will stay right here with us," Orin shot back. "You're on my stomping ground. Two of my boys are going to be here soon enough, now move. I'll plug one of the girls right through Patsy if I have to. I'm sure your companion doesn't want that."

"I'm alone." LaShaun shrugged. "We split up to search. Nobody thought the girls came this way or so far out."

"You're lying," Orin snapped. He started to go on, but a shout and then gunfire stopped him. "Now you're alone. I told you my boys would get here."

"Taking the girls was a bad idea, Orin. Let them leave. None of the killings can be traced to you, and nobody is going to listen to Manny." LaShaun's gamble paid off. Orin jerked in surprise.

"What does that mean?"

"He filled in the details that Willie Dupuis didn't provide for one thing. I know a lot about you now," LaShaun replied with a calmness she didn't feel. Her mind reeled with possibilities to get the children away from here.

"Manny wouldn't be locked up if he'd listened to me. Sloppy; just like my other son. And stupid to let you cozy up to him." Orin spat on the ground to punctuate his disgust with his offspring.

"You can still salvage this screw up in an otherwise perfect series of crimes. They can't link you to any of the murders. Far as the sheriff's department is concerned Willie was the killer. Case closed."

"That's great, Orin. She's right. We just let the kids go and then..." Patsy blurted out.

"Shut the hell up." Orin nodded at LaShaun. "I knew you'd be trouble the minute those two old bitches got you involved. I'll fix that little problem tonight."

"You said since I covered their eyes we could let 'em go." Patsy blinked at him.

"Orin likes little girls a little too much, Patsy. Ask him about his daughters," LaShaun said. She risked a glance around in an attempt to locate Chase.

"What's she talking about?" Patsy frowned at Orin.

"Stop being so damn dumb," Orin shot back. "She'd say anything to save her own skin."

"Ask him about how much he enjoyed being alone with his own girls when they were young. Long afternoons with daddy that they weren't supposed to ever tell *anyone* about," LaShaun said. She nodded when Patsy's eyes widened. "You've made a lot of mistakes, but I always heard you love your children. You wouldn't hurt an innocent child. He's looking forward to doing exactly that."

"Another word and I'll forget about having fun with you first," Orin said.

"I talked to his daughters, so I'm not making this up. Because of this man and his buddies, you're connected to murders and worse." LaShaun prodded Patsy as she kept an eye on Orin.

"My God. I wasn't there when they... You said Willie and T-Row did all that killing without you." Patsy backed away from Orin pulling the girls with her. "You're right. I've been really dumb to get mixed up with trash like you."

"That's really funny coming from the town slut. I should have known you couldn't be trusted." Orin trembled with rage. When he snarled at Patsy, huge canine teeth gleamed as though moonlight reflected on them.

LaShaun eased the derringer from the inside pocket of her jacket. When Orin turned to face her again, LaShaun pointed the Remington at him. "Let the children go."

Orin uttered a gruff laugh that ended as a rumbling growl like a mad dog. "I ain't scared of guns, especially not toys pistols. If you've talked to Manny you must know that."

"And if you know about the Rousselle family then you won't be surprised to hear my bullets are special. By the way, Manny wished me luck. He's not exactly sentimental about you," LaShaun said. She smiled when Orin's cocky grin slipped a notch.

"I should have smothered that little mutt when he was a baby." Orin blinked hard then quickly swiped a hand across his forehead.

"The pack you so carefully built up is torn to shreds. Willie's gone. I took out three more at my house the other night." LaShaun could smell the animal in him, a rancid mixture of sweat and hair, and something else. Fear. She could also sense Chase getting closer. "Your boys haven't shown up yet. Those shots didn't sound that far away."

Orin risked darting a glance around. "Hey, Shawn and T-Row. What y'all doin'? Get the hell out here."

"They're not coming, Orin. I'm going to pray you right into hell, Orin Graves Young. Monmon Odette learned the words from her mother and grandmother. You're not even the strongest we've faced." LaShaun stared at him intently with a fierce smile.

"Get back." Orin seemed mesmerized by LaShaun's words. He swallowed so hard his body jerked. "I'm gonna shoot."

"Let my prayer go up to heaven and rain down divine retribution on this tool of the devil," LaShaun said.

She switched to Louisiana Creole French as taught to her by Monmon Odette. With each phrase Orin grew more agitated. LaShaun heard Patsy's voice grow shrill with fear. The longer LaShaun prayed, the more Orin cursed. Everything and everyone else faded as LaShaun honed in on her target, the man who stood before her; the one who had chosen to live as a beast.

"Run, baby," Patsy said to Jessi. She pushed the children behind her to shield them.

"Get back here or I swear, I'll rip you in half," Orin shouted.

But he was too late, the girls slipped into the darkness of trees. He spun around and fired. Patsy shrieked and dropped to the ground. LaShaun stammered for a second, but kept praying.

"Stop that racket." Orin moved in a semi-circle around LaShaun, pointing the gun at her.

"You'll be able to sit and have a chat with Satan very soon, cher," LaShaun hissed at him. She started a second prayer.

"I'm going to kill you and deliver the bloody parts to St. Augustine church since you love to pray," he shouted at LaShaun.

Orin stumbled and started to shake violent. He blinked hard as sweat stung his eyes. His gun wobbled, and he grabbed his with both hands in an attempt to steady his aim.

Then Orin winced as a thin line of smoke rose from his hands. A hissing sound grew louder, like meat on a hot skillet. He dropped the gun and fell to one knee. The .38 landed several feet and out of his reach, so she took a few steps closer to him.

"You're nothing, and your God is a weakling." Orin sprang from his crouched position like a rabid dog, his lips pulled back and teeth exposed.

LaShaun shot him in the throat and jumped to the left to escape his forward motion. Orin clawed at the hole in his flesh, eyes wide as his mouth worked to form words or suck in air. His hideous gurgling sent chills through her. He dropped to his knees again.

"Please," he hissed. "Don't want to die."

"I know," LaShaun said, not an ounce of pity in her tone. "I'm glad to deliver you into the hands of the one you've followed so faithfully for most of your miserable life."

His glazed eyes widened in terror and seemed to be looking at something beyond LaShaun. Then he focused on her face again. "No, no stay away... help me," he croaked.

"Go to hell," LaShaun whispered in reply.

Chase rushed into the clearing but skidded to a stop when he saw Orin lying on the ground. Blood bubbled through Orin's fingers as he held his throat. His mouth stretched wide as he tried to speak. Seconds later two more Vermillion Parish deputies arrived followed by M.J. She let out a low whistle at the scene.

"Lord have mercy. LaShaun, you got to stop having these kinds of night time adventures." M.J. checked on Patsy, who had managed to crawl a few feet into the woods. She covered Patsy with her jacket and issued orders. The men rendered what first aid they could.

M.J. used her walkie-talkie to direct emergency medical techs to the area. Then she gave orders to her men to start securing the area as a crime scene. "She's been shot, but she's still breathing. Do the best you can, guys. Go back the way you came. Maybe we'll avoid tromping all over evidence."

"The girls okay?" LaShaun said to Chase.

Chase nodded and slung the shotgun over his shoulder. "I had to shoot one guy after I practically tripped over him sneaking this way. When the girls took off running I caught up with them. Dave is taking them back to the house."

LaShaun raised an eyebrow at the news that Chase's opponent in the election was on the scene. "Interesting."

"He's a senior detective," Chase replied. He shrugged when LaShaun continued to look skeptical. "Yeah, reporters are at the house. They somehow found out, probably a scanner. When they mentioned my name and yours, well, you know."

"Okay," LaShaun said. Politics. No doubt Dave didn't want Chase to grab the glory. She brushed that aside when two medical techs arrived.

The next four hours stretched on as Chase and M.J. took charge of the area. The medical techs got help from a second team. They carefully lifted Orin on to a stretcher. With a lot of work they took him down the rough path to a waiting ambulance. Another tech worked to stabilize Patsy. Ten minutes later they moved her as well. Blue lights flashed through the trees from two sheriff's vehicles. Red lights from the ambulances flashed as well. After detailed questioning M.J. allowed LaShaun to go home. Chase walked with her to one of the cop cars. A deputy drove them. Chase's father met them when they arrived at the Broussard house.

"Y'all okay?" Bruce, Sr.'s faces had deep lines of worry that made him look every bit of his sixty years.

"We're fine. What about the girls?" Chase put a hand on his father's shoulder.

"They're shook up, especially Melanie. Jessi seems to be coming around a little bit. She says you kicked butt, LaShaun." Bruce, Sr. managed a weary smile.

"I don't know about that," LaShaun replied.

Mrs. Broussard strode down the steps toward them with Sharon close behind. "You brought danger to our doorstep, no, right into our home."

"Mama, please don't," Sharon said.

"None of this would have happened if she hadn't come here," Mrs. Broussard said to Chase.

"Liz, c'mon." Bruce, Sr. shook his head. He put an arm around his wife and spoke gently to her. "Those sick bastards lured them away. You can't blame LaShaun..."

"I most certainly do blame her. Misfortune follows her, and everyone knows it." Elizabeth glared at Chase. "I want her away from this house and my family."

"Liz, lower your voice. The kids will hear you talkin' like this." Chase's father glanced at the deputy, his face red with embarrassment.

Elizabeth stood rigid and did not look at her husband. "Don't ever bring her here again."

"I'm sorry... I mean she's just close to hysterical about the kids." Bruce, Sr. said and rubbed his face hard. "We're all keyed up and exhausted."

"Don't speak for me, Bruce. I know exactly what I'm saying." Elizabeth stared at LaShaun.

"We're leaving, mama. If you don't want us here, then we won't be back." Chase grabbed LaShaun by the hand.

Elizabeth transferred her gaze to Chase's face. Her chin trembled and her eyes filled with tears. "Then you made your choice."

"And you've made yours," Chase replied quietly.

"This isn't right, Elizabeth, and you know it," Bruce Sr. said, his shoulders slumped even lower from the stress of more conflict. His wife ignored him as she walked away.

"Never mind, daddy. Go on back inside with the others," Chase said.

"It's gonna be okay, son. I'll talk to her." Bruce, Sr. hugged LaShaun and went into the house.

Sharon started to follow her mother, and then came back. "Thank you. We know you risked your life tonight." Then she followed her parents inside.

"And you've made yours," Chase replied quietly.

Chase turned to the deputy and spoke quietly. The man nodded as he listened, got in the cruiser and left. Then Chase used his cell phone to call M.J. Ten minutes later Chase and LaShaun were on the highway in his truck headed to Beau Chene. They didn't talk for the entire forty-five minute drive. When they arrived at LaShaun's house, Chase parked in her driveway, but neither of them moved to get out.

"Your mother is right about me bringing that evil to her doorstep, Chase. Orin Young followed me and used those sweet little girls as a weapon. They could have been killed because of me."

"You saved the kids. Believe me, my brothers and sisters are grateful." Chase wore a hard expression. "And Orin got exactly what he deserved."

"This is how it's going to be you know. There will be stares, whispers and your family will be hostile." LaShaun stared straight ahead into the night.

"We'll build our family from the ground up if we have to. Besides, not all of the family will act like mama. Adrianna and Sharon think you're great. I think you're Jessi's new hero." Chase forced his fingers between LaShaun's tightly clasped hands. "What about your family? I haven't had the pleasure of meeting them and being insulted yet."

When LaShaun looked at him he wore a smile. "Be serious, Chase."

"I'm dead serious. It's about time I meet the notorious Rousselle kin folks. " Chase pulled her against his body and rubbed his cheek against hers.

"Darlin', I know all about what we're gonna face. I'm in. What about you?"

"I love you," LaShaun whispered.

Chase answered with a light kiss on her forehead and held her tighter. Suddenly she could let go and not be strong; his embrace provided a place of refuge. LaShaun trembled in his arms, and Chase whispered words of love until she grew calm minutes later.

"Took a pack of rougarous to make you say those three little words. Guess I'm gonna have to find some vampires to get you to say, 'I do'," Chase teased.

She wiped tears from her face and gave him a playful swat on the thigh. "How can you joke at a time like this?"

"Cher, if this ain't the time to joke, there'll never be one," Chase quipped. He opened the driver's side door and got out. "Now come on inside. I'll get you all tucked in before I go back to purgatory."

"What?" LaShaun slid under the wheel and jumped down from the truck.

"That's what me and some of my buddies call a crime scene. You know, temporary, but still painful."

Chase dialed a number on his cell phone as they went to the house. LaShaun unlocked the door and disarmed her security system. As he talked to M.J., Chase went through the house checking each room. He waved away LaShaun's objection, so she gave up and allowed him be her protector. She went to the kitchen and put on some water to make a pot of peppermint and chamomile tea. Monmon Odette would surely have been the first to suggest she have a cup after fighting supernatural foes. Chase walked back into the kitchen. He put his arms around

LaShaun as she stood at the counter putting tea bags in the pot.

"M.J. says I don't need to go back to the scene. We'll go in tomorrow and provide more detailed reports."

"How is Patsy?" LaShaun turned to face him.

"She's in surgery. Orin's bullet hit her in the back. The doctor will know more after the operation, but right now her injuries aren't life threatening. Orin won't make it through the night."

"I know." LaShaun let out the breath she was holding.

"Let's not talk about anything else grim. We'll have enough of that to face again tomorrow." Chase let go of LaShaun, stretched and rolled his shoulders to work out the tension in his muscles.

LaShaun put on a serious expression. "Wait a minute, I'm getting a vision. I see a warm rainfall shower, soothing cups of tea and a warm bed in our future."

Chase grinned at her. "I must be psychic, cher, cause I see it, too."

They spent the rest of the night enjoying the warmth of their love, and the happiness of being together.

*****

The next morning LaShaun and Chase went to the station, refreshed and ready to face more questions. After two hours, the deputy assigned to take her statement wrapped up. To her surprise, Chase's election opponent sat in. Dave Godchaux came across as a friendly old boy from the home town. LaShaun knew that he had ambitions far beyond being the Sheriff of a rural parish. Still he didn't say much after introducing himself.

"Thanks for all your help, Ms. Rousselle. You had a very interesting night," Godchaux smiled at her.

"Interesting is one way to put it," LaShaun replied in a dry tone.

"Well hopefully we can make sure this parish gets safer with more patrols and strong leadership," Godchaux said with a crisp nod. The other deputy cleared his throat, which earned him a sharp glance from the candidate.

"Vermillion Parish isn't a hot bed of criminal activity now, so I'd say past leadership has done a good job." LaShaun stood.

"It's been pretty quiet until the last year or so." Godchaux stood with her. "But times change, and crime is up everywhere. You have a good day now."

"You, too, Deputy Godchaux. I'll be seeing you." LaShaun gave him a big smile. Godchaux blinked rapidly at her then left the interview room.

Minutes later LaShaun met Chase in M.J.'s office. The muted buzz of the station went on outside the closed door. M.J. wore a tired expression. Dark circles under her eyes made her look older than her thirty-seven years.

"The last few hours convinced me, Chase. That election can't come fast enough. I haven't been home to see my kid yet." M.J. rocked back in the leather desk chair. "But at least we've seen an end to Orin Young's brand of badass."

"Are you going to charge Patsy with anything?" LaShaun asked.

"We're still investigating, so that's yet to be determined," M.J. said.

"Those other two guys won't talk, one of 'em is sick and getting sicker. I'd say they were being cagey, but I think they're scared." Chase rubbed his chin and frowned. "Strangest thing trying to get through to them."

"Orin's influence is strong as the pack leader," LaShaun said softly.

"Maybe they'll change their tune once it sinks in he's dead. Can we all agree not to mention packs and rougarou to anyone else?" M.J. looked from Chase to LaShaun.

"Sealed lips," LaShaun said.

"Folks in town are going to whisper about this for years. Not to mention that ghost busting crew sniffing around. With everything that's happened, Schaffer may move his operation to town for a few months," Chase retorted.

"Don't even say that as a joke." M.J. rolled her eyes. "Now you, Chief Detective Broussard, can take a couple of days off. Out."

"Call me paranoid, but I think you want to get rid of me." Chase raised an eyebrow at her.

"A cooling off period would do us all some good," M.J. said pointedly. "A little *peace* and *quiet*, no excitement or eerie happenings."

"She's looking at me," LaShaun said to Chase using a stage whisper.

"Enjoy yourselves away from my station. Far away," M.J. shot back.

Chase and LaShaun grinned at her but took the hint. Moments later they slipped out a back exit of the station, but Schaffer had good sources. He appeared around a corner of the building.

"Good morning, Deputy Broussard and Ms. Rousselle. If I could just have a few moments..." Schaffer lifted a hand.

"No," Chase and LaShaun said at the same time.

"I could make your election a done deal," Schaffer called out as they walked to Chase's truck. "Some people believe you're the hero in this whole series of events. With one appearance you could be golden in the parish, and the entire state."

"Goodbye," Chase said.

Once they were in the truck and driving away, LaShaun glanced back at Schaffer. His videographer pointed his camera at them. "He's right. You could be missing your chance at political stardom."

"Pass. If I'm elected I'll do my best to make Vermillion Parish safe. If Dave is elected, I'll help him do it. I've got the career I want, a great place to live and you." Chase winked at LaShaun.

"You're my star already, cher." LaShaun snuggled close to him.

Chase hummed along with the radio as they drove. She didn't want to spoil Chase's sunny mood. Still LaShaun thought about the election, his mother's bitter words and Manny Young. Her extra sense told LaShaun she would see The Blood River Ripper again, and face the entity in the glowing mist that once again dwelled in her woods.

1 Read A Darker Shade of Midnight for more LaShaun Rousselle adventures in spooky crimes

2 Isaiah 53:3, KJV

3 In Two previous novels, Night Magic and A Darker Shade of Midnight, LaShaun was a murder suspect

4 Rougarou or Loup Garou - a mythical creater with the body of a human and the head of a wolf said to prowl the Louisiana swamps

5 In A Darker Shade of Midnight, LaShaun fought off a demon, and Chase witnessed it

6 In A Darker Shade of Midnight LaShaun was accused of murdering her cousin

7 Cajun French that translate to "Better safe than sorry"

ABOUT THE AUTHOR

Mix knowledge of voodoo, Louisiana politics and forensic social work with the dedication to write fiction while working each day as a clinical social worker, and you get a snapshot of author Lynn Emery. Lynn has been a contributing consultant to the magazine *Today's Black Woman* for three articles about contemporary relationships between black men and women. For more information visit:

www.lynnemery.com